THE GLEN

Prologue

The Glen woodland.

The Glen is glorious around April into May with sheets of white flowering Garlic and the Bluebells' blossom blanketing the woodland in a purple haze. The leaves on the trees give shade, a canopy of flickering green light, the beauty can only be dressed by the pillows of yellow, pink and orange wildflowers that fluff up on the edges of the pathways, and between the rocks. The sun shimmers on the leaves, as the breeze inspires them to dance, the river giving applause for their performance as it rushes by, light twinkling on its surface in the sunshine. The majestic waterfall's thunderous drum roll, fades into a low thrum, backing natures calming sounds as the water makes its way through the glen. Birds chatter, chirping, singing their songs, while Squirrels dash upward, a flash of fluffy tail, their tiny grey hands gripping the trees, ears twitching with the slightest sound. A crack of a branch alerts the Deer, they stop grazing, their gentle big brown eyes searching for any approaching danger, returning their gaze to the long grass with a flutter of long eyelashes.

The Seelie are the Faeries of the Glen, this is our dear green place, our home. We are more beautiful than the loveliest flower or the brightest butterfly. We have the gift of light, a warm glow dresses our beings, the colours shifting to express our mood, illuminating the dark.

All living beings have an aura which is visible to we Seelie, letting us know whether the being is good or evil; Only the pure of heart do we attach ourselves too, as their aura is kindred to our glow. Our powers are many, we can see all that has passed before but only into the immediate future.

Seelie use our power sparingly, only to give assistance to any being with pure aura if they are struggling in life. We will always shine our light for the lost or afraid. We are kind beings but can use our powers to hinder or harm if we are wronged or witness injustice.

#

Before the Mills were built we lived in peace in the trees, happily cohabiting with all-natural life. Rarely did we encounter a human as there were very few that entered the woodland. When they did, if their aura radiated love, we would show ourselves, even reaching out to touch them, blessing them with good fortune.

As the village grew nearby, young children with all their wonder would venture into the woods to play, auras shining like beacons, we would follow them enjoying their wide-eyed innocence, watching their games. Their unquestioning acceptance of our being, reaching out so gently to us, admiring our beauty, would make we Faeries glow bright with their joy. These were the days of old, full of love and peace.

#

When man started building the Mills, we Seelie were saddened at their intrusion for they disrespected each other and everything around them, we observed them from afar and wished them gone. The answer soon arrived, so we believed!

Around the 1560s a malignant entity came to abide in the Glen with the influx of humans to whom they trail. The Slaugh, fearsome creatures, they hunt in packs, ruthless for survival and through the centuries have evolved an enjoyment of cruelty similar to mans, ironic as the Slaugh maintain their hatred of the human race is due to their perception of men as cruel and selfish. The Slaugh also known as the Host, are believed by some cultures in human society to be the Fallen Angels or Demons that roam the midnight skies of the earth searching for lost souls; In reality they are an ancient race of creatures who have the power of telepathy. They can mimic every living being, although have no need for a spoken language of their own. The Slaugh are responsible for death among man and domestic animals, causing sickness even spreading disease. Seelie Faeries have tolerated the Host for thousands of years, blessing the best among them, encouraging the good in them. Time has created a strange bond between our broods, they are our neighbours, yet we avoid close contact when possible, as not to absorb their negative energies.

Once the Host were in number the humans from the village were suffering. The young people would leave us gifts in the woods with the false belief that we the Faeries could stop the Slaughs' evil deeds and their wicked tricks on them, sadly we rarely would or could.

#

In 1866 a huge Viaduct was built to accommodate the new Railway, it spanned Glen River with seven huge arches giving more access to the village, there were so many humans, so much noise that we retreated into the denser woodland higher up, we created homes in the steep embankments and rocky cliffs. We had to accept the comings and goings of the humans and learned to stay out of sight.

Various working Mills remained by the water for seven hundred years but as with everything they eventually declined and were abandoned, time and nature hiding them away leaving our woodland quiet once more!

A descendent of one of the Mill owners as a small child would roam the woods alone, playing with sticks and stones, he was a gentle boy with a pure heart. He was weak so the other children would tease and bully him, leaving him often with bruises and a bloody nose or lip. As he got older the beatings became fierce and we found it too painful to watch, we started to warn him of danger when we would see the troublesome children approaching the Glen. We Seelie were his only friends, we would play 'hide and seek' with him, letting him chase us through the trees, he would sit in the long grass singing his songs to us and us to him. Sadly, his visits became less and less as he became a man, as often is the way. We missed his joyful spirit, but he never forgot our kindness for in 1927 believing that he alone owned the Glen, he gifted the woodland as a park to the people of the Parishes in the hope it would keep, we Faeries safe by preserving the woods.

#

The Glen Park entrance sits at the end of a short one-way narrow street, one side is the embankment of the river, on the other a row of tenement houses. An overgrown garden with an old, dilapidated house which is still inhabited, but no one knows by who as they have never been seen. A small playpark is after the entrance with a grass slope which takes you to the upper field that lends to woods, then down into the lower Glen under the Viaduct into dense woodland which spans for at least twenty miles and of course the river. There are ruins and foundations of all the old buildings there on the riverbanks on both sides of the river.

#

Magpies are vigilant of our special place, they look down from the many trees that have grown tall, skirting the bare earth that surrounds the 'Sanctum.' In a perfect circle, the branches stoop forward providing a vault over the circle of ancient stones that were put here by the first. We the Seelie come here with the Slaugh in the presence of the Guardian spirits. We replenish our energy from the power below while we tell the truths from what has passed, to remind ourselves as we live through the centuries of the lessons we have learned.

#

THE HOST

Down by the river in the fern-covered glen,

The Slaugh Folk abide in the trees.

Far from the places of men and their kin,

you may hear the screams from their murderous din.

With long locks flowing as they swoop through the air,

Long-limbed but robust, they show the living no care.

Man, or beast alike, approach if you dare.

From the first sunshine to the blackness of night.

Their eyes glow the brightest of green:

Beautiful!

Yet the most hellish of sights to be seen.

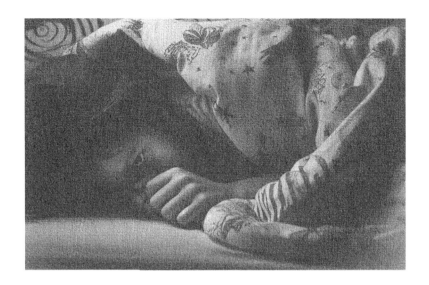

Chapter 1.

The Visitor 1959

"More Winnie the poo, please Mummy," asks Susan.

"No more, Winnie the Poo is going to bed darling," Linda replies.

"I don't like my bed Mummy; the man keeps touching my back."

"Stop it now Susan!" Linda sounds impatient.

"I'm not lying mummy," Susan speaks in a small pathetic voice, "he pokes me in the shoulder."

"Don't be silly, there is nobody in the house except Mummy, Daddy and you, there is nothing bad in your beautiful room, look how pretty it is with your lovely toys and your Magic roundabout wallpaper. Look at Zebedee how funny his moustache is," Linda replies with a fake giggle.

"Please leave the light on. Please mummy!" Susan begs.

"Just for a little while, now close your eyes," Linda strokes her daughters' brow, admiring her innocent face and long dark hair.

"Come on let's say your prayers that's a good girl.

"This night as I lay down to sleep," Susan joins in with Linda in reciting the words, "I pray the lord my soul to keep, if I should die before I wake, I pray the,"

"I don't want to die Mummy!" Susan interrupts in a sad small voice,

"I pray the lord my soul to take," Linda finishes and strokes the hair off her daughter's face. Linda starts to sing in a quiet soothing voice, "Close your eyes…., go to sleep, for the sand man is coming…. close them tightly….. close them now…. or he will put sand in your eyes." Linda kisses her daughters' head, tucking the blankets tight around Susan and then under the mattress. She leaves the night light on which is a little ceramic house with tiny mice in it; It has a very shallow tinted glow. The moment her mother leaves her room Susan wriggles the blankets free, pulling the covers up and over her head, she curls into a foetus type position with only a space for her to breathe and peep out the tiny round gap. She stares at the night light, apprehensive, until she falls asleep.

Susan wakes up, sweating and breathing heavily, she stares out and realises she is now facing the wall that her bed leans against, someone is tapping her shoulder, she has been through this many times and does not want to turn to see who is there! She lies frozen in fear, her bedroom lit in an eerie glow, the sweat trickling now down her back, breathing too quickly, she is trying to become invisible lying deadly still and quiet.

'Please go away, please go away,' she repeats in her head. After some time, she eventually doses off into a fretful sleep. Dreaming of walking through a wood at night, she can see well as her way is bright and glowing, it has what she perceives as many night lights similar to her own, little houses with tiny mice occupants, in the trees and in the undergrowth, she is not afraid, but laughing as she walks on the path lined with bright stones.

Susan jolts into consciousness, feeling great unease, now lying on her back staring ahead, there is someone standing at the end of her bed, with long grey hair and a long beard, robes with a skull cap on, she can't see the face clearly. Momentarily frozen by shock, she stares unblinking, then lets out a loud and long scream. Susan stops, pulling the covers up to her eyes, she shouts with all her might, "Daddddddy!" After few moments the door opens wide and Susan's father Mike appears, a fine big man with wavy dark hair, he walks through where the figure had faded away. "Hey, what's wrong honey?"

"I saw the man standing just there!" Susan points at the end of her bed where Mike is now stood. Mike walks round and sits on her bed, the bed dips under his weight. Stroking her head, he looks in her beautiful face, with her big green eyes staring up at him, 'she is the double of her mother,' he thinks then smiles. He says in a gentle voice, "It was just a dream Susie, you don't see him now, do you?" Susan shakes her head slowly, "that's because your awake and he was only a dream, do you understand!"

Susan speaks in a baby voice, "Noooooo, Daddy, he was here, he taps me or touches my back, I told you!" "I want to sleep with you and Mummy, pleeeeeease Daddy?" "I'm scared." "Your too big now to sleep with Mummy and Daddy you're a schoolgirl now, five years old." Susan makes little whimpering noises.

"I will stay here with you I promise, until you go to sleep Susie." Mike says reassuringly, lying back on the bed squeezing onto the small single bed next to her, half his body and one leg hanging off the side. Mike puts his arm around her small body.

"Will you leave the door open when you go to mummy, so you can hear me if he is there again?" Susan pleads.

"Okay," Mike sighs, "I will leave it open when you're sleeping and I will listen for you, but don't worry you won't have the dream again Susan," he is stroking her brow, his big hand moving up over her hair. "Think about nice things." He whispers as she closes her eyes.

Mike stays there for about half an hour until his daughter is asleep, he slithers his body slowly off of her bed, cautiously measuring every movement as not to disturb her and then returns to his wife in their bedroom.

"What kept you? I could barely stay awake?" Linda asks.

"It was that dream again; Now where were we!" Mike chuckles, pulling his pyjama bottoms off and making a jumping motion back into bed with Linda, the mattress springs creaking as he lands, "shushhhhhhhh!" Linda hisses her finger to her lips; they giggle and begin to kiss passionately!

A dark shadow figure passes through the open doorway of Susies' room. The temperature drops and Susie's breath becomes visible.

#

Chapter 2.

The Policemen's tale 1972

"A call's come in from a female resident of the village, she claims to have spotted a land mine down by the river, stuck in the mud." The Duty Officer Scott said as he handed Sergeant James Earshman the call slip, "she had noticed it whilst walking in the Glen lower woods this morning." James read the slip. "There is an old WW2 Army camp in the vicinity," Scott added.

"Aye I know the one, I've been up there!" James replied, "think it warrants a visit just to check it out?"

"Definitely, the caller a Miss Alma Fravardin has arranged to meet you at the Park gates at nine tonight, as she could not make it any other time."

"Okay, you are cutting it short, it's nearly nine now. I will take Alan and the new guy with me," James said, he asked "what's his name again?"

"Stephen Morne," Scott said, "nice young man Jim." He said while writing in the activity logbook. "Mind take a big torch with you; it is dense down there!"

#

"Hi, Miss Fravardin?' James said as he approached the elderly woman with shoulder length straight grey hair, she was standing in front of the huge gates, he thought she looked around seventy, she was wearing outdoor clothing in a style he had not seen before, and he noticed her big muddy walking boots.

"Hello, yes, just call me Alma!"

"Are you sure you want to do this at night?" James asked.

"Yes, I have only got this time as I am going away!" replied Alma.

"I'm James by the way," he looked to the two very young-looking Policemen, forgetting their first names for an instant. "This is Officers Morne and Anderson," he introduced them. Officer Morne looked about eighteen, tall and slim, with light golden-brown hair and a gentle face, he stood biting his thumb nail obviously nervous at the prospect of entering the woods at night. Alma smiled as he looked her way. "Shall we go in then?" she asked.

"Lead the way!'" James replied, as they walked toward the park. James pushed one of the huge heavy ornate dark green historic gates open, it made a loud metallic screech.

"Needs some oil," he said, as the others entered.

They passed the deserted play park to their right, Officer Morne was feeling very jittery especially as he had noticed one of the swings slowly moving back and forth with a low

14

creak, yet the other two hung silently still. Their feet crunched as they made their way along the gravel walkway, it led to the hill steps that took them up into the woods. The low continuous roar of the waterfall to their left, like white noise. The streetlights from the village lightened the immediate darkness to a sombre grey through the play park but once they had climbed the steps, the blackness encased them. James switched on the big heavy looking torch, he swept the beam of light around their surroundings as they walked, Alma was leading the way. The light from the torch highlighted the twisted shapes of trees and made the shadows animate as the shaft of light travelled away with the group of men.

Alma points "you see those three big boulder stones there?" the men all turn to the left and seek out the stones with the Torch light.

"Aye, what about them?" Officer Anderson asks.

"Would you like to hear an interesting local tale about them?"

"Aye, why not!" James replied.

"In Scotland around late fifteen hundreds witchcraft became a crime punishable by death," Alma stated. "Aye, I remember that from school," said Officer Morne.

"Well, the old story goes that there were three girls who hailed from the farms, Bonnie, Mirren and Fiona. As children they loved to venture into this wood, being innocent, thus pure of heart they attracted the attention of the Faerie folk, who would play with them filling them with laughter at their tricks, playing 'Hide and Seek,' laying Daisy chains upon their heads and lighting the way through the woods to the village when the sun went down."

"Is this a Faerie story Alma? I'm a bit too long in the tooth fir that?" James said rolling his eyes! "I'd like to hear it!" said Officer Morne, "if you don't mind Sir?" he looked towards James Earshman, who just nodded. Alma smiled.

15

"The girls as they grew up would bring the faeries bits of sweet bread their mother made, fruits they picked, dancing and singing through the Glen, the Faeries grew to love their ways anticipating each visit excitedly. The girls would lie in the Bluebells admiring the Faeries, giggling as they moved like the wind around their outstretched hands, the Seelie humming with joy. Sadly, as the lassies became teenagers, the times changed and talk of witchcraft was rife." Alma carried on with the tale while the men walked slowly just behind her.

"A girl from one of the farms Josie Devin, small and plump with a heavily freckled face was a friend of the lassies, she had often played with them in the fields as children, making dolls from bits and flowers. When they grew older Josie, and the girls would take turns of brushing and braiding each other's hair for hours on end; As Bonnie grew, she became very beautiful with a creamy clear complexion, slim but shapely too, the complete opposite of Josie who would eye her with envy. The farmers' boy who Josie wanted for her own, had turned his head for Bonnie taking a fancy to her, blushing and stuttering his words out if she was near. Josie noticed, she became bitterly jealous and full of spite, devising a plan to steal him away from her.

Josie began rumours in the village, she accused the three girls of gathering in the woodland conjuring up evil toward their neighbours, spells if you will! When the farmers crops failed and animals died, they blamed the three young women. A Royal commission was sent for to investigate Fiona Gorrie, Mirrin MacSween and Bonnie Lyndsey. Witch trials in Scotland allowed torture, so the poor souls were dragged away from their families and beaten by their interrogators, yet they would not confess. The Witch pricker was called to do his pricking with the long thick sharp pins. All three were roughly shaved by the villagers from head to toe and inspected for the devils' mark. The girls begged, pleading their innocence, beseeched for their lives, their calls were ignored! The pathetic young women were paraded in front of a panel of men; naked the girls hunched over trying to cover their breasts and

16

private parts, humiliated, faces burning with shame. The men taking perverse pleasure in their predicament, feasting their eyes on the young bare flesh."

"This isnay a Faerie story, far too sinister!" stated Officer Anderson.

Alma continued, "The lassies exhausted finally confessed, accepting their fate, sighting the culprits of the farmers misfortunes as evil demons called the Slaugh. They protested that they only danced with the good, true Seelie Faeries in innocence. This poured fuel on the fire that was to engulf them! The girls were given to the mob, who jeered them and threw stones at the poor souls as they were marched into the Glen, grappling with them, lifting the weeping women to hang them from the trees. Their treacherous friend Josie watched with a smirk on her mouth, a blush on her cheeks, her heart racing, excitement in her stomach and a fire in her groin. She turned away as they heard Fionas' neck snap as she dropped on the rope, Josie burying her head in her sweetheart's chest, the farmers boy! His eyes filled with tears as Bonnie was lynched up in front of them, she did not make a sound or cry out, but her mouthed moved as in prayer. Mirrin MacSween had watched her friends hang first, terrified she screamed out as she wrestled her executioners, shouting out to the Faeries of the Glen as her head was placed in the noose, "Seelie faeries let justice be ours, hex the descendants of Josie Devin, pledge gruesome death until her bloodline no more!" Then to the Slaugh she bellowed "Demons do you worst!" A young man punched her in her stomach with force. Silence fell over the crowd in the Glen as Mirren kicked and kicked until dead.

"Once the girls' bodies had burned to bone, the villagers were once again calm. Bonnie Lyndscy's' family came, rolling and carrying the great boulders up from the river, placing huge smooth rocks on top of where they buried the girls' bones and ashes, one stone for each." "What a horrible story," Officer Anderson exclaimed. "Upsetting," the younger Officer Morne said. "Oh, there is more than that story to this Glen" replied Alma.

James laughed, "you wouldn't be trying to scare us now Alma, would you?"

"Not at all," she smiled, 'just giving you some local knowledge.' The four were now descending deeper into the woods. "This Viaduct that we are walking under," James sweeps the light over the walls of the arch, 'CELTIC' in huge green, orange and white writing, screams out of the dark!

"Now that is horrible!" Officer Anderson and the younger police officer chuckles.

"Here you, watch it," James jested with him, "that's my team!" The men laugh.

Alma continues, "The Viaduct has seen many suicides since it was erected in 1866," they all stop and look up to the left of them.

"How can anyone jump off of that?" Officer Morne said shaking his head. He looks from the blackness of the very bottom of the structure all the way up to the top.

Alma resumes talking; "Death is associated with these woods; the latest death was not a suicide but tragic all the same. Only months ago, a boy of just eighteen came out of the local pub, the police believe he went down the embankment to urinate in the river, then fell in and panicked." Oh no!" Officer Morne exclaimed "eighteen!"

"He drowned; his body was found right there!" Alma points to the river they are winding themselves down too, the torch is shone down, revealing an oil black, fast river with a throne of large rocks rising up from a small beach area! "He was found at that outcrop."

They all look down into the murky depths. James tutted and let out a loud impatient sigh. "Where is the object you saw Alma?" he asks, "is it far?" he rubs his neck. He looks fleetingly from left to right, quickly turning to check behind them. Officer Morne is still biting his nails, his eyes flitting back and forth over the blackness around them as they are paused. Officer Anderson is solemnly staring into the shadowy woods, standing his arms tightly crossed. "Can we move on? I'm not happy with all this creepy talk?" he asks James.

"Aye, don't fret son, I want us to check this out as fast as we can!" James replies in a reassuring tone.

"Not far now, just down to this wee beachy bit and along," Alma points down a steep embankment.

"How come you know these woods so well even in the dark?" Officer Morne asks.

Alma smiles. "I love the Glen." The men can't see much and hurry on! The beam of light from the torch seems to be absorbed by the denseness of the trees. Alma glides down the embankment to the gravel sand beach, to the mens' amazement. James calls to the younger men, "you okay there?" as they slip and slide down the wet, steep muddy slope to the river that Alma had managed with such ease; gripping each other's clothing, grabbing at small bushes and trees on the way down.

"Here give me your hand," James offers Officer Anderson, helping him jump down the final drop onto the gritty dark sand.

"This way," Alma directs along a trail that follows the river.

There was a sharp crack of wood and the sound of bushes being moved strongly.

"What was that?" Officer Morne whispered, they all freeze, turning quickly to the noise, James eyes wide, searching, waving the torchlight trying to find the source. The youngest Policeman lets out a high yelp, as a large dark phantom figure arrived only six feet in front of them for a brief moment. It continued raucously splashing into the river reaching onto the other shore with one lengthy bound, only a flash of white backside visible in the dark as it disappeared into the trees. "Only a deer!" Alma reassures them, "there are many in here."

19

" Wooooooooooh! I nearly shat myself there!" Officer Anderson exclaims loudly with a huge exhale of breath.

"Oye lad, watch your language in front of the lady!" James says in an authoritative tone. Alma points up to the old foundations on the higher level parallel to where they are walking.

"Ruins of an old Mill up there! A village boy Adam was found hanging from that big tree, he owed drug dealers money and talk was that he either did himself in or his family would be murdered." Alma paused, "Drugs, the Devils work!" she said then turned away.

"Sure is" said James "and it is getting worse."

The men have been walking for what seems an eternity. "Surely we are near the place now Alma?" James sounds exasperated.

Alma replies "Aye," sharply, pointing down to a clearing made in the vegetation on the rivers' edge. All three men go down and stare into the muddy riverbank with the torch.

James excitedly said, "there! Look! is that what you saw Alma?"

"Yes!" she replies moving back as the police officers move forward to inspect the object,

"I couldn't touch it," she said quickly, "I reported it as there are a lot of children down here in the summer, I wouldn't want any innocent souls to get hurt!"

There was silence as the men inspected the metal object, then flipped it over.

Officer Anderson suddenly reveals in a high pitch mocking voice, "Fer Feck sake, It's the top off an old barbeque." He pulls the object up and swings it up so the others can see. They all laugh! "Sorry about my language," he says.

"No! I am sorry if I have wasted police time," Alma said.

James reassures her, "better safe than sorry." He has already turned making his way back along the trodden path they had made. "It is our job to check these things out, so don't worry!" They all retreat the way they came.

A blanket of blackness descended over them.

"The torch has cut out," James said loudly in a high voice, frantically he tries to get the torch to come back on, shaking it, clicking the switch back and forward.

"Oh no," "jeeeeez," "switch it on," Officer Anderson says, he is holding his elbows tight, rocking slightly, looking around him back and forth. "This is what happens in horror movies," he said loudly. "Oh don't!" the youngest policemen Morne replied in a whisper.

"Don't panic, I know my way through here in the dark." "I will take you through the 'Faerie Glen' it is quicker!" Alma tells them calmly.

"Lead the way," said James to Alma, "as this Torch is no fir coming back on!"

The small group follow Alma in the dark, silence descends upon the men, they are all breathing heavily with the exertion of the ascent and partly with fear. They approach a large thickset tree, snarled and knotted, its' branches like long arms with bony fingers grasping out at them over the pathway.

"A woman was frozen to death under that tree only a couple of years ago!" Alma blurts out. The men instinctively swerve off the path slightly to avoid walking under it. "She had suffered depression and walked out of her home only few miles away with no jacket on in the dead of winter, it is assumed she became lost in the woods and died of hypothermia!"

"I attended that case," said James, "very sad for her husband and children," his voice then became louder with an assertive tone, "But I think that's enough of the horror stories Alma if you don't mind!" "We all just want to get back now; I'm sure the station will have plenty of urgent calls waiting for us!"

Almas' pace quickened as she led them swiftly up the steep pathway that had been so easy on the way down. The men were all panting, "wait for me," "not so fast!" Officer Morne pleaded voice shaky. The blackness started to lift slightly as they emerged through one of the Viaducts seven arches, they followed the dirt pathway to a small slope into a clearing which was lined on each side with spaced out fluorescent white stones. The men all shuffled behind Alma passing the old wooden sign in faded paint, which read 'Faerie Glen.'

"Ah near home now," Alma said reassuringly. "Thank god," said James.

A small village of tiny houses came into view. "Are these Doll's houses carved out of the trees?" Officer Morne asked, "how can the windows be so bright?"

"This is cool man, way out!" Officer Anderson said with wonderment.

The men silently progressed on the pathway, eyes wide, mouths open, as it became more illuminated as they went ahead.

"Is that wee Faerie dollies around the housing?" James asked Alma.

"WOW they look alive!" Officer Anderson looked all around him, his mouth open, "who put this here?" but Alma didn't reply. The entire walkway was aglow with a warm yellow light.

"Can you hear a buzz," asked Officer Morne. "Yes, a hum! Is there electrics?" James asked.

"Who put this village here Alma." James asked again, more insistent.

"The villagers!" she replied. "The Faerie housing was placed here, through the Spanish flu pandemic in 1918, the villagers thought the woodland spirits would chase the disease away." "Later it became a place that children came."

"1918? Over fifty years ago!" James exclaimed; his heart was pumping so hard he could hear it thumping in his chest. The two younger men had stopped walking, the glowing orbs floated all around them, they seemed to change colour as they drifted! They stood in awe, Officer Morne extended his arm up as if to touch one of the small bright figures, but it floated away from his hand like a feather on a breeze. "Children didn't make these! no way!" Anderson said loudly.

"Why did we not see this Faerie glen wood as we walked in," Officer Morne mumbled to himself. "How could it last all this time?" he asked quietly of the others, in disbelief.

"The Faerie Glen story is for another day Stephen," Alma answered turning to stare in the youngest policeman's eyes. "You may understand next time we meet!" Stephen saw her eyes flicker like a bright green flame, he looked away quickly frightened, his heart fluttered quickly in his chest. Alma now seemed to radiate light around her head, the others didn't show any sign they had notice it. Stephen was transfixed as she moved on. 'I'm letting my imagination run riot,' he thought; He was sweating, and his hands were trembling.

As the four emerged from the Faerie glen, the men sped up with relief as they saw the light from the village and the huge gates ahead. James turned and looked back, but the darkness was solid, he felt confused, the Faerie village he had just walked through was not visible, not a twinkle or even a tiny glimmer from the hundreds of bright glowing lights he had just seen? He walked as fast as he could, his legs felt like jelly.

Back at the parked police car, James hurriedly opened the doors and the two young men jumped in the back and slammed them shut, pushing the lock buttons down,

James turned to offer Alma a lift, but she was gone! he scanned all around, looking quickly everywhere, he shouted out her name "ALMA," but his voice sounded eerie in the quiet, he walked back up to the big gates and called out again, "ALMA," but his voice seemed hollow and small in the vast darkness. James swallowed hard, his throat suddenly dry, he shivered as he stared up at the black woodland. Alma did not reply. There was only a deafening silence! James jumped in the car and swivelled round to face the guys in the back, 'did you see where she went?'

"No, I thought she was right behind you! You were talking to her," said Officer Morne.

"I am sure she was talking to you when I got in my seat!" Officer Anderson said to James. Officer Anderson turned to the younger Officer next to him, "What's wrong with you, Stevie boy? You look awfy peely-wally?"

"I never told her my name," Officer Morne replied, "I'm sure I never told her my name, but she called me Stephen!" He looked deeply troubled. "Did you see the glow around her head?"

"No!" said Officer Anderson, he turned away and stared straight ahead.

James radioed the station, the Duty Officer answered, "To report there was no 'Land mine' it was a Barbecue lid," the listener laughed loudly on the other end of the connection.

"Uck weeshed!" James said disgruntled. "Give me Alma Fravardins' address, could you?"

"This doesn't seem real," said Officer Stephen Morne, "I want to go back to the station."

"Don't be silly son, the woman has just walked on, that's all, don't let her rattle you with awe her spooky stories. We will go to her hoose, I'm sure she will have got there before us." James reassures the others and himself, although he wasn't so sure. He silently drives round to Bon Accord Street which is not even five minutes away.

"It's nearly half past eleven," Stephen said looking at his watch.

"The roads and streets are awfy quiet." Officer Alan Anderson said. "We have been in there two and a half hours!"

Stephen raised his eyebrows, shaking his head, "Jus canny believe it?"

"What number is it?" Alan asks.

"Number 13" answers James, "Of course, it is!" Alan snorts, "there are no house number thirteens Sir!".

Stephen asks "Is this some kind of 'new boy' wind up? Because it is just no funny guys! I feel as though I'm in the twilight zone!"

"Maybe we are on candid camera or something, Stephy boy!" Alan teases, then laughs loudly even though his own heart is beating fast, and his laugh doesn't sound like his.

Alan and James get out the car and walk up the street, which is a dead end. Cottage flat style council housing line both sides, two houses face forward at the end, it is a nice street, the houses are well-kept. "See there is no number thirteen!" Alan whispers to James.

"Why are you whispering for fucks sake!" said James, he snorts then spits on the road. Alan lowers his eyebrows; he knows to keep his mouth shut this time! The men get back in the car and lock the doors.

"There was no number thirteen was there?" Stephen asks, but already knew the answer!

"NO" Alan and James answer together. The three men sat in the car for some time.

"We are not going to mention anything about this back at the station, right!" James was insistent, "we would be a laughingstock, with our Faerie story and disappearing old woman!"

"Whatever you say sir," Stephen said. "I'm no gonna tell anyone, that's fir sure, it's a pure riddy!" Alan said to James.

#

They never discussed Alma Fravardin with anyone back at the station, the whole episode was put down to a 'crazy hoax' and over the years they individually questioned themselves whether they all had really seen the Faerie Glen. As time passed the men forgot about the whole episode, but not Stephen.

#

Chapter 3.

The Revelation 1980

Linda Fulton, Susie's mum, is now 54 years old, she reluctantly agreed to a divorce from Mike a few years after moving out of their home in Giffnock.

Linda and Karen were in Bonis Café at Clarkston. Karen had been Linda's dear friend since they met in their teenage years and had always kept in touch, writing post cards and letters, as Karen loved to travel and was always away working in different countries. They had seen little of each other in the last few years.

Bonis Café was the place they liked visit when Karen was home, it seemed to be stuck in a time warp reminding them of their younger years. The cafe hadn't been decorated since the early 1960s, it still had the old Juke box they had used as teenagers when they would sit for hours on rainy days with one Milk shake each, trying to make it last. The Money slot locks still remained on the doors to use the ladies' toilets, although they now were obsolete. The wallpaper is dark brown with an orange flower pattern, now faded and away from the wall at the seams. The built in varnished wooden seats and Formica tables were as they had always been, uncomfortable! The café was situated on the main street and had one large glass window at the entrance with venetian blinds that were always half closed. The women walked in, the familiar high counter ran down the right-hand side creating a narrow pathway to the back of the café, the café was a large 'L' in shape. There were no other windows in the building so the interior was very dull, on an overcast day it seemed almost dark; teenagers loved it! The café has been owned by the same Italian family since it opened, and they still worked there even though they should have retired years ago.

Karen watches as the elderly plump waitress wearing a white frilly bibbed apron over her black dress, shuffled over with one coffee, she puts it down on the table spilling some of the coffee into the saucer, she toddled away, then after a few minutes she came doddering back with the second cup. "She has Fluffy slippers on!" Karen whispered, Linda lifted her eyebrows, squeezing her lips together trying not to laugh. Karen had a stupid grin on her face with trying to force the laughter back! Once the old lady had disappeared behind the antiquated coffee maker, into the kitchen, Karen and Linda burst into laughter.

"This place is hilarious!" Linda said. Karen took a sip of her coffee, "ugh my coffee is bloody cold!" "No wonder it took her half an hour to bring it over!" Linda said, they both laughed. "Don't you dare ask for another one or we will be here all day!"

Karen laughed then snorted, they both laughed together.

"Remind me again, why do we still come here?" Linda asked.

"Because we bloody love it! That's why!" they both smile at each other.

"I watched that Exorcist film last night." Karen said, "I eventually managed to 'summon up' the courage," "pardon the pun!"

"Pfft, that's been 'doing the rounds' for years!"

"I know, I have always been too feart to watch it before even though I don't really believe in all that spirit stuff," Karen said, "but it still frightened me out my wits!" "I can't get the jitters to go away since Steve and I put it on."

"Ugh the bit where she projectile vomits! "Karen does a boaking motion.

"Oh, stop!" Linda chuckles putting her hand up in front of Karen.

"Have you seen it?" Karen asked.

"No chance! I would never watch it!" "I am frightened enough with stuff that happens in real life!" "I know spirits are real, I don't need any horror film to tell me that!"

"How can anyone know for sure Linda?" Karen stares quizzingly arching her eyebrows high.

"I do!" Linda insists, staring back intently.

"How?" Karen probes.

"Because of all the carry on we had with Susie when she was a kid," Linda states.

"What carry on?"

Shaking her head slightly, Linda sighs, looking across the table into her friends' face. "I haven't thought about this for a long time, I've never spoken about it either." She paused with a heavy sigh.

"Susie would see a man at the end of her bed, he would tap her, whisper things in her ear or poke her hard in the back. For a long time, we thought it was a recurring nightmare, but then the visits were more often. Things started moving around her room or disappearing only to reappear in another place. Mike and I both witnessed it!"

"Oh my god, really, you never mentioned anything to me before?" exclaimed Karen, the hair on the back of her neck standing up.

"You were in Germany at that time I think." Linda said trying to remember.

"Tell me, what the hell happened?"

"Well, Susie started constantly screaming and crying in the night. We insisted she slept in her own bed, thinking she would settle down, but things got worse, much, much worse. Mike and I could not get a full night's sleep, we were up and down all night trying to settle her. We became ill and felt totally exhausted with the stress. Finally, we gave in and allowed Susie to sleep on a mattress in our room, hoping it would just stop! This caused terrible unhappiness in our home, doors would suddenly spring open then bang shut. The three of us felt uneasy every minute we were in the home," Linda looks at Karen eyes wide. "Arguments erupted daily about what we should do next. We had no private life anymore with Susie in our room, we felt bullied, depressed, trapped! We eventually decided to leave that house, but by then it was too late to save our relationship." Linda's eyes filled with tears.

"Such a shame, you two were so good together!" Karen said.

"Yes, we were!" Linda wiped a tear away quickly before it had a chance to roll down her face; "but he is happy now with his new life and a new wife in Ireland." Linda said with more than a tinge of sarcasm.

"What did Mike make of it all?" Karen asked.

"Well, you know he was a Catholic right? Karen nodded. "Mike decided to call a priest to come to bless our home, which I wasn't pleased about, being a sceptic at that time." Linda sipped her coffee. "I was sure there was a logical explanation for the goings on. I had told my next-door neighbour Patty that I felt it was really creepy having the Priest there."

"Patty was such a gossip; I should have known better than to confide in her! Soon everyone in the street were talking about our haunted house and exorcisms. Mike was really angry at me for discussing our private business with a known gossip!"

Karen looked at her sympathetically. "It did help us understand what was happening though." Linda smiled. "An old man, who had heard everything about the priests' rituals at the house from Patty, came round to visit Mike and I. His name was Howard Silver. Howard told us that he had lived around the corner for thirty years. He had known the previous owners well as they were both Jewish. He told us the house had belonged to the Synagogue and a Rabbi had lived in our home before we bought it. Seemingly the Rabbi was a good, kind, honest family man with a friendly, pleasant disposition." "What's a synagogue?" asked Karen.

"A Jewish church," Linda said. "The Synagogue had sold the house to us not long after the Rabbi had been found dead." "Found dead? In the house?" Karen exclaimed.

"Yes, the Rabbi had become inconsolable after his son had disappeared, the boy was only ten years old when he went missing. The Rabbi would search the woodlands nearby, day in day out, trying to find his missing son, calling out his name. He would walk round the home wailing and reciting prayers. His wife tried to help him, but she just could not deal with his grief as well as her own and left him." "Oh, my goodness, what a tragedy!" Karen said sadly.

Linda continued; "Once he was on his own, the Rabbi's neighbours had contacted the police several times as they thought something bad was happening to the Rabbi. He was heard shouting and screaming. The neighbours would hear him banging doors shut as he roamed the house crying loudly." Karen leaned forward elbows resting on the table. "After the Police visits, the Rabbi had hidden away from everyone. His family said he had become mentally unwell and refused to see them." Linda shook her head slowly from side to side.

"Grief can do terrible things to people," Karen said.

"When his wife finally divorced him, the Rabbi hung himself in the garage. His younger sister Roslin found him." Linda sighed. "Poor woman, he had been hanging there a while!"

"Once Howard finished telling us all this, I was totally shocked, and it changed my whole way of looking at what happened to Susie!" Linda looked at Karen with eyes full of sadness.

"No wonder, it would make me question everything too!" Karen gave Linda's hand a reassuring squeeze over the table. "Bloody hell, I can hardly believe you went through all that and didn't reach out to me!"

Linda shrugged, "I guess I should have; I probably didn't want to worry you as it all sounds nuts!" The two women sat quietly for a moment.

"I remember Mike and I just stared at Howard as though he had grown horns, we just looked at each other horrified with the realisation it was not a dream our daughter had been having for over a year; she was actually being contacted by the ghost of the poor Rabbi!"

"That is terrifying Linda! Really scary!"

"Stranger still!" Linda said. "Howard asked us both as he was leaving our home where the Mezuza was above the front door. I asked, "what is a Mezuza?"

"It is a Jewish blessing, Gods word," Howard explained.

"Oh," said Mike awkwardly, "I removed them all!"

Howard had looked at us both, his face deadly serious, "Oh! that is very unfortunate."

"We asked the old man if there was anything he could do to help us, but he said the Torah forbids Jews from contacting the dead!" Karen squeezed Linda's hand again.

Linda said, "I guess I kind of blamed Mike for removing the Jewish blessings, I cast it up to him too many times. I didn't really think it was his fault, I was just angry at the whole situation!" Linda stared down at her hands. "We sold the house six months later at a substantial loss, Mike and I were just desperate to get out of there, to be honest." Linda sighed.

Karen was shaking her head her eyes wide, "Wow," "I've got chills, the hair on my neck is tingling!" "Between you telling me that tale and the movie last night I feel quite sick, that is a very weird and unsettling story!"

Linda leans over the table nearer to Karen, "Susie to this day still thinks as a child she bad dreams. We told her she was an over sensitive child who had night terrors."

"Mike and I agreed never to tell her what Howard had told us, so I trust you keep that info to yourself!" Linda said quietly, "I wouldn't want her to have to think about anything upsetting, like that, she would worry."

"Of course, the secrets safe with me!" Karen said, but she felt a terrible unease about the whole story.

"Let's go and have a walk around the shops, take our minds off of ghosts and cold coffee," Karen suggested. Linda gave a small laugh as they stood to leave.

"I will get this," Karen said.

"No, not a tall, it is my turn," Linda insisted.

"I will fall out with you if you pay Linda, you got it last time!"

The old lady shuffled over to the counter, "was everything satisfactory ladies?" she asked.

"Oh yes, wonderful," they both responded together, then giggling, "Snap!" they both said.

#

That night in her bed, Karen couldn't sleep thinking about the Rabbi and his son. She wondered if it was all true.

#

Chapter 4.

The Battered Wife 1985

Linda Fultons' health had deteriorated over the years, she had never remarried, she lived near her daughter Susie. Susan Irvine was now a thirty-year-old, slim, stylish and very attractive woman with long dark hair, she had piercing green eyes just like her mum. She is married with a daughter Fiona (wee Fee Fee), five years old. Her husband of seven years David Irvine is a big cuddly bear of a man, handsome with sandy hair and blue eyes. Wee Fee's dad.

Davie had been crazy for Susie, with her striking good looks and bubbly personality he fell hard within weeks of meeting her, he had 'pulled out all the stops' to win her love, his fantastic sense of humour had sealed the deal, they married a year to the day they met. Both enjoyed the others company; they were rarely apart. It was apparent to all that they were very much in love.

When old friends complained that they hardly saw Susie, she would joke, "I can't bloody well shake him off!" But the truth was she loved being around her husband, they were a happy couple. As time went by, they both lost touch with most of their friends.

#

The problems started just before Wee Fee Fee was born. The couple had become friendly with their new neighbours who were of a similar age, Rab Brown and Rita Riley, they were not married and did not have children but even so, they seemed to be in a pretty solid relationship. Rita ran the local greengrocers at Clarkston which was her own business and Rab a 'big character' a stunning Italian looking man, with high cheekbones and jet-black hair, owned a nightclub in Glasgow and he was there most nights except a Monday as it was closed. Rab was great company for anyone who loved to party. Rita Riley was a petite strawberry blonde-haired woman with huge breasts for her tiny frame, people would constantly compare her to Dolly Parton or Barbara Windsor, which she would always reply with "Aye, well I may have their looks, but I've no got their fame or fortune!"

Rita was up at half past four in the mornings to buy at the fruit market, so she would be leaving the house as Rab was getting home. The couple had only socialised together on a Sunday night, until they hooked up with Susan and Davie, who had always had an active social life together. The foursome began enjoying 'good times' regularly and had even been over on holiday to Rabs' flat in Spain. The holiday had been wonderful, the foursome had complimented each other so perfectly, that they had laughed the entire two weeks Susie and Davie felt more in love than ever.

Once they had returned from Spain, Davie asked Susie to stop taking contraception so they could try to start their family. They had discussed having children before they married and both had said they wanted a family; But Susie was apprehensive, she wasn't sure they were ready as they did love to party. Davie seemed so keen, so she agreed. The couple were overjoyed when Susie found out she was expecting their first child.

#

Davie had spoiled Susie rotten for the first few months, fussing around her, being overly attentive. "You are more beautiful than ever," he assured her. She was so happy. During her pregnancy she had made an effort to keep an attractive appearance, finding clothes that complimented her now womanly curves. "I just love those big boobs," Davie would say, snuggling into his wife's bosom. The foursome continued their social life right up into Susie's eighth month of pregnancy. She had hardly looked as though she was having a baby! But in her last eight weeks' her 'tummy' grew huge, she was tired. "I feel fat," she complained, "I'm fed up," she grumbled. Her skin was horrendous for the first time in her life. Susie told Rita "I just want it out of me, I want it over with!"

Susie stopped going out; But Davie didn't! He continued to party with Rab. Rita now was rarely invited. Davie had become bored of Susie being exhausted, he told Rab, "She is on my back the whole time for never being home and blaming you and the club!" Rab nodded in empathy. "The lassie is having your kid, you need to be patient Davie, it's just a big change for you!" Davie was tired, his work had suffered. He was repetitively late in the mornings, 'burning the candle at both ends!' it was having a negative effect on his quality of work.

A month before the baby was born Davie received a final written warning from his employer.

Susie paced the floor, "why the hell is he doing this to me?" she said aloud.

She called the club, the Chargehand answered, "Is Davie there?" Susie asked.

"No," he said.

"Is Rab still there?" Susie asked.

"Hold on, I will see," there was a long pause, she could hear muffled talking in the background.

"Hi Susie, you just caught me, I am finishing the money love and locking up! You, okay?" Rab asked in an upbeat tone.

"Davie has not come home Rab, he promised to be home earlier at night as I'm near my due date."

"Oh! Susie love, he must have forgotten to give you a call. He has been helping me out in the club. He left with another friend not long ago, a guy we do business with." Rab told her.

"It is nearly four in the morning Rab! What man? And what kind of business do you do at this time?" she asked.

"Oh, I don't think we have introduced him to you yet, just a supplier Davie was keeping him entertained!" Rab muttered.

"What is the man's name and address?" Susie questioned him.

"Hold on Susie," another long pause, more muffled voices. "I need to go love; I need to let the guys out to their taxis!"

"Rab please where is he?" Susie said desperately.

"Susie, stop worrying love, he will be home at some point Davie just got full of it!"

"Go to bed, you need your sleep!"

The line went dead. Susie stood staring at the phone as she laid the receiver down. "Full of it! What the hell does that mean?" She said loudly to the phone. Her heart was beating so fast, she felt sick with worry, her head was pounding. She went into the kitchen and took two paracetamols with water, then went through and plonked herself down on the couch. She sat there with her fat stomach and swollen aching breasts, knowing in her heart Davie was up to 'no good with another woman!' She was in the living room all night on her own, rocking with grief, then pacing back and forth with anger, she did not phone her mother or any old friends as she felt ashamed that her husband would do such a thing when she was so near to having their first child.

#

Susie was exhausted lying on the couch, when Davie eventually came home. She had cried so much, she barely opened her swollen eyes when he walked straight through the living room and upstairs into the bathroom, locking the door behind him. She heard the shower and lay listening to him move about. She dosed off, sleeping the day away. Davie was not there when she awoke, she only got up to drink water and eat a sandwich. She felt too emotionally drained to call Davie to discuss anything with him. Climbing the stairs to her cosy bed, tucking the fresh brushed cotton sheets around her, she was out like a light. When she woke in the morning, Davie was lying in their bed, she didn't wake him. She couldn't bare the thought of another argument. All that day Susie had the urge to organise the house, her 'Hospital bag,' her cupboard, she hardly stopped, she had been feeling restless and her back had been exceptionally achy.

#

"I hear you were on the blower to Rab the other night giving him grief about me!" Davie said as he walked into the kitchen, she was looking out the window at the three Magpies that were devouring furiously the bread she had thrown. Her back was to him! "You not talking?" Davie asked sternly.

"Not much to say to that Davie!" Susie answered dryly.

"I was with a supplier, I had too much to drink!"

"Yes, Rab said!" she exclaimed.

"Aye, well if you're going to be like that!" Davie said.

"Like what Davie exactly?" she snapped.

"How would you feel if it was you, if I had stayed out all night, if I was not pregnant, eh Davie?"

"I would trust you, that's what!" he shouted as he turned and marched out of the kitchen.

Susie shouted after him, "Oh would you really?" "Liar!" she screamed; she heard him lift his car keys from the hall table. "Before I was up the duff, I couldn't breathe for your jealousy!" she shouted, then she heard the front door as it was slammed shut.

Susie felt her tummy heavier than usual, so she lay on the couch the rest of the day watching daytime TV, eventually climbing the stairs to run a warm bath. She was miserable.

"This is not the way it is supposed to be god," she prayed, "please get us back on the right road!"

Once in the warm water her muscles and joints seemed much more relaxed, she could barely dry herself off before collapsing into bed. Early that morning, about four Davie crept into bed falling immediately into sleep.

"Susie, Susie, wake up," Davie was sitting up in bed shaking her shoulder as she roused, "you have wet the bed!" he looked disgusted. Susie immediately sat up, she looked under her, her nightdress was wet, the bed was damp with a pink streak on the sheets.

"Oh my god, my waters have broken!" Susie said excitedly, "I must be having the baby!" Susie was in labour for a long twenty hours before she was given a caesarean section to bring the baby safely out into the world! Davie was there to see his daughter being born and was 'love struck' for his wife and child. He looked down on his tiny girl, then up into Susies eyes, tears ran down his face. "I am so, so sorry Susie, I'm going to be a better man for you and the wee one." He held on to his wife sobbing, "I promise, everything will be wonderful."

Susie believed him.

#

For six beautiful loving months Davie stuck to his word. The Irvines were happy and content, it was as if the problems in the marriage had disappeared with the birth of Wee Fee. Davie stopped the nights out, he seemed to dote on his new daughter and was there for his wife one hundred percent. Happiness was short lived for Susie though as Davie slowly slid back in with Rab!

#

Rita came to visit Susie and baby Fee early one sunny morning. Susie was sitting at the kitchen table with the sunlight steaming in the kitchen window, when Rita opened the back door popping her head round,

"Hi Susie, safe to come in?"

"Yeah, Reet, he is still in bed." Susie smiled, "Coffee?"

"Yes please," Rita said. "I needed to see you, as I have some news, "she paused.

Susie walked over and closed the kitchen door quietly.

"What's the news?" Susie asked, screwing her face up questioningly.

"I'm moving!" Rita giggled opening her eyes wide.

"I'm at the end of my tether with Rab. I'm moving out!" Rita proclaimed.

"No, no, tell me you're joking Reet. I don't want you to go!" Susie's face fell, she looked at Rita pleadingly, "you're what keeps me sane!"

"Sorry, Susie love, I just can't put up with his womanising anymore. He has given me a venereal disease and if that isn't bad enough, completely humiliated me by shagging the local Newsagents daughter who is eighteen!" "Debbie!" Rita said the name with distaste.

"No, Reet, surely not the Debbie that works a Thursday student night in the club," Susie looked shocked, "she seems such a lovely girl!" "Are you sure?" Susie asked.

"Yes, I am positive! Rita was adamant. "Everyone is talking about them it has been going on for months!" "Rab and that wee lass!" "Her parents are livid!"

"That is disgusting!" said Susie looking grim, "but, where will you go Rita?" She asked with concern.

"I know this older guy, we are good friends through the fruit market, I've known him a few years now, we always joke around, and he has great 'banter.' He has a chain of greengrocers. Well anyway, I confided in him about what Rab's been up too and that I wanted to leave him. He just blurted out that he has always been crazy for me but didn't want to say as I was with Rab! He has offered me a room in his house until I decide what to do." Rita said excitedly.

"Oh wow," "Are you sure you will be okay? I mean is this guy okay Reet? Will it not make things a bit complicated living in his house if he fancies you." Susie looked into Ritas' face wide eyed.

"No, he is a lovely man Susie, not a womaniser like Rab, don't worry I will be fine. I will be back soon to see you and Wee Fee soon as I can." "This is all very sudden Rita; I am worried about you making a big mistake!" "No luv, no mistake! I've been thinking constantly about leaving for the last six weeks. My health comes first, Rab is selfish, he didn't even have the decency to put a 'johnny' on it!"

"Will you phone me and give me your address?" Susie asked, her eyes were full of tears, "you are my only true friend Reet."

"Of course, you have been a great friend to me, I don't want to lose touch." Rita gave Susie a big hug and held her close. She clasped Susie's face with her hands, looking into her eyes seriously. "Watch your Davie, Susie, he is a selfish bastard too! I do not want to hurt you, but you need to know the truth. Davie has told everyone at the club he is divorced." Susie's eyes widened her mouth in a gape. "He is behaving as though he is a single man luv!" Rita paused, looking sadly into Susie's face. "You are far too good for him, you know that don't you?" Rita whispered loudly. "I know." Susie said softly, "I am going to miss you so much Rita!"

"I'll call you as soon as I have a new number and am settled." Susie just nodded, wiping away her tears. She stood at the living room window sadly watching as her friend as she drove away. 'It is true,' Susie thought, 'Davie is messing around.'

#

A month later Davie is pulling his socks on while sitting on the bed. "Can you believe it?" Davie blurts out.

"What?" Susie asks as she is tidying around the bedroom.

"Rab gave Rita a settlement for half of the deposit on their house and a bit more, even though they were not married!

"Rab was glad to see the back of her I think." Davie snorts.

"She deserves a settlement." Susie states. "Rab has accepted the split with good grace he knows he was to blame; he was messing around!" Susie said as she picked up Davies wet towel from the bedroom carpet. Davie watches her intently as she speaks. "I mean was he really going with that wee girl Debbie?" Susie asked.

"Wee girl! Davie exclaimed sarcastically, "Don't be so naive Susie for fucks sake, "Debbie is no angel, she is a wee slag, she was practically begging Rab for it! She was shagging a few of the guys at the club, no just Rab."

"Why would he go with her then? I mean Rita is beautiful and so much fun!" Susie genuinely wanted to know.

"Rab wasn't getting enough! Reet was too busy getting banged by big bananas down the market," Davie snorted a sarcastic laugh. "Reet was hanging about with some old codger, fucking him behind Rabs back!"

"That is not true Davie! Rita loved Rab, but he gave her a disease!" Susie said with indignation loudly, not thinking. "So, I doubt she would be having sex with anyone!"

Davie lowered his eyebrows, his eyes became dark, his face contorted.

"Did that wee cow tell you that?" he spat the words, jumping up off the bed onto his feet. Susie started to walk out the bedroom, but he came up behind her, grabbing her arm, she burled round dropping the dirty washing, as she did Davie slapped her hard across her face. Her cheek burned hot after the sting of pain, she put her hand to her face in shock.

"Don't you ever say that about Rab again, do you hear me? That's a fucken lie!" Davie spoke loud and clear into her face. "Do you hear me?"

"Yes, I hear you!" Susie said in a whisper, still in shock. Susie went to check on Fee Fee in her Play pen. Davie walked past them on his way to the front door he said nonchalant,

"Rab offered me the Managers job in the club full time, I've accepted."

#

Davie was enjoying his new position way too much for a married man with a small child. He loved the power he had. People wanted to be his friend, to be around him, they would buy him drink, give him drugs, so they could get in the club, he loved it.

Most of all he relished the attention he got from the opposite sex as the manager.

His personality completely changed; he became short tempered, lost weight. Davie now took sun bed sessions and spent money on fashionable clothes. Susie and Davie were rarely together, by the time Wee Fee was five years old Susie was deeply unhappy with the marriage, she threw herself into making her wee girl's life as good as possible despite her husband's disinterest!

#

It was yet another weekend where her husband was not home. Susie awoke, she looked at the digital clock on the bedside table, it was four a.m. she lay eyes wide open staring at the ceiling, suddenly she heard her husband's laugh. She sat 'bolt upright' her hearing straining in the darkness, again she heard his laugh, she got out of bed, pulling on her dressing gown, she went downstairs, the house was silent, he wasn't there? Susie heard his voice this time mixed with a women's laugh, the muffled noises were coming from Rab's house next door.

Susie's heart was racing, she felt shaky, the sounds were toward the rear of the house, she slowly 'tip toed' through the kitchen and slid the glass patio doors open, just an inch or two ajar, she stood out of sight. Rab was in the jacuzzi with a young woman, she looked around twenty years old. Susie gathered all her strength together, her breathing quickened, wrapping her fluffy dressing gown around her, she pulled the door quietly open enough to step out, she walked over the grass silently on her bare feet to the slatted fencing and peered through; She could see a man's bare legs stretched out on a sun lounger, over his thighs was straddled a woman, the side of the woman's leg and naked bottom were visible, she was sure the man's leg was Davies. Susie's face was on fire, she froze, then trembling she moved to return to the house.

"Hey who's that?" "Is that you Susie?" Rab called out!

She stopped, listening, there was a flurry of movement from the patio and then she heard the sun lounger scraping against the ground as it was moved, then the Bi folding doors that Rita had proudly showed off to her the day they were installed, were closing slowly as if someone was trying to be quiet entering Rab's house.

"Are you there Susie?" again Rab called out.

"Who is Susie?" asked the young woman.

"My neighbour," Rab replied loudly, then he was whispering something to her, the woman started giggling.

Susie ran into the house, she quickly went to check on Wee Fee, who was sleeping soundly, curled up, cosy and snug in her small bed. Susie stared at Fee's innocent face; tears stung her eyes. Susie closed her daughter's bedroom door quietly, then ran downstairs, straight round to Rab's front door, she was going to ring the bell but then by chance tried the door handle, the door opened!

Susie stood with the front door open for a moment breathing heavily, as if there was a line she didn't want to cross, but she knew she had too! She stepped inside.

Susie walked down the hall of Rab's house into the lounge, there was Davie sitting in an armchair obviously very drunk. He stared straight at Susie, she looked at him with disgust.

"I heard you outside, I saw you" she said accusingly.

"You saw nothing," he growled.

"Where is she?" Susie raised her voice.

"Who? You crazy bitch?" Davie spat the words at her.

She turned to go up the stairs where she knew the woman must be! Before she could take another step, Davie sprang from his seat grabbing her hair, pulling her backwards away from the stairs to the ground, he kicked out at her, his foot connected with her stomach, she curled up in pain, he kicked her again on the back and she screamed!

"Davie Stop" shouted the voice of a young woman coming down the stairs.

"Rabbbbbbbbbbb Stop him," the woman shouted.

Susie heard her husband being pulled away as she was curled up on the carpet.

The young woman who had been in the jacuzzi had come in through the Bi folds, standing bare breasted and wet, she hurried over to help Susie up.

"That is uncalled for, totally out of order Davie" she said sternly.

"Help her next door," Rab directed.

The woman grabbed a man's shirt that was on the floor and put it on before she helped Susie out into the front garden, then into her house.

47

"Go in, lock the door! Leave the keys in the lock on the inside so he can't get in."

Susie stared at her trembling. "Just until he has time to get his act together, he is out his head on coke!" the young woman said. Susie stared at her numbly.

Once inside Susie stood with her back against the locked front door, "Oh god, what is happening, I don't understand what has happened to my husband, to my life!" she whispered.

#

From that night things with Davie only got worse. Susie wanted to leave, but she had nowhere to go with a small child, she had no job, no savings of her own. She had put her heart and soul into making their house a beautiful home. Davie walked in and out of the house like it was a hotel. He was still paying all the bills, but she had to practically beg him for money for food. She suspected what the woman had said that night was true, he was taking drugs; She had found a small plastic pouch in his Denims 'pocket when putting a washing in the machine, she had approached him about it. "Davie, I found this!" she had held out the clear bag of white powder to him, Davie snatched it out her hand.

"I am worried about you, maybe this is why you have changed, maybe this is what is wrong with you!" Susie had said in a concerned voice.

"Mind your own fuckin business, there is fuck all wrong with me, I haven't changed, you have you moaning cow. Look at you!" He pushed her so hard against the wall, pinning her there. "If you mention anything to my folks, you will be very, very sorry, do you hear me Susie!" Davie fiercely said into her face, Susie nodded.

Susie never mentioned the drugs again.

When she ever complained or contradicted Davie he lifted his hand, he'd punch her hard, right on the back of the head or in the stomach, where there would be no visible bruises.

48

Susie withdrew from the few acquaintances she had and her mum to avoid the awkward questions about her loss of weight and hellish appearance; She would sort it out soon, something would change, something had to change, she reassured herself.

#

The only thing that brought Susie and Wee Fee joy and peace was their regular walks to the local Glen. Susie would take her daughter to the small playpark often and after a push on the swings and a few slides down the shoot, they would wonder down the pathways through the woods to the river. Susie and Wee Fee loved the Glen and they never failed to stop and admire the view of the Viaduct from their favourite spot. They felt happy here in the Glen, it felt safer than being at home.

Sitting on the big rocks by the river, Susie would pray out loud, "Please God if you're listening to me, please give me strength to leave Davie, show me a way. Amen."

Susie and Fee Fee were unaware that they were constantly watched from the trees, every word they said was listened too.

On one of their regular visits on a warm sunny day, Susie had bought Wee Fee a Childs' fishing net, a bright yellow one to much her sunny disposition and sun dress, they chatted on about what fish could be found in the river.

" Do you think I will catch one today Mummy?" Fee Fee asked cheerfully.

"You can try!" said Susie, "But we must put it back in the river if we do, remember."

"Can I catch a shark in the river Mummy?"

"No, thank goodness, there are no Sharks here Fee Fee," Susie laughed,

"Not even a Baby Shark?" Fee asked.

"No Fee, no Sharks, they have big teeth that might bite us!" Susie made big biting motions with her mouth, "the Mummy Shark is coming to get you!" Susie laughed chasing Fee Fee down the pathways, Fee screaming with laughter down to the 'Beachy bit.'

Susie and Fee Fee were sitting on the top of the rocks sipping out of Ribena boxes of juice, enjoying eating the sandwiches they brought with them. Susie was raising her face in the direction of the sun and enjoying the warmth on her skin, when the hair on her arms stood up, she sat up straight and looked straight ahead. Wee Fee was waving at a figure with long grey hair, standing on the pathway halfway between them and the Viaduct, the figure put their arm in the air and let go of something white, Susie thought it was a plastic bag, it drifted away in the air, something didn't feel right. Susie waved, she wondered if it was someone she knew, the figure whoever it was did not wave back. Wee Fee stood up; Susie took her eyes away from the figure to put her arms around her daughter so she wouldn't fall off the rocks into the river. When she returned her gaze, the figure was gone, she scanned the pathway up to the Viaduct, 'not there!' Down to the Beachy bit, 'no, not there!' 'Where did they go? There was nowhere they could have gone to be out of sight so quickly! She thought.

"Let's do our fishing mummy," Fee said moving down the rocks pulling at Susie's hand. The sun glimmered through the trees creating beautiful patterns on the ground. White light twinkled on the water as they fished, putting tiny fish in their plastic bucket. Susie and Fee chatted and played in the gritty sand, they tried to skim stones until no more flat ones could be found.

"Can I take the little fishes home Mummy?" Fee asked.

"No darling, they would be sad. The little fishes want to go home to their Mummies." Susie said.

"Please, just one?" Fee begged, but as the sun went down Fee Fee watched as Susie gently emptied the fish back in the river.

They happily walked up slowly towards home, Wee Fee stopping to look at leaves and pick up snails. Under the Viaduct arch they went, the charcoaled wood from an old fire lay with empty cans and broken Buckfast bottles.

"Watch your feet," Susie said while guiding Fee around the debris, Susie realised it must be late as it is getting rather dark by the time they reach what the locals call 'Faerie wood.'

As they made their way along the path, the stones that bordered the pathway became bright in front of them, lights appear everywhere, beautiful glowing orbs, dancing in front of them.

'I'm dreaming,' thought Susie, 'tiny fluttering,' from what Susie thought looked like little people, whispered as they passed her ears "your safe," "we are here for you," "we will help you." 'I'm going mad,' Susie said in a whisper! 'I am a crazy bitch, just as Davie said,' she thought. Wee Fee let go of Susies' hand, she was chatting away to herself, giggling, she started singing. The bright whisps dancing around Fee Fee. Susie remembered something she had learned at school:

"How now, spirit? Whither wander you?"

'A Fairy Song'   by William Shakespeare

Over hill, over dale,

Thorough bush, thorough brier,

Over park, over pale,

Thorough flood, thorough fire!

I do wander everywhere,

Swifter than the moon's sphere.

And I serve the Fairy Queen,

To dew her orbs upon the green.

The cowslips tall her pensioners be.

In their gold coats spots you see.

Those be rubies, fairy favours.

In those freckles live their savours.

I must go seek some dewdrops here,

And hang a pearl in every cowslip's ear.

The song played in Susie's mind repeatedly, as the tiny houses lit up one by one in the tree stumps and rocks as Susie and Fee walked past.' Susie was mesmerized, by the beautiful floating beings of light.

#

Abruptly, it was dark when they emerged from the end of the stone lined pathway, the lights were no more, they were back in the dark grey dullness of the park. Susie frantically searched the darkness behind them for the lights, but there were none. She lifted Fee who wrapped her legs around her mothers' hips. Susie walked quickly past the dark playpark and out the gates feeling someone's presence behind them, she hurried out toward the street. Susie turned to see an older woman with grey hair at the park gates, even at that distance the woman's eyes were magnetic, drawn in to her own, a bright green, she was drifting closer and closer. Susie felt paralysed with fear for what seemed a long minute, she wanted to scream but couldn't, until the woman passed right through her. Susie shuddered, 'someone just walked over my grave!' Terrified she broke into a jog holding Fee Fee close to her tight, until she was out on to the village Main Street under the light of the lampposts, the streets were deserted.

#

When Susie arrived home, she is shocked to find that Davie was in the house; he opened the front door. "Where the fuck have you been?" he spits.

"Sorry we didn't realise the time, we were fishing in the Glen River," Susie explains.

"To four o'clock in the fucking morning, do you think I'm stupid?" Davie shouts. Wee Fee starts to cry, "Stop it Daddy." Susie takes her daughter quickly up the stairs.

Davie shouts after her, "I'm going to bed, you're not welcome in it, you smelly cow. I don't know who you've been with!" Susie's heart is pounding, she is confused about the time.

She doesn't even undress Wee Fee, just pops her under her duvet as she kisses her cute wee face. "They were lovely Mummy!" Fee mumbled; she is asleep within seconds.

'How the hell did we spend all afternoon and night in the Glen?' she fretted, 'did I fall asleep and dream the whole Faerie walk? She wonders, 'No, because Fee saw it too!" 'Have we been hallucinating together?' 'Oh god, for Wee Fees' sake, I hope I'm not taking some sort of breakdown!' she worries. 'Who was that woman, a ghost?' Susie recognised her but from where?

Too scared to go into her bedroom to face Davie, Susie rests her head on her daughter's bed and after an hour or so with the first signs of light, she creeps downstairs to the empty couch, pulling a throw blanket over her and falling into a deep sleep.

#

Chapter 5.

Retribution 1990

Rab had sold the house next door a year or so after Rita left him. He bought himself a flat in Merchant City, Glasgow, he liked the buzz of the city life, and it was local to the club. He had given Davie more control over the running of the Glasgow business, Rab now took more to do with the club and his other interests abroad, he loved the fun holiday atmosphere, flying out to his flat in Palma, Majorca when he could.

#

Susie is now 36 years old she had eventually escaped Davie in 1987. The night Susie had walked out; Davie was home.

"Any chance of something decent to eat in here before I go to work?" he shouted from the Lounge. Susie walked through and stood at the door,

"Wee Fee and I have already eaten spaghetti bolognaise, there is plenty left, I was going to freeze it." she said.

"Leftovers is it for the man of the house!" Davie sarcastically jibed.

"Not at all Davie, it is just so rare for you to eat here!" "Don't go far Fee Fee!" Susie said in a loud sing song voice. Wee Fee had gone outside to cycle up and down the Avenue with her friend from two doors down. Susie reheated the pot and put a large portion of spaghetti on a big plate for Davie, she set it on a tray with a glass of milk and took it through to him, he was watching the news as she laid the tray on his lap. "Do you want Parmesan cheese with it?" she asked. "Aye, I want Parmesan cheese with it!" he mimicked with a sarcastic tone. Susie collected the tub of dried cheese and put it on his tray.

"What the fuck is that? You would think with all the money that I give you to buy food, you'd at least have grated fucken Parmesan cheese and not this dried shite!" he spoke in an all too familiar aggressive tone.

"Sorry, it was all they had at the local shop, I didn't get to the Deli," Susie said quietly. "What did you say, speak up, I can't hear youuuuuuu!" he said loudly.

"Sorry, it was all they had at the local shop, I didn't get to the Deli," she repeated but louder. Davie shakes some of the dried cheese on his pasta and starts to eat it, he spits a mouthful out onto the plate and said, "take this mushy muck away, I canny eat it, it stinks just like you're cooking."

"The Pasta is softer as it's been reheated, it was lovely, if you had eaten it with us!" Susie said. Davie ignored her completely, staring at the Television.

Susie stared at him, she envisaged picking up his fork and sticking it in his eye and popping his eyeball out his head! She smiled to herself.

"What you fucken grinning at, you crazy bitch? You want something to fucken smile about?" He suddenly threw the tray up in the air, the plate, spaghetti, sauce, cheese, milk came down, covering Susie and the carpet. Davie picked up the tray and started banging it off her head, with each slam of the tray he insulted her, "Susie (slam)is (slam) a stupid (slam slam) cow"(slam) Susie knew not to hit back as it just made the beating worse, she just stood hunched with her arms pulled over in front of her face. Fee Fee had come in the front door and saw her father battering Susie.

"Stop hitting my mummy," she screamed, she ran over to him and started pounding her fists on him as best she could. Davie swatted her like a fly, her small body flew over the Livingroom onto the floor, she started howling. Susie ran to her and pulled her up and ran upstairs with her to the bathroom and locked the door. Fee was terrified, she had wet her pants and was shaking. "Shuuush, she whispered to Fee," putting her finger in front of her pursed mouth, she held her daughter tight. All was quiet, Davie banged the bathroom door, Susie and Fee both jumped and gasped.

Davie shouted, "you better get that mess you made cleaned up by the time I get home! You hear me Susie?"

"Yes, I hear you Davie!" She could feel his rage emanating from outside the door, then after a few minutes they heard the front door slam. They stayed there huddled in the Bathroom until they heard his car reversing down the gravel driveway. Davie had never hurt Fee before, he had shouted at her, but never lifted his hand. Susie put a cold cloth on her daughter's forehead.

"Your okay sweetheart, let's get you into something nice and dry;" she proceeded to put her in the shower, then found her some clean clothes. Susie knew now, she had to leave him!

She phoned her Mum Linda, who was nearly sixty-five years old with poor mobility, she lived in a one bed ground floor mobility flat and didn't keep well. Susie told her mum what had gone on.

"I don't want to phone the Police Mum as last time they told Davie to leave for one night then to come back in the morning when he had calmed down! I even saw one of the Policemen pat Davie on the back as they walked down the path with him. When Davie got back the next day, I just got a worse time of it Mum, honestly."

Her mother listened then said, "go to 'Glasgow's Women's Aid' as you can't come here, it will be the first place he will look."

"Grab what you need, once your safe, I will bring you some money, contact a lawyer about the house," "your entitled to something and money for Fiona," Linda said.

"Okay Mum." "I hate leaving my lovely home." Susie said in a sad voice.

"You will have another home." "He will really hurt you or even kill you eventually Susie," Linda said with purpose, "no house is worth your life!"

A month or two after Susie left, she and Fee were living in a bedsit type flat, that was all she could afford on unemployment benefits, but it was safe.

#

Davie was practically living in the club, he and Rab were sitting in the right back corner of the tables surrounding the dance floor, it was about four a.m. All the staff were at a near-by table waiting on their staff taxis; 'One by one, 'the staff left until Rab and Davie were alone. Davie was complaining to Rab about his situation, over a drink.

"I'm totally skunnered with that house now," said Davie, "it's like a ball and chain round my neck!" Rab took a sip of his jack Daniels and replied. "Look Davie, you've got a wain, you should do the right thing man, just sell up! Give Susie a chunk to get her a wee place. Susie is a nice bird, you shouldnay be tight with her. We all had some great times together."

"You don't know her Rab!" Davie swallowed the rest of his drink.

"People split up all the time, look at me and Reet." Rab said.

Davie furrowed his brow, "I'm not gonni get that much Rab, once I pay back everything," he took a long drag on his cigarette, "I will be lucky to get twenty grand!" Davie sighs.

"Come on, who you tryin tae kid!" Rab said with disbelief!

"You've been selling plenty of that shit in here, you must be loaded?" Rab laughed.

"Aye, I've made a bit, but I've got a right dirty habit to take care off, you know that!" Davie downs another whiskey.

Rab leans back stretching his legs out, "I need to take care of the guy who's bringing the gift in next month, so I need to do another wee holiday to the flat (referring to his apartment in Majorca,) you gonni be able to cope here?"

"Sure, I can cope, I always do." Davie smiles.

"I want us to sell up here Davie, for the two of us to open another club in Spain, a joint ownership, you can sink your house money in."

"Sounds like the best plan," said Davie "after all if I stay here, I'm gonni end up doing that bitch in!"

Rab shakes his head and rolls his eyes. The men lock up the club, it's now about five in the morning.

"You goin back to yours?" asked Rab.

"Aye, I better make moves to smarten the place up, I've got it like a shit hole." "I need to contact a Cleaner and an Estate agent and I really do need to get a divorce," Davie exhales heavily.

"I don't want her trying to get anything from our future ventures." "When you heading over Rab?"

"Gonni get a flight for this week, let you know, "Rab replies. "Watch out for the Polis you've had a bucket the night Davie!" he adds before walking in the direction of his flat in Merchant City.

Something makes a loud flutter noise above them; Davie looks up. 'A pigeon,' he thinks.

Davie gets in his Ford Escort and puts some coke on the Cars' Manual he had sitting on the passenger seat for that purpose, he chops it into a line with a 'Stanley blade' and takes a strong snort, "ahhhhhh," he sits squeezing his nose and wiping his nostrils, he sits back then forward, looking in the drivers mirror to make sure his nose is clean. He put the manual under the passenger seat and started the car and drove toward Renfield Street. Down through Glasgow city he travelled, enjoying the high, some Phil Collins music and the drive out toward Shawlands, there was still people stoating about from their night out.

The Petrol light on the dashboard caught his eye! "Damn, I forgot about that, I wonder how much is left?" he thought as he continued up to Merrylee shops but the garage he intended to visit, is closed, he cuts through a back road, toward the road leading to Giffnock police station. 'I should have enough to get me hame!' he reassures himself.

Up toward Clarkston he drives as fast as he can, he passes the local train station when the car starts to splutter, it stalls on the hill.

Davie tried to start it, again, again, pushing his foot down angrily on the accelerator, but nothing happened, he was rolling back, he pulled on the hand brake.

'Thank fuck the roads are empty' he thought. He manoeuvred, rolling the car back into a parking space.

"Fir fucks sake!" he shouted, hitting the steering wheel with the flat of his hand, in anger.

"If it wisnae for bad luck I'd have nae luck!" he raged.

'I will just jump through the rear of the Glen come out a couple of streets from home, rather than walk up the main drag, in case there are any 'bams' about, I'm too pissed for any scrapping!' he thought, he got out checked the boot for a petrol can, to go get petrol after he had a sleep, but there was no petrol can." Typical!" he slammed the boot shut hard. It was getting lighter now and he started walking. He entered the small gates of Overlee park walking toward the woods, it was eerily quiet, not a soul in sight. Past the Pavilion he marched along the path toward the walkway under the Viaduct.

Davie jumped, "Oh! What the fuck?" as something darted in front of him and disappeared into the woods, 'probably a cat or a big rat he thought.'

Davies' legs were pulled away from under him, he heard laughing as he fell and hit the concrete path heavily; He stayed down for a minute then sat up, rubbing his head then his shoulder. He looked around frantically. His heart was pounding, 'what happened there,' he wondered.

"God, I'm so fucked up!" he said.

'Felt like something tripped me up? Or pull me down?' he wondered.

He made moves to stand when he saw a cat, no not a cat, he tried to focus on the shape, it is a wee man, he stared not believing his eyes, a very robust wee man with almost illuminous eyes, but the man is only about nine inches tall! He stood about three feet away and was staring right into Davies face. Davie is bemused, he giggles, then smiles then laughs out loud! 'I'm hallucinating,' he thinks, "You're not real!" he said loudly into the stillness of the morning. The small man speaks directly to him slowly. "You're not real!" his voice is deep and low, devoid of all emotion.

Davie shakes his head, trembling, he starts to move, making efforts to stand, when something pulls his head back by the hair, he realises in horror that he is being held down by more of these creatures, the back of his head, his arms, everywhere, whatever these things are, they are very strong. He can only stare up to the under the Arch of the Viaduct.

He thinks, 'this is a nightmare, too much drink and drugs.'

He shouts out to himself. "Wake up Davie, wake up! this can't be real!"

The wee man is now standing on his chest staring down at him. "Wake up Davie, wake up! this can't be real!" the little man said in a guttural voice.

Davie tries to scream, but no sound comes out, the wee man stretches his neck, sticking his chin out and from behind him appears large black wings, he grins, revealing a huge mouth of hideous jagged teeth. Davie is panting, he is uncontrollably shaking. The creatures he can see are all staring at him with their grotesque grins, he suddenly feels his clothing become tight everywhere, as he is lifted, he seems to float into the air as though he weighs nothing at all, up and over the paths' fencing, he was elevated up, up, above the Viaduct itself, high above. Davie shrieks as he looked down to the huge drop and the river and the rocks below.

" Stop!" he yells out, one of the creatures bites him hard tearing away half his ear, "Ahhhhhhhhhh," he felt warm blood trickle down his neck.

"Pleeeeeeease don't," he begged, he felt a stinging bite on his side.

" Oh god help me," he shouted. The creatures mimicked him, "Oh god help me," they chorused, biting him again and again. The little monsters were delighted with his agonising cries. The Host dropped him from a height on to the railway track, breaking his lower leg at the shin with a loud crunch.

Now on top of the Viaduct, they descended on him like a swarm, whooping with enjoyment, biting and ripping his flesh until he passed out.

#

Davies' ears were filled with a loud horn noise, which jolted his eyes open, he looked up at the blue sky and for a brief moment he felt a wave of pleasure 'I am alive!'

In agony he pulled himself up, to sit. The train slammed into him, it was travelling at speed and his body exploded on impact, his body parts flew through the air backwards and outwards against the direction of travel, a leg was dragged under the train, a ragged and torn lower leg dangled on the fencing hanging by a foot, pieces of him were washed down river but strangely a piece of his heart lay on the rocks where his wife and child had sat with their picnic many moons ago. It remained there for a while, until a fox sniffed it out then sat there enjoying the meal in the early morning sun.

#

Twenty seconds before, the train driver thought he saw something on the track, a cloud of darkness or a flock of black birds, he sounded the horn, the birds or whatever rose disappearing into the sky, then he realised it was a body on the tracks, a somebody, panic strikes, he hit the brakes, his heart was beating so hard he thought it might burst, but it was too late, he hit, then had to run over what was left of the body. The train eventually stopped further down the track, he made the emergency call, he knew who ever it was, is definitely dead. "I am very sorry to say there is an obstruction on the line, please stay away from the doors and windows." he announced to the few passengers on the train.

#

The day after Davie died, Susie was in her bedsit when two Policemen arrived at her door, "Mrs Susan Irvine?"

"Yes," Susie answered, a tall, slim man about thirty-five addressed her.

"I'm Officer Stephen Morne and this is Officer Gary Pierce, can we come in?" He held out his identification.

"Yes, of course, what is this about? Is it my Mum or Dad?" she sounded panicked.

"No, Mrs Irvine."

"Thank god!" she said.

"I'm sorry it is about your husband; can we all take a seat please?" Officer Morne asks.

Susie led them through and let them sit on the bed as she sat on the one chair there was in the room, pulling it to face them.

" So, what has he got himself into now?" she asked with cynicism.

Officer Stephen Morne leaned forward, "I am so sorry to inform you, but your husband has been found dead, he was hit by a train!"

Susie just stared into Stephens' kind face, her eyes unblinking.

"Is it okay to call you by your first name Mrs Irvine?" Stephen asked,

"Yes," she softly replied.

"Susan, would you like a cup of tea or a sip of water?" She didn't respond.

"Gary, could you make Susan a cup of tea," Stephen said, nodding to the kettle on the table. Stephen had a strange feeling, he was sure he recognised this woman's face, but he couldn't remember where from, she looked so familiar.

He held her hand, "are you okay Susan?"

"Yes," she nodded. Stephen let go of her hand as Gary handed her a mug of tea.

"There will be an investigation, so I will probably be back or one of my associates will call to ask you a few questions about your husband." Susan is nodding.

"You okay Susan? Is there someone we can call to be with you?"

"No, no, no need, I will be okay, honestly," she said, she sat staring numbly at nothing.

"Would you like us to sit with you for a while Susan?" Stephen asked.

"No, No, I have to pick up my wee lassie from school," Susie replied.

Stephen nods, continuing, "Okay if you are sure, here is my card, if you need to know anything, just call."

"Thank you very much for your kindness," she says as she takes the card. Their eyes met for a second, Stephen thought 'she has the greenest eyes I have ever seen," he felt a shiver run up his spine.

#

Once the Policemen leave, Susie sits on the bed, she wants to cry, tries to will herself to feel something, but she is numb.

The Transport Police attended the scene and then a further Police investigation concluded that Davies' death was suicide, probably due to the breakup of his marriage, a spiralling drug habit and the pressures of work. Susie became the sole owner of their marital home, she was also able to pay off the mortgage with the insurance money, the Life policy had thankfully passed the two-year suicide clause. Susie tried not to feel delighted, she had loved Davie once, he was still Fiona's father after all; but pure joy is what she felt.

Susie and Fee started to visit the Glen again enjoying their "Dear green place," taking flowers and brightly painted stones laying them in the rocks and the foot of trees, not to remember Davie but as a thank you, to whoever or whatever answered her prayers.

#

Chapter 6.

The Tale of the missing hand 2004

Officer Stephen Morne, now 49 years old, was in Reardons snooker hall in Shawlands. "Yay, I'm clearing up the day, eh!" Graeme his old pal said with a huge smile.

"Oh man, I'm playing so badly!" Stephen said letting out a huge sigh.

"You're always shite!" Graeme joked.

" Let's have one more game then, give me a chance to redeem myself" Stephen urged.

"Sorry no can do big man, I need to go, she is going aff her heed, I was supposed to be back ages ago!" Graeme said referring to his wife.

"I'm gonni stay for a couple more drinks before heading home, my 'pussy,' doesn't mind if I'm late!" They both laughed loudly.

"Lucky you!" Graeme said in good humour, knowing that Stephen was referring to his cat.

Since Stephens' wife and he had divorced last year, he had adopted a stray Black cat with amazing green eyes, he named him Skraggy. The cat now would hardly leave the house he was so comfortable with his new environment. Stephen loved the cat, much more than he loved his x wife; in fact, he was very relieved to find out she now had a boyfriend and had abandoned the idea of reconciliation!

Once Graeme had left, Stephen sauntered over to the bar and ordered a drink. He had been there a while when he had overheard a guy on the next bar stool complaining about the Police to the guy next to him. Stephen had been in the force most of his adult life and enjoyed it, so the conversation had caught his attention.

"I know the Glen Park like the back of my hand, do you know it?" the man next to him asked his friend loudly.

"Not sure mate, canny think of it!" the older man replied.

Stephen turned round interrupting, "I know that park," he commented.

"Oh, Aye?" said the guy turning to Stephen.

"Joseph O'Devlin mate!" he offered Stephen his hand to shake.

"Stephen Morne," Stephen shook his hand.

Joseph continued talking and Stephen leaned in to join the conversation.

"I enjoy walking my dog through the woods there now, as I feel close to my brother and my Dah. Sometimes the place still gives me the chills as it did back when we were young and my brother John and I would go with a team of lads fishing and drinking, having a laugh."

He took a big sip of his drink, "Our father died down there when we were teenagers."

"Sorry to hear that," said the other man.

Talk of the Glen had sent a shiver up Stephens back and the hair on the back of his neck bristled.

"I've been in that Glen at night, it's a very strange place, with a very interesting history and a record of death as long as your arm," said Stephen.

"Aye creepy alright," Joseph replied, "I searched it every day when my brother went missing in 2002, he was found two years ago hanging from a tree, but he didnay do himself in I'm sure it was murder!" "What happened?" the other guy asked.

"It is a bit of a long story mate!" Joseph said.

"Uck give us it anyway Joe," the man smiled. Joseph took another big glug of his drink and began.

"My brother John was a good-looking guy, he was much younger looking than his years which got him into trouble, as plenty young women fancied him." "He could nay leave them alone," Joseph chortled. "He had a big personality too; he was a right 'fanny magnet; single or married it made no difference to him!" "Women and girls would pull each other's hair out fighting outside the pub over him when he was younger!"

 Joseph had obviously had a few to drink as he starts to include the bartender in the conversation, all three men are now listening intently.

"I was shocked at John as he fell hard and fast for a young lassie called Michelle Henderson who was only twenty-two years old, he had been seeing her for a few months despite the objection of her family, especially her dad Robert Henderson a recently retired cop."

Stephen had heard of Robert Henderson but kept that to himself.

"The Mrs and I told John the lassie was far too young fur him!"

"Wish I could get a twenty-two-year-old bird!" said the barman and they all chuckled.

"No chance you've got a face only your mammy could love!" the older guy jested, the men all laughed loudly. "You're no that braw yourself old yin!" the barman quipped.

Joseph continued on, "two months before Johns disappearance Michelle had finished the relationship sighting family pressure as the problem, John said he was gutted; But he continued to contact Michelle, he wanted her back and had even convinced her to go out with him a few times in secret, meeting in the Glen for fast sex in the woods."

"John liked the outdoors and nature!" Joseph snorted a short laugh and winked. They all laughed together.

"Michelle told me that she received repeated phone calls from John pleading with her to get back together. She said the day before he disappeared, he called her threatening to harm himself if she wouldn't take him back." "The last call Michelle received from John was supposedly around six pm when she was finishing work in the Village hairdressers, but she refused to walk round to meet him in the Glen. "We now know that he had parked his prized Toyota at the local train Station and walked into the nearby Glen Park."

"But what is strange, is that a couple of hours after Michelle got home from work, Michelle's father alerted the local Polis station, letting them know John may have been genuinely suicidal. I mean, why would he do that? The guy hated John?"

"You want another?" the man next to Joseph offered, nodding to the bartender to get them all a drink.

"I think it was due to Michelle's father being an x cop that two days later when John didn't show, the Police were out interviewing his former girlfriends and sending divers into the waters that run through the Glen Park." Joseph paused to down a whiskey.

Stephen agreed, "they don't usually bother for a man missing for 48 hours."

"John and I had been dragged up, we were great pals though, we only had each other," smiling he said, "we were always in trouble!" He gave a small laugh, "just petty stuff, you know." "Despite our upbringing, John was always a big softy really, cheeky but lovable. He hated pain of any sort, would avoid fights and would never take any unnecessary risks."

"We were very close; John even came to stay with me and the Mrs, but he had recently bought himself a nice wee flat. I ask you, why would he bother if he was gonni top himself?"

Everyone nodded in agreement.

"You know, I am Johns' next of kin, but the Polis never even told me John was missing, it was an old mate that contacted me! It wiz Michelle Henderson and her Da that were being contacted by the Polis?" Joseph shrugged and shook his head.

"Why?" Stephen asked, "that's weird, not the usual way things are done!"

"We contacted the police to let them know that we were Johns' immediate family, the O'Devlin, not the Henderson's!" Joseph stated.

"Me an Yvonne started hunting for John in the Glen woodland the minute we knew he was missing." Joseph said.

"The Glen is huge, it is dangerous, steep cliffs and uneven ground, an awfy large area for you and your wife to cover!" Stephen added.

"AYE! Don't I know it! Joseph raising his eyebrows and nodding.

"One good result was the Polis knew he must have his car and house keys plus a mobile phone."

The bartender signalled he would be back and went to serve some other customers that were standing waiting.

"Despite the Polis initial urgent response, now they didn't seem to give a fuck and implied that John was known as a womaniser and was probably with some bird as he had gone off before." "But he had never done that," Joseph said, "never!" "I always knew if John was going out of town, I tried to tell the polis that. They wernay interested."

"Me and Yvonne visited Michelle we wanted to hear her story again. "Michelle talked about John threatening suicide, she seemed very calm not overly emotional or upset, cold in fact! Her Dah insisted on being in the room with us and he seemed calm even rehearsed too!" Joseph raised his voice.

The bartender was back again, "What did I miss!" he asked.

Joseph replied, "I'm just saying something fishy about that bird of Johns and her Da!" "There is no way my brother committed suicide; he was such a big coward. He had always said he couldn't understand how anyone could be that brave or crazy to do that sort of thing!"

"Yet according to that Michelle lassie, our John was threatening to kill himself several times!"

"Yet he didn't call me once or even send me a text?"

"It all seems strange; it just doesn't add up for Yvonne and me."

"Seems a twisted tale right enough," the older man said.

"Even though we thought it was all very suspicious, we did think it was possible John had an accident in the Glen, so we continued to search for him daily, with friends and neighbours."

"Another on me?" asked the Barman.

"Thanks mate, much appreciated," Joseph said.

"Aye thanks," Stephen and the other man chimed in.

"The Polis announced they had a breakthrough; they had managed to trace a signal from Johns' mobile in a part of the Glen Park so would be searching that area section by section."

"But even so they still had not found John three months later!"

"Then Yvonne got a call from a friend Jessie, she said:

"I'm out at the park searching," "I bumped into an older lady, Alma, she was helping with the search too and led me to something she had found. Not John! But you'd better come and have a look." Stephen ears pricked up, "Alma did you say? Was she very old?"

"Don't know mate," Joseph replied, "I never met her."

"Can you remember if her second name Fravardin?" Stephens' heartbeat had quickened."
"Sorry no, when me and Yvonne arrived at the park to meet Jessie Gorrie she was on her own." "Why?" Joseph looked at Stephen quizzically.

"Oh, nothing!" Stephen replied but he had a strange, unsettled feeling, his throat felt tight. He momentarily thought of his night in the Glen as a young officer. He shivered.

"Carry on Joseph, sorry," Stephen said, shaking off the feeling.

"Jessie had a bag containing an entire police uniform folded. It was found lying in the area the police were meant to have searched?"

"We handed it in to the station thought it could be relevant."

"The plot thickens," said the Barman.

"A few weeks later, the polis confirmed it was genuine! The uniform number belonged to a female officer based in Giffnock, but the polis would not elaborate any on how or why the uniform was there! They refused to make any connection between the uniform and John's disappearance."

"Yvonne and I wondered, if John had been messin about with a female officer that was married or something?"

74

"Sounds like it!" said the older man.

"It certainly could be a possibility!" answered Stephen.

"Johns' phones contact list had a few well-known Glasgow small time gangsters, we both knew them growing up, a couple of the contacts were very well known criminals but as far as I know his only business with them was to try and flog them something or an odd game of pool, John knew what they were capable off, so would never have crossed them."

"Aye well he was a smart guy then!" the Barman said.

"However, there is someone I am still not so sure about." Joseph said.

"Who?" asked Stephen.

"A man John used to party with, the guy had moved away, but had suddenly turned up again a few months earlier. When ma brother saw him in the local pub again, his face fell."

"Jimmy High Tower!" he paused, "some call him Jimmy HT!" Joseph said.

"Oh aye, I heard of him," said the older man, pulling an inverted smile.

"Aye so have I!" said the Barman pulling a grimaced face. "Nasty piece of work, so I've heard!"

"Yep, me too! I've never met him though!" Stephen added.

"Man, he is huge, must be at least six foot five, dark curly hair and ice-cold blue eyes, he is always smiling or laughing, there is something about him though, very scary!" Joseph told Stephen.

"Jimmy HT would seek John out." "John would go with him, which I just couldnay understand as I could feel John didnay like him." Joseph said, "sorry guys I need a slash, be back in a quick shake of the lambs tail!"

"I wish I'd never asked to hear this bloody story!" the older man said, the three men laughed, "I need to get hame fir ma tea, but I wantae know whit happened!"

"Ano, I got work to do!" the Barman said, they all laughed at his remark as there was no one at the bar.

Joseph hurried back to his stool. "Where was I?" he asked.

Stephen replied, "Jimmy High Tower!"

"Oh Aye! Well, many times I asked John, what it wiz between Jimmy and him."

"All he would say was, "it's all in the past, Joe don't worry it's all sorted."
"Since John disappeared, I've spotted Jimmy parked around the corner watching our house; Or driving by slowly, I mean, why does he not just come in, I know him, for fucks sake?"

"Then this bird turns up at our door, saying she was worried about John and asking questions about the search for him. It just didnay feel right. When she left, Yvonne snuck round through the neighbours back yard to see where she went and spotted her getting into Jimmy High Towers car!"

"Pffffft, now that is suspicious!" the older man piped up.

"Definitely worth looking into!" Stephen suggested.

"Whit? I wouldnay be looking into anything to do with HT, if it were me!" the Barman scoffed, shaking his head. "Leave it alone mate!"

Joseph finished his drink, "stick another one in there, will ye pal!"

"Six months after my brother went missing, a project worker for Glasgow City Councils' cleansing Team, was carrying out some litter picking duties after many complaints about broken glass from walkers near the nursery beside the Glen, when he stumbled across John, hanging by a noose from a branch of a tree. "

"Aww that's tragic mate!" the Barman sympathetically said.

The others just nodded empathetically.

"John was found over a mile away, a real hike from the section of the park where the Polis had insisted his phone signal was.

"Poor big sod was hanging in the grounds at the back of the Nursery School, less than a hundred yards from the school building itself. Teachers and staff from the school were shocked, horrified, really mystified as they'd passed that tree nearly every day in term time. How did they not see John?"

"Can you believe it? You couldnay make it up!" Joseph sounded angry.

The other customer and the bartender are shaking their heads, muttering in agreement, "somethings just no right, about it all," "Sounds like he has been moved!" they all agreed.

Stephen agreed too, "the whole story smells off!"

"The very same guy who found him, swears he and a team had regularly cleared the area of litter yet had never seen John!"

"The Polis tried to explain this by saying that the body was hanging extremely high up in the tree, camouflaged with the branches and leaves."

"Fair enough," said Stephen.

"It's total shite mate, come on!" Joseph snapped.

"Okay okay," Stephen said holding his hands up.

"Two months later Yvonne and I discovered John's trousers, keys and wallet on the ground just yards from where his body was found."

"How could the Polis miss such items? And why were Johns' trousers on the ground?"

Stephen wide eyed with surprise said, "I don't know how the Police missed that; it seems impossible?"

"Because they are all bent mate!" the older man growled.

Stephen ignored the comment.

"We put in a complaint to the Polis!" Joseph states, "not that did John or us any good!"

He sighs, takes a deep breath and tells the men in a quiet voice.

"The most horrible part of this entire nightmare is that Johns hand, foot and dick were missing!

"Oh my god!" exclaims the bartender.

"His hand has never been found nor his cock, but his foot was found by a member of the public. The polis didnay even tell us his body was incomplete, we did not know until the foot was found."

"Wild animals, a fox, that's what the polis told us!"

"I am gutted wi it all!" Josephs voice trembled.

"Of course, you are, "Stephen empathised.

" No wonder mate," said the barman.

"Aye an that's when the Polis changed their story about how high John been hanging in the tree." "Suddenly John was not too high in the air for passers-by to notice him, now he is hanging so low, foxes could get his hand, foot and dick!"

Josephs' voice breaks as he fights back emotion.

"The foot was found near the area the Polis had picked up his mobile signal! "

"Something is just no right." Joseph looks at his hands, head bowed.

"I am positive it is revenge for some woman, the fact that his dick was cut off!"

The men look sombre as they all nod.

"My Dah and my brother in that Glen now, that's why I walk there!"

The other man gets up from his stool and sways, "woops," he steadies himself and pats Joseph on the back.

"That is some sad story Joe. See you again pal, chin up" he says, "I've got tae go, I'm late awready!" as he staggers away.

"Aye, Bye." Joseph said.

Stephen said to the barman and Joseph "think we all need another drink after that, eh?"

The Barman poured the three of them a large whiskey, Stephen 'knocked it back,' he sat for a moment then stood up, he shook Josephs' hand and held on to it tight for a second.

"I hope you get answers about your brother, I really do!" "All the best Joseph, maybe see you in here again."

" I'm Joe mate, call me Joe next time!" Joe and the barman threw their drinks back as Stephen walked out.

The Barman leant over the bar and whispered to Joseph, "he is a copper, quite high up you know!"

"Ano," whispered Joseph and chuckled.

Stephen took a deep breath of cold clean air as he stepped outside, he walked up to Shawlands, he felt jittery, unsteady, 'he had drank too much' he thought, but the walk helping to sober him up and settle his nerves.

#

Chapter 7.

Descendant of an unfortunate liar 2002

John O'Devlin had been laying it on thick trying to get into wee Michelle's knickers again, he had even tried the 'I canny live without you,' line and had told 'the wee lass,' he was 'gonni do himsel in.' He was sitting in the Glen, at the top of the big hill slide, hoping she was going to turn up when she finished her work in the Village hairdressers at six. He called her 'dead on' five minutes past.

"Come on, please Michelle just come round for half an hour!" he begged.

"John, we are done, that's it, no more! I know you been messing around with that dirty cow."

"Who told you that rubbish?" John demanded.

"I've been told, you're going to end up with your balls cut off if you don't stop!"

"Am telling you!" "I'm going to laugh; you know that John? I am going to wet myself laughing!" Michelle said with malice.

"What you goin on about? He exclaimed,

"Who told you that shite Michelle, you know you're the only one, people are jealous of what we got, you know that?" he paused waiting for her response, but she was silent!

"Come on, your amazing, I don't need any other bird."

"No John! "She interrupted forcibly.

"You know I love you and only you, I'm not messin with anyone" John pleaded on.

Michelle shouted down the phone "We are finished. Leave me alone!" then hung up.

'Oh, well, John thought, 'that's that then!' he sniggered to himself.

He wondered who had been 'bumping their gums," about him again! 'If Jimmy High Tower, got wind of that bit of juicy gossip, he would be a dead man!" Feeling naughty thinking about it, John makes a call.

"Hi, it's me,….. are you working?" ……. "Uh huh,…." I have some very important information for you,"…… "can you come now? ..Well not now…. but you will soon!" John laughs loudly. "The usual place? ……. Okay gorgeous, I will wait, you're worth it." He hangs up.

John grabs his jacket and makes his way slowly starts walking slowly toward the pathway with the white stones, there is a loud buzzing noise coming from somewhere, 'probably a bees hive or wasps,' there was a lot of fluttering in the trees, he looked up expecting to see birds, but only the cloudy sky through the trees, it had been a dull afternoon but not cold, but it was going to get a whole lot better, he hoped. John made his way into the lower Glen, then edged along the Kittoch water to a hidden sandy bank at the foot of an overhang in the cliff, an enclave. He took off his jacket and smoothed the ground and then laid it out. He lay down eyes shut, just enjoying the peace and the sounds of the woods and the water. After about forty-five minutes, he heard some movement above, he stood up.

A tall, slim, attractive policewoman appeared in uniform, "Mr John O'Devlin? "She enquired loudly as she made her way along the waters' edge.

"Yes, what's the problem officer?" John smirked.

"I have some serious questions for you sir!" she says,

"Okay," he giggles.

"This is no laughing matter Mr O'Devlin," she says sternly,

"Sorry Officer," he says sheepishly.

As she comes closer, she purrs" Are you in possession of a dangerous weapon, Mr O'Devlin?"

"Why don't you come over here and search for my big truncheon!" they both laugh and meet in a passionate mouthy embrace, John slides his hands over her body, reaching up and under her skirt, his fingers brushing over warm smooth upper thigh, she pulls away and begins to take off her uniform in a burlesque style.

"Mmmmmmmm, come on, "he moans, he sits back down on the ground and beckons her, as she removes her uniform, folding each item carefully and putting them in a medium clear bag she had in her pocket.

"Patience O'Devlin," "I know how you love a girl in uniform, but we don't want any 'evidence' getting on my clothes now!" they both laugh.

"Shuuuuuuushh," John whispers, he has lay down on his jacket watching her show intently. The woman stands to his side now in a black bra and pants with 'hold up' black stockings.

"Wow, your amazing," he says with appreciation, she removes her bra and shakes her ample breasts at him and giggles, her nipples going hard in the fresh air, she turns around her back facing him, bends over and slowly pulls her pants down over her bottom to the ground and steps out them, she wiggles her bum at him then turns around and stands astride John naked. John unbuckles his belt and pulls his zip down.

"Is that a gun in your pocket or are you just pleased to see me," she laughs noticing the huge bulge now fighting its' way out his trousers.

"Very pleased to see you," he says, as she squats down revealing everything to him and pulls his trousers and boxers to his knees, revealing his hard penis. He reaches up and grabs her down into a sitting position over him, he strokes her breasts then pulls her onto him, they fuck hard, their cheeks burning pink with pleasure.

The Slaugh, all this time, had been watching from the top of the trees, many pairs of green eyes seething with venom, waiting for their own type of satisfaction.

#

Michelle Henderson came off the phone to John after her work and decided to do her worst. She had been plagued with the whispering in her head, urging her to hurt John since she found out that he had been shagging a Policewoman the whole time he was with her; The only Policewoman anyone knew in their circles was 'big Angie,' and she was Jimmy High Towers prized bit on the side. Jimmy knew Angie since way before she joined the force. It was common knowledge he had a major crush on her, but so had everyone!

Her desire to do John a dastardly deed took over Michelle. She text 'Jimmy HT

"John O'Devlin been fucking Angie for months, took the actual piss right out you, he took you for a mug mate, he is in the Glen Park right now!"

Jimmy was in the Beechings pub with a couple of associates down Clarkston Road, they were having a rare old time, the banter was mint, Jimmy was laughing wholeheartedly when his phone beeped, he read Michelle's text. Jimmy stood silent for a few moments.

"You alright HT?" Stu, one of the men he was with asked.

"Aye!" he answered slowly with a cold smile, as he was contemplating O'Devlin's demise. 'Angie was a very sexy bit,' he thought, 'addictive, she was a hard act to follow, he knew that more than anyone! But John, I canny believe he would risk going with her again, he was a big shite bag? He should have known better than to take the cunt out me! Johns' wee bird' Michelle, her text it's the truth, he felt it!' 'Aye nothing worse than a woman scorned!'

He tutted, 'shame I liked John!' he thought.

.   Jimmy recalled when he returned to Glasgow, he had suspected that John was messin with Angie, he heard the rumours before he had even set foot in the Village. He remembered he had grabbed John one night round the side of the Cartvale pub, pinned him up against the wall by the neck, John had looked terrified.

"I'm only gonni say this once." He had spoken clearly, his face only an inch or so away from Johns', "whatever happened with Angie when I was away, comes to a halt now I'm back! Got it?"

"No problem Jimmy, I never meant you any harm mate, I didn't think you were coming back!" John said in a soft pleading voice, his eyes wide looking straight into Jimmys', like some big soft puppy.

"You think I don't know that John? You think you'd be standing here if I thought any different? Eh? Do you?"

"No, I know that Jimmy." John stuttered.

He had tightened his hands around Johns' throat, his whole body was shaking.

"This is your only chance John, I'm warning you, there will be unimaginable consequences for you if you touch her again!"

"I won't Jimmy, no way, I know Angie is yours." John croaked.

"Good man, knew you'd understand," he took his hands from Johns' neck and patted him hard on the shoulder! He then flung his arm around Johns' shoulders roughly, holding him close as they walked up onto the street.

That was many months ago. Jimmy took a deep breath, breathing slowly out of his nose. He threw the remainder of his drink down his throat, then turned to his guys Stu and Tony who were leaning on the bar chatting up the new barmaid.

"Come on, we got a job, I will fill you in on the way!" they were about twenty minutes' drive before they were in the Glen.

#

It was getting dark, the three men made their way stealthily through the park, down the pathway, splitting up to check both paths, upper and lower, leading in to 'Beachy bit' at the river and rocks. "Nothing" Jimmy whispered.

Both men shook their head in a 'no!'

Making their way along the old foundations they headed to the Kittoch river cliff path, Jimmy put his hand up to his mouth, gesturing to the men to be quiet. The three stood straining to hear. Jimmy heard that familiar sexual groan of Angie's, he gestured to the men pointing for

Stu to get down to the river from high up on the right, signalling to Tony to follow him down to the left. They dropped down to the river from both directions and crept along toward the couple, not making a sound. Angie and John were oblivious to the approaching danger, in the final throes of passion staring at each other, as they moved together, John with his hands on Angie's pendulating hips. Stu had crept around and was hiding in the undergrowth on the other side ready to pounce.

Angie threw her head back and became still as John and she finished. Jimmy HT stepped forward quickly in that moment and punched her full force on the side of the head and face with his huge right fist, she was immediately knocked unconscious falling crumpled over John, the men rushed forward and grabbed her by the arms and dragged her roughly onto the dirt. John struggled to grab at his trousers which were at his knees, in an attempt to pull them up, to stand, but Jimmy kicked him full force in the balls, John folded into the foetal position exposing his bare backside, he was holding his private parts wailing in agony. Stu at his rear, booted him with all his might on the arse catching his perineum, John howled, his face contorted into a long silent scream! Jimmy stood over him and put his size twelve foot on the side of his face as he lay in agony, he pressed it down as though he was putting out a cigarette butt, grinding his heavy tread boot into his cheek. John chose to stay curled up, believing if he didn't fight back Jimmy would give him a lesser beating.

The Host were everywhere above them in the trees, they delighted in Jimmy's vindictiveness and Johns' agony; their eyes glowing with the charged atmosphere.

#

Angie's nude body moved as she started to come round, and the three men's eyes scanned her nakedness.

"Shame really, isn't it?" Jimmy mockingly addressed his men.

"A waste," replied Tony playing along.

"Poor thing is a nymphomaniac, "she just can't get no satisfaction." He mimicked Mick Jagger by sticking out his lips.

"One man at a time is just never enough!" the men cackled.

"Pleeeease Jimmmmmmy," Angie cried, now fully aware of the situation, "I'm sorry."

John was still curled up, Jimmy took a step off of his face and then kicked him full force aiming for Johns' eye, which seemed to disappear into its socket, his nose took the blow too and burst open at the bridge, John passed out with the pain.

"Stand her up," ordered Jimmy, the men grabbed her roughly under her shoulders, Angie struggled and started to scream loudly, Jimmy punched her hard on the mouth, her lip bursting open, blood flowed down her chin, she became quiet, her head hung forward.

Jimmy ran his hands over her shaking body, slapping her breasts, down her flat stomach, he removed her hold up stockings ripping them off each leg, rolling them into a solid ball, he gripped her hair wrapping it round his hand and pulling her head back, she began to cry loudly, "shut the fuck up Angie," he forced the ball of stockings into her mouth, she tried to fight it, but he was so strong, she struggled as she gagged.

"I should have known, once a pig, always a pig, eh boys?" Jimmy sneered.

The three men started making grunting noises and making grabs at her bare breasts and genitals, Angie knew what was going to happen, she started to panic, her heart was thumping so hard she felt it could stop. She started to fight the men, kicking and struggling, Jimmy grabbed her around the neck with his huge hand and squeezed it tight dragging her down onto her knees on the course sandy grit, he dragged her "stay on your hands and knees little Piggy."

The two men were like hyenas pacing back and forth, waiting for their share of the flesh. "I'm going to give you what you need, what all dirty nymphos want, eh guys,"

Angie tried to get up, but they kicked and pushed her back down, roughly holding her. Everything was happening so quickly. Her thoughts were darting through her brain.

'Just let them get on with it. Stop fighting,' 'maybe they will let me go,' 'let him humiliate you!' 'He won't kill me if I don't fight.'

Jimmy didn't let go of Angie, holding the back of her neck, as Stu dropped down onto his knees behind her and pulled his joggers down, he admired the view and then started pumping away inside Angie, she started to boak but managed to swallow hard as she feared she would suffocate on her vomit. Jimmy looked down on her the whole time while Stu was raping her, mocking her.

"You were a shite ride Angie," he spat as he squeezed his hand around her neck.

"A smelly cow." Jimmy taunted her.

Angie began reciting prayers in her head, saying the lord's prayer again and again, trying to block this nightmare out, the man gripped her hips and pulled her closer urgently, another second until he pulled away but to Angie it felt like forever.

He stood up sorting himself. "Nice Jimmy, very nice," he said.

"Glad you came?" asked Jimmy and they chortled.

There was movement from John, they all turned to see he had rolled onto his knees, Angie's' rapist walked up and booted him hard, 'up and under' into his stomach, John dropped onto his front, his bottom still exposed.

"Neeeeeeext!" Jimmy said mockingly, pushing down on Angie's neck when she tried to resist, Tony moved behind her and skelped her bottom hard. Angie flinched making a muffled screaming sound. "Yeah," he whooped, "I'm doing this!" he began slowly, enjoying his task, until Jimmy scowled, irritated, he growled. "Hurry the fuck up, we're no shooting a porno Tony."

"Okay, okay," Tony said, he grabbed her breasts from the side and squeezed so hard Angie thought she would pass out, she was frantically pumped for a few seconds, then he stopped, stared ahead groaned for a moment, before he got up.

Jimmy pulled Angie onto her feet.

"Have you had enough, or you want more? He cocked his head to the side looking down at her face, he took the ball of nylons out her mouth.

"No more Jimmy, I've had enough, no, no more" she whimpered, taking big deep breaths, "let me go Jimmy, I won't tell, I just want to live, please Jimmmmmy, pleeeeease," she was pathetic, dirty, scraped knees a huge black eye, bloody lip, he looked at her disgusted.

"I don't know how I ever fancied you. Look at yourself, your filth." he spat the words at her, then slapped her with a full open huge hand right across her battered face, Angie stumbled and fell. Jimmy pulled her over next to John, he forced her face down, laid out on the grit. She was shivering now, cold in the approaching darkness. The three men stood around her, Jimmy was smoking a joint with them, she could smell the weed, sickly and sweet. John was lying pretending to be unconscious, he moved slightly and when Jimmy looked down at him, he suddenly lifted a large heavy stone with two hands, striking it down on John, smashing his head on the side with a sickening thump.

Angie lay stunned, her thoughts raced, she couldn't believe that Jimmy had taken it so far; He was always smiling and laughing. She was racked with grief, she had never seen this in him, he was like a totally different man, evil! She lay shivering, waiting for her head to be smashed in. She could see out the corner of her eye that John looked dead. 'All my fault,' she thought, 'all my fault!' "Fancy another poke before we go," Jimmy asked the guys coldly.

"Nah, I'm wrecked" said one, "that smokes strong, I'd be in there fir hours," they laugh.

"Good stuff" said the second man.

"Aye, DD doesn't sell shite," "I don't get from anyone else now! I buy in bulk from him otherwise his stuff sells way too quick!" Jimmy chatted cheerily, as if John and Angie were not at their feet.

They stood for what seemed to Angie to be an age, their conversation became a mumble while she and John lay side by side, both curled up on their sides, hidden from view in their secret spot in the Glen, in the dark, she had been shaking but then felt warm and had drifted into a dream state.

#

Awake with a jolt, Angie listened intently, she realised they had gone, the men were gone! She swallowed hard, her tongue was swollen her mouth it tasted bloody but dry and sticky. She reached over slowly and laid her hand on Johns' chest to feel if he was breathing, there was no sign of rise or fall. She put her fingers to his neck shaking, she could not feel anything. "John, John," she whispered into his ear, trying to wake him but she couldn't, his face was cold. She felt for his phone, it wasn't on or around him, it was gone! She stood up looking into her black surroundings, terrified that the men were still near. She frantically scanned the ground looking for the bag with her clothes, but it was missing too. She was naked, her teeth were jittering! She pulled and pulled at the jacket that was stuck under John, eventually she got it, stumbling back a little with its' release, he rolled with its removal but didn't make a sound; She quickly put it on, smelling Johns' aroma and familiar aftershave, she started to weep. "Oh John, Oh, god, John, I'm so sorry."

She found her pants and trembling stepped into them, her shoes sodden through in the shallow water, she managed to squeeze them on. Overwhelmed with fear, feeling disorientated in the darkness, she tried to remember which direction it was to get her out of the woods. Angie stumbled shakily along the water's edge until it reached the main river, her eyes were getting accustomed to the dark and although she could see very little, it didn't seem so black.

Ahead she saw tiny lights moving around, then a silhouette moving toward her, she crouched down in the undergrowth afraid Jimmy had returned, she was scared to look, trembling as the spectre came her way, the lights danced around the figure illuminating the features, Angie could see now it was an older 'woman!'

The woman called out, "do you want our help?"

Angie stood up, "yes, yes I need help," "oh yes, yes, thank God!" "I'm a policewoman, I've been," Angie stopped herself from saying it, she had a flashback of what Jimmy had promised if she told anyone.

"I'm hurt," she said.

The old woman faced away from Angie and said, "follow me, we will light the way,"

Angie followed wondering what these lights were that surrounded the woman, the lights were so many now, it looked like the woman was glowing, they lit the way in a yellow glow, the woman who had long grey hair to her shoulders, seemed to wait on her, as if floating, she could hear her talking.

"A beautiful woman who lacks discretion is like a gold ring in a pig's snout, my dear," she muttered on. Angie is trying to keep up, straining to hear what she is saying.

"For the lips of an immoral woman are as sweet as honey and her mouth is smoother than oil but, in the end, she is as bitter as poison, as dangerous as a double-edged sword to men." Angie recognises where she is as they walk under the viaduct, a wave of relief washes over her.

"The Lord says, "Beautiful Zion is haughty, craning her elegant neck, flirting with her eyes, walking with dainty steps, tinkling her ankle bracelets. So, the Lord will send scabs on her head; the Lord will make beautiful Zion bald." On that day of judgment, the Lord will strip away everything that makes her beautiful: ornaments, headbands, crescent necklaces." The old lady turned to face Angie, "your beautiful ornaments, headbands and crescent necklaces have been stripped away, Angie, do you understand dear?" Angie didn't, she just wanted out of this nightmare.

The woman and Angie were at the end of the pathway, the play park was ahead, she turned to the woman and thanked her, the woman's eyes were a bright striking green.

"Don't thank me dear, it is not you that has to 'pay the piper' it is the descendant of the wicked one, the blood of the 'false witness!"

Angie did not understand what the woman was talking about, she felt confused, there were only a few bright orbs around her now and Angie thought they had faces?" she thought out loud "I'm probably dead on the ground."

"You're safe," she heard a voice say faintly, but the woman was gone!

"I'm on the brink of madness!" her head said, she hurriedly walked through the big gates, then she began to run as fast as she could, as far as she could.

#

Chapter 8.

To Pay the Piper

John lay where Angie had left him, his head was aching like no headache or hang over he had ever felt in his life.

'Why do I do this to myself, 'he thought, he rolled onto his back with difficulty, he stared into the blackness, something was wrong with his eye, he put his hand up to it, only to realise his eye was completely shut and the entire side of his face was swollen to an enormous size. He lay silently, trying to recognise what his injuries were; His private parts were on fire, burning hot, he tried to pull his trousers up, managing to get them to his upper thighs, but the pain in his groin stopped him from attempting to lift his hips to pull them up further.

'No woman was worth this!' he thought. 'Jimmy had nearly killed him; he probably thinks I'm dead! Angie is lovely woman, great fun but worth dying for? He wasn't even in love with her, never really been in love with anyone in his whole life!' John wept without tears his body racked with grief and pain. Trouble followed him because of the way he treated women, he knew that!

The ravine where he lay became brighter, filled with a million small glowing orbs the golden light lit up the rocky cliffs and the river, it was the most wonderful thing he had ever seen, the orbs surrounded him and he became frightened, aware they were tiny people, Faeries?

John thought, 'Am I dead, is this heaven?' the tiny creatures were chattering he saw, communicating, it became a loud hum, he had heard this noise before. 'A voice or a thought from elsewhere, was in his brain, in his ears.

It said, "It is better that we the Seelie give you your destiny rather than leave you to the Slaugh to deal you your fate, as you have suffered enough!'

Then in front of him, like an old projector screen, a story was revealed, he was in the movie! He was a girl wearing antiquated style clothing, the face then changed, flicking through various lives, various decades, centuries; He was a man, a woman, a man, tall, short, all horrendous deaths, until the face was his, he was pointing at three girls to what looked like a court but more like a gang of men, then the horror unfolded; the girls, shaved from head to foot, paraded naked, tortured with long pins, girls screaming, begging, then their bodies hanging then burning; John understood with complete despair he and his brother Joseph were the descendants of the accuser; They were cursed!

John felt the Seelie lifting him up, the beauty of their being was overwhelming, he felt love, an overwhelming feeling of love, for the first time in his life, he felt complete, it was the most wonderful emotion, his pain was not present, he was happy, smiling, they buzzed around him, guiding him, floating him just inches above the ground. Through the woods the cloud of light carried him to a large tree with a hangman's noose. John now understood. 'The curse must end, it had to end with him to save his brother!'

The thoughts said, do not cry, do not be sad, the universe is you and you are the universe, death is not the end, do this willingly and the curse ends.'

He felt unafraid. Pain gone. Johns' mind raced, he had done little good in his life, now the Seelie wanted him to do a completely unselfish act, to cease the generational suffering to come, to take responsibility for his ancestor's treacherous act.

Johns' trousers were now around his ankles and the Seelie steadied him as he stepped out them, he walked unsteadily to the tree, the Seelie lifted him to sit him on the large thick branch, this had to be his decision, they told him.

John willingly lifted the noose from his lap where it now sat and placed it over his head. He looked all around at the thousands of faeries as three young deer appeared near the hill slide where he had sat what seemed to be a lifetime ago.

He cried inside but he was doing this for his brother and his future children and all the O'Devlins to come.

There was a flapping from above, John looked up, the pain returned like a bolt of lightning shooting through his entire body. He became terrified when he saw one of the Host grinning down at him. 'No, no! He didn't want to die!' and in that moment of thought, John was pushed off the branch by the Slaugh with force from behind.

The Seelie rose as a swarm horrified, their lights changing from a warm glow to a cool green with the presence of evil aura, as the cloud of black wings descended with cat like screams. The Host in numbers, engulfed Johns body as it thrashed around, they were biting and tearing at his hand as he groped at the rope around his neck, many Seelie tried to fight them off but were destroyed, their energy absorbed into the woodlands. The Slaugh ripped John's hand off and threw it to each other, they swooped with it around the deer who bounded swiftly away into the woods. John, his brain still alive for a second, experienced this nightmare before he died.

The Seelie retreated swiftly to the woodland, extinguishing their glow and hiding in their safe places.

Enjoying their evil deed of thwarting the Seelie from ending the grudge, the Slaugh rejoiced that the curse would continue, the 'hairless hogs' suffering would remain. They violated

Johns dead body, by opening and closing his mouth and making animal noises, pulling open his eye sticking their jaggy fingered nails in his ears and nose, they bared their jagged teeth, eyes illuminous, a manic yellow green, they pulled at Johns penis, mocking him, biting the base to allow them to rip it off. The cloud of black wings flew over the waterfall, tossing it among them until the piece of flesh fell in the water for the fish to feed on.

Once the Hosts' pandemonium was over; The Seelie emerged feeling great sadness that Johns' death had been worthless. They laid a protective spell that camouflaged Johns' body in a cloak that had the illusion of foliage, it would hide his ravaged body from all prying eyes. The Host could not penetrate the cloak to defile Johns' body further. The cloak however only lasted two hundred and sixty-two thousand and eight hundred minutes.

#

Angie ran until her burning lungs screamed for her to stop, keeping away from any main roads, a few cars passed her, she hid as best she could, now at the avenue at the back of the Clarkston library, she started to contemplate what she was going to do. Angie knew she was lucky to be alive, but she knew that Jimmy would get to her somehow if she reported what had happened. 'She was a police officer for god's sake, she had to report it but how could she? She was in the woods with a known criminal having sex, not only that, but behind the back of a very well respected and liked X Chief Inspector Hendersons' daughters' back!' Her mind was in overdrive, different scenarios in the station and ultimately in court were played out one by one! If John was dead, would she be implicated, would Jimmy and his pals cast her as the villain? Everyone would know about her sexual history with John O'Devlin, Jimmy HT and her promiscuous past plus that Tony and Stu had raped her. She knew she would not have a job; she would be left with her reputation in tatters. Her parents were so proud of her, she thought. She couldn't bare it, she started crying. 'Her family!' 'Her mother!' "Oh God," she said aloud, the shame they would feel, the ordeal they would have to endure. She fretted, 'I can't do it to them, I just can't!'

Angie made her way down the lanes until she came to the pitches, creeping around the back of the primary school and up to her flat which was above the Ice cream parlour. She dug deep in the earth of her flowerpot for the spare key. She was in, the door quickly shut, chain, bolt and key locked, she did not put on a light, she headed straight for the shower. There was no window in the bathroom, she shut the door and put the light on, shrugging off Johns' jacket then struggling off her wet shoes. Putting her swollen bloody mouth over the cold tap she 'glugged down her fill of water,'

Angie stayed in the shower for at least an hour, weeping quietly, letting the hot water heat her bones, scrubbing her bruised privates despite the pain, unable to feel clean despite removing every trace of John and her rapists. Wiping the steam from the mirror she stared at her face, her right eye was nearly shut, and the huge swollen lower eye area merged into her swollen cheek which had a gravel burn from cheek to chin, her mouth was split and swollen. Her neck had a red hand of bruising around her throat. She was sore everywhere. She looked for the Co-codamol, she had when she twisted her ankle a few months before and took three with a few more glugs of water. She put the light off and went to her bedroom and put on her 'Onesy' in the dark, the soft fluffy material made her feel cosy and comforted, she hugged herself. Her lounge had a big bay window that looked onto the main road, over to the chippy and shops, the room was dully lit orange by the street lighting outside, it was so quiet in the street below, she lay on the couch with a throw and after an hour or so the medication put her to sleep. She awoke to the sound of traffic and the morning sun, momentarily it was as if nothing had happened. Then she remembered the pain searing into her thoughts, hideous flashbacks of her and Johns' ordeal. She called the station reporting she was very sick and would be absent at least a week and she would send in her sick line. She spoke to her doctor on the phone explaining that she had been feeling 'burnt out,' for a few weeks and now had come down with an awful flu, she said she felt unable to return to work for now; the doctor gave her a 'not fit for work' note for a month.

The day after that with still no news of John, she put on a dark track suit and skip cap pulled low over her bruised face, she walked back to near the Glen park, up through the lanes to retrieve her car, she drove it home through all the side streets where there were no cameras, parking at the back, in the last parking space which was the least public. She spoke to family and friends on the phone as though she was in bed with a very bad flu, asking them not to visit in case they caught this awful bug, every day they called to check on her. She put John's jacket in the sink in the kitchen with the extractor fan on full and set it alight, it slowly burned away for an hour. She scrubbed the sink clean and flushed the debris down the toilet.

Two weeks later at night, Angie smashed the passenger window of her car with a towel and hammer, creating a fake break in.

After ten days a member of the public noticed the window smashed in her car and reported it to local police, they contacted Angie, she explained she had been very ill in bed for weeks and had not been out to her car, but she would check it.

When the Police arranged a visit, it had been over three weeks since that night and her bruises were now hardly noticeable when covered with thick make up, she just looked very tired and unwell. She wore her leisure clothes, a scarf to hide her bruised throat and held a hanky up to the mark on her lip, frequently blowing her nose. She recognised the two young officers, they kept their distance from her coughing and nose blowing, asking quickly if there was anything missing. Angie looking through the car, firstly responded "No," then looking up at them shocked, she said "Yes, my gym bag." "Oh No! my uniform too, it is in a clear bag in it, I was taking it to the Dry Cleaners!" she exclaimed, she sighed a heavily.

She blew her nose loudly. "I had completely forgotten all about it being there, I've been so terribly unwell for weeks, I can't seem to shake it off!"

The young Officers nodded, "Don't worry, it is not your fault." They reassured her.

They hurried away, not wanting to catch whatever she had.

After a month, with still no news of John, except that he was reported missing by Michelle Henderson and her father, Angie reluctantly returned to work, she felt scared and had lost her confidence, her spark for life had been extinguished and everyone noticed.

#

Jimmy HT, Stu and Tony left to get 'the kit' to deal with Johns' dead body and remove it from the Glen, the guys made their way back through the darkness of the woods. "Too fucken spooky down here," said Tony.

"Shut it ya pussy," laughed Stu cloaking his fear with bravado.

"wooooooooooooooooo" Tony imitates a ghost noise, "it feels like we are being watched." Tony looked all around him.

"Fucken dope making youz two para," said Jimmy totally oblivious to the Faerie activity everywhere.

Down to where they had left John and Angie, the men made their way.

"Where the fuck are they?" Stu said in troubled surprise!

"Are we in the right spot Jimmy?" asked Tony "were we not a bit further along?"

"Nope, they are gone!" said Jimmy calmly, "he must be alive! Angie must have helped him out."

"Right let's get the fuck outa here before the polis or anyone turns up!" Stu said anxiously.

"No one is goan-tae report anything!" HT said with a confident sneer.

They hurriedly made their way up the pathways of the Glen, when they heard a strange loud buzzing followed by a series of cat type cries, which was enough to set Stu and Tony off running. Jimmy mumbled "for fucks sake," and took off after them.

Once out the park and back in the car, driving over the back road past the Cathkin Braes.

"Stu said, "there is something not right with that Glen and this whole scene, I am telling you now, I want nuthin more to do with that place."

"Me neither, never again, the vibe is too heavy!" Tony said.

Jimmy was staring at the road, driving at speed, he started to laugh loudly, manically.

 The men looked at each other, their eyes met, they stared filled with terror at each other.

"Slow down Jimmy for fucks sake, I don't want tae die tonight!" Stu pleaded.

Before Jimmy dropped them both off, he parked round the corner from Stus' house, the men sat in the car talking about the different scenarios and how they should answer any questions.

"Best if I don't see you guys until this is sorted."

"So, we clear? I dropped you here after the Beechings if anyone asks, that's it, you don't know where I went." "I don't know where you two went!"

"Sort your own alibi as to where you two went after you got dropped off!" Jimmy instructed them. "When will you square us up?" asked Tony.

 Jimmy laughed, "you want paid? Is it not enough you got a shag at a prize bird you'd never get the chance off in your life, you ugly bastard?"

"You goatti be having a laugh Jimmy, come on!" Tony said irritated.

Jimmy stared at him with a dangerous look, then like a flick of a switch, he started laughing, "only noising you up Tony!"

Tony's heart was racing, and he had sweat on his top lip. There was silence in the car.

"Fir fucks sake, you guys lost your sense of humour?" Jimmy chortled "I will get it to you both you have my word!" Jimmy gave them a big, beautiful smile and both men exited the car in haste, relieved to be away from HT's frightening vibe.

Jimmy kept his 'ears open' for any news of John or Angie. After a few weeks he heard through the grapevine that Angie was back at work after a spell of illness, he did not contact her or go near her; he had felt fleeting moments of remorse about her ordeal, but then would convince himself that she deserved it!

After about two months Jimmy persuaded a lassie John had shagged a few times to go to his brother Josephs' door. Joseph answered, the girl he recognised as someone his brother had fooled about with now and again. "Hi Joe, sorry to bother you but I am so worried about John, have you heard anything about his where abouts yet?" the lassie put on a sad face, but Joseph could feel she was hiding something. "No, we have not heard anything, have you?" he asked her. She looked nervous looking around quickly. "No, I've no heard, nothing, such a terrible shame, I miss John being around, I hope he comes back soon!" Joseph just nodded with an expressionless face, he knew she was not genuine, he could feel it. "Okay then," she looked around again twitching, "thanks Joe, I hope he turns up soon." She turned and walked at speed away from the house. Jimmy was sitting in the car an avenue away and round a corner, he was itching to know what the hell happened after he and the boys left. "No news," she said as she jumped into the passenger seat and shut the door.

After three months Jimmy heard that a policewoman's uniform had been found in the Glen Park, he thought 'why the hell did I not think about her clothes? Too angry, too stoned!' "Silly, silly boy, Jimmy boy!" he said to himself. 'It would not be long before things were going to get very sticky for him if he stayed in Glasgow!'

#

"Your uniform has been found in Glen Park," Angie's partner for the week Dave said. "Do you know if I will get it back, even though I've been issued with another one?" she asked, while trying to calm her racing thoughts and stop herself from shaking. "I doubt it Angie, I imagine it's been run over for any evidence to the crime, even though it was just a smash and grab!"

She had a flashback of Jimmy throwing the rock down on John's head! She shuddered visibly. "You okay," Dave asked, "Yes, fine," Angie needed to talk about what happened she knew that, she knew the signs of Post Traumatic Stress Disorder and she had them all. Her colleagues had assumed what she had hoped they would, that the opportunist thieves who had ransacked her car had thrown the uniform away. "Must have been kids!" Dave said, "if it had been anyone of any criminal standing, they would have kept it! Maybe used it to commit a serious crime." "Yes, thank goodness it was just kids!" Angie agreed.

After four months Angie was speaking to colleagues regularly about leaving the police force, stating she felt she was not up to the job anymore as she was feeling depressed. She sought out the help of the 'mental health services,' through her employer, attending frequent sessions but never opened up truthfully about the actual reason for her issues. Five months after the attack, Angie submitted her resignation, and it was accepted.

Six months had passed when Angie was told that John O'Devlin's body was found and it is presumed suicide, she was surprised that no one seems to be suspicious except his brother. Angie didn't know how John's body ended up hanging from a tree, but she was sure Jimmy must have hung him there!

106

There were plenty of rumours circulating the village, predominately that Michelle Henderson's father had probably killed John and that's why the police were not investigating his supposed suicide further. No one had made any connection between John and her, 'Yet!' she thought.

Seven months after Angie's rape she was shopping in Shawlands when she saw Jimmy High Tower in the street walking towards her, Angie looked around her frantically, there were plenty of people walking about, her heart was beating so hard she thought she could hear it, her face flushed a hot pink as their eyes met, he smiled a long sickening smile as he walked past her, his eyes cold as ice, she looked away quickly, feeling faint. Angie darted up a side street, quickly checking he didn't follow her, bent over vomiting into the gutter. Tears stung her eyes. Angie thought, 'I can not live here anymore! I might meet Jimmy the murderer or his filthy mates.' 'I have to get out of Glasgow now!' Only four weeks later she left Scotland to work in Europe, she had an exciting new job she told friends, but didn't tell anyone exactly where, not even her family.

#

Michele Henderson went through to the lounge, where her father was sitting in his comfy chair watching the Golf.

"Dad, I need to talk to you!" she said anxiously.

"Can it not wait until after the Golf love?"

"No Dad, I've done something stupid." Michelle blurted out.

"Uck, we all do stupid things love just forget it and move on!" he never took his eyes from the screen.

"What a shot!" He loudly exclaimed.

107

"Dad! Stupid, dangerous thing!" Michelle said with urgency.

Her father turned around to look at her. "Dangerous in what way?" he asked.

"Don't hate me! Okay!" she said in a small voice.

"Just tell me what is wrong!" her dad said in a demanding but concerned voice.

"I've still been in contact with John O'Devlin!"

"Ugh! You are a stupid lassie Michelle he is scum," her dad looked furious.

"I know Dad, but that's not it!"

"Well! What is it then?" he said impatiently, "spit it out!".

"John called me after work asking to meet up in the Glen, I said no, he said that he would kill himself if I didn't go back with him. I knew he was lying as John has been messing about with Jimmy High Towers girlfriend, I found out a couple of weeks ago!"

"HT, that piece of evil filth," her father spat the words.

"I felt so used and angry about him two timing me, I sent Jimmy High Tower a text a few minutes ago telling him about Angie cheating on him, letting him know John was in the Glen!"

Her fathers' face was red, he looked as though he might explode.

"I'm sorry Daddy!"

"Where is your phone?" Michelle handed her phone over, he removed the sim walking out the Patio doors, he placed the phone on the ground and smashed it into bits with his foot.

"At least you had the good sense not to use your contracted phone to contact him." He continued as he paced in front of Michelle.

"If anyone asks about any text to Jimmy deny it! Where did you buy this wee phone?

"I can't remember Dad it was a long time ago, from a second-hand shop in Glasgow, I think." Michelle looked at her dad with huge, worried eyes.

If it is traced back to you, say you lost it in the pub; If anyone asks you about John, you've dated a couple of times, but you have not been interested for a long while, but he has been bothering you! If they ask if you knew he was seeing anyone else say no!" "Yes Dad."

"Understand this lady, you have put yourself in the picture if that piece of scum gets murdered by that hood!" "Ano Daddy, I am so sorry!" Michelle whimpers.

"If John gets badly hurt and finds out it was you that gave him away, he may very well break more than your heart." He said loudly, as he stared at his daughter with anger.

"Tell me the truth, have you used your contracted phone to contact any of these criminals?"

"No Dad, I promise." Michelle sounded defeated.

"Well at least that is something you did right!" he sat back down in his chair.

"I have built up an exceptional reputation in the force, I will not let you and your inability to keep your pants on, take that away from me!"

Michelle's eyes were wide, her mouth open, her face chalk white!

"You could be implicated in any crime that maybe committed, you idiot." He stared at her straight in the eye.

"Daddy, I'm so sorry!" Michelle started to cry. "I feel so guilty now," she sighed heavily, "I wish I hadn't done it!" Huge tears washed her mascara down her cheeks, streaking her makeup. "Too late!" her dad snapped back! "Go clean yourself up!"

He lifted the receiver of the phone next to him, Michelle stood silently just outside the Lounge listening to the call.

"Hi Dave, it is Robert Henderson here, ……yeah Golfing mostly,….. he laughed. I don't want to make a formal complaint or charge or anything, as you know I've just retired and am going out to Canada to visit family and I really don't need the hassle but remember that pair of brothers O'Devlin, Aye, Aye that's right, reset mostly, nothing major! No not Joseph, John !.... Well, he has been bothering my Michelle, bugging her,…… yeah he has a bit of a crush, she is not interested, obviously! No,…….. yeah that's right. We are just a bit concerned, he called her after work from the Glen Park and he said he was going to kill himself!"

The other man made a sarcastic humorous comment and both men laughed down the phone.

"Aye, one less right enough!" he laughed. "Maybe give the local station the heads-up Dave, if they get a missing person in,….. yeah, of course give you a call for a few rounds up at the Bonnyton course when I get back. All the best to Anita." Robert replaced the handset.

Michelle quietly returns to the Lounge, "you are going to Canada?" she asked her dad.

"I am now and you are too!" he said with authority.

#

After two months and Johns body still not found. Michelle and her dad take a holiday to his sister Irene's home in Toronto, Canada. Michelle loves Canada she wants to stay, she starts working in her Aunties Gift shop, applying for an extended visa as she hopes to stay as long as possible.

A month later Michelle finds out she is pregnant. "You must tell your dad," Irene said, "I can't I'm too scared," Michelle said looking at her Auntie with huge eyes rimmed with tears, "could you tell him for me," Michelle pleads. "Oh god!" Irene said as she nods her head in a yes. Robert Henderson is furious and disappointed in his daughter; it takes him a full week before he could even look at Michelle.

#

"What do you mean you want to keep it?" Robert screams at Michelle, "no daughter of mine will have a child to scum like that!" Michelle is sat, head down at the kitchen table with Irene at her side. "Calm down Robert!" Irene said," you are scaring her!" "I do not want an abortion Dad; I can't live with that on my conscience." Michelle sounded pitiful. "There are worse things than a new baby Robert!" Irene said with warmth. "You better change your mind lady or your no daughter of mine!" "Robert!" Irene exclaims disapprovingly.

Robert does not back down, he is insistent Michelle have an abortion, but she refuses.

Mr Henderson returns to Glasgow alone.

#

Chapter 9.

The Curse

Angie was a different person than who she had been in 2014. She had avoided getting involved with any of the opposite sex for at least five years, avoiding even the slightest flirtation or sexual advance; she was still healing from her terrible ordeal and eight years later she had been reinventing herself as a sophisticated, attractive woman of class. She had been very cautious about being anywhere that could leave her vulnerable while travelling until she had met her now husband. Angie had found it fairly easy integrating into French culture as she had learned French at school and after a year of living there was fluent in the language and now spoke with the regional dialect, people would mistakenly believe she was French with her long dark hair with tanned skin.

Angie started working for Jacques Archambeau a French Lawyer about three years ago and they had an instant attraction that had turned into deep respect and love over that time; she was working as his Legal Administrator, Receptionist for his office in Cap-Ferrat in the Côte d'Azur, France, one of the playgrounds of the rich and famous. Angie adored this region and the tourist energy, their positive, relaxed vibes of being on holiday. She was now at last starting to feel happy again.

Jacques (Jaks as she called him,) asked to marry her after six months of a whirlwind romance, but she insisted they had to wait two years to be sure. They married in a simple, beautiful ceremony with the few friends they shared, it was a wonderful day, sunny and relaxed. They had decided for their honeymoon to travel to Spain for two weeks, visiting some places they both wanted to sightsee, Barcelona, Tarragoni, Castellon de la plana, if they wanted beaches, they had them where they lived and could take another week on their return.

Angie and Jaks had really enjoyed their Honeymoon, they felt complete and content in their own company. On the last day they spent the afternoon shopping for gifts for their family, friends and office staff, they had eaten the most wonderful meal and feeling full went to the hotel to lay down. On top of the bed, they started kissing tenderly, holding each other's faces in gentle caress, looking in each other's eyes intensely as they were making love; wrapped in each other's arms afterwards they drifted in to sleep for an hour or two, they both showered and made ready to go to a club for a night of dancing.

#

The couple were in a club called De Mambo, it was packed, hot, but it had a really friendly atmosphere, the music was fantastic, the beat vibrating through them from head to toe, they were drunk, high on life, laughing as they finished dancing and made their way through the crowd to the bar. They couldn't squeeze in anywhere, it was at least three deep, as they were edged to the side by the moving bodies, Angie noticed a space next to a man about fifty on a bar stool in the corner, he had his back to the wall, as she moved into the spot holding Jaks hand she asked Jaks what he wanted to drink in French, which now was Angie's first language. "

"Bonjour, mon ami" the man in the corner said, he was very handsome, he looked maybe Italian.

"D'où vendez-vous en France" he asked.

"Cap-Ferrat sur la Côte d'Azu France, » Jaks replied.

« Notre dernière nuit de notre lune de miel » pouvons-nous parler anglais, j'ai du mal avec Français, » the man asked.

« Of course, we can, » said Angie loudly over the noise.

"Hi, I'm Rab, Rab Brown, I'm the owner of the club."

"Great club, we are having a fantastic night," Jaks said, nodding his head to the beat of the track playing. "Are you English?" Jaks asked.

"Awwww nawwww, I'm Scottish," Rab replied faking a broad Scots accent.

Jaks laughed and smiled as Angie turned round with their drinks.

"Oh, pardon me, what would you like to drink."

"No thank you love, I've still a wee one here, anyway I've had enough for tonight." He smiled.

"Where abouts in Scotland are you from, "asked Jaks.

"Glasgow city, "Rab smiled.

"Angie was born in Glasgow, small world, eh?" Jaks said lifting his eyebrows.

Angie looked uncomfortable as Rab continued the conversation, he seemed genuinely happy to be chatting to a fellow Scot.

"Where in Glasgow do you come from Angie," Rab asked.

"Oh, not the city just out in the suburbs, a south side village." She replied.

"No way, I am too," "I came here and opened this club when my business partner was hit by a train on the Glen Viaduct line in 1990, it was supposed to be suicide, but I'm not convinced." Rab eyes saddened, "I miss that big bastard," Rab said with a chuckle.

He raised his nearly empty Glass "Too Davie!"

Angie lifted her glass to Rabs' but Angie's, blood had run cold at the mention of the Glen; it was if the crowds had disappeared muffled in the background. Her heart was banging loudly in her chest! She swallowed hard.

"That is very sad, isn't it Jaks," she turned around, but her new husband was chatting to another man at his side, laughing and bobbing about to the tunes. She turned and returned her gaze to Rab.

"What's wrong Angie, you don't look well?" their eyes connected, hers unblinking.

"No nothing really Rab, it is just such a coincidence, before I left to come to Europe, a man a knew growing up hung himself in the Glen not far from the Viaduct, he wasn't the type to do that either," she said sadly.

"But I guess there isn't a 'type!" added Rab. "The Glen has a bad reputation when it comes to death!" "In fact," Rab continued, "I heard from a pal back home last week, that a guy and his dog had a horrific accident there only a few weeks ago!" Rab continued, "Yeah guy called Joseph O'Devlin, maybe you know him?" he looked at Angie questioningly.

Angie legs were shaky, they buckled slightly, and she felt she might faint.

"Hey, you two look very serious," Jaks said, "nice to meet you Rab but I am taking my 'wife' back to the dance floor." As he took hold of Angie's waist from the back and shuffled her through the crowd onto the dance floor. She looked back at Rab, but he was talking to the girl behind the bar now, she had wanted to ask him more about Johns' brother Josephs death, but then she thought it was better not to know. She was relieved it had been noisy and neither Jak or her had told Rab anything more about where they lived or their business. Angie did her best for Jaks to look like she was enjoying herself, but in truth she felt sick to the bottom of her stomach.

When Angie and Jaks got back to the hotel and into bed,

Jaks murmured "Je t'aime tellement Angie bébé," "Angie bébé," then fell sound asleep, with a slight snore.

Angie snuggled into Jaks' back but couldn't shake the uneasy feeling Rabs' conversation left her with. When she eventually did fall asleep, she dreamt of a glowing old lady in the woods floating up the pathways, someone was saying "you're safe, you're safe!" She woke with a jolt, Jaks was sitting up, rocking her in his arms, repeating in a comforting voice,

"Un cauchemar, ce n'est pas réel, vous êtes en sécurité. "

#

Two months before Angie met Rab in Spain, Joseph was walking through the Glen. It was a changeable day as it so often is in Scotland, but at that moment the sun was shining

116

bright and twinkling through the leaves on the trees. He took his dog Ben there to walk most days. Joseph loved Ben; he was his companion since his brother had been found dead. Yvonne had bought him the puppy when she couldn't pull him out of his grief, she had felt the dog could bring them some happiness and a welcome distraction from their obsession with John's suicide and the Glen. She was right! Ben had helped heal Joseph, as much as he could be healed.

Joseph had always an uneasy feeling in the Glen, especially around the 'beachy bit' but at the same time it made him feel close to his dead brother John and he would sometimes talk to his brother as though he was still alive as he walked. Joseph walked down the lower pathway that encircled the 'Fairy glen,' he followed the small group of steps heading down to under the lower Viaduct archway. The trees overhang the path on both sides and on a day as today create a beautiful, curved canopy of bright light green, he walked through the shaft of nature, emerging at the viewpoint of the Viaduct. The view was stunning, and he stood enjoying the blue sky while the sound of the river burbling below. Ben ran up, Joseph walked on toward the old foundations, he picked up a stick and threw it down to 'Beachy bit,' for Ben who dashed down the steep bank straight into the river, splashing about, Joseph watched him laughing, "ya big dafty," he shouted down at his happy dog. Joseph edged his way down and sat on the big tree root that had fashioned itself into a natural bench next to the rocks and threw the stick repeatedly for Ben. Eventually Ben tired of splashing about and sat next to Joseph. They both took in the beauty of their surroundings until Joseph felt a cold breeze on his arms. The clouds had become grey when they proceeded along the rivers' edge then headed up the edge of the cliff to 'Bluebell woods.'

A deer appeared, bounding up toward the fields of wheat, Ben took off at speed chasing. Joseph shouted after him, then whistling loudly when the black Labrador didn't return, 'Fuck, fuck fuck, "Joseph barked. He quickly made his way through the small upper

117

wood, ducking under the branches and around the large holes where the young guy comes to dig with his metal detector. Shouting then whistling, then shouting again, "Be……n! "Joseph emerged from the darkening woods into the field. There were tractor tracks at the side and through the field which were the only mud paths, the wheat was tall, swaying in all different directions in the now strong breeze, it was quite hypnotic as he scanned the field for Ben. Joseph was worried now, he hoped the deer had not led the dog back into the denser woodlands, as he would never find him!

Joseph saw something Black out the corner of his eye, pop up out of the wheat then disappeared again. He started whistling. "Ben, there you are, come on boy," silence, except for the sound of the wheat rattling like a whisper, moving in the wind. "Ben, time to go home now!" Joseph shouted, desperately staring at the spot where he thought he saw him; there was a low rustling and then the most terrible whining.

"Ben, Ben, "Joseph yelled urgently fighting his way through the wheat to the spot twenty or so feet away, A sudden loud sound pierced Joseph's ears. He was startled, stunned he stared in disbelief as he realized it's coming from his dog; A cloud of black crows, he thought, rose from the tractor valley in front of him, Ben is screaming, he seemed to be inside the cloud. The screech is intense, it sounds so painful, but Joseph is frozen, he has no idea what's happening or how he can help him. Abruptly the screaming stops. Silence. The dog's body lands next to him in a loud thud, Joseph looked down, Ben was dead, his shiny black hair torn off his flesh in clumps, his eyes missing, a bloody hole where his nose should be. Joseph looked up, the black cloud now rising, moving his way, there were shapes writhing within the swarm, it was 'big bats, he thought,' 'no! it's something else.' He took off running, heading for the old railway bridge at the end of the field to the right that leads to the main road. He ran faster than he had ever ran in his life, each breath burning in his throat and chest, until he made it to the end of the field, he quickly glanced back but didn't see them behind him.

118

The Host were enjoying playing with Joseph, they were gaining strength from the fear he was omitting, they could have caught him in seconds, but they let him get only a few steps from safety, just before the bridge they descended upon him like an evil plague.

They dragged Joseph at speed through the gully toward the woodland, his upper body ricocheting, his head hitting every rock. Joseph was hauled into the top wood, sharp branches and thorned twigs, tore his flesh, he was barely conscious. The Slaugh were buzzing with excitement relishing their victims suffering, they had him now by the feet and had turned him upside down, their wings beating fast, the swarm rose holding Joseph high, they held him in the air, one of the Host, strong and muscular, stood in front of Joseph's upside down face staring, his eyes glaring yellow green. Joseph opened his swollen sockets and through the slits stared in shock, confused to see a beautiful perfect small man with glorious black hair, black translucent wings spread out behind him.

In his mind, he heard the beings' thoughts infiltrate his brain, insulting him 'filthy liars, your blood is poison, a vile breed.' Josephs mind shut down as he went into severe shock, a pain ripped through his heart and down his arm, the pain was unbearable, he passed out. The Slaugh man opened his mouth to reveal rows of razor-sharp teeth, he leaned forward biting off the tip of Josephs nose, then swallowed it, the Host whooped, the Slaugh's fun was over, they flew over the rocky cliff, still holding Joseph's feet, rising higher and higher, tossing Joseph like a bag of rubbish to his death.

Once the Host were gone and dark had descended upon the Glen, the Seelie came cautiously out their homes, glowing and glorious, they knew what had transpired, saddened that the curse still remained, but for now at least, this vein of the cursed blood of the O'Devlin was at an end. They retrieved Bens' body and lay it beside his master, companion, friend Joseph; the same spot his brother had lay with Angie.

Their bodies were found later the next day. A tragic accident, both fell off the cliff, there was no other explanation for it. The injuries on the dog and on Joseph would have been animals during the night, the initial Police presence had assumed.

However, the medical examiner, did have doubts, most of the injuries on the man were similar to someone being dragged by a car and both the man and the dog, suffered rips and bites, but they could not be explained by any known animal, they were very similar to a brown bat's incisors, but indicated two rows of teeth, akin to Piranha fish, but much bigger, he couldn't explain it! He was far too near retirement with an unblemished record, a very respected forensic pathologist, he was not going to start putting his neck on the line by putting that information out there, he would leave that to someone else in the future!

'Accidental death, heart attack it was, it was the fall that killed them both.'

#

Yvonne, Joseph's wife, did not believe it; she and Joseph knew that wood like the back of their hand, Joseph did not accidentally jump or run with Ben off the cliff edge! She became obsessed with the Glen, spending hours and days online researching its' history and deaths. She stopped taking care of herself, she had stopped eating, becoming very unwell. Her family were extremely concerned. Yvonne would rant about her findings repeating the same old stories over and over to anyone that would listen. It was only a few months since Josephs' death, when she suffered a nervous breakdown and had to spend a month in Dykebarr Hospital for mental health; On release she did well for about three months then had to be re-admitted for her own safety as she had become suicidal, suffering from severe paranoia and obsessive behaviours. She never truly recovered.

#

Chapter 10.

The curse on us all? 2020

Susie Irvine and daughter Fee were very happy living in the village, Susie now
sixty-six years old was pretty fit for her age apart from a little arthritis, her hair now grey she
looked good and had few wrinkles. Fee was forty years old, she was recently divorced from
her husband of twelve years, they had not had children, so it was an easy, amicable split. She
was back living with her mum for some moral support and to 'lick her wounds.' Fee like her
mother kept her hair long and was still attractive, tall and slim; she worked in a large retail
unit in Glasgow full time. Susie had just retired, she still did a lot for the community by litter
picking, she would stop her car for anyone she recognised from the village and give them a
lift, people would ask her to look after their children if they were stuck and she lent money to
those she probably shouldn't have, never asking for it back. Things were going well. The two
women were walking early in the mornings usually in the Glen, their favourite place. They
chatted and enjoyed the peace as they rarely would bump into anyone at this time, not even
the few old locals that had walked there for decades.

In January 2020 There had been intermittent reports on mainstream media of an
outbreak of a type of flu in China, the reports blamed a 'wet food' market where people had
eaten Bats, the flu was said to be killing many people. At the end of the month, all flights to
China were cancelled, due to the outbreak. On the thirtieth of January, the first two cases of
COVID-19 in the United Kingdom are confirmed. By February there were more cases. On
the twenty six to twenty seventh of February there is a COVID-19 outbreak at
a Nike conference in Edinburgh, from which at least twenty five people linked to the event

are thought to have contracted the virus, including eight residents of Scotland, although the First minister at the time kept that quiet.

The first British death from the disease is confirmed on the twenty eighth plus the first confirmed case in Wales.

#

Susie is out walking in Cathkin Braes which is a woodland that is divided only from the Glen by a small village of mostly cottage type housing and a Petrol station garage. The sun shone bright, Susie feeling the warmth on her skin, smiled as she walked, content she soaked in her surroundings, looking up at the bright blue sky, over to green fields with wildflowers. Susie strolled along the gravel pathways leading to the 'Big Wood.' Smiling nodding and saying 'Hi' to those she passed, once in the woods she sat on a fallen old tree having a rest, when a woman stopped to chat, sitting down next to Susie.

"Do you walk here a lot?" asked the woman, "I'm Anne by the way," extending her hand. Susie shook it "Susie," "No, only occasionally, I walk in the Glen in the Village, I love it there, but it is nice to get a change of scene!" Susie smiled.

"I'm on my days off, I work two weeks on, two weeks off rota." said Anne.

"I am retired," Susie said as she stood up, "are you walking?" she asked Anne.

The women continued the walk together.

"I'm a nurse, I travel to England to work as the agency are paying nearly three times the usual nurse's rate!"

"That is great pay!"

"I don't know if I will continue though as the rise in Covid patients in the hospital where I work is going through the roof, I must admit I am frightened for myself and my family!" Anne sighed, "but then I think about my patients!"

"It is an admirable profession, I don't blame you feeling scared, I would be too! I'm sure you will make the right decision though," said Susie.

The two women had a lot in common and chatted throughout the entire hour or so.

"Next time you are home, phone me, here I will give you my number." Anne took the number into her phone.

"We can meet up to walk again, I can take you into the Glen." Susie said smiling.

"Now that would be interesting," said Anne, "my great grandmother came from the Village she used to tell us spooky stories about it!"

Susie laughed, "I suppose it can seem spooky sometimes!"

Anne hugged Susie as they parted, as Susie walked away she heard Anne was coughing loudly.

Within a week, Susie was incapacitated, coughing continuously, she felt like she was drowning with mucus from her nose to throat, constantly swallowing, she had a fever and was absolutely exhausted, but she could not lie down, or she felt she was suffocating, she could not sleep. For one month she was in bed. During that time, on March the twenty third the Prime Minister Boris Johnson, in a televised address to the nation, said "people should only go outside to buy food, to exercise once a day, or to go to work if you absolutely cannot work from home." "You will face police fines for failure to comply with these new measures." Susie and Fee watched the statement feeling anxious and fearful. Later the First Minister addresses Scotland "Let me blunt," she states, "the stringent restrictions on our

125

normal day to day lives that I'm about to set out are difficult and they are unprecedented."
"They amount effectively to what has been described as a 'lockdown."

#

Susie was sitting propped up, Fee was sitting on the end of her Mums bed. "Let me phone the hospital mum, your breathing is not getting any better, you can't go on like this!" she pleaded.

Susie answered," If I am going to die, I will die at home, not in some hospital alone, with people in masks all around me; Think about it Fee, how horrible must that be!"

"I know mum, but they could help you, give you oxygen!"

"Fee, I have watched the news, now they seem to be putting anyone with Covid into an induced Coma!" "Is that what you want for me?"

"I could come with you Mum just to see what they think about your chest?" Fee took her Mums' hand.

"No Fee, with the restrictions no one is allowed in hospital with covid patients, no husbands, wives, sons, friends, no DAUGHTERS!" Susie raised her voice.

"Okay mum, I understand, but I think you're taking a chance with your life which is crazy. I mean the news are quoting deaths on the sixth of April from Covid as five thousand in the UK. The total number of reported cases is nearly Fifty-two thousand Mum! Fifty-two thousand! You are playing Russian roulette!"

#

Susie woke up, it was still dark, she felt as though someone was sitting on her chest, "oh god," she whispered a sharp pain was across her heart.

"Dear god, please help me, I do not want to leave Fee Fee alone, please she only has me, let me live."

Eventually she fell asleep into a vivid dream, she was floating through the Glen smiling and laughing, surrounded by Faeries all a glow, they buzzed in the air in front of her face, she could feel immense love radiating from them into her soul, eyes glowing green looking in hers, the Faeries mouths did not move but they spoke to Susie.

"You are strong, you can go on, you have an important task, you must choose, to leave or to stay." Susie woke up. She lay her heart racing, sweat on her top lip, she was accustomed to crazy dreams, her mother had told her when she was a child she suffered from 'Night Terrors.' Susie forced herself to breathe uncomfortable huge breaths in, struggling to pull in the air, then out again, again and again, each time forcing more air in.

'I want to stay; I want to live!' she thought and, in that moment, she knew she would survive whatever this was.

Susie recovered, but slowly. She suffered 'long covid symptoms,' for at least eighteen months, she slept sitting up on a pile of pillows. Fee insisted she get help from the doctor, speaking to him on the phone. She was prescribed inhalers and nasal sprays to help her breathe but there was nothing to give her the 'get up and go' that she needed, she felt totally drained, but she was determined, forcing herself up and out of bed. Susie would pant when she walked and had to stop frequently but she was committed to walking in her beloved Glen again.

#

Fee was still at work every day deemed one of the 'essential workers.' Stationed at her cash desk; the store was busy. A woman approaches her trolly piled high with tinned

127

goods, "If there are any with dents don't ring them through!" the woman says briskly motioning to the tins she is putting on the belt.

"No problem," Fee says then adds; "Sorry madam, you will have to put one of the packages of Toilet roll back on the shelf as it is rationed to one pack per household!"

"Are you having a laugh?" the woman replied sarcastically from her heavily lip-sticked red lips.

"No, it is the store restriction, due to people panic buying" Fee said pleasantly.

"Says who?" the woman sticks her chin out in straight lipped defiance.

Fee walks round and takes the Toilet roll out her trolley "I don't make the rules!" Nodding to a male colleague to come and put it back on the shelf. The woman grabs the Toilet roll and she and Fee proceed a comical 'tug of war' with it.

Fee let go, rolling her eyes. The male colleague steps forward taking the woman's elbow.

"I'm afraid I will have to ask you to leave the store!" The woman's face is purple with anger, she throws the big packet of Toilet roll at Fee.

"Get off me!" she shrugs his hand away! "Leave, I will, with fucken pleasure, your store is shit and I hope you all die with Covid!" she shouted storming out the store.

Fee and her colleagues shake their heads as they all look round from their stations, in empathised support.

"How many is that this week now?" Fee asks her male colleague.

"Five, nut jobs!" he said. Fee pulled at the surgical mask she had to wear all day, it was making her cough and gave her spots around her mouth.

"I cannot wait to finish this shift," she said loudly to the other customers in the line. They all smile sympathetically. When she returned home that night, she stripped in the entrance hall, put all her clothes in the washing machine, then ran upstairs to go shower.

"Hi mum, just doing my Covid routine! Be through in a minute!" she shouted to Susie who was in bed, "what a day!"

#

Susie had been walking around the streets trying to build up her fitness, within the following month she had started to walk in the Glen again despite the front gates being locked, due to Scottish water doing some type of sewage system upgrade, which had to go through the lower play park area. Susie had never seen any workmen. She had to go further up to the Nursery school and cut around the back through a Wheat field to the rear of the Glen, it made the walk much longer and at times she really struggled.

Susie was very grateful that she had not died and put it down to her connection with nature and the Faeries. She thought, 'yes, it is true,' but it was hard to admit it to herself, 'the Faeries help her! I don't know why, they just do!' Susie thought that there was a chance they might help everyone in the village through this pandemic. She slowly walked through the 'Faerie Glen,' trying to think of something wonderful she could do to encourage the Seelie to bless the village. A thought forced its' way into her mind, rebuild the 'Fairy village!' She remembered the tale of the Spanish flu epidemic in the village when the children brought the Faeries gifts and made small houses. 'The children would come; they would make the Seelie happy by spending time in the Glen.'

That night Susie was sitting with Fee.

"I'm going to rebuild the Fairy village of old in the Glen," Susie said out of the blue as they were watching Coronation Street.

129

"That's a crazy idea mum, why would you?" Fee furrowed her brow.

"The kids in the village will love it, it will be a surprise when the park reopens," Susie replied.

"Like everyone else mum, you are doing things you would never have dreamt of doing before Covid," she sighed, "you're not well enough! The idea is nuts!"

"It is for everyone Fee!" "Maybe the Faeries will bless us all!"

"Oh my god Mum, give me a break from your Faerie tale nonsense!" Fee said getting up and thumping up the stairs. Susie laughed inside and shrugged her shoulders.

#

Firstly, Susie painted the faded white stones that lined the Faerie Glen pathway, collecting wood and stones as she walked every day, building rooftops and gates with small twigs and branches, tied together with twine. She had a local woodsman, cut up an old tree into large chunks twelve to eighteen inches high, carving the insides out to create rooms, the woodsman Davie Brown even joined in her task, creating well-made slatted roofs for her houses, Susie painted flowers on them and beautiful patterns. She attached them to the tops of tree stumps that were hollowed, creating windows with curtains and screwing on functional tiny doors. People in the village who had small children heard of what Susie was doing and came to see, placing beautiful stones they had decorated around the small pathways to the houses. It gave Susie something other than Covid to think about. Two houses appeared one day that a local man had made, that had doors and steps leading to them. Susie was delighted that some of the Villagers seemed to be coming together for the Faerie Glen.

She tied crystals from the trees, bright colourful beads. She had sowed wildflowers in the dirt around the path and they had appeared in their delicate splendour, it was all beautiful.

At first the just watched, glowing with amusement as Susie went about creating the 'Faerie village' she would always bring seeds and bread, which the birds would enjoy, the rabbits and hare would dare to come close as they knew she meant no harm, her aura shone like a coat of colour around her being, it was so bright that the Slaugh wouldn't approach her, they watched her from a distance sneering. The Seelie Faeries began to show themselves to her, sitting in the grass near her as she worked, then eventually entering the houses she had made for them they lay in the tiny soft beds; they talked to her, but not in words, communicating with her thoughts, answering her questions about what they knew of the Earth and the Universe.

One bright day as Susie sat at the Beachy bit, to Susie's amazement, one of the Seelie Faeries softly descended resting gently on her arm. The Faerie spoke to her of the Glen. "There has been much death within our Glen, we have witnessed it throughout the lifetimes. We do not interfere; it is the natural order of the woodlands."

"Are Faeries flesh and blood?" Susie asked. "No, we are eternal energy, if we weary in one existence, we ask to be reborn into another, passing on any knowledge!" "Asking who?" Susie wondered. "The Universe." The Faerie glowed brightly.

"One of the oldest religions of man is called Hinduism, they believe we can be reborn after death too!" Susie said, the Faerie glowed brighter.

"The only creature on earth that can cause we Seelie pain is the Slaugh, as their negative energies can become so strong it can cause our glow to fade, draining us of life, in that instance our aura is returned to the universe for eternity. That is why we fear them!"

"Who are the Slaugh?" Susie asked.

"They are the beings who gave you justice!" the Faerie revealed.

"I don't understand! Gave me justice?" Susie asked, bewildered.

"The man who was so cruel to you, the father of your child, they killed him!"

Susie was stunned. "They killed Davie?"

"You called out for justice to all in the Universe!" the Faerie said, "we heard you!"

Susie tried to remember; she had wished Davie gone so many times! She knew it was true!

The Faerie continued, "the Slaugh will be at one with Seelie to assist in giving us retribution for any grievance or injustice we may feel."

A great sadness came over Susie, for the man she once loved had been murdered because she had asked for it. A tear slowly rolled down her cheek. The Faerie felt her thought. "You bare no guilt; you are a pure soul. You were suffering, we felt your pain." In that instant, Susie remembered the man Davie had become and the pain he had put her through. Susie admired the exquisitely lovely Faerie; she radiated love to the Seelie and deep gratitude. They sat together feeling each other's warm glow.

The Seelie Faerie told Susie, "We have had many human friends in this Glen; friends like you, with the bright glow, they all loved us and we them. Centuries ago, three such friends, young women, were accused unjustly by their own kin, tortured and killed by the lie of a treacherous ally. One of the pure hearts, as she faced her death, cursed the bloodline of the human Devlin, calling out to we Seelie and the Slaugh. The Slaugh are the deliverers of that retribution! The curse still has not been satisfied, we tire of the bloodshed, but it must be settled, it is the way." The Faeries glow dulled as she thought of it. Susie was captivated by the Faeries tale. The Faerie floated upward Susie smiled following with her eyes, the sun momentarily blinded her, and the Seelie were gone.

#

The deaths due to Covid were rising every day, very few people came to the Glen for their hour of exercise with their children as it was too far to walk for most, the gates were locked still but Susie continued to come, walking around the long way, spending more and more time with the Seelie. They would buzz around her in numbers, following her through the woods, listening to her thoughts about the life she had lived and the human condition. Fee became increasingly concerned about the amount of time her mother spent in the Glen.

Fee confronted her mother when Susie did not come home until after dark one night.

"Look mum, I'm really worried about you!" "You will end up getting murdered down there!" Fee said with a concerned tone.

Susie took off her jacket and sat down in the living room.

Fee followed her "what the hell are you doing down there all day and night? "

"Stop it Fiona, you sound like your father!"

"I'm nearly sixty-eight years old, I can do what I want, I want to be with the Faeries," Susie says matter of fact.

"That's my point mum, you're not far off seventy years old and you're talking like you're 'away with the faeries already!" Fee raised her voice. "There is no such thing!" Susie stood to go upstairs, Fee reached out and held her arm, looking into her mother's face.

 "Bad people creep about the woods at night, Mum." "You must be careful." Fee said with a concerned tone.

Susie hugged her daughter. "Sorry for worrying you, but they look after me, I will be okay."

Fee looked into her mothers' eyes, "I love you mum, but I am very worried about you."

" I love you too dear." Susie said, "Please stop worrying."

#

Chapter 11.

New life, New you? 2022

All restrictions were lifted on the twenty first of March in Scotland and there is no more need to distance yourself from others or wear a mask, the majority of the population have had three vaccinations but not Susie, she believed it to be unnatural, a poison, made worse by the fact that a young lass in the village had been taken to hospital a week after being vaccinated with blood clots near the heart, Susie would remind Fee of this every time she tried to talk to her about getting vaccinated! Fee thought her mum was crazy, becoming difficult and stubborn with old age.

Susie was in the Glen every day, sometimes even at night, if Fee was on late shift, she would be oblivious to that fact. She loved to see the Seelie glow and would sit for hours watching them and listening to their wonderful tales.

The Slaugh had been very quiet. The Seelie had learned from the deer that they had an illness which was killing them, they had retreated deep into the woodland, into their underground burrows near the ruins of the old Army camps. They were staying away from the human population believing the illness was spread by them! They hunted and foraged what they needed for food and nothing more; they had no energy for mischief, malice or murder. Their numbers had depleted considerably.

#

It was around June when a crowd of teenagers met down at the 'beachy bit' in the Glen around early afternoon. The boys were there first with the bags of cheap booze and snacks, they were impatiently waiting for the girls to arrive, they had planned to stay all day and have loads of fun. After about an hour some of the girls they knew turned up, playing their music loud, singing along to the tunes, showing off their bodies dancing on the rough sand, splashing and pushing each other into the river, they all were drinking and smoking weed, they felt relaxed and happy enjoying the sun. A couple of the guys 'copped off' of with girls they fancied, drifting into the woods in pairs, then heading home content as the sun went down; But Mark, Jamie and Sean, Carla and Zara were still there.

"It's getting dark, let's go under the Viaduct and start a fire!" suggested Mark.

"Yeah, we already have 'Fire starters' up there from when we were down last time." Jamie informed them.

They made their way up collecting dry sticks and leaves on the way, so when they got there, they got the flames going pretty quickly. They all 'cooried' in around the fire. Carla really fancied Mark, but Jamie fancied Carla, Jamie was Marks best friend so there was no way Mark was going to get with her! Despite her very obvious efforts.

Zara and Sean were flirting and after the last of the Buckfast tonic wine was guzzled they drifted off towards the fields to go home together. Zara whispered to Sean, "I'm scared, I thought I heard something,"

"Okay take my hand then ya fearty," he extended his hand and as they made their way home, he felt a bit uneasy himself so put his arm around her for his own comfort.

#

The last three sat around the fire, Carla didn't care to go home yet, her mother had died from a drug overdose a year gone and her dad was going the same way soon she thought. 'If he didn't care, then neither did she!' There was never any food in the house and sometimes no electric, she had nothing to go home for!

Marks' mum and dad were both drinkers and with-it being Friday night they both would be in the local club; his mum was pregnant when she was fourteen so both his parents were not even thirty years old. They went out a lot! They had never had any other children and even though Mark was an only child he had spent most of his time with his grandparents, now he was fifteen he was left to his own devices. He and Carla both were lonely, both loved to go where other people were, they were always the last to leave.

Jamie on the other hand, had his mum at home, he had never known his dad, but he thought he had the best mum in the world, she was always there for him and great company, he was only hanging on later than he normally would tonight as he hoped that he would get to 'cop off' with Carla.

The fire was nearly out, it was very clear that Carla fancied Mark, Jamie felt angry and very jealous. An hour passed with nothing happening, so the three decided to go through the Faerie Glen path and climb the fence to get out rather than walk all the way around the woods and then the big field to leave.

"Let's go," Jamie said abruptly jumping onto his feet.

"Okay," Mark and Carla said following, when they got up to the Faerie Glen it had a glow, Mark commented on it, "has someone put 'solar' in here?"

They followed the white stones of the pathway as they shone in the dark, "who put all this stupid Faerie shit in here?" asked Carla.

"That crazy old woman Susie from down the other way," Mark replied.

"Fucken stupid old cow!" Jamie said, laughing he ran up to one of the houses and kicked it as hard as he could, there was a loud buzzing, a 'woosh and a thump' before the glow was extinguished, as the house toppled over. Mark laughed and Carla joined in, the three started to pull at the doors off the houses, pulling out the tiny fencing, smashing the wee pots, all the lights went out as they made their way along the village destroying what they could. Suddenly the three came to a halt.

"What was that?" Jamie said quietly "shuuuuush," listen, the three stood still concentrating to hear.

"I hear fuck all," said Mark, the three turned as a figure rose up in front of them, it looked like old Susie but something else! She was floating towards them, her grey hair moving around her head like Medusa's head of snakes, her mouth opened, a hideous noise arose from it, then in their heads they heard in a loud voice, many voices that overwhelmed even their own thoughts. "GET OUT!" then again, "GET OUT!" The figure rose up above them and they ran. Mark tripping then scrambling up and after his friends, the glowing figure was on the hill staring at them floating above the ground, even at this distance the illuminated green eyes were burning into their soul. Trembling with terror, they started to climb over the fencing, scrambling along the embankment, hearts pumping, mouths dry, panting, back over the side fences onto the street.

"What the FUCK," shouted Jamie as they ran up the Main Street, Mark and Carla stopped outside the Cartvale pub, hands on knees, heads down trying to catch a breath, sweat on their brow, faces red and hot. The pub was busy, and they stood on the street, not old enough to be allowed in, but it made them feel safe.

"What was that?" said Mark, he was still shaking.

"It looked like that old woman that walks about the Glen," Jamie panted.

"But she was fucken floating, wasn't she? …..Or did I imagine that?" asked Carla.

The boys stared at her nodding, with solemn faces.

The three stayed near each other, arms around each other's backs, they made their way up Church Road, up to Birch where Mark lived. In Marks home they all sat in the living room, not really sure what to say or do, the atmosphere was charged with fear.

"Do you think we have been spiked?" suggested Jamie, "a mean, how could an old wummin float? 'An awe' that light from around her, "whit wis that?" Mark was wide eyed.

Carla spoke, her voice serious," I think we should go to her house and see if she is in, if she is, then we know we were 'trippin' and we've been spiked!" Mark was not happy about going to Susie's house, he didn't want to say to his friends, but he was terrified.

The three walked down to Susie and Fees' house. The lights were on downstairs. They walked up the path slowly and stood discussing in whispers who would do the talking. The boys dropping back, Carla stepping forward. She wrang the bell, a voice came through the doorbell.

"Yes, how can I help you?" Fiona spoke through her phone. "Eh, em, it is Carla, Mark and Jamie, eh, we wondered if Susie was there? Please," stammered Carla.

"What is it you want to speak to my mum about?"

"Oh, it was just, about the Faerie Glen." Carla said in a polite voice.

The door opened and Fiona stood, she gave the teenagers a big smile.

"Just to let you, you're on camera guys, okay?" Fiona said.

"Yeah, okay," said Mark, "is your mum in?"

"Yes" said Fiona, "she is in her bed. Why? Is it urgent?" The teenagers all shook their heads.

"I can wake her up if it is!" Fiona stated.

"No, no, that's okay, we don't want to disturb her!" Jamie said pulling Carla's jacket sleeve indicating to leave.

Fiona watched them as they hurriedly went down the path.

"Spiked, I knew it!" Carla said to the boys.

"Or it could have been something else in the Glen!" Jamie said.

Fiona returned to the living-room where her mother was sat, still with her muddy jacket on. She had just come home!

"What have you been up to mum?" she asked.

"Nothing Fee, The Faeries just told those three kids to 'get out' the Glen, they were destroying the wee Village. The Faeries helped me give them a scare, lifting me up! That's all!" Susie said with innocence.

"Mum, FAERIES! Just stop! Fee raised her voice, "You didn't do anything to them did you? "Fee asked in an angry voice.

"No,…… of course not," replied Susie "I wouldn't." There was silence for a minute.

"Stay away from them, stay away from all teenagers mum, they are not the same as when you were young, they carry knives, they take drugs, they could hurt you!" Fee said with emotion and concern, her voice breaking.

"I'm okay love, no one can hurt me, stop worrying Fee," Susie replied looking at her daughters worried face.

"And Stop with the Faerie stuff, that talk is weird!" Fee's face was solemn.

"That was okay when I was a kid, painting a few stones or throwing seeds for the birds, but it has gotten way too much mum, honestly, it's too much! People are talking about you!"

Fee went in the kitchen to put on the kettle for tea, she could hear her mum talking to herself in the other room, she shouted through, "Tea mum?" No reply, just Susie's continued mumbling. 'Maybe she is getting Dementia,' Fee thought.

The next day when Fee woke up, the morning light was filtering through her curtains, she looked at the clock, half five, 'ugh, is that all,' she thought. She got up and on her way to the bathroom looked in on her mum, her bed was unslept in. "Mum, mum?" Fee called out; Susie was not in the house! Fee threw on a sweatshirt and leggings and quickly slipped on her shoes, 'I need to put a stop to this,' she said out loud. Fee jumped in the car, driving round to the Glen, she parked at the dilapidated old house, climbing hurriedly over the side fencing and made her way up to the Faerie Glen.

"Mum, mum," "it's Fee," she shouted, the woods were eerily quiet, no answer, she made her way down the pathway. There, halfway down the path was Susie on her knees in front of one of the Faerie houses, she was repairing the roof.

"Mum, there you are!" Fee said loudly, "why did you not answer me?"

"I'm busy" said Susie, "I need to fix the village," "I can't let the Seelie down, they have been so good to us!"

"Mum come on, at least come home and have some breakfast, its' not even six o'clock," Fee begged.

"I am not hungry; I must fix this." Susie stated sternly.

"Have you been in here all night mum?" Fee stared at the back of her mums' head as she continued to repair the wee roof.

"You don't understand Fee" said Susie with emotion in her voice, "the Seelie got rid of your father for us, he had become a selfish, cruel man!

Fee squatted down facing her mum.

"They gave us our life back, gave me back our home!" added Susie sincerely.

"Mum for god's sake, Dad was a Coke head, he was dealing with dodgy folk, he committed suicide!" Fee pleaded.

"NO!" "You don't know the truth of it Fee, I do!" "I love the Faeries and they love me!" Susie looked into her daughters' eyes, but all her bright green eyes saw was pity looking back.

"Mum come home now!" Fee commanded.

"NO!" Susie shouted finally.

Fee stood up straight shocked at her Mums behaviour. Susie continued mending the roof on the small house ignoring her daughter's presence. Fee hesitated, before turning to leave the woods.

"I expect you to come home before dark mum or I will need to get you professional help!" There was no reply. Fee started crying as she drove home.

Susie did come home before dark.

#

Carla, Mark and Jamie could not keep their mouths shut about what had happened in the Glen, they sat in groups telling the local kids that Susie was a witch, some thought they must have been hallucinating, 'full of it,' or they were 'winding them up,' but there was a significant group that believed their tale. When Marks parents heard about it in the pub they questioned Mark the next day, he told his parents his story, but he failed to mention that Susie was surrounded by a glow or that she was floating, in the fear that his parents would think he was taking drugs. Mark had told them the old woman had chased them, threatening them in the Glen, he omitted the fact that they had been smashing up the Faerie houses; Jamie and Carla backed up Marks story. The Police were called.

Fee thankfully took the call from the Police and managed to have her mother there for their visit. "I mean it Mum; this is getting out of hand! Do not open your mouth about Faeries or being in the Glen or they will lock you up!" Fee instructed her before the Police visit.

Susie sat quietly when Fee ushered the Policemen in.

"We are here to ask you some questions about an incident that has been reported to us," said the Policeman. Susie just stared straight ahead not acknowledging what had been said, Fee interrupted, "as you can see officer my mother is not a well woman, she is in my care, she has had Long Covid which has had a terrible effect on her. My mother is nearly seventy years old and does not go anywhere without me, maybe if you can tell me what this is all about?"

The Policeman continued. "There has been a complaint that your mother chased and threatened three young people in the Glen Park, Friday evening last week."

"What? Does my mother look as though she could chase anyone?" Fee said sternly.

The police officer continued, "Can you tell us your mothers' where abouts, at that time."

Fee answered. "Last Friday night, that's easy, where she is every night, at home usually in bed by ten o'clock!"

The Policeman turned and looked at Susie.

"Mrs Irvine, is that correct? You were at home in bed at the time? "He asked.

Susie stared straight ahead.

"Sorry officer, I'm in the process of having my mother assessed for dementia," Fee stated. "Okay Miss I understand what you're telling me, I hope you are able to get your mum the appropriate help."

"The incident has been noted as the youths corroborate each other's story, so although we are taking your mothers health into consideration, if there are any further complaints your mother could receive a caution or be charged, do you understand?"

"Yes, I understand, thank you officer," Fee led the men to the front door, she bid them farewell with a sincere looking smile.

144

Once the police left Fee knelt down in front of her mother and looked into Susie's face, "Mum, you understand what they said?"

"Yes, of course I do" said Susie with indignance.

"You must stay away from the kids, away from the Glen."

"I will stay away from the kids," said Susie.

#

Susie continued going into the Glen; She avoided times that the teenagers were around like weekends and early evenings. When her daughter was staying overnight at her boyfriends' home, then going straight to work the next day from his, Susie would visit her Faerie Glen from about three in the early morning until three in the afternoon, lying in the undergrowth among the Seelie in their village.

#

Fee had met Josh at work and although he wasn't nearly as handsome as her first husband, he was a decent man, he made her laugh, she hadn't had much laughter in the last few years with Covid and now her mums' mental health, so she was enjoying being with him so much. They were spending more and more time together and she thought that there could be a future with Josh. Fee thought her mother was now listening to her at last, as she seemed much more settled at home. When Fee was there Susie seemed almost her old self, she was reading and drawing, she had also rescued an old black cat she called 'MyKat,' that followed her everywhere and curled above her head in bed.

#

In reality when Susie was home, she was very unhappy, the people in the village would whisper when she walked past or stop their conversation when she approached. The

145

locals stared at her as though she had horns and if she did pass children in the street they would shout 'Witch' or 'Old Crazy." Susie had a new neighbour, a woman with two children one eleven years the other thirteen years old, they were not originally from the village, so Susie did not know them. When she would sit in her garden, they would stare at her or say nasty things under their breath. The boys next door would say "stop following us," or "you're a horrible lady," when other people were passing! The passers-by would turn looking at her angrily as though she was doing something wrong to them. They would fire bullets from their BB guns at her cat through or over the fence, making him 'meaow' and run and hide. Susie would sit in the front garden reading in the sun until the two boys would kick their football on the fence really hard next to her repeatedly to disturb her, she would move going to sit in the back garden, then they would follow kicking their ball against that fencing, Susie was scared to say anything in case it brought the police back to her door, so she ended up not going out in her garden at all when Fee wasn't there. The neighbour spread nasty rumours about her, saying she burst the boys' footballs or that she shouted at them. She told neighbours in the street that Susie was a 'weirdo', that talked to the Black cat; 'She did talk to the cat!' but the woman was making it seem like that was abnormal. Soon anyone that had been friendly stopped talking to Susie. The rumours were rife. Susie's heart was heavy with sadness as she had always done her best, before she became ill with Covid she had helped within the community, she had always thought of them as her friends; but she realised she had no true friends here! Anything good she had ever done seemed to be forgotten. The truth was Susie was only now happy in the Glen and her only friends were the Faeries and the animals who lived there. She didn't want to upset her daughter with these facts as she seemed so happy in her job, in her relationship, in fact now all the time, Susie did not want to spoil Fees' chance of a happy future.

#

Two years passed with daily visits to the Glen, nothing changed except the seasons, all with their unique beauty. The Faerie Glen village was regularly vandalised by teens, Susie was depressed by the damage, but she would clean it up, repair or replace what she could. The Seelie had abandoned the village due to the teenager's onslaught of hate and the negative energy they omitted. Only if Susie visited there the Seelie would come to her buzzing around as she repaired the housing or sat on the tree trunk seat, she had asked one of the woodworkers to carve out of a tree that had fallen down in the Faerie Glen. Often the old lady would lie in the long grass and fall asleep, they would keep watch around her in case any of the disruptive humans arrived, they would stroke her face, sending her loving dreams. Apart from her daughter, the Seelie were the only positive contact Susie had in her life.

#

It was Susie's seventieth birthday, Fee and Josh took her out for a tasty meal in her favourite restaurant. Susie looked over the table at Josh, he was leaning as far across the table as he could, stroking Fees' hand, his eyes were bright filled with admiration, hanging on Fee's every word. The conversation turned to families.

"Fee has told me everything about her dad and you Susie, but I want to tell you a bit about me." Josh said.

"Yes, I'd like to hear it," Susie answered with a smile.

"Sadly, both my parents are now dead, but I have four wonderful siblings and a large extended family, we all get on well. I'd like you to meet my sister Marina, she is the one I am closest too!" Josh said.

"I'd like that very much Josh" Susie smiled.

147

Josh rummaged in his jacket pocket, it hung on the back of his chair, pulling something out. "Susie, or should I call you birthday girl? I have a suprse for you!" he pushed a small black square velvet box across the table in front of Susie.

"Oh, you shouldn't have Josh." Susie said, patting Josh's hand.

"It is from the both of us," Fee said as her mother opened the box. It was the loveliest gold Faerie on a beautiful ornate chain."

"Oh, my goodness, this is just lovely. Thank you both so much it is beautiful."

"How sweet of you both." Susie was delighted.

Fee had beamed as Josh fastened it around her mothers' neck. Susie smiled and laughed the rest of the evening until they dropped her off at home.

"It was a lovely evening." Susie said beaming with happiness.

"Susie, I would you like to meet my crazy family this Saturday night, if your free?" Josh asked.

"Of course, I'm free, is it a special occasion?" questioned Susie.

"I intend to marry Fiona, but I would like your blessing!" Susie was delighted that she had been asked and blushed like a girl.

"Of course! I give you my blessing. The Lord God said, 'It is not good that man should be alone, I will make a helper comparable to him!" Susie looked into Joshs' face, "You are a blessing Josh!" "Please be kind to my girl." Susie said.

Fee smiled broadly at her mother. Susie was genuinely happy for both of them.

Susie was excited for the future, she thought 'maybe now I shall be part of the happy family I always wanted.'

Susie lay in the Glen the Faeries all around they absorbed her thoughts and excitement about her possible new family, she showed off her Faerie necklace, her glow bright with joy. The Seelie looked at the tiny replica of their image with fascination. Susie didn't even seem to notice that the Faerie village had been damaged again and was looking broken down and shabby. She was singing old songs she knew as a child and walked slowly down to the Stone throne at the 'Beachy bit,' she perched herself high on the rocks and enjoyed the view of the viaduct. A Fox approached tentatively, sitting near and they sat there together heads held high faces to the sun.

Saturday arrived, Susie had bought a new dress online and nice but comfortable shoes. Fee blow dried her mums' long grey hair, once she had styled her own and it looked very nice indeed. She put a little mascara, blusher and lip gloss on her mothers' face and Susie stood up in front of the mirror and admired her look.

"You look lovely mum," said Fee and Susie smiled and did a twirl in front of her daughter.

"This is going to be a special night! Fee said hugging her mum.

The woman next door was standing at her front door, arms crossed sneering as usual at Susie and Fee as they got into the car, but they did not even notice her, they were so engulfed in their own happiness!

Josh's sisters' house was in Claremount Avenue, Giffnock a few avenues away from where Susie was brought up; it was a beautiful red sandstone across from the Community Hall at the end of the lane. They opened the wrought iron black gates, walking up the pathways that were lined with Fuchsias.

"What a gorgeous house," commented Susie.

A woman about fifty opened the door.

"Hi, you must be Susie, Fees' mum, "Marina Josh's older sister said as she held out her hand. Marina was plump in a colourful smock type dress, she looked like Josh except with curly hair, she had a huge welcoming smile. Susie took a deep breath and took a step inside. The evening was going very well thought Fee, her mum had been charming and had made a good impression on all of Josh's siblings Marina, Alison, Rodger and Stephen plus all the nieces and nephews, she had not mentioned the Glen and more importantly for Fee, the Faeries! They were all ushered through to a long mahogany table in the dining room.

"Please find your places," Marina said, small cards with their names were on the table helping them find their seats. Susie was at the bottom of the table facing Marina, Josh at one side, Fee at the other everyone else in between.

Susie asked, "I hope I am not being rude, but I have not had homemade Apple pie and cream in years, it is wonderful, is there any seconds?"

"Mum!" Fee sang out, they all laughed.

Marina said, "I am so happy you enjoyed it Susie, I shall get you some more."

Once they had all finished the scrumptious meal, Marina held up her glass.

"A toast," she said, "a toast to Josh and Fee!"

Everyone said "cheers!" they clinked their glasses.

Then Josh lifted his glass "a toast," he said, "to Susie my future Mother-in-law!" "Cheers," the family all clinked their glasses. They chatted some more, Rodger telling some very corny jokes, everyone, groaning but laughing all the same.

Stephen lifted his glass, "everyone, a toast,", "to Josh's new job," everyone held up their glass once again, "cheers, "they all repeated together.

Susie thought she saw Fee shaking her head briefly at Stephen but thought nothing more of it. The night had been an enormous success, at the end of the evening, Marina phoned Josh, Fee and Susie a taxi.

Fee spoke to her mum as they approached their home, "I'm going to stay at Josh's mum, I will see you in, okay?"

"It was a lovely night, thank your sister again for me tomorrow," said Susie as she got out the taxi, as she and Fee walked up the path.

MyKat, appeared and started to follow Susie. "Hello MyKat, coming into bed?" She suddenly remembered, turning to Fee, she said, "you must tell me all about Josh's new job." Fiona looked worried. "Yes mum I will, I'll be home early tomorrow, we can go a nice walk in the Glen if you want?" The women hug closely on the doorstep and Susie goes in, "lock the door mum," Fee said as she returned to the cab. The car drove away, Susie stood behind the locked door, she knew her daughter better than she knew herself; something wasn't right! Susie went to bed with MyKat and fell asleep straight away, she wasn't used to alcohol.

#

The next day Susie is up bright and early, she is feeling 'chipper,' as her mum Linda used to say. MyKat weaved his way around her legs as she prepared his dinner and laid it down for him. She sat on the bench in her garden sipping tea enjoying the peace as it was too early for her neighbour and her boys to be up. Fee text to say she was on her way.

#

Susie and Fee started their walk, it was a fresh morning, but the sun was shining and although there was still a chill in the air it was a nice beginning to the day. The women walked chatting about the night before passing the local hotel.

"It is beautiful there Fee, you should find out about their wedding package."

By the time they reached the Glen the conversation had turned to Josh.

"Well, spill the beans on Josh's new job then," Susie said.

"Well, it's an amazing opportunity mum, he has been offered a position in his cousins' business in New Zealand which would allow him to get a working visa. He has his savings which are over fifty-one thousand and if he sells his flat, he would have more than enough to start his own business once established there."

Fee was talking quickly as if she had to get all the information out before Susie could reply.

"He had applied for a residency before he met me and presented them with a business plan and it's amazing news mum, he has been accepted" Fee beamed.

Susie is silent.

"It's a wonderful chance for a new way of life in an amazing country mum!" Fee says in an excited voice.

"Scotland is an amazing country Fee," Susie said.

"I know, I know mum, but we both have a past here and not always a happy past, so it would be a new start for us both." Fee stops on the path, Susie stops too.

Fee takes her hand, "Mum, you could come over as often as you wanted, if you liked it, you could sell the house, you could emigrate too!" Fee looks sincerely at her mum seeking a response.

"I'm old Fee, I'm seventy, I love Scotland, I love it here in my Glen," she said looking around, "I cannot leave, what about my Faeries Fee! I can't leave them!" Susie said her voice getting higher.

Fee looks shocked and confused, "Mum, I thought you'd been getting better, I thought you'd given up these fanciful stories!"

Susie looked angry her green eyes bright and staring: "The Seelie are real Fee, I don't care what you think or what anyone else thinks of me, they are here, they are real!

"I can't do this anymore mum, "Fee said sadly.

"Do what exactly Fee?" Susie said as she walked ahead as Fee just stood, she watched her mum walk away.

Fee shouted after her mum, "just think about it mum, I know your angry just now, but just think about it!"

Susie turned and stared at her daughter, sadness in her reply "I'm not angry Fee I'm just disappointed, disappointed I won't spend my last years with you!"

"But I want you to be happy and if your happiness lies in New Zealand with Josh then that's what you must do."

Fee walked up to her mum and hugged her tightly. "You will have Josh's family if you need anyone, you don't need to worry, you can visit them anytime and as soon as we are established you can come out."

Susie was not listening. They finished their walk-in silence. While walking home Fee started to have doubts, she wasn't definite about New Zealand, she was worried about her mum. The fact that she wouldn't give this Faerie fantasy up and people in the village had hardly been kind about it! Fee knew she was being selfish, but she wanted happiness, she wanted her new start, she wanted Josh and if she wanted him, she had to leave mum. She thought about referring her to social services for home care or paying someone to look in on her once a week, she would discuss it with mum nearer the time once the shock of it had eased.

#

Six months later, Susie and Josh had been married quietly at Eastwood house, with only Susie and Josh's best friend since school Iain present, as they were keeping all cash for starting their new life, it was Fees' second marriage after all! Fee had helped her mum arrange the sale of their house and it had sold within a week of being advertised, as it was within the catchment for all the desirable local schools, they had received thirty thousand pounds more than the asking price.

Susie had found a one-bedroom flat just before the local village shops and near the local public transport. The flat was ground floor in a block of six flats, all the residents were of retirement age. There was a secure entry system and Josh had set up a camera doorbell that was downloaded on to her laptop. There were three blocks of the flat's beautiful well-kept lawns plus woodland at the rear that led down to where the dilapidated old lower Mill stood on the other side of the river from the Fairy Village. If she stood right down at the rear of the flats, she could see the woodland of the Glen. The woman in the next flat seemed very friendly, she had told Susie that Deer sometimes wondered into the gardens, all types of wildlife. There were landscaped gardens with trees and flower beds that were maintained for an annual fee at the front of the flats, and they looked across the Main Road to the local Church Hall; The flat also was only five minutes from the Glen Park which was the most important point for Susie. Fee thought her mum and MyKat would be happy there and seeing her mum arranging her precious things in her lovely new home took away some of the guilt she had for leaving her! Fee was also happy that her mum would be away from the toxic next-door neighbour and her horrible boys; The people in the flats seemed much friendlier and closer to her mothers' own age.

#

Now only six months after the wedding and a very quick year since Fee first told Susie of her plans, here they all were at the airport saying goodbye. The couple were elated, and Josh's family were visibly excited for their future. Susie had been trying to put on a happy face for weeks for Fee and Josh, but she was secretly devastated at her daughter's departure and was silently screaming inside, fighting the feeling that she was empty and totally alone now.

She held Fees' face in her hands, staring into her eyes.

Susie said, "I love you my wee Fee Fee, please be safe. Be happy."

"Don't forget me Fiona!" Susies' eyes filled up, but she blinked back the tears.

"How could I forget you mum, I'm part of you, we will see each other again soon."

"I've shown you how to use Zoom, so you can talk to me face to face anytime you want." Fiona said sincerely holding her mother close.

Then that was it!

Susie's beloved daughter was gone, walking away down a passageway to her new life, they all stood watching Fee and Josh go, with one last turn and a wave goodbye, they disappeared out their lives. "Love you all." The couple shouted as they disappeared out of sight.

Susie sat down on the nearest seat and started to cry, sobbing, huge, big tears ran down her face. Marina sat next to her and put her arm around her back, it was heart wrenching to see a woman of that age crying so hard. The other family members walked away slowly feeling helpless and awkward seeing Susie so distressed.

"You're a brave lady Susan, holding all that in until she was gone. She will have a wonderful life out there, Josh and Fee are made for each other," Marina said kindly.

Susie was nodding her head through the sobs.

"It won't be long until we are all out there on holiday, making a nuisance of ourselves!" Marina said as she squeezed Susie tight and helped her to her feet.

#

Back at the flat, Susie tried to feel at home, she put on her lovely old lamps with their soft warm glow, fluffed up her sofa cushions. MyKat was already incredibly happy there, he was sprawled out in front of the fire with its fake but very real looking coals with flames. He had lived happily with a Policeman for years, but his human had moved house and he had gone out enjoying chasing squirrels and mice for many hours, roaming far and wide, then when exhausted he tried to return home, but he could not find his way. He had survived in the wild for months but was tired and lonely when he saw this woman, she had such a glow he knew she was full of love, so he followed her, she took him home and loved him, he now loved Susie dearly.

Susie had made herself some toasted cheese with tomatoes and red onion with a big cup of tea, she was trying to concentrate on Coronation Streets most recent storyline, but her mind kept giving her flashes of the Glen and the Faeries. It was Friday night, she cannot go there on a Friday night, nor a Saturday, nor a Sunday, she promised Fee, she repeated the chant in her head.

'Not a Friday nor a Saturday nor a Sunday, she promised Fee,' she repeated softly.

"Not a Friday nor a Saturday nor a Sunday," she promised Fee.' Susie said it out loud,

"Not a Friday nor a Saturday nor a Sunday, she promised Fee," then louder,

"Not a Friday nor a Saturday nor a Sunday, she promised Fee."

Then again shouting, MyKat looked up at her, their eyes meeting, he stretched a long stretch. "Sorry MyKat, I'm just a crazy old woman, so I've been told!" Susie spoke to the cat; in Susie's mind she believed the cat spoke back in thought.

"It is you that is sane in the craziness of the human existence!" Susie laughed then laughed and laughed.

Susie's new neighbour Jean in the flat above, sat quietly doing her crafting, she heard the woman below chanting something again and again, then manic laughter, she thought 'I hope this is not a sign of the things to come!' She had heard some of the rumours about her new neighbour but had decided to wait and see what the woman was all about herself.

Susie had managed to resist the urge to go down to the Glen the night before, but she was 'up at the crack of dawn walking down Main Street towards it now, MyKat sauntered with his own particular style a few steps behind her. The postman passed her and smiled, she tried to smile back, but her sadness was such that her smile was a grimace and he recoiled at the sight of it, hurrying on. He turned when he was further up the street, watching in surprise at the Black cat following her!

#

Susie's upstairs neighbour Jean was standing at Janet's door, who was Susie's downstairs neighbour, when the postman walked up the path.

"Saw your new neighbour at six o'clock this morning walking down the road with her black cat," he chuckled, "I think she was going to the Glen!"

"Walking? I've heard she usually flies by broomstick," Janet said, they all laughed.

"Oh, don't joke about it! That woman should be locked up! I heard she attacked some wee wains in the Glen a few years ago, nearly got the jail for scratching their faces and chasing them through the woods, terrified they were, scarred for life!" Janet said her tone full of venom.

"Poor wee mites," Jean empathised. "You should have heard the chanting from it last night," Jean said, "frightening! It really was! Any more of it and I will be phoning the Polis."

The Postman laughed.

"Aye laugh if you want, it'll no be that when you're croaking it as a frog! Janet joked.

The three laughed loudly as the Postman went on his rounds. The Postman being the friendly sort stopped to say hello to everyone he met on his way and relayed the story of Susie and her cat, the wains and the chanting.

#

Susie sat in the Glen on her wooden seat, MyKat on her lap. The Seelie buzzed about her and her friend, feeling her thoughts and giving her their warm empathy, they could feel her loneliness, the grief of her loss. They gave her solace with their warm positive energies. 'Time doesn't seem to exist in this world' Susie thought, as she noticed the darkness slowly fall. MyKat jumped down and Susie stood, they both stretched, the Seelie lit the way for their old friend up the pathway until she could see the gates. She sent them loving vibrations, her aura shining brighter than ever for them, all the colours of the rainbow like a crown around her head, they thought she was the most beautiful creature in existence, they felt a love for her and reciprocated by glowing brightly as they rose into the air, their wings like translucent Mother of pearl, smiling and singing tinkling tunes, tunes of comfort and hope.

#

Susie and MyKat walked home. She thought 'how strange my life has been in comparison to others,' She spoke to what she perceived as the creator of all existence.

"Thank you God for everything, my life, my daughter, the Seelie, MyKat, the Glen and all its natural wonders, my health, thank you God."

As Susie walked past the pub the Beer Garden was full, there was the loud murmur of lots of conversations. There were men standing at its gate smoking and as she passed, she heard them say something about her, she didn't quite catch it, but it made her feel afraid. She hurriedly walked past the blocks of flats, noticing the curtains moving, the blinds being lifted, she thought she saw a dark silhouette at her low-down neighbours' window and heard someone say loudly," witch!'",

'Stop it, you are imagining things' she thought, 'your being silly, just a silly old woman.'

Susie and MyKat had something nice to eat and settled down for the rest of their evening. Fee had sent her an email promising to zoom on Monday night as they were just getting settled in now. Marina had left her a message on her house phone asking if she was okay and to call her back, Susie thought it was too late at night to return the call, but she would talk to her in the morning. She picked an old movie from her DVD collection, 'The Green Mile.' It was a movie that she could relate to, she had watched it so many times but never tired of it. She lay on the couch enjoying the movie once more. MyKat was sound asleep on the sofa so she didn't wake him as she got up to go to bed, he would come through in his own time.

Susie woke with a jolt, it was three o'clock in the morning, 'the witching hour' she thought as she looked at the clock. Someone was pressing her flat buzzer, she peeked out her venetian blinds, but couldn't see anyone, it was dark, the road empty, a loud metallic buzz as again the buzzer was pushed, the noise was intrusive! She answered through the telecom,

"Who is it?" Susie asked, no answer. She hung up. She went into the kitchen to get a drink of water. 'Buzzzzzzzzzzzz' again!

Susie answered, "who is it?" "Are you looking for someone?" Silence.

Suddenly there was a loud smash as her lounge window crashed in, damaging her blinds, a large rock landed on the floor with shards of glass. She heard footfall on the flight of concrete steps to the right of her flat that led to the Main Street and many people laughing! She phoned the police, she was trembling, she paced as she waited. The police arrived an hour later, they took the details of the vandalism, they were sympathetic and due to her age called an

emergency joiner who arrived an hour later and put a plywood cover on the large broken

window. Susie cleaned up the broken glass carefully and was at her front door saying thank

you to the joiner as he was leaving, when her downstairs neighbour appeared in the 'close.'

"Thanks again, "Susie said as she waved to the joiner as he carried his tool bag to his van.

"Here you," Janet her neighbour beckoned Susie, lifting her chin up in a thin-lipped

confrontation, "I paid an 'awfy' lot of money to live here you know! Every penny I own! I'm

no gonni let the likes of you drag the price of my property down," she stated with a hate filled

tone, "stop being evil to wains you bad witch, you've brought this oan yersel!"!"

Susie retreated into her doorway, looked straight at Janet replying calmly.

"My conscience is clean, but be assured Janet, God is watching you!" and closed her door

locking it and putting on the chain.

The next morning was Sunday, Susie was busy hoovering up the remaining glass

particles, she had phoned the only glazier that would come out on a Sunday and booked them

to come later in the day. She and MyKat ate breakfast, she stood sipping a tea at her kitchen

window watching the fox creep around the trees. MyKat sat on the window ledge watching

the birds come and go from the washing line. She ran her hand from his head down his back,

"like Black velvet you are MyKat," she said with affection, he purred loudly, pushing his

head lovingly into her hand.

Marina called around noon, "Yes, Marina I'm fine, don't worry yourself dear."

"Yes, I am missing Fee, but I have MyKat to keep me company! "Susie assured her.

"How is everyone?" Susie asked and Marina stayed on the phone chatting about what the

family were doing. Susie did not tell Marina anything about the incident night before!

The glazier arrived at two in the afternoon and a new window was quickly fitted. Susie thought 'looks like it never happened.' MyKat was asking to go out, so she opened the kitchen window. Susie opened the fridge, she needed milk, she looked in the cupboard, she needed bread, she grabbed her purse and a cardigan and went to the local grocery shop. Not one person spoke to her, not one person looked at her face, those who had to pass her on the street, diverted their eyes away from her. In the shop the man wrang up her bread and milk on the till, made the card transaction without saying one word. Susie felt deformed, a monster, a beast not part of humanity in any way.

Once back inside the flat, she paced around the rooms, extremely distressed, she thought 'calm down Susie, deep breaths,' she started breathing deeply; in, then out slowly.

She phoned the insurance company and made the claim for the window, she nearly hung up after having to listen to a pre-recorded message on repeat, it felt like an accusation, the voice advised the caller that fraudulent claims would be found out and prosecuted.

She lay on the couch and fell asleep.

When Susie woke up it was dark, she got up and put on a lamp. She had a cup of tea put on some music low. It was no good, she couldn't settle, she felt on edge, her stomach was full of butterflies.

"Not a Friday nor a Saturday nor a Sunday," she said.

"Not a Friday nor a Saturday nor a Sunday, she promised Fee." Susie said loudly.

Jean upstairs banged her foot hard on her floor, Susie looked up at the ceiling! '

Walls of paper!' Susie thought, 'Or big ears!'

Susie went for a look around the gardens for MyKat, he had been out all day she was a little worried as he usually didn't stay out long, she wondered if he had gone down to the old house by mistake. She really didn't want to upset herself going near her old home, but she wanted to check to see if MyKat was there.

#

The night was very cool as she stepped out, she was glad she had put on her jacket. Susie made her way up the side streets, past the Village school and down the lane, scanning everywhere as she walked for MyKat. "Chi chi chi chi," she repeated again and again, the sound he knew to answer too. Now in the avenue of her old address, Susie had a strong feeling MyKat was here, she called out for him the breath like smoke from her mouth, but there was no MYKat. She went round the corner and sat on the bench in the Nursery Park, in the dark and thought where she should look next. She glanced up briefly and saw a group of teens making their way across the field, "Oh No!' she felt immediately anxious. It was too late to move, they would see her and maybe start haranguing her, so she pulled up the hood on her jacket, put her head down in the hope they would not notice her sitting in the park. The group included her old neighbours two sons Jordan now fourteen and Harry sixteen years old. Susie's heart was pounding, she tried to sink into the bench hoping to become invisible. The group stood talking and smoking about twenty feet from where she sat. One started walking away in direction of the street, he turned, "see you the morra," he said, the others stood laughing about something and then too went into the street but turned left heading down towards Susie's old home and where the two brothers lived. Susie was sweating, she didn't move for at least ten minutes until she was sure they were gone. She quickly headed the other way heading to the little bridge, over the river, it was very dark, but that way would take her up to the Hotel and the main road which her new flat was at the top off. All the way she looked for MyKat. When she got home, she was shocked to see it was after one in the morning. She stared out every window searching the dark, in the hope her cat was there but he wasn't. Susie slept but she dreamt of her childhood bedroom, someone was touching her, she was crying. A voice said, 'in the Glen, in the Glen.' She woke up, her heart pounding in her chest, she lay awake unsettled until daylight.

#

Fiona was 'zoom meeting Susie today! Susie was so excited that she would see her child's face she could hardly contain herself. She went into the kitchen to prepare some breakfast, she got the pot, boiled water, and spooned two eggs in to boil on the gas stove. She was standing at the sink rinsing her cup when something caught her eye through the window near the grass.

There was a large group of various birds, and they were pecking at something especially the crows, it was black. "OH NO! Please God, not MyKat!" Susie ran out as best she could to the garden the edge of the washing green at the rear where the woods began, as she ran out the birds flew up in a 'woosh' of wings, revealing a black and bloody bundle, she stooped down, a wave of relief ran through her, it was not MyKat!

Many times in Susies' life, she had rescued injured and unwanted animals, she instinctively now knew what to do! She returned to the flat to retrieve an old towel to pick the poor thing up. She returned, carefully lifting the whatever it was. 'A big Mole perhaps!' she thought at the weight of it and returned to the flat. Once inside the kitchen she laid the bundle on the worktop and unwrapped the animal, 'it has wings?' Susie uttered in surprise; she peeled them back from around its body.

She stood aghast! It was a small man like creature! 'One of the Slaugh,' she thought.

Small but perfectly in proportion, the man was badly torn down one side where the birds had been pecking, his wing broken in one place. This creature was covered in a hair like fur, but it looked almost mossy, he was very bloody, his face was covered in dirt, his long hair on his head matted and muddy, his eyes shut. She inspected his wings they were stunning, similar too black onyx but with a translucent quality. He was about eight inches tall and smelled really rather strong, a kind of repugnant fox smell. She filled the washing up basin with warm water and lifted him very gently and lay him in the water, her hand supporting his head and shoulders, with the other she cleaned his wound. He opened his eyes very slightly viewing her movements through slits. She lay him back on the towel patting gently, He pulled one wing back over around his wounded body with a loud growl, when Susie lifted it back, he hissed and growled baring hideously sharp teeth, lots of small but yellowed spikes.

Susie spoke gently, "I am your friend, I will not hurt you, I am trying to help you."

The Slaugh man bared his teeth again, she ignored him and went to get her First Aid box. She found a small bandage and a pad to put on the wound, he was still laying on his back on the towel when she put a tiny amount of antiseptic on the pad and applied it to his injuries, he recoiled and made a cat like noise, but lay still as she manoeuvred the bandage around his torso. Susie retrieved a lollypop stick from the first aid box and lifted the tiny man's broken wing, he sharply screamed out, she placed the stick next to the broken bone and strapped it on with a light bandage, rolling the Bat like creature on to his side, folding the wing behind him.

"Can you speak?" Susie asked, the small creature did not answer. "I am Susie," she pointed at herself.

"You are?" she pointed at him as she asked, nothing, no reply.

"Okay, I will call you" she pointed at him, "BOB," she exclaimed.

He stared at her warily, he didn't seem to understand. She got a cushion from the lounge and lifted the towel with Bob on to it. Finding a couple of dish towels, she laid them over him. Susie retrieved a small syringe from her First Aid kit, filling it with cold water and slowly putting it near Bobs' mouth. She pushed a drop onto his lips, he opened his mouth slightly and he drank the water so she skooshed the rest into his mouth, he swallowed it down.

"I think you will live, if you lie quiet and sleep, it will help you heal." Susie said. She went out the kitchen and shut the door tight behind her. Susie felt excited, her heart was beating fast, her tummy felt in knots. She went back in the kitchen about noon to check on Bob, but he was sleeping soundly, so she didn't wake him.

She returned in the afternoon at three, after she had walked around the block looking for MyKat, but there was still no sign of him. Bob was lying his eyes wide open as she entered the kitchen. She approached with another syringe of water, he drank it without a struggle, she then opened a tin of tuna and put it in a bowl mashing it into the sunflower oil until smooth, then putting a little on a tea spoon she held it under his nose, Bob sniffed and opened his mouth, his rows of teeth were fearsome and Susie thought, they could take her finger off in one bite! She put the tuna in his mouth, he swallowed it down, then opened his mouth again, he ate a few more spoonful's. Susie watched in wonder at his mouth, although the lips looked human, his actual mouth spanned beyond the lips, wider, his mouth was huge for the size of his head. Susie tried not to look at his teeth as it made her fearful. His dark green eyes stared at her the entire time, then he turned his head away and closed his eyes.

Fiona phoned her mum about dinner time and asked her to go onto zoom so she could see her. Susie sat with the laptop on the coffee table and opened zoom. Her daughters' face stared out the screen. They both smiled at each other for a full minute their eyes locked. "Have you been okay mum?" Fee asked.

"I am fine love, it is just wonderful to see your face," Susie said.

Fee laughed, "It's only been days!"

"It has felt like a lifetime, my dear." Then feeling guilty for making Fee worry, Susie added, "I am enjoying my wee flat though."

"Have you been talking to your new neighbours? Bet they a lot better than Jordan and Harrys' mum?" Fee snorted.

"I've not really seen them, apart from in passing." Susie answered.

"Phone Marina, if you need a chat if I'm not answering, okay?" Fee said.

"I know, I Know!" Susie sighed.

Fee then continued, telling her mum about 'Sumner' where she and Josh were now based. "They have an Archbishop of Canterbury here too!"

"Really?" Susie asked.

"Yes, it's a seaside suburb Mum, it was seemingly named in eighteen forty nine in honour of John Bird Sumner, the then newly appointed Archbishop of Canterbury."

"Ahhhhh, quite interesting, it has a little history." Susie said, while she watched her daughters face, animated, excited by her new life.

Susie felt happiness for her.

"It's such a lovely beach; Imagine, it has this big Rock sticking out the sand called 'Shag Rock!' Fee laughed. "Shag rock!""

Susie just looked lovingly at her daughter.

"You will see it soon enough!" Fee said cheerfully.

Josh appeared on the screen at the rear of Fee, "Hi Susie," he waved.

Five minutes more chat and then they were gone again.

Susie popped in the kitchen, but Bob was still asleep, she stood watching over him, she thought he was the most beautiful creature she had ever seen. The Seelie had told her that the Host were dangerous and totally devoid of any kind feeling toward any living being but looking at this angelic face she found it hard to believe. She moved around quietly making herself tea and a sandwich and the remainder of the tuna. She saw Bob peeking at her out one eye. "Do you need me to help you lie on your other side?" Susie made a lifting and turning movement in the air and to her surprise Bob nodded slightly. Susie cared for Bob for four days, feeding him, giving him water and bathing his wounds, He didn't move much, his wounds were visibly improving, although the wee man did cry out when he would move into another position.

MyKat had not returned, Susie went out daily looking around the village for him and had phoned the Cat and Dog home to find out if he had been handed in! Susie was genuinely concerned but her worry was distracted somewhat as her mind was on caring for the Slaugh man Bob, so much so she had not been in the Glen for a week.

#

Chapter 12.

The Boomerang boy

The Sunday night that Susie had been out looking for MyKat, the brothers had been down at the fields at the back of the school with a few pals smoking weed, they started making their way home about midnight cutting across Nursery field and having another 'one skinner' before they all headed home.

Their mother Clara was sitting up waiting on them getting in as they had forgotten their keys. As soon as the boys walked in the door, she said in a disgruntled tone, "take your keys next time, I wanted my bed an hour ago!"

"Alright, alright, get off my back" said Harry, "we just forgot."

"Aye well don't!" said their mum Clara as she headed upstairs.

#

"I've got the munchies, "said Harry. "Me too," Jordan concurred.

The boys went into the kitchen and were making toast with Chocolate spread, pouring big glasses of milk, they sat at the kitchen table once it was ready, munching into their toast and looking at their phones, occasionally showing each other Tik Toks they found funny.

Harry turned around, he heard a cat, he looked at the window and saw a pink mouth and bright green eyes.

"No way!" he exclaimed with glee, "look who it is!"

Jordon laughed, "Is that that crazy's cat?"   "Yeah, it sure is, "confirmed Harry.

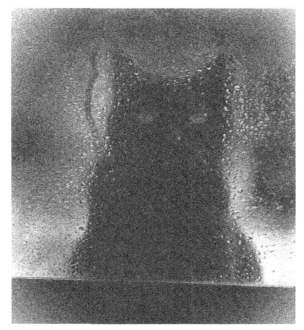

They went out the back door and quickly blocked MyKat into the kitchen window! MyKat hissed and raised his back up, sensing the boy's intent to harm, MyKat couldn't escape so he stood himself up onto his back legs and tried to scratch them with his claws. Harry punched the cat on the head hard, MyKat fell off the windowsill and Jordon booted him hard against the house wall, the cat lay still.

"Film me" said Harry, "we can do another crushing!" Jordan turned on the phone's camera, filming Harry as he went over to MyKats' injured but breathing body. Harry put one foot on the cat and pressed down, the cat tried to struggle free, but he was old and weak. Harry then stood with both feet on MyKat and pushed his weight fully down, the cat screamed.

"Ha, look shits coming out its arsehole," said Jordan.

Harry continued to crush the life out of MyKat.

Clara appeared suddenly in her nightie, "what the fuck are you two doing?" Jordan stuffed the phone in his pocket, but Claras' eyes had gone to the dead cat illuminated by the kitchen light shining through the window at Harrys' feet.

The light came on in the neighbour's bedroom window.

"Get that cat the fuck away from this house now," Clara hissed with venom "and don't let any cunt see you."

The boys put MyKat in a plastic bag.

"Lets' head doon the back way to the Glen Park." suggested Harry, "no street cameras."

"Okay," Jordan traipsed behind Harry.

Down at the Glen the boys climbed over the side fence and into the park, it is densely dark, but they know the way, they continue up past the Faerie Glen.

The Seelie silently watch the brothers enter the Glen from high above in the trees.

Harry and Jordon scrambled their way up the small slope at the side of the Archway of the Viaduct, pulling themselves up high enough on the metal security fence to see on to the top of the bridge, they pulled the cat out the bag by the tail and Harry grabbed both its front paws and swung the broken body as hard as he could up and on to the railway tracks.

"Lets' get out of here! It is as creepy as fuck at night." Jordan said. The brothers started to run back the way they came.

Once the boys had left the park the Seelie floated down in a glowing cloud to where MyKat lay. They encased the body in their glow and lifted MyKat off of the tracks. The Seelie considered Susie's love for MyKat and the warmth and companionship she had given to the being; The Cat had been full of love for her. They could see the death of the cat replayed and they knew it was evil thoughts toward Susie that had caused MyKats' suffering at the hands of the boys. They decided to right the wrong.

#

The lady who bought Susie's house was up first thing in the morning to hang her washing outside before she started work, she glanced over to Clara's Garden and saw something black hanging from the washing line, 'what the hell is that?' she thought. She walked over to the dividing fence and looked closer; it was a black cat! It was 'Susie's black cat!' she was sure of it. She thought 'that must have been the noises I heard out back last night, those nasty, nasty boys.' She quickly went inside feeling upset but not wanting to get involved with any trouble.

Clara got up at eleven and made her way downstairs into the kitchen, she lit a cigarette and took a big draw, inhaling the sharp taste of the smoke deeply into her lungs; she

173

switched on the kettle. The boys were still in bed, Jordan hadn't bothered to go to school and Harry was unemployed. Clara sighed and looked out the kitchen window inspecting the day.

"What the fuck!" she exclaimed and headed outside, she recognised the cat from last night, she knew it was Susie 'the witch's cat.'

Clara ran upstairs and pulled the duvet off of both boys' beds, she was shouting "what the hell did I tell you last night? eh, Harry, you tell me! What the fuck did I tell you to do?"

"What you nagging on at me about now, ya mad wummin!" Harry uttered in a weary voice, rubbing his eyes.

"Look out the window and you tell me, what the fuck I'm nagging about!" Clara demanded.

Both brothers get up out of bed and go over to the bedroom window. Looking down they see the cat they had killed hanging by its neck on the washing line.

"I don't understand it," Jordan said quietly, "we threw it on the train tracks."

"Aye well it's no on the train tracks now, is it!" Clara said sarcastically.

She went into the garden and cut the dead cat down, she wrapped it in an old towel, she went back upstairs and tossed the bundle on Jordans' bed!

"Ooooooh yuck!" Jordan moved away from where it landed.

Clara stared at her sons her nostrils flared, she was breathing heavily, she said, "get down to the river right now and throw that thing in, then you get to school you lazy wee fuck; And you Harry! You get back here and start using that phone of yours to find a fucken job or your out of here! I'm no joking!"

Both boys sat on their beds with their heads down, neither said anything. They had never seen their mum so mad.

MyKat's broken body floated down the river, passing the wee bridge and old Mill houses, then three riverside homes at the hotel. Down under Main Street bridge, his body was dragged down the huge waterfall, bobbing back up and then on to the smaller falls, past the derelict Lower mill. The Seelie watched his body travel through the beautiful woodlands with the birds chirping, onward under the Viaduct and to the Glen 'Beachy bit.'

MyKats' body was snagged at the rocks there and the Faeries took him once more.

#

Clara had woken up, she went into the bathroom to pee, then proceeded down the stairs to the kitchen. She lifted the kettle and filled it under the running tap, she looked up, the kettle dropped into the sink, water splashed over her dressing gown. There was the cat, but skinny and bedraggled looking, back where it was two days ago in the exact same place!

The three stood in the garden they didn't even want to touch the cat they felt uneasy, scared even, but once again, they cut MyKat down and after some discussion they decided the boys would take it up to the old army camps and set it on fire.

Clara said, "whoever did this won't have a body to bring back."

The brothers walked through Overlee Park and down to the Army bridge, they crossed the river heading up the mud path, through the deep woodland, it is a very steep hill a bit of a trek. Jordan had the cat in a rucksack on his back, Harry with a small cannister of lighter fuel in his. It was a sunny and warm day. The boys both were puffing and panting as they climbed. The Seelie watched them from high trees as did the Slaugh who were hunting squirrels in the opposite copse.

175

Once at the top the boys walked through the field to the ruins of the World War two Army base, the sun shone brightly over the fields, fluffy white clouds slowly drifting overhead.

"Where will we build the fire?" asked Jordon.

"Let's fire up this spliff first!" Harry said heading toward the two big slabs of concrete that lay in the shape of a huge sun lounger. After a smoke, lying on the makeshift lounger the boys started to collect dry leaves, sticks, any old bits of rubbish putting it in the shallow hole they had dug out. Jordon pulled the cats body out the bag and put it in the hole then Harry poured the fuel on to it.

"Stand back," said Harry as he lit the pile with a long piece of newspaper that was aflame, it set alight immediately, and they stood well back as the smoke plumed up into the blue sky.

"What are you boys up too?" a man said in a loud voice as he approached, "don't you know it's dangerous to start fires near woodland when it's dry weather?"

Harry and Jordon turned to look at the guy, he was a muscular man, about thirty and carrying a metal detector and a small folding shovel, he had sleeves of Celtic tattoos on his strong forearms.

"It's in a pit, so it won't spread!" said Harry defiantly.

"Is that petrol?" asked the guy with concern when he noticed the small canister next to the boys' feet, "you two up to no good!" he made a statement rather than asking. As the man stepped boldly toward them, Harry picked up his rucksack and put the canister in it quickly, zipping it shut, he signalled to Jordon with his eyes to go!

The boys took off at speed running straight down the steep path, the way they came. The man went over and started kicking the dry earth on to the small fire, 'bloody wains,' he thought, 'dangerous, could set the whole place up at this time of year,' he continued to put dirt on the fire, 'what is that they are burning anyway?' He stared in the small fire pit, clearing off some of the earth with his foot now the fire was out. There was a black charred lump in amongst the dark smoke, "oh god, it looks like an animal," he thought as he bit his bottom lip. The man called the police to report it, they told him to wait, but he waited an hour, no one came, so he continued over to the site further away that he had been digging in the day before. He returned to the pit a couple of hours later, the burnt remains were still there and there was no sign of any police. "Bloody state this country is in," he murmured, "when the police don't even show up!" He threw lots of dirt on it, 'poor thing,' he thought who knows what those neds subjected it too before it's death.'

#

Clara had been drinking with her mate 'big Shaza,' all of that day knocking back Voddy and Cokes, until about ten at night, the boys didn't show face until late evening when she was crashed out on the couch.

"Did you torch it?" she mumbled when they entered the living room.

"Aye, we done it! Alright!" Harry said with a cheeky tone as the boys headed up to bed.

#

The next morning, Harry was still in his bed sound asleep; Jordan was out of bed, he thought since he had woken up before nine o'clock, he may as well go into school and catch up with a couple of mates. He knew is mum would not be up until well after noon as she had been drinking. He had poured himself a bowl of coco pops and looked out the kitchen window, to his relief the cat had not been returned to them. He had a quick wash and dressed for school. "I'm away," he said loudly outside his mothers' door. Then headed down the stairs and opened the front door. There on the front doorstep were the charred remains of MyKat, a paw still visible sticking out of the charcoaled lump.

"Awwwwwwww naw" he exclaimed in a high-pitched loud voice. "Harry!" he shouted as he ran up the stairs for his brother, his legs felt weak under him, throwing open the door barging back into his bedroom, Harry sat up with a jolt. "Wha….t is it for fucks sake?" Harry said.

"It's back! The cat's back!" Jordan said breathlessly.

Clara was now awake and behind Jordan.

"Where is it?" she asked.

"On the step," Jordan said, "I don't want to look at it," Jordan cried, he started weeping.

"What you fuckin greetin for?" His mother stared at him unmoved by his tears.

"Because she must be a witch, that old Susie she knows what we done, she is gonni do us all in!" Jordan said whimpering.

"Calm it, she's no really a witch, she must be 'noising us up,' trying to give us the fear" Clara said mockingly.

"Let's take the cat up to her new house and leave it there, so she knows we know it's her and we're no feart!" Harry said defiantly.

"Ma heeds bangin," "I canny be doing with this hassle this morning!" said Clara.

#

The wee man Bob was much improved, he was now accustomed to this human and her powerful aura, which at first had hurt his eyes, he could not understand why she had helped him. He had been taught all humans were hateful, vile, disgusting creatures that waged war with nature, that they used and abused all beings on the earth and poisoned water and the sky above. The Slaugh were taught to stay hidden from them but to reduce their numbers with fervour when possible.

Bob was now able to sit up although his wound was still bad, he had given a good fight to the fox that had caught him as his meal of that day, Bob had torn at him with his teeth and nails until the fox had to let go, whimpering away with a badly torn snout. 'The Seelie must have blessed him that day,' he thought. The woman he knew now as Susie, put out her hands to his and tried to pull him gently up on to his feet, he understood and tried to lift himself up but it was too painful and he groaned aloud, Susie slowly lowered him back down, she removed the 'puppy pad,' from underneath him and replaced it, then fed him some cooked sausages. He had never tasted anything like it and had made enjoyment noises as he ate. She smiled at him; he stared back with his green eyes.

'Her eyes were not unlike the Slaugh's, how strange!' he thought.

Susie heard her inside front door buzzer, she looked at the lap top screen it was her upstairs neighbour, Jean. Susie spoke through the intercom on the doors' camera bell, "Hello Jean, how can I help you?" Jean looked round then realised the voice came from the doorbell.

"Oh, Hello Susie, sorry to bother you but I'm afraid, I've found your cat."

"That's great," said Susie opening the door.

Jean stood in front of Susie looking sombre. "No, it's bad news I think, if it is your cat."

"Where is he?" Susie said, looking into Jeans face questioningly, Jean led the way to the front 'outside close' door, and there was a black charred lump, vaguely resembling a cat lying outside on the front step. Susie was horrified, she stumbled back slightly. "Oh, my god," her voice trembled. "My poor boy." Jean caught her arm; Better get you back inside Susie."

"No, no, I'm fine, it is just the shock. I need to call the police!" Susie was aware she couldn't let anyone in her flat as they might see Bob.

"I will go get MyKats' blanket," she went back in her flat and retrieved the cat's blanket and shut the kitchen door tight." Susie went back outside but Jean had returned to her own flat. She scooped her beloved Mykat in his blanket and took him inside, she went into the kitchen and laid him down on the worktop on the opposite side of the kitchen to Bob. Susie opened up the blanket and the sight of her poor dead cat, broke her heart, she let out a terrible howl of grief." Oh, what have they done to you my dear friend," she cried out. Bob sat up with a start, he didn't understand at first until he saw the old woman shedding tears over the animal, he realised it was her friend, he wondered what happened to the beast. Susie got her trowel, going down into the woodland at the rear of the block of flats back garden; On her knees the old woman dug a deep hole, she returned to the kitchen, Bob was sitting up, she looked at him directly, "I loved this cat." Susie said with emotion, "I hate the people that did this, I hope they suffer!" Bob understood her thoughts, he could see her pain reflected in her aura. Susie returned to the garden, gently lowering the cats remains into the hole and buried him.

#

A week after Susie buried MyKat, Bob could stand up without crying out, a day after that he could walk very slowly. He was now feeding himself. He even enjoyed the bathing Susie insisted he do for his wound; rarely would he go into water in the wild but the warmth of the bath she prepared helped ease any pain. Bob snarled as she approached him with comb and scissors, Susie combed a little of her own hair and snipped it, Bob watched, he stood quietly as she combed his long hair cutting out the many matts then showed him his reflection in a mirror.

"We are not so different you and I Bob," Susie said as he stared intently at his image, he had never seen his self so clearly before, he cleared his throat with a few choking sounds then said in a low growly voice, "We are not so different you and I Bob!" he mimicked. Susie stood aghast, "you can talk?" He stared at her, "you can talk?" he copied.

She realised then he didn't comprehend fully her language and he was only repeating her sounds, but brilliantly! Bob became stronger, healthier, he was curious about Susie, watching everything she did, he felt a stirring of affection for her, something he rarely felt for any being.

#

Susie was walking through the Glen in the very early mornings. She was delighted to see the Seelie had not forgotten her, they floated around her, she smiled feeling them warm her soul with their loving thoughts; They buzzed around her knowing what was in her mind, they were amazed that she had one of the Host in her home without being seriously injured, they told her his name was Fynn! "I better not call him Bob anymore then!" she laughed.

Eight weeks passed quickly, Fee was meeting with Susie every week by zoom and she was delighted to find her mother settled, Susie did not reveal the truth!

#

Susie took the splint off Fynn while he stood, he stretched his wings out, the old woman was surprised, looking on with admiration. "Oooooooooooooh…. You are beautiful Fynn, "he looked around quickly, surprised at the mention of his real name.

He flapped his wings once, rising to the ceiling, she looked up as he buzzed loudly, he floated down. He looked into her eyes, she felt in her soul that he was thanking her. He stretched his wings out fully, then flying through the flat, Susie ducking and laughing as he swooped at her, they rested for a couple of hours in the afternoon. They ate together in the kitchen. Susie looked at Fynn, he stood and walked to the window looking out into the darkness, his eyes suddenly illuminous and glowing. Susie had a small silver bead that had fallen from her old bangle that her dear mother had given her as a child, she threaded a piece of fine twine through it, she held it up to Bobs' chest and indicated she wanted to tie it on him, he allowed her to, he looked at her then touched the bead with the talon like nails on his strong hands. Susie said "We are not all bad! You are not all bad!" Fynn looked at her sadly and spoke.

"We are not all bad! You are not all bad!" Susie wondered if he understood the words he said, she was sure he could feel what it meant. She opened the window, they both took a deep breath of the cool air and in a 'wooosh,' he was gone, he did not look back.

"I hope I see you again Fynn," Susie whispered. She stood there for a while, the loneliness embracing her once more with its' ice-cold fingers.

Chapter 13.

Brothers in arms 2026

"So has your Mum agreed to come over yet?" asked Marina.

"No, she is adamant at her age she just doesn't want to fly that far, she says it's too much for her!" replied Fee.

"So, are you coming over to her then?" Marina asked.

"Josh can't get away from work just now. I am just in the door at my job, I don't want to ask for anytime off until maybe the end of this year."

"She is fine, isn't she? She sounds quite happy when I 'zoom' her?" Fee stated positively.

"Your mum is a tough old bird; she does miss you though Fee! Surely you realise that?"

Fee sighed, "I'm sure she will be okay until the end of the year," she replied sounding irritated.

"Oh, I meant to ask you, what number did your mum live in Wellfort Avenue when she was a kid?" Marina asked.

"I'm not sure, why?" asked Fee.

"Well, it's quite interesting, supposedly a house in that street has been the subject of an extensive ghost investigation, seemingly there have weird things going on for years! There is plenty on 'YouTube' about it, have a look!" Marina suggested. "The exciting thing is, there is a new documentary about the most haunted homes in Scotland; The house in Wellfort is starring as 'the most haunted home in Glasgow!"

"Wow," exclaimed Fee. "That is exciting. I will have to ask Mum."

Later that day Fee contacted her mother on 'zoom' they chatted about the mundane, Fee's work, the weather. Fee asked once again. "Come over to visit New Zealand mum, I miss you. I want you to see where I live, how beautiful it is!"

Susie was silent.

"Mum?" Fee urged for a response.

"Fee, I miss you too dear, so much, but I can't come over, I feel it is just too much for me, you know how I hate to fly!" Susie answered sadly.

Fee had a heavy feeling of remorse that she had not made more of an effort to visit her Mum. "I am hoping to get over to visit you then at the end of the year, just myself, so we can spend lots of time together." Fee said with an upbeat tone.

"Really? Oh, that would be wonderful Fee, it would mean so much to me, it feels like forever since I held you." Susie's voice lifted, it was filled with emotion. Happy tears stung her eyes.

"Oh, mum don't cry, I will give you a huge hug again soon!" Fee had a heavy feeling in her heart as she knew she was making false promises.

The conversation drifted on, then Fee remembered, "Oh before I forget, I meant to ask you what number did you live in Wellfort Avenue when you were a child?"

"What a strange question, why?" asked Susie.

"Well, it's a funny old story, Marina told me a TV show has been made about a house in that street, the media state there has been undisputable evidence of paranormal activity, the researchers say it is the most haunted house in Glasgow! It will be on a show called 'Most Haunted.'" said Fee.

"That's interesting, I must watch it, when is it on?" asked Susie.

"Not sure yet Mum but I will let you know, when I find out."

"Anyway, what number were you? "

"Eleven" Susie said, feeling a cold shiver up her spine.

#

Susie was in the Glen mid-afternoon, she was tidying the old Faerie village, it was very shabby now, there wasn't a lot left of the original beautiful Faerie houses, but she just kept the wee homes intact for any children that might be visiting the Glen to give the younger among them delight and wonder. She hung windchimes of bright beads and sticks, others

who walked there left their own small fairy figures or painted stones. Susie had made a wooden mask with hair made from twisted sticks that looked like Medusa, she put green sea glass in the eye spaces and hung it on a tree where the teenagers sat, to try to remind them not to break anything. She chuckled to herself when she thought of them possibly being scared away.

Susie sat on her wooden tree chair, listening to all the woodland sounds as the wind blew gently on her face and through the trees. After a while the Seelie appeared in a bright cloud, they buzzed around Susie, some settled on her head, shoulders and legs, she spoke to them with her mind as they did with her, it was a transference of warm feelings and positive affirmations about their being. They hummed as they enjoyed her love for them. Time sped by and it was soon getting dark, the Seelie urged Susie to leave. She soon was sauntering contentedly home. As she walked over the bridge, she saw a crowd of boys coming around the corner towards her, she quickly ducked into the pathway that led up behind the old tenements and the Cartvale pub, she did not want to risk coming face to face with the brothers, or any of their pack as they seemed to hold great animosity toward her. She knew they had killed MyKat! The Seelie had confirmed what she had already seen in her 'minds' eye,' she had felt it. She had wondered many times in her life if she was a little bit psychic. It frightened her what the brothers were capable of doing to her now they were late teens and twenty years old, men not boys anymore.

Susie slinked up the rear of the houses, one of the young men, Stevie B turned and caught sight of her and turned to the others. "There is that creepy old woman."

"Pure weirdo," sneered Harry.

One of the other guys, Kevin said "uck, she is just an old woman, she looks about ninety for fucks sake! Leave her alone."

"Scared she will put a curse on you ya wanker!" Jordan laughed, the rest joining in, Jordan wrapping his arm round the back of Kevin's neck.

"Get aff me ya prick!" Kevin shouts, they start wrestling each other roughly, along the road, the group headed to the White Cart pub for a pint.

The brothers Harry and Jordan were sitting with Stevie B, Kevin, Alex and Dunkie, in the Pub.

"This is shite," said Kevin "they are turning all the pubs into fucken old people's homes since Covid, there is nae where to go round here anymare, no music, nuthin!"

"I bet everyone is down the Glen wae a carry oot." Alex said.

"Aye let's head down to 'Beachy Bit!" said Dunkie as he stood up and brushed down the back of his trousers with his hands.

The brothers were not keen, "Nah, a hate it down there now," said Jordan.

"Aye it gives me the 'heeby jeebys'!" said Harry, them both shaking their heads.

Stevie B stood up laughing "heeby jeebys, I've no heard that fir ages!" He started to walk away with Kevin, Alex and Dunkie.

"Fir fucks sake cum on!" Stevie B said with annoyance.

"You go if you want," Harry said.

Jordan piped up. "I'm staying here fir a bit!"

The four boys walked back the way they had all come in. Half an hour past and the brothers sat outside in the Beer Garden, smoking their last ciggy between them.

"Well, this is boring, in it?" Harry sighed.

"You wanna go catch them up, eh?" Jordan asked standing up.

"Beachy bit? "Asked Harry.

Jorden nodded his head as he took the last draw of the ciggy, threw it down and put it out by grinding his trainer on it. "Nothin else fir it I guess."

The boys left the pub, turning right, then left toward the old farm entrance. There was a burnt-out tractor to the left of the field and a path to the Wheat fields and down to the rear entrance of the Glen. It was the quickest way to the 'Beachy bit', but it also was very creepy.

Jordon tried to call the others on his phone, but it did not connect.

"They willnay get a reception doon there!" said Harry, walking on into the darkening field.

"Will we go to the Fire pit first see if they're there?" Jordan asked.

"Aye, may's well," Harry replied.

The brothers walk down and head to the left side of the field next to the railway track, through a small coppice.

"Hope Kevin still got a bit of blow," said Harry.

"Don't think they will have done it aww in," replied Jordon, "we should-a got a bit aff him before they left!"

They followed the small path that led to the gap in the fence next to the Viaduct.

"Kooooo Eeeeeeeee!" shouted Harry, the four young guys sat under the Viaduct on a huge, big log, at their usual place, the fire pit.

"Kooooooo Eeeeeeeee," the four friends shouted back. Harry laughed as they walked round to the others who were sitting under the Arch around a small fire.

"Thought you two, too feart to come doon here the night," said Stevie B.

"Ha ha ha! Funny guy!" said Harry sarcastically. "You smoked all that puff?"

"Nice timing, "Alex replied, "I've just rolled the last four skinner."

"Mint," Jordan said as he squeezed on the tree log seat beside him.

The Slaugh were in the Glen tonight. Fynn was among them, he watched the men under the Viaduct, he loathed them, the sickly-sweet smell of what they were inhaling made him feel nauseous and heavy headed. A Faerie from the Seelie passed by his ear whispering into his mind that the tallest man and the one on the end of the seat was the old Seelie woman's tormentors and her beloved cat's killers.

"Did you see that?" asked Dunkie.

"What," they all asked.

"It looked like an orb," he continued, it just flew out of that tree.

"It's an ember floating from the fire," said Kevin.

"Wooooooooooh is it an ember Kevin?" said Harry mockingly, "look who thinks he's fucken Mastermind!" They all laugh. "It's not my fault you're a dumb fuck!" said Kevin without humour.

"Who you callin a dumb fuck?" Harry retorted aggressively.

"You, "Kevin replied.

Harry kicked out at him on the log and Kevin fell backwards, all the men jumped up.

"Hey!" cried out Alex.

"Chill, chill," shouted Stevie B

Jordan was holding back his brother.

"Think you're a fucken hard man Kev, eh?" Harry roared.

"You're a piece of shit Harry, you're only good at picking on old women!" Kevin shouted as the others held him back. "Nothing but trouble, just like your maw!"

Harry flew forward past his brother and punched Kevin on the forehead, then it all erupted Jordan and Harry were fighting Kevin and Alex, Dunkie and Stevie B stood back. Harry went to punch Alex and caught Dunkie on the side of the face, he grabbed Harry by the jacket toward him, then swung a punch that dropped him to the ground, Stevie B took a kick at Harry as he was getting up.

Jordan shouted, "Come on Harry," pulling his brother toward the path that leads down to Beachy bit, the brothers start to run, and the four guys gave chase.

Alex slowed down, panting heavily, he shouted out after the others loudly,

"I canny be arsed with this, I'm away!" he turned and made his way quickly out the Glen. "Bloody arseholes, someone's gonni get really hurt and it's no gonni be me! Canny even come out for a smoke anymore," he mumbled to himself as he hurried along.

The three pursued the brothers down to the steep drop to the Beach, Dunkie gave chase but tripped on the small step that took them off the path and went flying, he landed badly, his ankle went over. "For fucks sake!" he screamed out! "My fucken ankle!"

Stevie B slowed and turned, coming back to help Dunkie up.

"I canny stand on it!" said Dunkie. Stevie B shouted at Kevin who was standing at the top of the steep incline looking down on Beachy bit to see where the brothers were.

"Come on Kev, he's just not worth it! Dunkies' fucked is ankle we need to help him!

"Fuck you, you arseholes!" Kev shouted down to Beachy bit.

Kev and Stevie B put their arms round Dunkie and helped him hop up the pathways, it took them ages to get out of the Glen, they had to stop twice to rest.

Kev ranting as they paused, "I swear I am finished with them, that Harry is a pure wanker, causes trouble wherever he goes!"

Dunkie nods, "Aye, someone always gets their weed nicked or their head kicked in!"

"I'm gonni give them a swerve for a bit anyways, I canny be doin wi this shite!" Stevie B added.

As they left the Glen through the huge gates, they heard an animal type scream, followed by quiet, "What the fuck was that?" asked Stevie B. Then again, the stillness was broken by loud scream then silence. "Sounded like a cat or a fox" exclaimed Kevin, "probably those two arseholes at the wind up!"

"Come on, who gives a fuck about them, I'm in agony I need to get hame!" Dunkie said urgently.

#

Clara woke, about eleven in the morning, she headed to the toilet, as she sat on the pan she thought 'the house seems dead quiet.' She finished peeing and went into the landing; she opened Harry and Jordan's bedroom door. They obviously had not come home last night as the room was still the stinking pit it was yesterday. She thought, 'they coulda bloody text me! "Men! Selfish bastards!" she muttered.

By six o'clock that night Clara was in the pub, she didn't know her boys were still not home.

They were never coming home again!

Chapter 14.

Most Haunted

Fee called her mum excited. "Did you look up the 'You tube' info on your old house mum?" Susie replied in an uninterested tone, "No Fee I forgot all about it." "I did not like that house when I was a wee girl, my mum told me it gave me night terrors. I suffered for years with them, not sure I want to be reminded of it, to be honest."

"But Mum!" Fee continued, "maybe there was another reason for the bad dreams. "The 'Most Haunted Scotland - Paranormal Caught on Camera' is on SKY TV tonight, SKY History at 9PM, I'm definitely going to watch it, you should too!"

"Maybe I will then, see what all the fuss is about!" Susie told Fee with a snort of laughter.

Marina had called Susie at eight thirty that night.

"Hey Susie, 'Most Haunted' is coming on at nine! You going to watch it?" she urged.

"I guess I will since you and Fee seem so insistent that I do!" she laughed.

"I'm going to watch it;" "It will be funny seeing our own neighbourhood on TV, maybe see someone we know!" Marina chatted on with her usual energy for quite a while, "Oh, quick that's it coming on now!" The line went dead.

Susie settled into her comfy chair, tucking a pillow behind her back, she had made herself a big mug of tea which was now lukewarm, she took a sip as the programme started.

The presenter 'Jax,' a young good looking American man, introduced the programme and proceeded to walk down Wellfort Avenue toward number eleven. He stated, "the house was built around nineteen thirty-five and approximately two years later was bought by the Jewish synagogue for Rabbis and their families to live in," he paused. "A man named Rabbi Shmuel Silverstein moved there with his new wife, they had a son the following year. Shmuel and his family visited the King George Playing Field which was a small park with a Pavilion and woodland at the edge of the field; Shmuel and his son Uri would play football there often."

"The park was only an avenue or two away from their home and by the time Uri was ten he was visiting the park and the woodland daily with other boys from the neighbourhood."

Susie recognised the street; she was watching with interest as she had not known anything much about her childhood home.

The presenter continued.

"Uri had gone to the park one summers day in early nineteen forty-nine and not come home. He had disappeared. No one had seen him that day. He had told his mother that morning that he was going to see if there was any of his friends at the park to play with and would be back if there was not. None of the local children who had been in the playing fields that afternoon had recalled him being there. The Police had been called and a search party assembled; his parents, neighbours and local people scoured the park, woodlands and the railways track that lay behind it. There was no sign of Uri!" "His father was frantic, as you would expect!" the presenter paused and said, "sadly Uri was never found!"

"Over the next six years the rabbi became obsessed with the now named, 'Huntley Park' and woodland searching through it daily. He became increasingly unhinged, talking to his wife about nasty creatures living in the trees. He believed his son had been murdered by small demons."

Jax lifted his eyebrows and stared into the camera briefly.

"His wife became very concerned and tried to help her husband but if he was not in the woodland searching, he would be reciting prayer, pacing the rooms of the house or wailing for God to help him. He refused to talk to anyone, she was forced to leave as he would throw things at her and destroy precious items around the house, she believed he had become insane."

A warning flashed up on the screen, that there may be an upsetting storyline or scenes.

Jax is still walking slowly down the avenue while he narrates, he pauses outside a small bungalow with an upstairs Dorma window!"

"The Rabbi remained in the home alone until he hung himself in the garage in nineteen fifty-seven just after his wife divorced him."

Jax nods with a downward mouth and sad eyes. The camera moves from 'Jax' to a man who he explains is a local man David Silver whos' father Howard Silver knew the Rabbi and the history of the house.

"So, what happened next David," the presenter looks to David Silver.

"Well, according to my dad a young couple bought the house from the synagogue in nineteen fifty-eight only a year later at a low price as no one had made an offer to buy the house once they knew about the suicide. A Mr & Mrs Fulton, they had a young daughter about four years old. They must have had some problems in the house over the following years, as according to my dad Mr Fulton being a Catholic had called a Priest to come to the house several times, performing rituals. My father visited the family and told them about the Rabbi hoping it would help them. After my fathers' visit, the couple sold the house at the end of that year, at a lower price than they bought it."

'Susie could not believe it, they were talking about her, her mum and dad! She had the strangest feeling in her stomach. Her parents had never told her this story. Why?'

Then Jax turns to an attractive, tall slim lady in her fifties, with long blonde hair. Jax said, "Alison you've been the local estate agent for over three decades." "What happened next with the house?"

Alison explains eloquently, "by nineteen ninety-one the house had been sold six times!" "No one stays in the property long, "she says, "they all report strange happenings, sounds, plus unhappiness while in this house."

She continues, "the house has now been unoccupied for ten years since two thousand and sixteen. The owner is abroad with his family, now retired, he has given us permission to enter.

By this time, Jax is standing with two other men outside the front door of the bungalow type house. He is speaking directly to the audience at home.

"Over the years the reports of the Rabbi have been so many that we cannot list them all or show all the footage!"

"The Rabbi apparition seems to want to touch, hold or tell the children something!"

"Yet the other occupants are attacked, scratched or items thrown at them."

"Scary stuff folks, I'm going to show you the best of the photo evidence and video footage from various residents of the house and neighbours over the years."

"Make your own mind up of whether you think the evidence if genuine or not!" he says staring at the camera intensely.

Susie feels he is talking directly to her and shivers.

The screen flicks to a photo of what seems to be a blurry dark figure coming out of a doorway.

The next item is an older video, the footage is set in a small Childs' bedroom, Susie recognises the room. A transparent figure in robes stands with a white smoke like substance drifting from its hand.

Another photo, a dark shadow on a child's bed, the bed has an indentation as though the weight of a person is present.

Next a video of lights flickering, an apparition passes in seconds across the hallway into a doorway the door slams shut.

Another photo has the image of a transparent head of grey hair with a skull cap on!

The next video is clearer, it's from a camera that has been put in a Childs' bedroom at night, the child is curled up sleeping, the duvet moves then an indent appears as if someone is lying behind the child, the child moves, sitting up, crying out for her mum. The footage shows a dark entity move across the room as the mother enters the bedroom, then a doll flies across the room and hits the mothers' shoulder as she sits on the bed.

Susie is crying, the tears running down her face. She understands what is happening and more importantly she remembers what the Rabbi was saying in her ear as a child. "Beware the Host!"

#

Jax says "this is my team tonight, Andy, Ted and of course our trusted cameraman Steve." The camera moves to each man, Andy waves, Ted nod and smiles. "The equipment we are using in tonight's investigation: GS2 Laser Grid System."

"Likely you've all been watching the latest paranormal investigation shows on the Travel Channel and have seen this device that projects a grid or small dots." Jax states.

He then lists the others equipment as "the Full Spectrum POV Camera, an EVP Recorder, EMF Meter and of course our old faithful the Ghost Box." Jax opens eleven Wellfort avenues' front door and enters.

The screen flicks to live camera coverage from inside the house. As they walk down the dark entrance hall, immediately Andy says, "I don't feel so good," they walk a little further stopping to move the detectors around the hallway. "Ahhhouch!" "I've been scratched," Andy shows his arm to the camera Steve is holding; It is fresh wound, burning hot, and red to look at! Andy speaks out in a desperate voice, "I'm feeling very threatened guys!" "Just calm down!" Jax says to him.

"ahhhhhhh" Andy yells, "I've been jabbed in the kidneys. Jax I am in pain!" Steve turns the camera to face Andy, he looks very frightened, his eyes are wide searching the dull hallway. Andy is breathing heavily, he drops down into a crouch and holds his head, "I need to leave guys. Something is wrong, very wrong!" His face pale as he excuses himself and hurriedly makes his way outside via the front door. Steve returns the camera to Jax and Ted, they continue slowly into the centre of the house. The men stop suddenly, "you hear that?" Jax asks Ted.

"Yes!" Ted turns around concentrating on hearing.

Jax holds out An EVP recorder he whispers while looking straight into the camera.

"This is a well-known tool in the ghost hunting industry with most investigators using them, this voice recorder is known to pick up even a mouses whisper." They both stand very still in the centre of the bungalow. The EVP amplifies the noise they hear.

Susie jumps as the sound of wailing is brought loudly through the TV into her home!

"I guess you all heard that?" says Ted into the camera with a deadly serious face.

"Are you Rabbi Shmuel Silverstein," Jax shouts out, all the equipment goes off the scale.

"I guess that's a yes," said Jax.

The low wailing starts again, so loud it can be heard without the EVP.

"Wow! we can hear you Rabbi; how can we help you?" Ted says loudly.

"URI" the EVP screams in reply.

The doors in every room start to open and bang shut, slamming repeatedly!

"Ahhhhhhhhhhhhhh," shouts Jax, "I've been scratched."

Steve follows Ted and Jax as they rush ahead to the front door, it slams shut in front of them.

Ted is panicking, he tries to pull it open, it is stuck, Andy is on the outside pushing on it hard. The noise from the doors banging throughout the house is thunderous. Ted pulls hard, the door flies open, they all scramble to get out, Ted hugging Andy as he emerges, the door banging shut behind Steve!

The camera has been laid down on the doorstep, it is still recording the noise that is coming from behind the closed Front door, a low wailing and intermittent screaming. Steve picks up the camera, Jax showing he has a nasty deep scratch on his neck. He looks visibly shaken as do Ted and Andy.

Andy reveals the area on his lower back where he felt he was punched, fresh bloody scratches read: HOST.

The team move quickly away from the house to outside the garden. Jax looks at the camera, "Is this the 'Most Haunted House in Glasgow? We definitely think so!"

The programme ends with a roll of credits. The SKY channel presenters' voice said deeply, "whew, now if that wasn't enough, Jax and the team are back the same time next week with more 'Most Haunted in Scotland!"

Susie switches off the TV and sits quietly thinking about what she has just witnessed.

The phone wrang a loud ring and Susie jumped.

When she answered it was Fee. "Oh my god Mum, poor you, your parent what a bloody terrible house, no wonder you were having nightmares!"

"It's given me a lot to think about Fee," "I must try to remember properly what happened to me as a child." Susie said.

Fee paused then replied, "I think that is a good idea, even try to go to one of these regression therapy people, to find out the truth."

#

Chapter 15.

Blood is thicker than water.

The brothers were lying down in the undergrowth, they were waiting for the rest of the guys to leave the Beachy bit. They heard Kevin shout down at them "Fuck you, you wee assholes!" Then there was muffled talking sounds as the guys slowly left the Glen.

"They gone?" whispered Jordan asking Harry.

"Aye a think so!" said Harry lifting himself up out of the long grass and weeds.

They both stand up, wiping themselves down. "Fucken boggin!" said Harry, wiping his damp dirty knees.

Walking along the thin, muddy path that skirted the river heading back to the beachy bit the brothers were quiet. The moment that Harry's foot touched the sand he heard a cat cry.

Then again, a long 'meaow.' Harry and Jordan stood listening. Silence. They began to walk again and stopped frozen to the spot as they heard another long loud 'meeeeeeaow' type scream!'

"That's they wankers noising us up," Harry said, in the second he stopped talking, a buzzing filled their ears. They looked all around them, as hundreds of what they thought were bats, descended on them, pulling them down onto the ground. Harry was hitting and batting them as they landed on him, tearing at them with his hands when they bit him, the fight invigorated the Slaugh's resolve as their attack became more intense. Jordan curled up like a foetus, pulling his arms around his face. The Host pushed Harry down flat, pulling his arms and legs out like a star, they put their body weight on him, hundreds of Slaugh pushing and grinding a heavy pressing force on to his chest. 'Another crushing!" he thought as an image of Mykat flashed through his mind, he battled to free his arm briefly grabbing one of the beings, biting hard into the creatures' leg, the Slaugh Faerie let out a high pitched short scream before they grabbed Harrys' mouth in numbers, tearing his jaw open, splitting the sides of his mouth with a rip, digging their long talon like nails into his tongue, clawing it out with a hideous peeling noise, throwing it in the river, the pain Harry felt was excruciating; He was trying to take a breath but he was choking, spluttering and gagging on his warm metallic tasting blood. The Host dragged him into the river pulling him under at the deepest point filling his lungs with water as he took his last burning breath. Jordan started crying, sobbing, "please," he wept begging, now on his knees, "please," he uncovered his face and saw Fynn beside him, his wings fully extended standing directly in front of his face. "Pleeeeease," Fynn mimicked, "Please." Jordan went into shock at the sight of the Faerie man and the hordes of creatures behind him. He tried to crawl away from them on all fours, but he was pushed forward. He rolled off of the edge of the undergrowth into the river panic stricken, eyes wide open in horror, when he saw the body of his brother who was just visible under the surface.

The Slaugh descended on him holding him under, until he stopped moving. Two

wide terrified, dead eyes staring out from his submerged face. A loud buzz was heard as they

rose into the air, eyes glowing yellow green, they were triumphant swooping and buzzing

loudly. The Seelie had watched from nearby they did not interfere, they were satisfied that

the old woman's friends' death had been avenged.

#

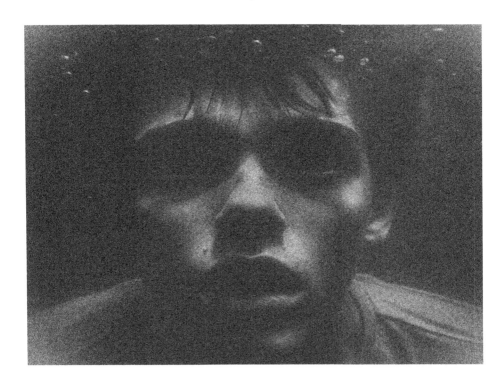

It started to rain at midnight, the rain came down heavier than it had for weeks, thrumming

hard into the estuary, the waters swelled and became strong and ferocious, it washed the

brothers down river. Harry's crushed broken body was moved roughly along in the gushing

water, his brother following him 'as in life!' They passed the Army bridge they had crossed with the dead MyKat in their bag, sailing along to the homes running down the back of the town, soon floating past the back of the primary school, which backed on to where Angie the Policewoman had lived in a flat long before. Through the dim, murky woodland they continued on their voyage, the rain pelting down upon them, the waters roared under the White bridge at Lynn Park, the brothers bodies crashing down the huge thunderous waterfall, the thrashing waters throwing them up to the surface briefly to proceed down the river, through the woodland near the Graveyards edge, where they had played when just boys. Cruising down to Snuff mill bridge the brothers travelled. Harry's body got caught at the rocks there. The Seelie had watched the boys tour with gratification at the Hosts work, glad that the evil seeds had been dug out before they grew into deadly poisonous plants. Jordans body travelled further being caught on the branches of a tree that had fallen at the waters' edge.

#

A week later a young woman was out jogging from Lynn Park to Cathcart, her earphones in and she was enjoying her 'happy' play list, she slowed to take a sip from her bottle of juice, when she spotted what she thought could be a dead body! She was panicked and scared, her heart pumping fast and hard she took off, sprinting over Snuff Mill bridge and banged on the door of the first house she saw. Panting she quickly told the householder what she had seen. The Police were called, the river was searched. Harry was found first, then Jordan, he was dragged from the river, his eyes still wide open in horror.

All the four friends who were with the brothers that night had been questioned at length. The investigation was closed and three weeks later the deaths were confirmed as accidental death. Their mother was told the boys had drowned, there was no foul play. Clara had protested, but her drunken rantings about a Black cat and a Witch, were ignored by the

Investigating officers and put down to extreme grief. The usual warnings were given on local television and social media about staying away from waterfalls and rivers! A warning notice was erected on the Village noticeboard and at the side of Glen falls. A warning was also posted on the White bridge at Lynn Park after a Public outcry pointing out that other young people had died there in previous years, yet no appropriate sign had been erected.

#

Susie stood at the rear of her garden, she had seen and heard all the commotion of the search through the Glen, the helicopters flying low over the river and woodland at the back of her home, repeating their search of areas again and again with the huge beams of light illuminating the treetops. Jean her upstairs neighbour stood behind her bedroom curtains with bad will in her heart, she watched Susie.

Susie stayed away from the Glen for a few days as she had been told by one of the Church elders that they had been looking for Clara's sons. 'The brothers Grimm,' she thought. The brothers' bodies were now found, once again the rumours were rife. The other boys that had been there the night when the brothers disappeared had told the police they had seen Susie creeping about when they left the boys in the Glen and of course that information spread like wildfire. They all, apart from Kevin had spoken of how they thought the young men feared Susie thinking she was a witch. The Police had not taken the story seriously so never approached Susie about the accusations.

Jean her neighbour had shared her fantasy story with anyone who would listen; "Susie was watching the Police search from the back woods, she stood for hours, she was smiling a wicked smile and looked very suspicious!" If that was not enough to enrage the locals, Clara's neighbour had now revealed that the brothers had killed Susie's Black cat, giving her a motive to kill them! The rumours were charging the negative feeling in the atmosphere of the Village and bad things started to happen.

#

Chapter 16.

Conciliation 2028

Susie walked through the Glen enjoying the quiet and the whispers of the wind through the trees, she looked down at Beachy bit, 'I wish I could manage down,' she thought, 'to sit on the Tree bench;' But the descent was too much for her aging limbs. Making her way up the path, she paused to admire the view of the Viaduct, a memory of her husband Davie flashed through her mind of when they were happy, cuddling and kissing, she shook it away; a tear stung her eyes. Susie continued up the dirt gravel pathway slowly, 'she would sit in the Faerie Glen the Seelie would pass her way there!' she hoped. Two young men approached her on the path as she neared the top woods, one said something as they passed, with Susie's increasing deafness she couldn't make it out, but she did hear them both bursting into loud laughter as the continued on. Her heart raced and she hurried up the small slope to the Faerie Glen.

#

Back in her flat, Susie was lying in her small bedroom with the blinds shut which made the room shady. She had been taking naps in the afternoon, sometimes dozing into beautiful dreams, other times drifting into memories of her home in Wellfort Avenue.

Susie lay awake now thinking, 'it is definitely the Slaugh the Rabbi is referring to when he said, 'Beware the Host.' She continued to ponder, 'Host,' scratched on the presenter of Most Haunted must be the Rabbi trying to warn of the Slaugh! I'm sure of it!' 'The Slaugh must know what had happened to the Rabbis son Uri!' Susie decided, 'the Rabbi is only hanging on in spirit in the house as needs to know where his son is!' She made up her mind to discover the truth of the boy's disappearance all those years before.

"I'm going to set you free Rabbi by finding out!' Susie said out loud.

She slept a bit longer, early evening sitting up stretching her arms up and out with a big yawn. Standing up, she opens her blinds, she sees what looks like mud all over her window. "What is that?" Susie rubs the inside of the window, "it's definitely on the outside!" She made her way out to the close, leaving her flats front door's snib up, then opening the Front close door and leaving it on the latch. She walked over her small lawn and went to the bedroom window, the outside was covered in smeared watery dog poo, looking over at the living room large window had what looked like, 'WITCH' smeared on it, the black poo bag still hanging from a chunk of poo on the letter 'H.'

"Oh god, not this carry on again!" she said aloud, her legs felt weak, a tremble coursed through her arms, her hands were shaking. "Tell Marina!" she told herself. "No not this time, well when then?" she asked herself. 'Maybe I should phone the police, but it could make it worse?' Susie thought, 'It's probably kids! Only dog poo!' Thoughts racing through her mind, she turned away from the window heading back into the flats, but the main front door was now locked, she pressed the buzzer for Janet. 'Buuuuuuuzz' no answer.

She pushed the buzzer for Jean upstairs, 'buuuuuuuzz,' no answer.

Susie pressed all the six flats' buzzers one by one to no avail. She was only wearing a pair of light leisure trousers and a t shirt, as she had been napping, it was cold out. Shivering, looking around for signs of life, Susie saw the curtain moving in Janet's window. "Janet, Janet," she shouted and pressed her buzzer 'buuuuuuuuuzz,' still no answer.

She walked around the back of the flats to see if she had an open window, she did not.

210

'Even if there was an open window, they are too high at the back, stupid!' She thought, shaking her head. "Oh god, my phone is in the flat," she looked down at her feet, she only had slippers on! Susie hurriedly walked down her street heading to the shops. 'Someone will surely let me use their phone, I will call the Police.' There was no life in the flats as she passed down the street, no one to ask!

There was a crowd of teenage boys at the local shop, hanging about outside. "I smell shite," said one of the crowd, as she passed through the open door; They all laughed.

Once inside the small grocery store, "I wonder if you could please let me use your phone? I am locked out!" Susie asked Ali desperately. He did not look happy. "Eh naw, I'd rather no," he said in a serious voice.

"Please," said Susie, "I'm locked out my house and it is cold." Ali stared at her unmoved. "Naw a said, I don't want any trouble with them outside or anyone else aroon here!" He turned his back on her quickly, packing cigarettes into the cabinet. Susie stood staring at his back hoping he would change his mind, he did not, she reluctantly left the store as she had to squeeze past the boys outside, who stood solidly in her way. She manoeuvred trying not to let herself touch any of them. She felt unsteady and was visibly trembling now as she was feeling panicked and there was a chill in the air. 'Who can I go to?' she thought. 'The church!' she hurriedly made her way around to the hall, to her horror the group of boys were following. She scurried along; her heart was thumping loudly in her chest. She managed to shakily get up to the front doors; they were locked. She let out a small cry, Susie felt like weeping, she put both hands up on the door, willing it open, her face now burning hot, she turned to face her tormentors who stood at the Church path entrance. She walked back down very tentatively, feeling intimidated, she paused holding the rail as she went down the steps, once again passing the group of youths, who laughed loudly. One particularly ugly boy with angry looking acne turned to Susie and sneered, "someone's gonni do you in hen!" Another piped up, "Aye, drown you, the way you drowned the brothers, ya old witch!" "No, I never did!" She tried to say loudly but heard her voice as a wavering whimper. She hurried away. The gang called after her. "You're getting it!"

She was terrified, feeling totally alone, shaking with the cold, she tried to run making her way round into her street, stumbling and nearly falling. A big, tall guy with red hair, getting out of his car, saw the old woman trip and stumble, he ran over to her to help, she got such a fright with him approaching her at speed, she fell down and curled up.

"Oh no, no, oh my god, I'm so sorry, I wanted to help you, not scare you like that," he said with concern as he put his hand round the top of her arm and aided her up on to her feet.

"I am locked out," she said trembling," my phone is in my house," "the church is shut!" "The boys were chasing me!"

"Calm down, calm down, you're okay now," he reassured Susie, "where do you live?" he asked. 'The man had a very deep soothing voice,' thought Susie. She pointed to her block "last flat on the bottom," she answered.

"I'm Patrick McSween," he said, "pleased to meet you?" he put out his hand and Susie took it. "Susan Irvine," she said shaking his hand, but he could feel that she was freezing cold and trembling. They got to her flat. Patrick looked at the state of the windows, "horrendous," he said. He saw her neighbours curtain move so pressed the buzzer long and hard, the curtain moved again in Janet's lounge window. Patrick banged on the window loudly, shouting, "come on, open up, I can see you!"

Then a voice said "yes, who is it?" through the intercom.

"Open up! Now!" Patrick commanded in his strong voice.

Janet came out into the close and unlocked the front door.

"I had to lock this," she said, "cause of all the trouble this yin here has brought to our door," Janet's tone was aggressive, as she motioned toward Susie with her chin. Susie moved quickly past her pushing her home door open, as she had left it on the latch, she turned to thank Patrick, just as he said to Janet in an authoritative manner.

"Shame on you Mrs, shame! Not to have empathy for an elderly woman that has done your person no harm! Your neighbour!"

"I beg your pardon!" Janet raised her voice.

"To encourage those teenage bullies who harass her." Patrick said loudly.

"I never did!" Janet spat the words.

"Oh yes you did Mrs! I'm her witness and I will be phoning the police to report this crime!" Patrick continued. "This is the village at its worst! Shame on you!" he said with disgust.

Janet skuttled in to her flat. He noticed the shadow of someone upstairs move off the landing and heard a front door close. "Shame on you too!" he shouted up the close stairs.

"Let me come in and make you a cup of tea Susie."

"Thank you Patrick, that is very kind."

They drank a cup of tea as he waited with Susie until she phoned the police. The Police call handler said, "Dog poo on a window is not an emergency, neither is locking yourself out but someone will be in contact in a day or two, we are very busy tonight." Which did nothing to reassure Susie.

"Thank you again, Patrick, so much. I doubt my neighbour would have opened the door if you were not there," Susie said warmly, genuinely filled with gratitude.

"Anytime," "I live in the next block, third floor number three, it was my mother's flat so I know well what the Village can be like sometimes." Patrick looked sad for a moment, "Sadly my mum died last year."

"I'm sorry to hear that, you must miss her." Susie empathised.

"Never hesitate to call on me in an emergency Susie okay?" Susie nodded.

'What a nice young man,' she thought, as she watched him walk down her path.

Susie called Marina once Patrick left, "Marina I am so sorry to bother you, do you think you could come over?"

"I'm right in the middle of something now, but I can be over within the hour, unless it is an emergency Susie?"

"No, not an emergency, that's soon enough dear, see you then!"

Marina arrived in forty minutes. "What the hell is that?" she said as she walked up to Susie's main door entrance, she stared passing the filth on the windows. She could smell it was excrement.

Susie now sitting on one sofa, Marina sitting on one of the two seats facing her. Susie looked down as she wrung her hands.

"What is going on Susie? Who put that stuff on your windows?"

"Marina, I don't know where to start. There have been terrible rumours about me because I visit the Glen!"

"Why does it matter if you visit the Glen or not?" Marina asked looking confused.

"My windows were smashed here one night after Fee had just left for New Zealand." Susie looked embarrassed.

214

"Oh my god Susie, why would anyone do that? Marina said her eyes wide and watery.

"There are rumours that I am a witch!" Susie looked defeated.

"A witch?" Marina laughed. "You are joking, right?" She looked at Susie faintly amused.

"My old next door neighbours' sons were found in the river drowned; the woman that bought my house told everyone the boys were responsible for killing MyKat!"

"Did they kill MyKat?" asked Marina with anguish.

"YES! I was told they crushed him under their feet! A woman from the church said the boys put a video of them hurting him online, along with lots of other videos of them doing bad things to other animals!" Susie said, a tear ran down her cheek as she thought of it. Marinas' mouth hung open, horrified!

"Now all of the village and my neighbours are bullying me, spreading slanderous gossip, they really seem to believe I drowned the boys in the Glen in retaliation!" Susie sighed.

"But you're an old lady! For goodness' sake!" Marina let out a sarcastic laugh, "I've never heard anything so absolutely ridiculous in all my life!"

"Now this, poo on my windows and my neighbours locked me outside in the cold with only pyjamas on!"

"Locked you out!" Marina stared at Susie her nostrils flared and her face deadly serious. "Why the hell have you hidden all this?"

"I didn't want to cause a fuss, upset you. I didn't want to upset Fee!" Susie said in a pathetic voice.

Marina was stunned. "All this time, you have kept up the pretence of being happy and safe to Fee and Josh! To me! I can hardly believe it!" she said as she stared at Susie in incredulity.

Marina was now ranting in anger. "You need to sell this flat Susie, you must!" "Move out of this damn Village, with their small mindedness." "They lead such boring lives they have to pick on old people! How disgusting! They make me sick!" "I hope you have phoned the Police and reported those boys and your neighbours?" Marina asked, her voice still raised with the injustice of it all.

"Yes!" a lovely man Patrick came to my rescue and sat with me while I phoned, but they say they can't do anything to help as no one has actually hurt me!"

"Well, if they won't help you, you must help yourself! Change your name and start again somewhere else." Marina said defiantly, "You can't live like this!"

"I'm seventy-four years old, I can't start again. I love the Glen and I don't want to leave it!" "We are never too old Susie! Never!" Marina said positively. They sat in silence both thinking. Marina continued now in a calmer voice. "The Glen spans for miles and miles, you do not need to live in the Village to walk in its woodland, it is huge! Move to the other side!" Susie nodded slowly listening and considering what Marina had suggested.

Both women went outside to throw buckets of hot soapy water on the windows, then cleaning the poo off with a window scraper on a pole. "Uneducated louts can't even spell Witch," Marina said loudly. Both she and Susie laughed.

"Please don't tell Fee and Josh," Susie asked as they went back in to the flat, "I don't want their happiness to be spoiled by this."

"Promise me you will let me help you move then and quickly!" Marina demanded, "You can stay with me until you sell this place."

"Okay Marina, maybe you're right. I will think about selling this flat and leaving the village, I can't go on like this. I don't feel safe!"

Chapter 17.

Alma Fravardin is born.

Alma Fravardin walked over the Army bridge, it was nearly a year since she had moved from the flat in the Village to Summerland, a small area with shops, a church and a garage. A leafy area as it sits near the rear entrance of the Glen, and it has a pathway leads from it to Lynn Park. Alma loved her small terrace house and felt at home instantly. She thought, 'Marinas' advice to change her name and move home had been proven right, she didn't miss the Village and had become accustomed to using her new name. She felt happy and safe, she felt reborn!'

Alma slowly made her way through the woodland to her favourite spot which now was high hidden on a hill that had a large circle of small standing stones, she had stumbled upon it quite by chance, but it had a strong positive vibe she felt from below. At some time in the past someone had fashioned a seat from a tree stump that had fallen, and she enjoyed sitting on it, tuning into the energies of the universe that may reveal secrets to her, or just listening to the sounds of the woodland.

The Seelie visited her often here, it was their special place they told her, they were happy she was away from the humans that had the negative energies that had rubbed off on her and made it difficult for them to be near sometimes. Alma's aura was brighter than ever.

She wanted to concentrate on the Rabbi's son Uri today as she was desperate to know where the boy lay. She knew he was dead; she had slowly pieced together the pictures shown to her in her mind, helped by the Faeries she now had a patchwork story of his death.

#

Uri had walked to the Woodland in Huntley Park as there was no one in the Pavilion, he thought the other boys may be playing 'Hide and Seek' in the trees. He was happy, he sang a song as he walked, which attracted the attention of the Slaugh, they watched him as he made his way through the woods. The boy sat, he became bored, none of his friends were there! 'Where could they be?' he wondered!

He threw a stone at another stone trying to hit it! He missed; Uri tutted. He tried again and missed.

A stone was thrown out from behind a tree, at his stone, it missed! "Missed" he said and laughed out loud. Uri thinking it was just a fluke, threw his stone again, once again he missed. A stone came from a tree at the other side of him, it hit the target stone. "Oooooh, you hit it!" he said out loud in congratulations!

A small slim man with fur all over his body appeared. Uri froze, staring in astonishment!

"Hello, "Uri said, "who are you."

The small man repeated "who are you?"

"I am Uri."

The small man picked up his stone and threw it at the target stone again hitting it.

"Well thrown," said Uri.

The small man walked nearer to Uri and the boy smiled, he could see he had folded wings on his back.

"Are you a bat," asked Uri, the man stared at him and smiled a huge smile that showed rows of jagged teeth.

"Oh, you have many teeth," Uri stated the obvious, "look at mine," the boy innocently said, grinning wide showing his teeth. The small man stared into Uris eyes coldly.

Uri stood up feeling scared, realising he was on his own for the first time.

He looked down on the wee man. "I must go," he said, "my mother will worry."

He turned to leave the woodland by the path he had come, but stopped dead, shocked as there was at least fifty of the little men standing on the path.

The one nearest him threw a stone that hit him on the leg. "Ouch," complained Uri, another small but strong looking man threw a bigger stone, it hit Uri on his chest, "ouch, that hurt," Uri exclaimed unhappily. The man directly in front of him said "ouch, that hurt!" He grinned a terrifying grimace. The front of Uris trousers became wet, as he felt the air crackle with their malevolence.

Uri began to cry; he trembled as he frantically looked for an escape.

The Slaugh started to throw stones at Uri fast and hard, again and again the stones hit him with force. "Stop!" Uri shouted, he tried to run away, but the Host rose up into the air with a loud buzz, diving down to him, punching him with their small fists, scratching him with their talon like nails, Uri fell immediately curling into a ball.

The boy started screaming loudly "Mummy help me!"

The wee man who had cast the first stone, mimicked him, "Mummy help meeeeee."

Uri's heart was pumping so fast and hard, like a drum, he could hear it banging loudly in his ears, his chest hurt. The swarm descended on the boy. Uris' heart stopped!

Disappointingly for the Host Uri died of fright within seconds.

Alma had not seen where they had put the boys' body or what the Host had done to it. She sat meditating, trying to relax, removing Uris death from her thoughts.

Alma started to 'huuuuuuuummmmmm, ooooommm, huuuuuuuuuuummmmm ooooommm,' the Seelie and the Slaugh all heard the sound, it appealed to their frequencies, they came to sit near the noise. Alma continued humming for a long time, more and more of the Seelie Faeries came, sitting in the circle, filling it, then creating circles around it, firstly the Seelie then the Slaugh on the outer rims. The Slaugh began to buzz, the Seelie began to hum, all together they made a song and right at the foundation of the song was Alma's humming chant. She heard the beautiful sound in her ears, her mind and her soul vibrated. Alma opened her eyes, every Seelie, every Slaugh looked to her with their glowing bright green eyes, she looked to them with her eyes bright. All the Faeries, Seelie and Slaugh saw Alma as a beautiful being of light her human body not visible, for the first time her Aura was like a huge crown of rainbow colours shining brightly, they stared at her in awe, their minds were filled with pure thoughts, all their energies became one and it was wonderful, they all jointly felt complete with each other and the world in the Universe.

People everywhere stopped in the street wondering what the low hum was, it was overwhelming for some, an emotional experience for others, many held their ears against what they perceived as the maddening noise. The hum stopped abruptly, as quickly as the Faeries came to this place, they left it!

#

Alma stood up once they had all gone, walking back down the pathways the animals had made with their comings and goings, winding her way through the woodland slowly to the Army bridge, she realised that she had been shown everything she wanted to know.

All she had suspected was confirmed, 'The Host the Rabbi mentioned are 'The Slaugh!' Uri's where abouts had been revealed, once the Slaugh had finished with him the poor boy's body had been thrown into one of the very old large tunnels at the local Quarry. The Quarry tunnels had filled with water once they were abandoned until a Steel company started using them as a dumping ground, which was around the time of Uri's death. The boy's body had been covered and after all these decades his bones could not be retrieved as it would be far too dangerous for anyone to venture on to such unstable ground. Alma felt a great sadness for the Rabbi and for his son.

222

Alma had seen Fiona's happy future with Josh and their family and that brought her great joy.

Her own future, her death had been revealed, she was unafraid as she knew that everything had an energy, and that energy is eternal.

We are all connected she now knew, everything! There is no time only existence. Every being's energy has a purpose. My purpose is a Guardian, "The Guardian of the Glen." She said smiling.

#

#

Chapter 18.

Manumit 2030

Marina was on the phone to Alma. "The house in Wellfort has been demolished Alma! The owner took his time," Marina stated, "he should have done that years ago!"

"Ano Marina, that poor man," Alma said.

"Oh, don't feel sorry for him, he will probably build flats on it or sell it on to a developer," Marina continued, "he will make plenty money either way, that's for sure."

"I wasn't talking about the owner," Alma laughed," I'm talking about the poor Rabbi stuck there and he will probably stay there whatever is built!"

"Yes, well they need to bless that space or something," Marina said.

"I'm going to see if I can get something arranged." Alma said, "I will give you a call and let you know if I make any progress.".

Alma thought, 'I need to contact the Jewish Synagogue,' immediately asking her 'Smart Speaker' to find it locally. Alma phoned and to her amazement the Rabbi Ariel Cohen agreed to come with her to the site and read a blessing.

Alma was now 78 years old, not as fit as she once had been, when she told Marina what she had planned, Marina was genuinely concerned. "Do you not remember the terrible ordeal of the 'Most Haunted' team? I really don't think you are able enough Alma, not at your age, I truly don't!" Alma smiled, "I know you worry for me dear, but honestly I am stronger than you think!" Marina didn't look convinced. "I won't stay there myself; I will leave the site as soon as the Rabbi Cohen does, okay."

#

A week later Alma took the train from Clarkston to Giffnock station walking up Forres Avenue, slowly onto Church Road, then down into Wellfort Avenue. Alma's heart was thumping in her chest although she was not scared, just apprehensive. She was focussed on trying to tell the spirit of the Rabbi what happened to his son Uri in the hope he could leave that place.

She descended the Wellfort Hill remembering herself pushing her dolls pram there many, many years ago, she smiled as she strolled past the well-kept homes. At the bottom of the hill the bulldozers and skips were visible on the road but there were no workers there.

For a brief moment she thought 'how strange.'

The big house on the corner next to the now demolition site, had the most gorgeous green garden, Fir trees and established flowering bushes and many roses; it was such a contrast to the ruinous site next door. Alma had a sudden flashback of a jolly looking woman hanging over the fence talking to her mum, Patty! That was the woman's name.

'She won't live there now silly!' she said to herself.

She stood on the pavement outside where number eleven used to be.

"Hi, Alma Fravardin I presume?" a man about forty said smiling as he approached her after emerging from a rather smart looking black car.

"Yes, thank you very much for coming Rabbi Cohen," said Alma extending her hand.

They both shook hands. "Please call me Ariel," he said.

There were orange cones spaced out in front of the site but as no one was there, they just walked onto a patch that had no rubble on it.

"Will I begin?" said Ariel very matter of fact.

"Please do," answered Alma.

The site where they stood seemed to darken ominously.

As Rabbi Cohen started to speak what Alma presumed was a prayer, she concentrated her mind on the spirit and the story of his son's death.

She spoke to the spirit directly in thought. "If you are here, you must know you must leave, be at peace, your son has moved on! Uri is dead, his bones lie in the Quarry at peace, as no one can enter that place as it is too dangerous."

All the while the Rabbi Cohen is speaking, he now is moving around where he can.

Alma speaks out loudly in her mind. "Move on your son Uri is not here!" then again, "leave here, your son Uri is not here!"

Suddenly a loud angry voice enters her head. 'The DEMONS TOOK HIM!'

Alma answers him in her mind 'why do you stay here? Uri is not here!'

The angry voice answers, 'I MUST WARN THE CHILDREN,'

The Rabbi Cohen jumps back as a stone comes from nowhere and hits him on his face. "Aaaah," he reacts rubbing the spot where it hit. He continues praying now, louder. Alma and the Rabbi Cohen are being blown by a wind, yet the trees next door, branches and leaves are not moving.

Alma speaks to the voice again, "Uri is not with Demons, his energy, his soul, has moved on, returned to the universe, as you must do!"

'AHHHHHHHHHHHHHHHHHHH' Alma nearly fell down with the screaming in her head, she threw her hands over her ears to no avail.

Ariel pulled her arm, "did you hear that?" "We must leave Alma," Rabbi Cohen said. Retreating through the rubble, another stone hit him with force on the back of the head and he fell to his knees, holding the bleeding gash on his head he tried to pull himself up.

Alma began to recite Psalm 23,

"The Lord is my shepherd; I shall not want.

He causes me to lie down in green pastures; He leads me beside still waters.

He restores my soul; He leads me in paths of righteousness for His name's sake.

Even as I walk in the valley of the shadow of death, I will fear no evil for You are with me; Your rod and Your staff, they comfort me.

Another scream filled Alma's head.

A stone flew past her face toward the Rabbi Cohen who was now standing looking towards Alma.

"GET OUT OF THIS PLACE," shouted Alma loudly to the spirit, her hair blowing high around her head, her eyes were glowing brightest green.

She walked over to Rabbi Cohen, he was now standing, his face was ashen, staring at her in horror. "Are you okay Rabbi, is your head cut?" asked Alma.

Ariel did not reply, he backed away hurriedly from her to his car, struggling to get in with his haste, he got in, not stopping to put on his seat belt or check his mirror, he started the car without a word or a glance toward Alma. The car shot up the hill at speed.

She stood on the pavement, the wind gone, the sky clear, everything looked normal in the avenue, except it was deserted, devoid of any life or traffic.

Alma was exhausted, she walked around the site of the demolished house, she now felt nothing. She hoped the Rabbi was now at peace. Alma began walking toward Marina's home, passing under the old railway bridge down to the lane over the tiny wooden bridge at the burn that led to Claremount Avenue. Marina opened her front door, "Oh my god Alma, look at the state of you, you look completely drained, come in, come in," Alma followed Marina into the entrance hall. "I'm going to be sick," Alma blurted, putting her hand over her mouth, Marina quickly guided her to the toilet to Alma's right, she could hear her violently vomiting.

After about five minutes Alma emerged from the toilet. "Marina, I've cleaned up don't worry."

"I don't care about any mess love; I'm worried about you." Marina spoke in a soft voice.

"I feel very guilty I've not said anything to Fiona or Josh about this, I feel you are in need of help!"

"Do not feel guilty Marina please," Alma said with a pleading tone,

"I have done my best, I doubt the young Rabbi Cohen, or I can do anything more."

"I hope that whatever you did has ended it?" Marina said. She made Alma a cup of tea and they sit.

"I am not sure if the Rabbi's spirit is still there; I don't know if he will move. He is consumed by grief and anger. He threw stones at the young Rabbi hitting him on the head, drawing blood."

"Oh my God! Really? I can hardly believe these things can happen in real life!" "Was he okay when you left him?" Marina asked, wide eyed, shaking her head unconsciously.

"I am not sure, he looked terrified and drove off!" Alma looked weary.

"The spirit screamed in my head so loud; I thought my head would explode!" Marina listened feeling unsettled, she had an awful feeling of impending doom.

"I wish Fee and I never told you about that damned TV programme!"

"I'm so, so tired," Alma said quietly.

"Come on, said Marina," "come and lie down in the spare room, it's got a lovely comfy mattress and after you have had a nap, you will feel much better, and I will make something lovely for dinner." She led Alma up to the bedroom and she lay down, Marina slipped off Alma's shoes, then fluffed up her pillows, laying a beautiful patchwork quilt on top of her.

"My mum made me that!" It's been my comfort blanket all these years, "let it comfort you."

Alma rested her head on the soft pillows, she swept her hand back and forth over the lovely silky quilt. Marina sat on the bed next to her, both women's eyes met, Alma and Marina smiled. "Thank you dear, you have been a true friend to me" said Alma softly, she closed her eyes. Marina sat on the bed with her hand on Alma's shoulder until she was sure she was asleep. She went downstairs into the kitchen and closed the door gently but tight. She phoned Fee, "Fiona, I really think it is time now to put your own life aside and come visit with your mum!"

"Why what's wrong Marina? She always seems fine when I contact her!" said Fee with a touch of impatience.

"She is 78 years old Fee, for gods' sake! Do you not think nearly seven years without a visit is a bit much for the woman that raised you all by herself?" Marina said with anger.

"I know Marina, but she could have come here at any time! I'm sick of asking her!" Fee said with indignation "Josh and I have been building our new lives, we don't want to return to Scotland!" Fee said curtly.

"Not even for a short bloody holiday Fee, to see your elderly mother?" Marina was furious.

"Look, I will speak to Josh again about Mum tonight, okay?" Fee said reluctantly.

"Talk about it? huh!" said Marina dryly. "How about you just get on a bloody flight!"

Fee hung up!

Marina then called Josh. "Hi Josh, it's me. You need to have a word with your wife, she just hung up on me!" Josh was quiet for a second as though taking a deep breath, "I'm in work Marina, can I call you back when I get home?"

"NO! You don't need to call me back; you need to tell your wife to come and see her mother immediately!" Josh was silent, "Are you there?" Marina asked after a few seconds, "Yes I'm here!" Josh said. "Well think about it Josh, would any of us have treated our parents with such disregard, would we have treated our mother this way?" Again, there was silence at the end of the phone, then in a quiet voice Josh said, "NO we wouldn't. I will speak to her when I get home." This time it was Marina who hung up.

It was five o'clock in the evening when Marina checked on Alma, she was sleeping soundly. At seven thirty p.m. Marina checked on Alma again, she was sound asleep, so she decided not to wake her.

'Poor thing is exhausted,' she thought.

She went upstairs about eleven, leaving a glass of water on the bedside table next to Alma, then went to bed herself in the next room. Marina woke up during the night, although she was still half asleep, Alma was standing in the doorway, she had delightful delicate glowing wisps all around her, floating as light as a feather, her eyes were bright, she didn't open her mouth and she was smiling when she said, "I'm going to go now dear, take care," she raised her hand in a small wave.

The next morning Marina got up and opened her curtains, "oh," she sighed as she looked out on a dull grey sky and heavy rain. She went downstairs and put on the kettle making she and Alma some Tea, then she remembered the dream!

Standing outside the spare room, Marina chaps the door, "Alma," she calls, then with a sing-songs voice, "Alma, I've made you some tea love."

There was silence. Marina opened the door slowly, "Alma?" Alma was lying on her side curled up. Marina pulled the Patchwork quilt back, Alma was still, Marina checked for a pulse of any sort, she put her face to Almas' mouth, there was no breath. Alma was dead. Alma's hand was at her neck holding the Faerie necklace.

#

Fiona and Josh did not return to Scotland for the 'insultingly' small funeral despite Fee being the sole beneficiary in her mother's will.

Marina said, "what a sad end for a woman that had tried so hard throughout her life and had shown kindness to so many!" "Life is a bitch!" she said to Stephen as they left the crematorium.

He replied, "Fiona is a bitch, a selfish bitch, I doubt I will be able to look at her again!"

"Nor I.," said Marina.

#

234

Chapter.19

Return of the Slanderer 2032

Michelle Henderson had never returned to Glasgow after she fell out with her father over the John O'Devlin incident; Now aged fifty-two she still had no inclination to visit. She had remained in Canada for thirty years and considered it her true home. Michelle loved the country and the Canadians, she loved their comedy, as it is the art of observation just like Scottish humour.

She met her husband Stacey Green, when she was twenty-five, marrying him five years later, which her father was absolutely delighted about as her new husband was a doctor. Stacey took the role of father to her seven-year-old daughter Jennifer, (Jenny,) treating her as if she were his own, made easier by the knowledge her biological father John O'Devlin was dead; Michelle and Stacey then went on to have a son Kevin Green. Michelle's father had rekindled their relationship and had enjoyed a good relationship with Stacey right up until he died. Michelle and Stacey had a wonderful family life and enjoyed their time together as a couple now their children were adults.

Jenny had grown up with 'a chip on her shoulder,' she felt the way a lot of children do that are adopted or have missing paternal information; Although Stacey had been the most wonderful Dad, Jenny was approaching thirty, she wanted to know more about her 'real' father before having children of her own. Michelle had not given Jenny much information except to say that she was incredibly young when she was with Jenny's father. Michelle had said that she and John were very much in love, but he had been a petty criminal and a bit of a 'bad boy' with the ladies as he had been very handsome. Her mother had stated that her father disliked John, thinking he was not good enough for any daughter of his, so she had reluctantly split up with him. Jenny's Papa Hendy had taken her Mum away to Canada to help her get over the romance but while there Michelle had found she was a few months pregnant while staying at her Auntie Irene's. Her father had returned to Glasgow in a rage when Michelle had decided to keep the baby. Not long after that, Michelle heard that John O'Devlin had committed suicide. Her mother had told Jenny she was devastated. Sadly, the only other relative on her father's side was a brother Joseph, but he was now dead.

#

Jenny said "I'm going Mum, I've only got one life! I want to see Scotland; I want to go touring then see Glasgow and the Village where your family came from! Why not?"

"I'm not happy about the holiday darling as you will be too far away! On your own! Anything could happen and we would not be able to get to you!" Michelle exclaimed her face drawn.

"I won't be on my own in Glasgow! I will be with Sophie!" Michelle knew Sophie as Jenny had brought her round for dinner a few times. Jenny had mentioned her a lot recently as the girls had been going out having fun while Sophie was on holiday.

"You know that Sophie Grain has been back visiting her dad in Toronto, she is returning home to Glasgow I can go with her." "She has recently moved into the Village where you were born, can you believe it, such a coincidence!" "It is meant to be Mum!" Jenny looked at her mother for a response.

Michelle just sat tight lipped. Stacey looked at his wife shrugging his shoulders and lifting up his hands, in a questioning motion, he pulled a funny face. Michelle shook her head at him in annoyance. He exhaled a heavy sigh and looked away.

"Sophie has offered to put me up for as long as I like!" "She has promised to show me around once I return from the Highlands and Islands touring!" Jenny said.

"That's nice of her!" Michelle said sarcastically.

"Scotland is beautiful Jenny, see as much of it as possible," her Stepdad Stacey said.

"Your Mum is just worried about being with me alone for so long!" He smirked. "She will be exhausted!" he chuckled and winked at his wife!

She rolled her eyes back at him, straight faced. He laughed.

#

The day Jenny left from Pearson International Airport, Stacey, Kevin and her Mum were there to wish her a safe journey and a happy holiday. Sophies' Dad was so sad to see her go, he chose not to come to the Airport and had said his goodbyes earlier.

"Stop worrying Mum, I am a grown woman, I'm going to be fine," Jenny held her mother close and said to her reassuringly.

"Glasgow is just so far away Jen," Michelle said looking stressed and worried.

"Mum it's only seven hours." Stacey put his arm around his wife's shoulders.

"Don't let her kid you Jen, we will enjoy the peace!" he laughed out loud.

"I will not," said Michelle with the pretence of annoyance, "Don't listen to him!" she playfully slapped her hand on his chest.

"Well, it be nice for me to have my wife to myself without you whisking her away to the thrift stores," he chuckled, "I will save a packet!"

"The only woman I know that can spend so much on second hand junk!" They all were laughing.

237

Kevin put his arms around his sister. "Please be careful, remember, not all nice-looking men are nice, it's only me!" They all laughed!

"Who told you, you are nice looking!" Jenny teased.

The flight was called, Jenny and Sophie hugged each one of them in turn.

Michelle held on to her daughter tightly, "I love you, Jen."

As the two women walked away, Kevin shouted after them, "Don't ask to see what's under the kilt!" "Oookh Aye the noo!"

They both turned and gave a last wave, giggling as they went.

Michelle started crying. "Stop Mum, for god's sake she'll be okay! "Kevin said irritated.

The three walked quickly back through the airport to the car park, as they approached the car, they noticed something lying on the bonnet.

"What's that?" said Kevin.

His father walked over and picked it up by the wing, "a Magpie," Stacey said as he lifted it and then laid the dead bird over away at the edge of the parking area.

Michelle heard an airplane take off and fly up and over them and, in that moment, she thought "One for sorrow!" she had a strong feeling of foreboding.

#

Jenny had left a few days after their arrival in Glasgow to tour around the Highlands and Islands, returning six weeks later.

Sophie and Jenny were in Glasgow in the Corinthian bar and restaurant, a world class, iconic venue which is steeped in history, situated in the heart of Glasgow's Merchant City just minutes from George Square and Royal Exchange Square.

"There are five floors all with a different theme" Sophie told Jen.

The women were seated in the Teller's Brasserie, they had been told it serves premium quality food in spectacular eye-catching surroundings and they were not disappointed. Jenny could hardly keep her eyes from the beautiful white ornate cornicing and stunning glass domed ceiling, both women kept looking up.

"This is amazing! I can't stop looking." Jen said rubbing the back of her neck.

"I'm so glad we came Sophie, thanks for bringing me here, it is fabulous and some of these Scottish men! woweee!" Jenny motioned with her eyes to three men that had just walked in, they both giggled.

"Mmmmm mmmmm mmmm," Sophie hummed through a big smile! All three men were smartly dressed, tall and well built. As they passed Jenny and Sophies table to be seated, one gave Jenny a huge 'film star' smile, he was quite dark skinned with dark hair that had a slight curl to it plus the brightest blue eyes.

Jenny returned his smile and looked down embarrassed hiding her pleasure at him noticing her.

"He was gorgeous," Sophie enthused.

"They all are, take your pick," Jenny giggled.

The women took their time with their meal enjoying every mouthful, while Jenny told of some of the sites she had seen on her trip. They had the full three courses and were enjoying their dessert, when the men they had admired passed their table again. Jenny had a mouth full of cake when the man who had smiled at her paused at their table and said, "I hope you have a great night. Where are you off to after this?"

Jenny put her hand to her mouth to hide that it was over full.

Sophie answered, "please excuse Jenny she loves a big pudding," and laughed.

"We are not sure, have you any recommendations as we are not familiar with Glasgow nightlife."

"My names Paul Noble, by the way and you are?"

"I'm Sophie and," Paul finished her sentence, "this is Jenny who loves a big pudding!" he made a funny face by puffing up his cheeks and then lifted his eyebrows, they laughed.

"My friends and I are heading upstairs to Charlie Parkers, maybe see you later?" he smiled.

Jenny smiled back and made eye contact for a second time with Paul, "maybe!" she replied.

The women sat enjoying their drinks for about an hour, then went to the toilet to fix themselves for the rest of their evening.

"Look at my stomach, it's huge, I look pregnant" Sophie said standing looking at her body side on, pushing her stomach out.

"Oh, stop it, just pull it in, you look fabulous," Jenny said, then put on fresh lip stick.

"Sophie was now quite tipsy, "Woo hoo, Jenny lets go get them guys!" she said enthusiastically.

"Okay calm it Sophie, we don't want them to think we are desperate!" Jenny joked dryly, then they both laughed loudly linking arms as they left the toilets and headed up to the Charlie Parker's bar.

The three men were in their late thirties, George Sinclair was the manager of a large hardware store, blonde with chiselled features, Ryan Daniels had dark blonde hair and was perfectly groomed in the latest style which included very long sideburns, he was the owner of a chain of barber shops and had a very infectious laugh.

Paul was a builder. "Ahhh that explains the dark skin and the great physique, "Sophie said.

"I know! I'm gorgeous!" Paul laughed. "What do you think Jenny?" Jenny laughed.

"Sophies kicked better out the bed!" she jested. The men all laughed.

"You might do though," Sophie said while giving Paul a sexy look, lifting her eyebrows and pursing her lips.

'Oh well,' thought Jenny 'that's him gone then!'

"Would you like another drink girls, it's my round," asked George.

"Oh yes please, Gin, Soda with Lime and a glass of water for Sophie please," laughed Jenny. "Oye you, cheeky madam, I will have another glass of house white please, it's rather good, thanks George," Sophie said.

The five of them had a fun night. Ryan ended up leaving with a girl he had been seeing who turned up unexpectedly, she had snubbed Jenny when she had tried to introduce herself and had given Sophie the most horrible look.

"Don't mind her, "George said, "she has jealousy issues.

"Who wouldn't be jealous of you two, eh?" Paul said.

"Oh yes we get it all the time!" Jenny replied, as she and Sophie strike a model like pose, overly pouting their lips!

The four walked slowly downstairs to the dance club in the basement, flirting and joking with each other, it was a relaxed and happy vibe. In the club they were dancing as a group until George was backing Sophie away dancing with her alone.

"Your friend seems to be moving in on your girl," Jenny playfully said.

"Not my girl! I'm not interested in Sophie, I've been trying to get your attention all night," Paul said in earnest.

"Oh, I thought you fancied Sophie, so I backed off!" Jenny said happily. "I like you too!"

"Good, because there is something about you Jenny!" Their eyes met and Jenny felt a strong connection to Paul.

The night carried on until three o'clock in the morning, George and Paul walked holding Sophie up between them while Jenny linked into Pauls other arm to the Taxi rank.

"You could come to the Hotel with us?" George asked hopefully.

"Not tonight, Sophies really out of it George! but I know she would love to see you again!" "Wouldn't you Sophie?" Jenny asked, Sophie grunted lifting her head momentarily then slumping back again.

"What about me?" asked Paul.

"Oh silly, you know I'd like to see you again," Jenny said enthusiastically.

Paul pulled out his phone, "give me your number then," Jenny obliged, Paul called it straight away to check he had taken it correctly.

It was the girls turn for a 'Black Hack' taxi, they all helped Sophie inside, she lay down immediately across the back seat.

"Yer pal better no puke or it'll cost ya hen!" the Taxi driver shouted through the glass.

Paul held Jenny in a tight embrace, kissing her passionately, "see you tomorrow?" asked Paul.

" Yes, let's do something." Jenny answered as she entered the cab.

Jenny sat smiling, stroking Sophies' head on her lap all the way home.

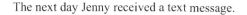

#

The next day Jenny received a text message.

'Hi it's Paul, remember me?'

'How could I forget?'

'Would you like to meet me for lunch today?'

'I would have, but Sophie and I are so hung over, I doubt we will be out our beds at lunchtime!'

'LOL lightweights!'

'Are you free Monday Jenny? I really want to see you again!'

'Yes, I should have recovered by then! lol'.

Jenny smiled, feeling flattered.

'Where would you like to go? Your choice as you're on holiday!'

'Kelvingrove Museum, it is a place on my list to visit.'

'Great see you at the front entrance at ten?'

'See you then!'

#

Monday arrived and Jenny had butterflies in her tummy at the thought of seeing Paul again, she showered and curled her hair, choosing one of her prettiest of tops, it revealed a glimpse of cleavage, but not too much. She pulled on a great 'bum shaping,' pair of jeans, admiring her rear in the mirror. Sophie was at work today but had arranged to meet George,

243

Jenny and Paul at eight that evening in town to have dinner, they had booked a restaurant with a great reputation for serving authentic Italian food.

In the Taxi, Jenny was reading all about Kelvingrove in an attempt to stop herself getting too excited.

"Thank you, "Jenny said to the driver, as she exited the Taxi. She walked toward the huge red majestic building. Looking up at the fairy tale towers, the vivid colour of the building contrasted beautifully with the bright blue sky and deep green foliage of Kelvingrove Park. It really created a magical castle picturesque effect. The entrance had a broad skirt of grey steps leading upward to the archways. Paul was standing at the bottom step in blue jeans and a crisp white shirt, he looked even more handsome than she recalled. He looked up and waved the moment he spotted her; she tried her best not to run over to him but gave him a huge smile, speeding up. They hugged when Jenny reached him, a warm lingering embrace, she breathed in his fresh but musky scent, they both looked up at the Museum.

"Quite something isn't it!" Paul said.

"Stunning," Jenny was impressed.

Paul continued as they mounted the steps, "The Kelvingrove is hailed as one of the most beautiful buildings in Glasgow but back in the old days it was criticised for ostentatiousness, plus it has English style windows!"

"Really, what is the difference between English and Scottish windows?" Jenny asked.

"The hell I know!" laughed Paul, "probably, just because they are made in England!" he laughed, Jenny joined in.

"Ostentatiousness! That is a mouthful," Jenny said, Paul smiled and lifted his eyebrows, looking like a cheeky boy. She shook her head, smiling.

"I shall take you round the rear entrance when we leave as it is more impressive than the front!"

Paul thought to himself, 'yeah, just like your impressive rear!'

Paul continued, "some say that the building was constructed back to front by mistake and the architect jumped to his death when he realised his error."

"Oh, how awful, poor man!" she paused for a long moment.

"Did I tell you my biological Dad killed himself?" Jenny asked.

"Oh, god, no you didn't I'm so sorry, I would not have said that if I had known!" said Paul apologetically, there was an awkward silence.

"Oh, that's me blown my chances then, eh?" Paul said.

"Don't worry, I didn't know him, I never met him!" they both were quiet, the atmosphere was strained, then Jenny blurted out, "so come on, what else can you tell me about this great place!"

Paul cleared his throat, "well," he said, "the building is inspired by many styles, the dominant theme being Hispanic Baroque."

"How do you know all this?" Jenny asked.

"I am a builder!" he exclaimed.

He sniggered, "I read a bit online before I came out, to impress you!"

They both laughed, he pulled the huge dark wood door with polished brass ornate handle open for Jenny.

245

"Seemingly the north front is inspired by the Cathedral of Santiago de Compostela, whatever that is!" Paul said.

"Ahhhhhh ha! That is something I do know!" Jenny exclaimed "It is in the north-east of Spain, Santiago Cathedral is a Catholic temple designed in the Middle Ages to hold the remains of Santiago, James the Apostle, one of Jesus Christ's closest disciples!"

"Ooooooooooooooh," Paul said in a funny voice, "get you!"

Jen giggled, "I too read that online in the taxi," she revealed, and they both laughed out loud.

They entered the main hall, "Wow! look at that huge organ," Jenny said as she stared up at the Pipe Organ situated high up on a balcony.

"Aye, I could show you bigger!" Paul laughed; he nudged her with his elbow!

"Uh!" Jenny shook her head, "so you say! We shall see!" Jenny laughed.

"Ahhhh, is that me on a promise then?" He asked jokingly, looking at her intensely with his bright clear blue eyes."

Paul took her hand in his, she looked at his handsome face appreciatively.

She thought 'stop it Jen, you don't even know him yet.'

They strolled slowly among the animal exhibits commenting on them as they sauntered past or stopping at those that were of particular interest.

"What were you saying about big organs Jenny?" Paul laughed as he stood looking up at the Giraffes underneath! Jenny shook her head, "you're such a big kid Paul. Behave!"

They walked around the upstairs Galleries appreciating Claude Monet, Camille Pissarro, Pierre Renoir, Van Gogh, intermittently admiring each other. The magnetism between them was at times intense, it was hard for Paul not to be too full on. They purposely brushed past each other, constantly touching, meeting each other's eyes.

Salvador Dali's Christ of St John of the Cross was in a tiny room, they waited in the small line of people to view this deeply moving painting.

Jenny and Paul stood staring intensely at the painting.

"They say the lack of signs the crucifixion gives a sense of hope," Jenny said seriously.

"I have high hopes," Paul raised his eyebrows with a big smile.

"Oh you! Does this not move you" she asked.

"I'd like to move you Jenny, deeply!" Paul answered smiling a lovely smile of white teeth. "Stop Paul, that's too much!" Jenny said in school mam fashion.

Paul looked sheepish. "Sorry," he said in a dopey voice. They giggled together walking on.

The couple stepped slowly down the huge off-white sandstone staircase in amazement at a Spitfire, a plane suspended from the ceiling; In this grand Victorian setting it had a startling effect.

"The plane was actually used in the 1940 Battle of Britain against the Nazis!" stated Paul. "Another interesting internet snippet," Jenny quipped smiling.

"That's me shot down in flames then! Boom boom." he laughed; Jenny joined in.

The couple walked through a lower room, a painting caught Jenny's eye, Edward Robert Hughes' Midsummer Eve, the information board at its' side read; 'a mythic and luminescent painting of the imagination, deftly capturing the spirit of Victorian fairy tales at a time when they were surging in popularity.

247

"This is interesting," said Jenny as she stood in front of the painting. "I wonder what gave the Victorians the idea of Fairies?"

"I like it," said Paul, reminds me of childhood somehow, even though I didn't get Fairy stories as a boy. I had a bit of a rough upbringing!" "Aww I'm sad for you," Jenny said with empathy, as Paul pulled an exaggerated sad face. "Aye, my dad was a bit of a hard man, Big-Jimmy, it was all Wrestling and Boxing in our house, I miss him though."

They stood for a few moments more until Paul pulled Jenny by her hand. Jenny had an

unsettled creepy feeling. "Come on!" Paul said pulling her away!

They strolled around the 'West End' enjoying the busy atmosphere, popping in one of the nice local Cafes near the University. The couple enjoyed a few alcoholic cocktails, which

248

loosened them both off before they jumped on the Tour bus. They spent the rest of the day hopping on and off around Glasgow's tourist attractions. They sat on the top deck that had no roof, the wind blowing their hair, Paul had his arm around her shoulders pulling her in towards him. They visited the Riverside Museum which Paul found amazing, they acted out the iconic scene from the old Titanic movie on the deck of the Glen Lee ship; Paul standing behind Jenny, holding their arms stretched out, both laughing so much Jenny had to stop to get a breath. Back on the bus Jenny looked up to admire all the passing architecture on Glasgow's fine old buildings and the wonderful modern street art. They exited the bus at the Gothic Cathedral and Necropolis which they wandered around for an hour until after six o'clock. They decided to go for another drink and relax before meeting George and Sophie at eight for dinner.

#

By the time Jenny and Paul turned up in the restaurant to meet Sophie and George they both were quite tipsy.

"Hey, you two, how was the big adventure day?" asked George jovially.

"Fantastic!" Jenny answered with a big smile, "I love Glasgow!" she and Paul took their seats at the table.

"Yes, it was great," said Paul, "I'm actually knackered already, Jenny has walked the legs off me!"

"How was work?" Jenny asked Sophie. "A nightmare to be honest, there is a new girl in the office, she was started as a junior but for some reason she thinks she is my boss!"

"Don't let her away with it, set your boundaries strongly but politely at the start," George advised her "or she will end up in your job!" he laughed.

"These young yins think they rule the world with their crap Uni degrees, Masters in eff all."

The four enjoyed a lovely meal and a couple of drinks, but everyone except Jenny was working the next day so it was decided a strong coffee rather than more alcohol would finish their evening.

"What are you going to do without us tomorrow Jenny?" Paul asked putting on a sad face with his bottom lip sticking out, she laughed.

"Oh, I don't know, maybe have a look around the Village, my mum was born there! I could visit the small Cemetery where my grandparents are buried." "Oh, and I thought I'd try and track down my dad's brother's wife, possibly ask her to visit with me the woodland park near where my dad died."

"Sounds an interesting day," commented George, "you enjoy it, whatever you get up to!"

"Let's all meet up again on Thursday night for a 'wild one," said Sophie.

"Yeahhhhh," They all agreed and left the restaurant walking together down to Glasgow Central train station as the main Taxi rank was there. Paul was dropping George first at Newlands, the women off at Sophies home and he would be last at Carmunock, the couples were cuddling and kissing in the Black Hack taxi.

When George got out, he asked," are you not coming in to mine Sophie?"

"No, I am not!" she laughed, "but nice try! I will get out and give you one of my magnificent snogs though!" she got out the cab with him, to say a very 'steamy' farewell, then jumped back in. "What a nice guy," she sighed.

When the cab stopped at Sophies home Sophie opened the Taxi door.

"Bye Paul see you Thursday!"

"Bye Sophie," she got out and headed to her front door.

"I don't want to leave you," said Paul to Jenny as she made moves to get out the door, he jumped out after her.

"Just a minute mate, okay!" he said to the driver. Paul held Jenny close to him on the pavement, then looking in her eyes said, "come home with me."

"I can't tonight Paul honestly, I am so tired, but I've had the most brilliant day."

"So have I. Would it be too much, to ask to come and meet you late afternoon tomorrow, Jen, if I can get away from work early?" Paul looked in her face hopefully.

Jenny replied happily, "I would love that Paul, I really would."

They locked lips in a strong parting kiss.

Paul thought to himself, 'bloody hell, she is amazing."

He waved out the rear window at Jenny, she stood on the pavement waving back as the taxi drove off.

#

Sophie was ready for work at seven a.m. Jenny got up too, they chatted over tea and toast, Sophie was looking at the local news on her phone.

"Oh No! did you see that post about the missing Village boy, Jen?"

Jenny shook her head, "the boy disappeared before we left Canada, but he still has not been found.

"That's awful," said Jenny, "What age is he?"

"He is only nine."

251

"What a terrible shame." Jenny said.

"It really is, his mother wants the Police to search the Glen woodlands again it says here, but they have refused, saying they have searched it thoroughly."

"She must be going out of her mind!" Jenny replied, then asked. "Is that the park my father was found dead?"

"Yes, maybe it is not a good idea to go there just now, with all that going on, the boy's family might still be searching in there!" Sophie said. "Yeah, you are probably right," replied Jenny.

"See you tonight, Jen, have a fabulous day," Sophie called down the path as she unlocked her car door. Jenny waved before shutting the door and heading for the shower.

#

Jenny meandered through the village and then into the local town Clarkston, popping into the Florists to buy some flowers for her family plot. It was a bright, dry day, she chatted to the Shop assistant.

"I've been very lucky with the weather since I got here," Jen told her. "My Mum said it rains most days in Glasgow even in Summer, but I think I must have brought the sun here with me!"

The assistant laughed, "your Mum is right, it usually does! Long may the weather continue for your stay!" "Leave the sun with us when you go!" the assistant added, giving Jenny a wave.

"Will do! Have a nice day." Jenny said as she left the store.

She continued down into the town which to her delight had many charity stores, she had a rummage in them all. She saw the bus heading up towards the stop through the window and quickly dashed out to catch it.

#

The small Graveyard was hidden away at the end of a street next to a farmers' fields. She walked up and down the avenues of headstones until she found her families' plot. There were two headstones side by side, her grandparents were on the same headstone and on the other her grandfathers' brother and a cousin who had died in a river near Aviemore on his way back from a party to the hotel he was staying at, he was only twenty-five. "Very sad." she thought. It was a beautiful cemetery, small with trees and convenient wooden benches.

dotted around, the graves were all maintained and there seemed to be flowers everywhere. Jenny stood at her Grandparents' grave and said, "Sad I never got to spend time with you all," she laid the flowers she had bought, creamy white roses, her mothers' favourite. "I may have been a mistake in your eyes Papa, but mum loves me so much. I love her. I promise to try to be the best daughter to her forever." She stood for a moment just thinking about her Mum. It became eerily quiet; Jenny felt a presence behind her, she quickly looked round, no one was there, she was completely alone, her heart was beating fast, 'what is that noise' she thought, it got louder, the sound infiltrated her brain, like Tinnitus, causing her discomfort. Jenny felt afraid, panicked, she retreated away from the plot and back up the path to where she entered. As she approached her exit in haste, she noticed a Magpie sitting on the last Gravestone before the gates, as she hurried past the bird turned its' head to follow Jenny, she felt it and quickly glanced round and as if in slow motion their eyes met. In that long moment it flew up in a noisy flurry. The buzzing stopped abruptly. A deafening silence. 'For goodness' sake,' she thought to herself, 'it was only a bird, why are you so spooked?' but it did nothing to reassure her, she was scared. She started jogging down the long back road to the Village, the route was bordered by empty fields of green with an occasional glimpse of sheep, a spot of white through the hedgerows. Jenny felt quite unsettled and alone. She was just emerging from the farm road breathing heavily and sweating, onto the main road to the Village when her phone wrang loudly, she jumped, stopped pulling off her bag from her back, rummaging in the Backpack trying to find it.

"Hi gorgeous, how is your day going?" Paul asked.

"Good now I've heard your voice, I was feeling a little sad and homesick," Jenny replied, "I was up at my families plot in the cemetery!"

"You sound out of breath?" Paul sounded curious.

"I was jogging back." Jen answered.

"Good for you, keeping fit! Now I know how you keep such a lovely figure!"

"Thank you." Jenny giggled.

"That is nice you went to visit, but better not to dwell on the past." Paul said with sincerity.
"I can get away at four if you fancy meeting me for dinner and a cuddle back at mine?"

"Sounds just what I need, can we eat locally tonight?" Jen suggested.

"Perfect I know a rather nice wee restaurant next to where I live in Carmunock, will I get you at Sophie's at six? I will book us a table."

"Great," Jenny said happily, "you have cheered me up already, see you at six!"

#

The restaurant was in a converted old cottage type building, Jenny looked at the twinkling lights that had been placed around the outside and said, "looks quite like the places in the old towns of Spain, don't you think?"

"A wee bit, I guess, except we don't get all that sunny weather!" said Paul.

"It has been lovely while I've been here!" Jen smiled. "You've been lucky!" he said.

Jenny and Paul chatted happily whilst eating their food.

"Everything satisfactory with your meal?" the waiter asked.

"Perfect," Jenny answered.

"Would you like the dessert menu?" we have a sumptuous Lemon Torte!" Jenny shook her head.

"No thank you, we won't be having a sweet or coffee tonight, we are just too full, thank you." Paul continued, "the main course was delicious as usual." He said with a nod. "Just the bill thanks."

"I will bring it over Paul," the waiter said in a familiar tone smiling.

"Do you come here often?" Jenny asked. "Now and again," Paul replied.

He gazed into Jennys' eyes, "I thought we could relax over a few glasses of wine at mine." "That will be lovely," Jenny meant it.

Paul's home was a small cottage, "I've kept my wee 'hoose' as true to original features as reasonably possible," said Paul as he led Jenny up the small path that was lined by white painted stones.

Paul opened the door wide then swept Jenny up as if they were newlyweds, she was giggling loudly as he carried her over the threshold. "That's a bit premature," Jenny laughed.

"Which one of my exes said that? Tell me!" He joked. Paul put her down on the couch, she was still giggling loudly. The ceilings were low in the cottage, but Paul had added rustic looking French doors that looked out on the most perfect Cottage Garden with mature trees. "I will be honest Paul, this is not what I expected, don't take offence, but I thought you'd live in a trendy flat with a huge TV, Mini fridge and a Dish washer!" Paul gasped and put his hand on his chest, pretending to be insulted and they both laughed again.

They kicked off their shoes and cuddled up on the couch with some 'easy listening' music on low. "We are like Strawberries and Cream, "Paul said.

"More like Cheese and Pickles with those smelly socks," Jenny joked.

"Humour aside Jenny, you have to admit, we were born to meet, it feels so natural, do you feel it too?" "Paul, I feel so much for you, but it all seems far too fast, too much too soon!"

"It's not too fast for me!" he said.

They lay down and were kissing passionately, Paul stood up and took her hand and led her through to his cosy bedroom. He sat on the bed and she stood in front of him, he put his hands on her hips then lay his forehead on her belly, she stroked his hair, running her fingers through his soft locks, he looked up, their eyes met and he started to undress her slowly, kissing every part of her skin as it was revealed. Throwing her clothes to the floor bit by bit. Jenny unfastened the buttons on his shirt and slid it over his shoulders, running her hands over his muscular chest and arms, his skin was smooth and warm over his strong firm muscles, he pulled her down onto the bed. They softly searched each other's mouths with their tongues, kissing with increasing passion. Paul caressing Jenny's neck and then down to her breasts, sucking her nipples. Jenny was laid down watching Paul as he removed the rest of his clothes, then he kissed her lower tummy caressing down over her Mons Pubis, he lay between her soft thighs, giving her pleasure with his mouth, they rolled naked feeling the heat from their bodies, the glorious pleasure of skin on skin. Jenny climaxed, loudly moaning, Paul smiled feeling pleased with himself, he looked at her face all pink with warm satisfaction. After a long moment. She rolled over and sat over his legs, bent over kissing all his stomach and down between his legs, she reciprocated the joy he had given her and when he finished, they lay, Jenny with her head on his chest, he with his arms around her.

Paul and Jenny caressed slowly taking time to recover, chatting in soft voices. Stroking each other's skin.

Enthusiastic hard and fast sex followed. They thrashed around the bed and at one point falling heavily on to the floor, rolling around, joyously laughing loud.

They fell asleep waking a few hours later.

They continued their love making, having sensual, slow, emotional sex, sharing prolonged intense eye to eye contact. They were moving together, taking time now, Jenny holding Paul's face as he kissed her, then dozing off entwined.

Jenny had such an intense feeling of happiness tears nipped her eyes as they both orgasmed. Paul woke with the sunlight peeking through the blinds, he was laying with Jenny tucked in front of him, he had spooned into her all night. He thought' I've never done that before, ever!' "You feel so good,' he whispered into her hair. Jenny was still sound asleep.

'This one feels so right!' he thought, before dozing off.

#

Chapter 20.

The Wifey

Stephen Morne was now retired from the Police force, he was watching the news in his kitchen in his Bungalow in Bearsden, he was now 80 years old, but all there and more! Yes, he admits, he is slower in walking and does not have the same energy, but his mind was still sharp. The story of the boy that went missing a few months ago, Jamie Callahan was being aired again, this time the boys' mother, Betty, a young single parent who the media had gleefully revealed was a drug user, was being interviewed by the Press. 'They must suspect her,' he thought, 'an easy target for them.' The woman looked pale with huge dark circles around her eyes, she looked in pain. "Poor soul," he muttered. 'The Glen Park and woodland

259

had such a terrible history of tragedy,' Stephen thought of his own experience and knowledge of the woods, he thought 'if the boy is in there, he is not alive, not after all this time; Surely, they should have found his body by now! But then he remembered the case of O'Donnell, no! O'Devlin, that was the name! The O'Devlin brothers, they both died in the Glen. The supposed suicide, which was very peculiar, his body was not found for six months, despite the Police insisting they had searched thoroughly.'

Stephen remembered the conversation with the man's brother Joseph in the snooker hall, horrible story it gave him a shiver. He finished his porridge and decided after he had been to his Opticians appointment, he was going to the Village about an hour drive away and have a snoop around, may be even have a walk through the Glen later in the afternoon, it was a lovely day and he had not been back there for decades.

'Why not it will be daylight,' he said to himself.

#

Jenny had been dating Paul for over a month, she was now staying at his home! Paul had asked her to spend the rest of her vacation with him, after they had spent their first night together! It had just felt natural for them to be with each other as much as they could be as Paul worked forty hours a week so it just made sense that she would be there when he was home.

Sophie had been very shocked when Jenny had told her she was moving in with Paul until she returned to Canada. Sophie worried it was just a case of 'lust at first sight,' for Paul and would be 'a short holiday romance,' but she didn't share her feelings with Jenny as she didn't want to hurt her feelings. Sophie had advised her to 'slow her emotions down a bit,' But Jenny had already confided that she thought Paul was the one! Her soul mate!

Sophie and George spent many an evening, discussing the progressing romance and the heartbreak that may ensue once Jenny had to return home. George and Sophie were more like friends than lovers, 'a no ties' friendship, they had a good rapport and enjoyed seeing each other a couple of times during the week, they enjoyed playing pool or watching movies at Sophies, occasionally having satisfactory sex.

#

Paul sat on the side of the bed next to Jenny, who was propped up on a couple of pillows. "So, what are you up to today Jen?" he asked. "I've arranged to meet my Uncle Josephs' widow Yvonne. We are meeting at Clarkston in that little posh coffee shop, I can't remember its' name." Jen said but asking. "KOFFY," Paul answered and laughed. "I forgot you were trying to arrange that. What does she sound like?" "Seemed really nice on the phone," Jenny said as Paul finished putting on his shoes. He leaned over and gave her a quick kiss, Jenny put her arms round him and pulled him down on top of her.

"No, no, I have to go to work, don't tempt me wench!" he said jokingly, as he freed himself, he leaned in and gave Jen another kiss, this time on the cheek.

"Let's go out tonight, we have been in this bedroom for weeks," Paul suggested.

"Sick of me already?" Jenny exclaimed with hurt in her voice. "No! don't be an idiot!" he sounded irritated. "Okay, how about Bowling? Pool? or we could go for a swim," Jenny offered. Paul shrugged.

"You decide this time Paul, message me later." Jenny blew him a kiss as he left the bedroom.

"See you later," he called out as he shut the front door.

#

Yvonne O'Devlin was sitting at a small table situated at the window in KOFFY, that looked out onto the Main Road. She was an extremely thin woman; Jenny knew she was in her late fifties, but she looked much older today.

"Hi, Yvonne?" Jenny asked as she approached the woman.

The woman stood up and extended her hand, "Yes, Yes and you must be Jenny." "Oh my god, your so like Joseph and John, I can't believe it." Yvonne's eyes welled up.

"Oh, please don't get upset," Jenny said as she put her arms round the woman and gave her a warm hug.

"Sorry, I promised myself I wasn't going to do that." Yvonne gave a weak smile.

"What would you like Yvonne, my treat!" Jenny offered.

"Just a coffee, thank you, milk and sugar," Yvonne smiled.

Once both women had their coffee in front of them the conversation started in earnest.

Jenny nervously began; "Thank you so much for meeting me today, Yvonne, I know it is probably painful for you, but I would love to hear more about my real Dad and your husband, my Uncle Joseph. "

Yvonne replied staring intently at Jenny, "I can hardly believe, how like them you are, tall and dark; I mean considering your mum was so small and blonde."

Jenny replied, "Yes I'm very different from my Mum and brother, I guess that is why I have come to Scotland, to find out more about my dad and his family as I feel I must have more of my father's genes!" Jenny gave Yvonne a huge smile.

"Oh, yes your definitely an O'Devlin, you've got your Daddy's winning smile for sure." Yvonne replied smiling warmly.

Jenny could see she had once been an attractive woman, she thought, 'what a shame what grief can do.'

Jenny asked, "What kind of man was my dad, good or bad, I'd like to know the truth, if you don't mind talking about him."

Yvonne took a deep breath, "He was a handsome big bugger that's for sure, women loved him, he was funny, so, so funny," she smiled, "charming, cheeky and there was not one woman I knew off that did not think your dad was sexy."

She took a sip of coffee. "He had women fighting over him, I am not joking! His whole life!"

"He sounds as though he could have been a bit of a rascal, Yvonne. Was he a nice guy?" Jenny asked.

"Yes, he was a lovely, gentle man, he didn't like trouble or fighting, that was his favourite saying, I'm a lover not a fighter!" Yvonne smiled, "and he was most certainly a lover from the stories I heard over the years!" she chuckled, Jenny smiled an awkward smile."

Yvonne continued looking serious. "John and Joe had a terrible upbringing you know Jenny, their mother Glenda and father Mathew had been drinkers, Glenda had been a stunningly good looking woman but tragedy struck when seemingly her face had been hit by the mirror on the side of a bus as she stood at the bus stop, the driver was new and had pulled in sharply too fast, the entire half of her face was struck and permanently disfigured; the bus company paid out thousands in compensation, they had to redesign the side mirror for all buses!"

Jenny listened intently as she knew nothing of her fathers' family, she wanted to hear everything.

"Poor Glenda hated her face and couldn't bear to look at herself so started drinking, Mathew their dad was then made redundant, and both soon became alcoholics; drinking their way through all the money she had been awarded, she died of alcohol poisoning, liver failure. Sadness then gripped Mathew, he became an angry drunk with no wife and no money, who would look for any excuse to beat the boys. They would stay outside, hanging about the streets, rather than go home, staying out of harm's way."

"How sad," Jenny empathised.

"Their Dad spent most of his time with a man called Alby, a nice wee man who liked fishing or drinking Buckfast wine round a fire in the woods, he had the most lovable dog called Ema, a fat wee Staffordshire terrier that went everywhere with him. The men would 'stoat' home drunk, late at night if at all."

"That is awful, the poor kids!" Jenny said. "Yes, it was a damn shame for those boys!" Yvonne agreed.

"My Joe was a tough cookie he could take care of himself, but your Dad was a big softy and Joe said that after they lost their mum, John would make big sad eyes at the women in the village and as he was the youngest with a lovely face, they would mother him, bringing food round to the house for the boys, handing them bits and pieces of clothes passed down from others. Joe said your dad was always being cuddled and kissed by women wherever he went! I guess that's how he learned to use women, he didn't intend to hurt people, but he did." Yvonne stated.

"What happened to their dad, Mathew, my grandfather?" Jenny asked.

Yvonne replied, "From what I know, he was with the man Alby, they got very drunk and had a fight, which wasn't unusual. Alby said that Mathew had battered him and knocked him out cold and when he had come round, Ema his dog was missing, Mathew was face down in the mud at the edge of the river dead. The police did not believe Alby, neither did the court, he was charged with involuntary manslaughter, they said Alby had drowned Mathew under the extreme influence of alcohol; he was later found guilty and spent eight years in prison despite his insistence of innocence, but he just could not remember." "The dog was never found."

"Sad to say the death of the boys' father was a relief for John and Joseph, but they were separated, put in different foster homes so they ran away and basically turned to petty crime to survive on the streets; but they were together!" "They hung around the Gorbals."

Jenny was listened intently.

"Joseph and John always said they felt as though the O'Devlin family was jinxed."

Jenny looked sad, "That is such an unhappy story, I hate to think of my dad and Joseph suffering like that as kids." "I've been so lucky; my stepdad Stacey has been such a wonderful father I couldn't have wished for better."

Yvonne smiled, "I am happy to hear that Jenny."

Jenny sipped her coffee, "What do you know of what happened to my dad Yvonne?"

"My mum told me she thought he killed himself because she finished her relationship with him, and she had immigrated to Canada!"

Yvonne drank the last of her coffee and looked fixedly at Jenny. Yvonne now spoke seriously. "Joseph and I did not believe your dad killed himself, in fact I still believe in my heart he did not!"

"I do not want to offend you or your Mum, but since John and Joseph died, I've been doing a lot of investigating and research. Now more than ever, I believe there is something sinister to the Glen; Their fathers murder and both their deaths are more menacing than I thought before!"

Jenny urged, "What do you mean, something more menacing?"

265

Yvonne continued, "Well the research I've done into John and Joseph's family has been extensive. The records give good information up to a point, but they only go so far; then it just gives cause of death and age, no whereabouts, but the information has shown that "all!" Yvonne emphasises, 'all,' "of the O'Devlin bloodline have died un-natural deaths!"

Jenny responded, "Sorry I'm not following you," she looked confused. "Unnatural deaths?" Yvonne replied very, matter of fact, "No one died of old age Jenny, no long-term illness, all the O'Devlin's, drowned, committed suicide, had accidents, were murdered, disappeared, 'all!" she emphasised again.

Jenny sat quietly she was bemused by what Yvonne was getting at. She thought as she stared at Yvonne, 'surely an unhappy coincidence.'

"So, what are you saying Yvonne?" Jenny asked, "Are you saying the O'Devlin's are 'Jinxed' as Joseph and John said?" she stared into Yvonnes' face intensely.

"Or are you saying John and Joseph were both murdered?"

Yvonne became energized, over excited in her manner, she spoke quickly.

"Yes, yes! Both! I don't think your dad killed himself I think he was murdered, and I don't at this stage want to say by who. I believe my darling Joseph was pushed to his death. I know there is something terribly wrong with the Glen, it's all just too much, all the deaths, there is more you know, much, much more! I can only thank God we never had children!"

Jenny thought 'what the hell does she mean, she thanks god she never had children?'

Yvonne looked manic, Jenny felt unsettled, she moved about in her seat, feeling uncomfortable. Her heart rate was elevated, something was frightening her about this entire conversation, 'She is crazy!' she thought.

Yvonne stated, "There is a boy missing now, you know! But he has not been the first, there have been many, the Glen is haunted some say, you can feel it when you walk there, it is a horrible place! A death trap of some sort!"

Jenny tried to speak quietly and calmly to Yvonne in the hope she would lower her voice as others in the Café were turning, they couldn't help but listen to the conversation. Jenny's cheeks were flushed, and she felt as though she was on fire.

"Yvonne, relax, I'm listening to what you're saying. Tell me did you go to the Police with what you say you discovered?"

Yvonne lowered her voice somewhat, "Yes of course we went to the Police, we told them everything about your dad, but they didn't want to know, I think it was because of your grandfather. Even after Joseph died, I told them time and time again, Joseph knew the Glen inside out he would not have run with the dog over the cliff edge, he knew it was there, our dog did too, there is no way it was an accident!"

Jenny sounded stern, "What do you mean 'because of my grandfather?'

Yvonne retorted, "Well you grandfather was high up in the Police, he had just retired, he really hated your Mum being with your dad; many in the Village believed your grandfather killed your dad and that's why the Police never found his body for six months. His penis was cut off, you know! Who else would have done an atrocious act like that?"

Jenny was horrified, she stared at Yvonne in shock! "I need to go Yvonne, this is madness, my father's penis was not cut off by my Papa or anyone else! For god's sake, he hung himself! I don't want to listen to accusations that have no factual basis about my Papa Hendy." She pushed her chair back, creating a horrible scraping noise and stood up, everyone had turned round as she started walking to the door. As Jenny stepped outside Yvonne grabbed her shoulder roughly from behind. "Listen to me! What I've told you is true, you might not like it, but you can verify it yourself!" "You are in danger being here, leave the Village, you are cursed! Something or someone will kill you, you're the last one!"

Jenny shrugged her shoulder away from Yvonne, "Sorry, I don't believe you, I think your ill, please get some help!"

Yvonne shouted back as she ran across the road, "Don't have kids!" Directly in front of Jenny, a car just missed hitting Yvonne by inches, Yvonne let out a scream then ran on, not looking back.

The pedestrians who heard Yvonne shout, stared at Jenny as they walked past, she stood, visibly shaken, 'What the fuck?' she thought, suddenly she was pulled by the arm, Jenny jumped in fright and let out a yelp.

"Sorry I gave you a scare," said the Café server, "you have not paid your bill!"

"Oh my god, I'm so sorry, let me come in now and pay, my friend was just a bit upset."

The girl noticed jenny's hands were shaking as she tried to get her phone from her purse to pay. "You okay," the girl asked, "do you want a seat?"

Jenny nodded her head, "Thank you, could you call me a taxi I don't know the local cabs;"

#

Jenny went straight back to Pauls in the Taxi, she felt so jittery.

After she steadied her nerves, she Skyped her mum in Canada.

"Oh, Mum it is so good to see your face, I have had the most terrible shock today. I just needed to tell you about it!" Jenny blurted out what Yvonne had said to her in full.

There was silence and a long pause.

"Mum, You, okay?"

Michelle answered quietly, "Yes darling, I'm still here!" there was another long pause.

"Yvonne is deranged Jenny; the poor woman has been in and out of Mental health facilities since your father and her husband died. It was just too much for her, Joseph was her life!" Michelle sighed heavily. "Please, please do not listen to a word of it, the woman is just looking for anyone or anything to blame for her loneliness."

"She seemed so nice at first, then she turned into this raving nut!" Jenny said sounding stressed.

Michelle said concerned, "Listen, it will just upset your holiday and the great time you have been having if you give this woman another minute's thought, please try and put it out your mind."

"Okay Mum I shall try; I love you so much."

"I love you too sweetheart." Michelle paused again. "Be assured that my father did not kill your dad John. That is just crazy talk, okay Jenny? Thank God I'm in Canada or I would have been arrested if I had heard her say such things about your Papa." They both laughed.

"Stay safe until I see you again, I love you, more than you can imagine." Michelle ended the Skype call; she was as white as a sheet and trembling.

#

Chapter 21.

The Old Policeman

Stephen Morne wandered down the Main Street of the Village, it had changed quite a bit over the years. The Historic houses were gone, a modern block of flats stood in their place, The Cartvale restaurant was there but a pub no more, the Historic library and tenements still stood but it didn't look like the beautiful village it had once been, it was more of a through road to the main towns. Stephen stopped to look at a bust of a man with a football that had been situated on the Main street's car park, 'strange place to put a monument,' he thought, 'it is quite ugly.' He popped into the library; it was still the same as he remembered a large room divided into sections creating a cosy atmosphere.

"Hi," said the library assistant.

"Hi, is it okay if I have a look around and use a computer, I am just passing and not a member?" Stephen asked noticing the seven computer desks were free.

"Let me have a look and see if we have any vacant spots!" said the Librarian, Stephen laughed inwardly, staring at the top of the man's bald head as he pretended to check. "I shouldn't really let you use anything without a membership, but we are quiet today."

"Oh yes, you can use number six for half an hour!" he stated and led Stephen over to a desk a few steps away. "Can you use a computer?" he asked Stephen, who couldn't help but chuckle. "Yes, I think I will manage, thank you."

Stephen started to search for a map of the old Mills and the Glen, he found some amazing photographs on an old Historical site that hadn't had any views or reviews for years. He went deeper and deeper into the site until he discovered here was a map that seemed to show a large, long tunnel, but it was situated on a rather dangerous area under the ground at the Lower Mill site, he had never seen this information before, despite searching the history of the Glen many times.

He moved on to other information pages but kept returning to the photo of the tunnel and the old map. He had a gut instinct that the Police possibly didn't know the tunnel was there as it was not highlighted on any of the current or more recent maps.

He thought, 'I'm too old to try to access the tunnel myself! I can have a look, if it's dangerous I can come back out,' he debated with himself, 'don't do it your crazy, your too old!' 'Uck, what have I got to lose?' he decided.

He closed down the PC and went over to the assistants front desk. "Thank you," Stephen said, the man looked up and nodded.

"Did you get everything you were looking for?"

"Yes, thank you," Stephen said. "I wondered if the Glen is open as I had heard about the boy that was missing!" he asked.

The assistant looked serious, "Yes, it is open, but it shouldn't be, it's dangerous! Some of the locals have been on to the Councillors about it! That poor boy is still not found!"

After a pause Stephen said, "I am interested in the Lower Mill, I'm a Historian and I wondered if you locals knew of an easy way to access the grounds?"

The librarian thought for a moment and replied, "I wouldn't go there alone it has been derelict for decades, but the easiest access is through the Lower Mill Road, across the Road from the group of shops just before Sheddan's roundabout." He spoke seriously to Stephen: "But be careful and tell someone where you're going or put a tracker on your phone. Personally, I would never venture into the woodland from the site, it is treacherous and if you don't mind me saying, 'at your age!'!" the assistant lifted his eyebrows and nodded.

He smiled then started to type getting on with what he had been doing.

"Okay thanks for the info, see you again." Stephen called out as he exited the main door.

"At my age!" he mumbled, insulted by the remark. He drove down to the shops at Sheddans, parking next to the flats that were on the Main Road. Stephen sat for a moment debating whether he should wait and take someone with him or not. He decided despite his better judgement, to go look.

#

He made his way down the twisty dusty narrow track road, the tarmac was broken and strewn with hard core, it was a difficult walk down to the derelict Mill. Stephen passed a garage with several cars squeezed into the awkward car park; the next building was a small Bakery factory. A fat man with a beard, with a hair net on and a white apron covered in flour, stood outside smoking, from his elevated position at the top of a stone stairway he looked down on Stephen as he passed. "You lost mate?" he shouted. "No, no thanks, I'm okay," replied Stephen with a wave.

The man did not smile but watched Stephen until he was out of sight.

Once at the Mill building, Stephen snooped about, someone was using the land to store stones outside as they were all piled up high and tidy in a corner. There was a couple of cars parked which Stephen suspected belonged to the Garage as his space looked very restricted when he passed. He walked around the side of the old Mill building heading down to what looked like a path into the undergrowth that led to the woodland that edged the river below, he managed to cover quite a distance but then the path trailed off into dense weeds, tangled vines and jungle like foliage, it confirmed his suspicion that the police had not searched the area that led in to the tunnels. He tried another less overgrown route only to trip, he tried to save himself, arms outstretched, but he fell hard on his hip. Stephen sat for a moment to recover, 'what the hell am I doing' he thought, then rolled onto his side, pulling himself onto his knees in the mud, taking a step on to one foot, finally he pushed himself up onto both feet. "Too old for this!" he mumbled to himself, he felt a sting on his cheek, he saw a black wing swoop past in front of his face, he put his hand to his cheek;" Bloody hell, somethings bit me!'" he said aloud, wiping blood from his face, he turned to exit the way he had come. Stephen was pulled down backwards by a great force. He called out, "ahhhhhhhhhh," as his head hit the ground with a thump, he was briefly stunned. A moving mass of black was biting him wherever his skin was exposed, "ahhhhhhhhh!" he screamed out in pain. Suddenly a glow too bright for Stephen to look at was ahead of him, he couldn't comprehend what was happening, but the attack had stopped. He lay still trying to focus on what he saw in front of him, a translucent figure glowing brightly stood between him and the black cloud that was now rising up away to his left towards the tunnel. The figure seemed to solidify; it was that of a familiar elderly woman, but he could not remember where he had seen her before. Then as quickly as she became solid, she was gone! Stephen lay in shock, his face and hands were bleeding badly, his eyes glazed over, everything became a blur, then all went black.

The Bakery owner Alec had seen the old man walk down the road to the Mills, he thought at the time it was strange for anyone to be down this far. You'd expect to see groups of teenagers maybe once a year in summertime out exploring the Mill, rarely anyone else, most locals hated the place! It had been over three hours and he had not seen the old guy return. It was time to shut the Bakery. He shouted his brother Eddy, "Seen an old guy head down the Mills, he didn't look very stable on his legs, he has-nay come back oot, so lock up ana will have a quick shooktae doon there," Alec told him.

"Aye but don't hang aboot as I got shit to do the night!" Eddy barked back.

Alec 'stoated' down the wee road, outside the Mills he shouted out toward the dilapidated building, his voice was deep and loud!

"Hey, is there anyone in there?" He walked up to the doorway it looked black inside, 'it smelled rank.'

"Hey, anyone in there!" shouting louder this time, it was eerily quiet!

"Place gives me the creeps" he mumbled. He walked around the perimeter of the building noticing an indent in the vegetation.

"Hey anyone down there?" He shouted again, he turned to leave when he heard what sounded like a loud human moan. He shouted, "where are you?" A loud groan came in reply, but he couldn't make out what direction.

He ran back up to the Bakery, "Eddy, Eddy," he shouted for his brother. Eddy came out from inside the driver seat of his car. "What is it," he said with a cigarette hanging from his mouth.

Alec looked flustered and panted "I'm sure the old man is hurt; I heard a loud groan!"

"Damn it," Eddy spat his ciggy into the mud and ground it out with his boot. "See you wi your shite at finishing time!"

The brothers headed into the undergrowth but stomped through the deep thick copse not following the flattened path that Stephen had pursued.

They stood silently listening, "there did you hear that?" asked Eddy.

"A cry," Alec replied. They both heard a loud, "uuuuuughhhhh," so they hurried on.

"Fer fucks sake," Alec exclaimed as a huge nettle stung his lower arm. "Where are you, old man?" Eddy yelled. "Shout out if you can!" Alec called. Every few steps they would stop and listen, going in the direction of the sounds, then another cry coming from lower down, but they were hearing moans and sounds from all different orientations, they forced their way forward, the river was nearby. "I can't believe the old guy made it down here Alec, you sure he's no come back out!" Eddy said loudly from behind his brother.

"Eddy we can hear him, what you on about?" "Just over here!" They both stopped dead. They had emerged from the trees and now stood in front of the tunnel entrance, crying noises were coming from inside! Eddy and Alec stood peering in the tunnel, it was long and dark, pitch black after twenty feet.

Eddy shouted loudly, his voice echoing, "Hey, is there anyone in there?"

"We need to go in the tunnel and look." Alec stated staring into his brother's face!

"Am no going in there Alec, no fucken way!" Eddy said.

"Phone the Polis while I look then, ya fucken shite bag!" Alec slowly edged his way along the tunnel as there was about twelve inches of water in the floor so he couldn't see what was under foot! He made good way calling out as he moved, disappearing into the blackness of the tunnel. Eddy was frantically trying to get a connection when there was a loud animal like scream!

Alec froze where he stood in the dark, he couldn't make anything out clearly, but he could hear an increasing hum!

Eddy stood like rock, listening hard at the entrance, scared to move, a low buzz was coming from the tunnel. "Get out of there Alec!" he shouted to his brother.

Alec was retreating as fast as he could, splashing his way to his brother.

The low hum became a buzz, the buzz was increasing in volume until it was unbearable. "Run!" screamed Alec before the blackness in the tunnel became alive.

Eddy ran, he turned for a second only to see his brother folding at his stomach, being sucked back into the depth of the blackness, he vanished into the abyss, he could hear dreadful screaming.

Sweating, fighting his way through the jungle of underbrush, "you fucken coward Eddy," he shouted at himself, "you've left him, you've fucken left him!"

All at once a blackness surrounded him and he was off his feet, running through the air up high. "Hellllllllp!" he bellowed, he was dropped on the ground outside the tunnel, then dragged on his back through the water into the dark shaft by his head and his jacket, but he didn't know how or by what, he looked up and saw black wings, then faces, lots of faces all grinning their horrific grins. The beasts were making the crying noises that he and Alec had thought was the old man.

Terror struck him, then he was gone.

#

Stephen Morne lifted his head and groaned, he looked around, he was lying in the undergrowth where he fell but it was now dark. He felt very afraid, 'he was eighty years old, too old to be lying in the woods in the cold,' he thought. He strained to sit up, after two failed attempts, he sat on the third try and checked himself for any injuries, he seemed to be okay. Once on his feet, he shakenly made his way very slowly through the woods, it was deeply dark, he struggled to see anything, 'am I even going the right way?' he fretted; Until he saw the wall of the old building to his left. "Thank you god," he whispered as he managed to get himself out of the undergrowth into the grounds of the Mill. He cautiously shuffled up the dark road he could hardly make out anything, as he approached the Bakery, he noticed a car in the driveway sitting with its door wide open, the interior light is dull, but on. Stephen calls out, "hello," then again, his voice trembling, "hello!" he looked in the car, the keys were in the ignition, 'something is wrong, very wrong!' he thought, pausing briefly, he contemplated taking the car but he feared he may be putting someone else at risk so he walked away, intermittently checking there was no one behind him. After the most difficult walk uphill in his life, his hip and lower back screaming with agony, he reached the main road where his car was parked.

Two women walked toward Stephen they stared at him looking fearful, they turned as they passed him with eyes wide, then quickly hurried across the road. He thought 'I must look a state.' He rummaged in the pocket, deep in the inside of his jacket, and was extremely relieved to find his keys. Once in the car he checked himself in the mirror, he recoiled in horror, his face was covered in cuts with skin hanging from them, there were round chunks of flesh missing from his cheeks, his face was covered in dry blood. He suddenly felt tremendous pain everywhere. He started the car and drove slowly, he could hardly press his foot on the acceleration due to the excruciating pain in his hip, he was heading to the Princess Kate hospital.

#

The hospital Accident & Emergency staff were concerned about his injuries and had him attended to straight away.

"These look like small animal bites all over your face and hands," the Doctor said while attending his wounds. "Where were you when you were attacked?" "Did you see what type of animal or animals' bit you?" The Doctor quizzed him.

Stephen said, "Sorry, I cannot remember, I fell when walking in woodland, I must have passed out." The Nurses were cleaning him up, dressing his injuries then they administered a Tetanus shot.

"As your hip and thigh are badly bruised, we will pop you along to Xray, just to be on the safe side," the young nurse said, "we will give you something for pain once the Doctor has spoken to you.

"Nothing was broken, you will be glad to hear!" the Doctor told him once he viewed the images.

"Due to you not having any recollection of this attack?" the Doctor said. "I have to keep you in hospital overnight for observation, just in case you are suffering from concussion, okay?" The Doctor wrote something on a clip board and put it on the end of the Hospital bed.

"Yes, thank you Doctor! I'm totally exhausted to be honest, and a bit shaken up!" Stephen responded wearily laying his head down and closing his eyes.

During the night as he lay in his hospital bed Stephen had a dream of Alma Fravardin walking him round the Glen, she was glowing, he woke with a jolt!

He thought, 'I remember, that was the woman! The vision he had seen at the Mill; The woman who had protected him from whatever attacked him, it was Alma!'

'That's impossible though,' he thought, 'she was about seventy years old when I was in my twenties, she must have died a long, long time ago.' He remembered the Faerie village and all of Almas' stories, it gave him a chill, as though someone had walked on his grave.

#

When Stephen was discharged from hospital in the afternoon the next day, he phoned a Chief Inspector friend of his explaining about his suspicions that the missing boy was in the tunnel in the Glen. He told him about going to look at that area, the attack from some sort of birds or bats and also about the vision of Alma that had stopped him being killed.

The Chief, James Stewart had known Stephen for years, he had worked under him, Stephen had been his Inspector when he was a Sergeant; So James trusted him completely, he believed his story but he also took into consideration that he was now 80 years old, maybe had been suffering from Dementia or some other affliction of the elderly that he wasn't privy too which would explain the apparition, but he would not dismiss his story altogether as

Stephen had always had great instincts when working on any case. James responded when Stephen had finished his account of the events.

"That's some story Stephen! I will send a couple of nice guys round to get a statement, if you don't mind?" Stephen sounded worried.

"No I don't mind making a statement, but I realise it all sounds farfetched, it sounds crazy as I say it, but I'm telling you it is true and even though it sounds unbelievable about the bats or something, the hospital staff can confirm I have animal bites all over me. I accept the spectre may have been a trick of my mind, a hallucination due to the shock, but please James, promise me you will check the tunnels down in the Glen for the boy!" Stephen sounded desperate!

"I will, I will definitely do that for you, I trust your proven gut!" James reassured him. "Ping me over the maps you have found of that area, and the tunnel you were trying to get too; Then I will get a team back down to look at the Mill area."

Stephen sent him the map he had on his phone of where the tunnel lay, adding a message asking to be kept updated.

#

The next day, James examined the map, he contacted the leader of the Major Investigation team, Ivor McDonald who was dealing with the Jamie Callahan disappearance. "When the search for the boy was carried out did you search the Mill or the old tunnels down there?" James asked.

"No, what tunnels!? We definitely had a couple of men search the Mill building though." Ivor exclaimed. "We concentrated our search in the Glen Park, the Viaduct area and the woodland leading up to Castlemilk and the old Army camp plus down through Lynn Park. These were the areas where the boy was known to frequent." Ivor replied, then continued. "Just to make you aware James; Another incident involving the Mill bordering the Glen came in yesterday at six thirty am, the owners of a small Bakery next to the Mills have gone missing under very strange circumstances."

James was intrigued, he asked "What were the suspicious circumstances?"

"Their car was in the Bakery driveway with the door open, cigarette packet and lighter on the dash, jacket on the back of the drivers' seat with the Bakery keys in the pocket. The car keys were in the ignition." Ivor replied.

Whatever happened they left in a hurry then! "James added, "I have had some good information about that car, the Mill site woods, and I think it is worth pursuing with one more search Ivor."

"I agree with you James. We completed a risk assessment on the missing men elevating the status quickly, when we spoke to the family, they alerted us to the fact that the Bakery had old security cameras, which are sometimes on, sometimes off!" Ivor paused.

"We got lucky the footage shows an elderly man walking down the hill then returning in the dark after the men disappear. Edward the younger brother is seen getting out his car urgently as though something is wrong, Alec the older brother is seen in the corner of the picture briefly, looks like he had come up the hill to get his brother, they both must have run down toward the Mill and woodland."

"Great news," responded James.

"The audio is poor but maybe we can enhance it!" Ivor said positively. "The men do not return on camera! The old man is seen in a very bad way, many hours later but the footage is grainy as it's very dark."

"The old man is my source, he is a retired Cop, I know him very well. He contacted me yesterday after being discharged from hospital, I've already arranged someone to visit him to get a full statement." James said. "My gut is telling me to look for the men, as with the boy at the Mill site tunnels as quickly as possible!" James stated.

"Okay, so you don't think the elderly man has anything to do with the Bakery brothers' disappearance then?" Ivor asked. "No, no definitely not, take my word on it!" stated James strongly. "Let's get another search organised for the old lower Mill site, the Tunnel and the surrounding woodland, need dogs, possibly a Helicopter plus get a specialist team for investigating the tunnel." "I will send you over the old map I have. Ask the Search advisors to check 'properly' this time, for any current maps of the tunnel site and foundations of previous Mills!" James instructed. "Keep me updated immediately of any progress regarding the Bakery owners. Okay Ivor?".

"Yeah, thanks for all the information, James, I will get this sorted as soon as possible. Find out what the hell is going on down there and hopefully find the boy alive!"

#

Chapter 22.

The Bare Bones of the Matter

The top of the small road that led down to the Mill had a Police car blocking the entrance, a Policeman stood on duty restricting any access. Down at the bottom of the narrow track road the entire lower Mill site was taped off. There was a Dog Handling Unit van, a Police vehicle in the car park of the Bakery and one in the Garage forecourt, two large black Specialist search team Police vans were situated in the grounds of the old Mill.

The Police search force was split into small teams, Units A, B and C, led by Tommy, included the two Dog search units. The Camera footage monitor Mark and six regular Policemen patrolled the Mill site. Helicopters were on standby if required.

The two Alsatian dogs had camera units strapped to the top of their heads, Leo the dog handler was keeping the dogs calm and under control, he instructed the dogs to lie down as he spoke to Tommy.

"Have you and your other guy been given your protective face masks, we need to cover neck, ears and hands?" Tommy asked.

"Yes," Leo replied. "What is all this, having to wear face protection masks?"

Tommy stated, "there has been a report of a species of bats that can give multiple nasty bites near or in the tunnels; the bats have not been identified or confirmed, but let's not take any chances."

"No problem!" Leo said as he flattened out the paper map on the bonnet of one of the vans, the others joined them, discussing their best strategy for the search. "Mark was already in the 'Camera van' he would be monitoring Tommy's camera and the dogs' cameras' footage.

Two men were to investigate the inside of the Mill building, being very aware that the floors were extremely unsafe, also there had been various reports previously that the Mill had been used as a drug den, so the men would need to be careful in case of any contaminated needles. Two men would search the surrounding grounds reaching up to the entrance of the track road; There were two men to explore the grounds of the Bakery and they would also search the grounds at the back of the Garage. The main Units would search the woodland to the river and the woodland heading down to the Viaduct.

"Okay everyone, do we all know what we are doing and where we are meant to be?" "Yes," the teams, replied, all nodding to Tommy.

"Remember everyone, put on all your protective kit." Tommy instructed before pulling the shiny 'balaclava like face mask down. "Okay, Unit A, clear the way as best you can to the tunnel," he directed. "Unit B as discussed you focus on the area going down in opposite direction." Unit B nodded and they set off. Unit C, follow ensuring we have not missed anything in the previous search.

"Leo, after you." Leo and the accompanying dog handler Geoff instructed their dogs to their feet, both talking to their dogs calmly, stroking them fondly. Walking them over to their allotted areas of search. Leo pulled the Baker brothers clothing from the clear bag and let Honey smell the clothes, she sniffed the air then the ground and took off pulling Leo, Tommy following.

Geoff pulled the Jamie Callaghan bag out and put his dog Henry's snout in the bag, he gave him a moment. Henry walked slowly off the path, stared straight ahead sniffing, he stalled at the undergrowth, he sniffed around pulling Geoff in a slightly different direction at speed. Geoff and Henry passed Unit C who were already deep in search through the tall vegetation.

Henry the dog was following a definite path, he was pulling Geoff hard, it was too overgrown for him to let him off his restraint just yet. Henry stopped, he sniffed the air and started pulling Geoff back the way they had come, the dog seemed confused. Geoff got out the clear bag again, Henry wouldn't co-operate, he shook his head from side to side, wrestling against the restraint, he whimpered, baring his teeth, all the hair on the back of his neck stood up, he was growling looking straight ahead. Henry began pulling Geoff back in a desperate strong retreat. Geoff was struggling to keep a hold of him. "You're okay Henry," the dog snarled at him, Geoff had never seen his dog behave like this. "What's wrong boy?"

Geoff felt something tug at the back of his head protection, he turned quickly, there was nothing there, next thing he knew he was pushed over, off his feet and on to his face, he let go of Henry. The dog took off at speed. "Henrrrrrrrrry" Geoff lay still before pulling himself up, he shouted, "Hennnnry." He took out his dog whistle. Geoff could hear a buzz and his dog barking. Loud yelping suddenly pierced the quiet, followed by a sudden silence. He blew the whistle and waited, only silence answered. Geoff looked around frantically for the dog or any sign of Unit C.

Geoff contacted Tommy over the 'walkie talkie', "I lost my footing, the dog has run off, he was spooked by something, he has never done anything like this before." Geoff was breathing heavily. "Ask Mark if there was anything on his camera!" Geoff said, "I heard him yelp, he may have fallen, I need to go find him in case he is hurt!" Geoff looked around, "I can't see Unit C either, I've lost them?" "Copy that," Tommy replied.

Tommy spoke into his handset directly to the men in Unit C who had been in the area not far behind Geoff.

"Do you copy," "come back to me with your present location guys," there was a loud buzzing through the 'Walkie talkie,' so loud, Tommy pulled it away from his ear.

Tommy contacted Mark in the camera van. "Any footage from Henry the dog's camera?" Mark clicked onto Henry's monitor, "Don't understand it! Strange!" Mark was momentarily confused, "the camera is very high up, it is showing the tops of trees and is looking down on to the river, I think the dog could be situated near or on top of the Viaduct, I will play back the footage, see what's there!"

Just then Leo shouted out. "Over here Tommy!" Tommy followed his voice he could see him standing at a large black entrance to a tunnel, it was partially disguised with Ivy tendrils. This is what we have been looking for!" Tommy said satisfied, pushing back the hanging leaves.

Mark contacted Tommy, "The footage shows Henrys' camera was moving through the air Tommy?" "What? Couldn't quite catch that!" Tommy said loudly into the handset. The 'Walkie talky' buzzed with a horrible metallic static noise. Tommy switched it off.

Tommy and Leo stood together at the mouth of the dark tunnel, there was low level water on the floor." Honey had a definite scent, she was eager to go, but Leo was holding her back. Tommy activated record on his Body Worn Video camera. Honey was pulling to go in the abyss, Leo switched her head camera on, "he patted her rear, "go in girl," unclipping her restraint. Both men switched on the long beam torch on top of their helmets and proceeded in after the dog.

The dog splashed ahead disappearing into the darkness beyond the reach of the beam of light. Tommy tried the 'walkie talkie,' "anything on Honeys' Camera Mark?"

There was a long pause, then Marks voice broken up, crackled through, "No not yet!"

Tommy and Leo followed carefully, the ground under the water was rocky and uneven. The smell was atrocious and getting worse as they proceeded. The men were coughing despite having their nose and mouths covered.

After a few minutes, Mark exclaimed through the Walkie Talkie loudly," it looks like she is approaching a large blockage in the tunnel, she is moving around it. "Yes, she has got something Tommy!" he sounded excited.

"There is something huge! She is pretty far in, be careful." Mark said as he looked intensely scrutinising the dark image on the camera monitor. "Oh my god!" he suddenly cried out. "It looks like bodies!"

Tommy and Leo waded at speed into the dense darkness to Honey, splashing as they moved. The stench was becoming unbearable, recognisable as dead rotting flesh, the sickeningly pungent sweet sulphur or methane type smell invaded every pore. They were surrounded by thousands of flies, they could feel the small hard insects as they moved through them, swatting them out the way as they proceeded. Rats dived in the water hurriedly swimming away from them as they approached.

The beam of light illuminated a hill of what at first looked like rocks or mud; But as the two men got closer, their lights became brighter, they realised in utter shock and disgust that the pile was human remains! "Carnage!" Tommy whispered. Before them a festering mass of bodies, the flies were unbearable, beetles scuttled over the putrefying flesh, maggots were on every inch of the pile it was nauseating. "Thank God for these masks," Leo said holding his gloved hand over his masked mouth and nose, his stomach was heaving, he was swallowing the saliva in his mouth repeatedly trying not to vomit. Honey was pulling at a body that was sat at the edge of the heap, back leaning on the wall, the lower half of the corpse was under water, apart from the boots. The flies angrily rose up in a cloud as Honey tried to retrieve it, she was excitedly wagging her tail. Tommy moved the beam of light round shining it through the hundreds of flies. The shaft of light illuminated the face of the corpse, it was Alec the older Bakery brother! "Leave!" Leo shouted the command, she reluctantly let go and went to him. "Good girl," he said, "good girl," he patted her shoulder. Alec's face was partially missing, there were maggots already imbedded in the flesh that remained, slugs covered his bald head as though he wore a slimy shiny wig. The right forearm and hand were missing.

Tommy contacted Mark; the connection was poor. "Mark, get a specialist team and Forensics down to the tunnel!" "We may need anthropologists or archaeologists to assist in the recovery of the bodies there are many at various stages of decomposition, I can't even say how many! We need everything related to the remains mapped in situ." "We still don't know what this is, who or what did this." Silence then a buzz like crackling noise, "Okay boss, I w…. get…. it n….w! You are brea.. ing.. u" said Mark before losing connection.

The gut-wrenching stench was too much for Leo, the acid burning his throat, he started to boak. He choked up vomit and pulling his mask frantically out from his face, projected it out. Tommy scanned the huge pile of bodies with the torch light, his eyes had grown accustomed to the blackness, he walked around the hill of flesh going deeper into the tunnel, he thought there were other bodies further in, his heart was beating fast, the sweat now running down his back profusely, he returned to Leo. "Hideous, this is what hell would look like," he said to Leo, 'something you'd imagine from a Stephen King Horror story' he thought. A skeletal hand was sticking out the water as though it was waving goodbye to them as they turned to retreat. Leo turned to look back, a skull with hair sitting on top of what looked another bodies leg, stared at him through its dead black eye sockets, terror crawled up his spine, Leo shuddered. There was a glimpse of denim. A wellington boot sticking out from the oozing mass.

Tommy swept his spotlight up, a rat sat feasting on a child's body near the top of the pile, "Jeeeeezuz!" he exclaimed loudly. The rat sat motionless, staring at Tommy. A small once white sports sock and a filthy white trainer hung down; "Jamie Callaghan!" Tommy said sadly his eyes welling up. Leo made a jumping movement splashing toward the Rat, it scurried down the pile, plopping into the water. "Let's get out of this Hellhole, let the specialists deal with it!" Tommy told Leo.

#

Graeme from Unit A had been split up from his team, he was standing at the tunnel entrance as Leo and Tommy trudged their way back through the water. Leo put his hands on his knees bent over retching, he started to cry, Honey his dog, sat quietly looking up at him. Tommy spoke to Graeme quietly, "it's a mass grave, too many bodies to count! One of the Bakers is in there and I think it's the boy too!" Graeme's eyes widened as Tommy spoke, Leo turned his head to listen to what was being said. Graeme put his arm round Leo shoulders, "you will be alright mate, you and your dog, done a brilliant job!" Tommy was devoid of colour, he stood staring into the woods, he said quietly," I must be in shock as I don't feel anything now!" "I just can't believe what we have found! Who or what in hell could have done this?"

Graeme asked Tommy "where are Jimmy and Ron situated?" "Should you not know Graeme? They are in your Unit?" Tommy responded agitated.

"I thought they were with you," Graeme said anxiously, "I lost them, I couldn't keep up the undergrowth was too thick, so I stopped here!" Tommy was silent, Graeme paused, "Sorry Tommy, I could not contact them, the talkies they are down and there is no mobile signal

292

here." Tommy stared at him with a grave expression, then his eyes returned to the woodland, he stood staring as if stunned. His thoughts flashing images of the poor souls in the tunnel! Leo was praying until Graeme broke the silence, "Tommy we should get back!"

#

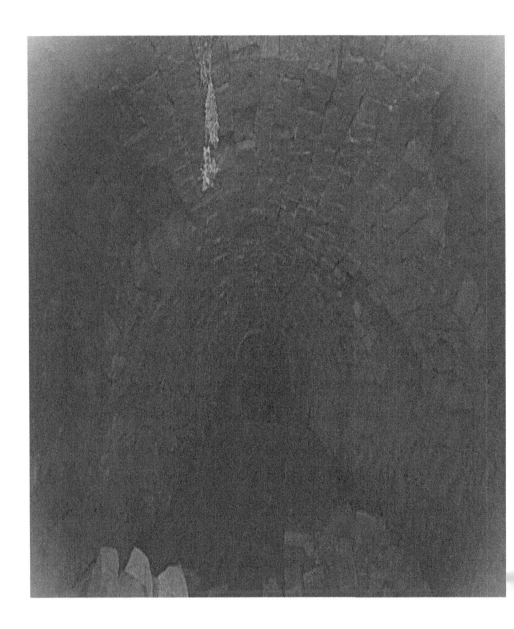

Back at the Mill, Mark was outside the Camera monitor van, updating all those present. "Nothing has been found in any of your assigned plots, thankfully," he paused; "but we have a major incident here guys! Tommy and Leos' Dog unit have found numerous dead in the main old Mill Tunnel, they suspect some of the fatalities are historic. One of the corpses looks to be Alec or Eddy Baldy the brothers from the Bakery; The missing boy has been found dead but as with correct procedure, we will need to wait until identification confirms who these bodies definitely are!"

The men all gasped, mumbling among themselves. Mark took a breath. "Two men from Unit A are missing, Unit B and C have not returned yet and have not been in contact for ninety minutes. There have been severe problems with communications! Tommy requested Helicopter assistance before he was cut off; they are on their way! "

One of the team piped up," What are we looking for now?"

Mark sighed "To be honest at this point we do not know! It may be a serial killer who has been hoarding his victims over time or more than one, best not to speculate at this stage!"

He paused again, "We are still looking for the other brother."

"The other dog is missing. Geoff is distraught searching the lower woodland for him, he has been in contact with Tommy, who is now on his way back with Leo and Graeme, they should be back in five." "Once Tommy is here, we will know how we can best proceed. Rest up, get a drink until he appears."

#

Geoff was down near the river searching along the embankment for Henry, using his whistle for 'recall,' when an old woman appeared from nowhere.

"You looking for your dog Geoff?" she asked. Geoff was shocked to see anyone; he lifted his mask up off his face to his forehead. "Yes, how did you know it was me? He wrinkled his brow. "Do I know you?" Geoff asked.

"I know everyone down here" she replied.

"Oh! Okay," said Geoff sounding a little perplexed, pulling his mouth to the side.

"Geoff, your dog is dead! The Host took him! What is left of his body is near the 'Beachy bit," she said in a direct but sympathetic voice, she looked directly into his eyes, he felt himself drawn into them, like a green flame! 'This is weird,' he thought, he felt spaced out, unsteady but Geoff had an overwhelming knowledge that the woman spoke the truth.

"Who took him?" Geoff asked. She didn't answer. "Where?" he stammered now visibly upset and confused! "I know how much you loved your animal friend, but you must 'get out' the Glen now it is not safe!" the old woman said. Geoff felt terribly vulnerable, tears stung his eyes, he put his hands to his face to hide his grief, but when he wiped his tears away and rubbed the sweat from his face, he looked up to ask the woman more about Henrys demise, but she was gone! Geoff frantically searched around him, his eyes darting around everywhere. He heard a loud whisper 'GET OUT' in his ear as he stumbled on over the uneven, rocky edge of the river, disorientated, he was finding it hard to keep his balance.

'I need to get out of here! It's the shock!' he thought, 'something is wrong here, very wrong!' He tripped nearly falling stopping to steady himself, fumbling with the Walkie Talkie, he eventually spoke to Tommy.

"One of the locals has managed to get down here, I'm near the river. She said my dog is dead that the 'Host,' took him." Tommy fired questions at Geoff with an agitated tone. "What the hell is one of the locals doing in the Glen? Who is the hell is the Host? Where is the woman now?" Geoff answered quietly, "I will give details when face to face Tommy."

Tommy sighed into the handset. "We have men at every access point how did a women get down there!" Tommy asked loudly. "How the hell am I supposed to know, Tommy? I'm coming back, now! I don't like this fucken place something is not right here. My dogs dead!" Geoff uttered in a voice full of grief. Tommy was silent, his eyes wide, he had never been spoken to like that, but he thought 'the guys were all under enormous stress." He let it go.

#

Unit B, Julie and Dougie were crouched down with their handsets switched off as they had picked up a terrible buzzing noise. They had spotted a colony of large bats flying overhead as a cloud, they seemed to be carrying large pieces of something, gyrating as they passed overhead. As they both looked up, a big dollop of blood sploshed onto a large Dock leaf next to Julie, her eyes were immediately drawn down to it. Julie knelt down, one finger touched the dark puddle on the leaf, "BLOOD!" Julie said quietly. She quickly switched record on her Body Worn Video.

Dougie signalled to Julie with a wave to follow the swarm as fast as they could on the opposite side of the river from the legion of flying creatures. They fought their way through the thick bushes, neither had ever seen anything quite like the moving mass of black above them.

The dark cloud moved over the trees then swooped down precisely like an arrow, moving as one entity, a loud flurry of noise as they descended at the old foundations near the beach area, they just disappeared into the ground. "Where the hell did they go?" exclaimed Dougie.

"Not sure, there must be an opening!" "Let's get back," Julie said urgently, "we don't know what this is!" "Yeah, Let's go. Bats are nocturnal! Seems to me these things are out hunting in broad day light!" Dougie said.

"We need advice, they are definitely much larger than any bat I've ever seen, "Julie said."

Okay, we can let Tommy know everything when we get back up!"

#

The Seelie had been watching the comings and goings of the Police." Collectively they directed their thoughts to all the Slaugh. "You have become too bold, not only killing for need or justice but for the sport of it! You knew it would bring human negative attention to our home, you had no care for all your fellow beings."

The Slaugh's eyes flashed yellow. "You cannot deny, the Hairless Hogs are a plague on us all! The Host will do as we please!"

"It is not for the Host to declare who or what is a plague! You become too important in your own minds!" The Seelie advised them. "You have disregarded the need to be discreet around humans, only taking what you need. You have brought negativity to the Glen with your blood lust and gluttony!"

The Slaugh stood defiantly. "It is you! The Seelie Court who believes in your own minds, that it is your right to decide for all! "We the Host have decided! It is our intention to rid ourselves of the human disease forever."

The Seelie converse among themselves.

"The Guardian has done well to protect the innocent but cannot not warn them all of the Sloughs' true nature."

"The Host have brought danger to the Glen, for all living beings here.".

"It is not the positive natural home the woodland creatures and we Seelie had once enjoyed. The Seelie court must prepare."

"What about our neighbours the Slaugh?" asked one.

"They have brought this upon us, the Seelie must protect our own kin!"

The Faeries directed their attention to the Slaugh once more.

"You must do as you see fit for the Host, and the Host alone!"

They Slaugh bared their teeth in rage, sending negative angry thoughts in reply to the Seelie's rejection.

The Seelie flew up and away in a hurried flurry not wishing to absorb any more of their ill will.

#

Unit C: Danny and Max had been following Geoff and his dog, but the dog had veered off in a different direction pulling Geoff along, despite the under growth being thick

Geoff moved much faster than they could. Max in particular had gained weight over the past few months and was struggling with the effort, sweat ran down the inside of his mask and down his lower back, they soon fell behind, once Unit C realised Geoff must have taken a different route they tried to contact Tommy but there was some type of interference on the walkie talkies. Danny tried his mobile, but it would not connect. "We should continue to search this route then return to base, okay with you Max?" "Fine with me!"

Searching through the woods they found a Childs' trainer, then a sculpture of balance made from stones, they took a photograph of the shoe where it lay and bagged it, they also photographed the piles of stones. "Looks like a child's been playing here. Could be relevant." Danny said. "Keep in mind Danny, lots of kids come down here in Summer," Max replied.

They worked their way along the deep undergrowth, following the curve of the river, searching. "What's that over there?" Max pointed to a square black hole on the opposite side of the river. "Looks like an opening to a shaft!" Danny said.

"Maybe the out-pour of an old drainage system, look at the age of the wall around it, centuries old that is!" Danny stated."

"Take a photo Max, I think Tommy will want us to get a team over there, the waters too deep mid-way to try go over ourselves!" Max smirked, "thank god you don't want me to go over there now, I'm dying as it is!"

"You need to cut out the triple Cheeseburgers mate and the packs of Crispy crème doughnuts!" Danny jested.

"You calling me a fat bastard Danny?" they both laughed. They tried the handsets again, this time there was no interference." Danny spoke into the handset, "Walkie check, Unit C" "Breaker 1-9," "Do you copy?"

Tommy responded "Affirmative," "What's your 20?"

Danny answered, "Before Viaduct, lower waterfall." "10-17, Found small Tunnel no access from here need assistance!"

Tommy answered "10-19, Return to base."

Danny says, Copy that."

Tommy then "Over and out."

Danny and Max turn back, working themselves up the pathways they had trampled down, climbing the embankment back up to base.

#

Unit A had been having problems with their handsets and had no signal on their phones but had continued with their search. They passed the Tunnel entrance continuing to the big waterfall on the opposite side of the river from the huge Glen entrance gates.

"Where the hell is Graeme?" Jimmy sounded concerned, "he was lagging behind me by at least five minutes!" Ron answered. "He will catch up, if not he will see Tommy once he is at the Tunnel. Don't worry!"

"This is a nightmare with no communication!" Jimmy huffed.

Once they had worked their way up through the heavy foliage to the Upper mill foundations, they found openings leading underground.

"These historic buildings have left a maze of disused tunnels, probably old sewers and drains," Ron said, "bloody dangerous the council should have had these filled in years ago!"

The men were noting down each openings location as they photographed the area.

"Will we head back to base now?" asked Jimmy, "we have been out of contact for too long and we need to check in and find out where Graeme is."

"Yeah. Try the walkie again." Ron said.

"Will do," Jimmy answered.

"Just be two minutes, I want to take a video of this deep shaft," Ron said as he leant forward near the mouth of the opening which was dark, about three feet wide by three feet, buried deep into an old wall in the undergrowth, "it looks as though it goes quite far in."

Ron peered into the opening. "Fuck!" he yelled and jumped back, landing on his rear, eyes wide. "What is it Ron, what's wrong?" Jimmy asked. "There is something in there Jimmy!"

"What was it?" Jimmy asked sounding worried.

"I think, I think it was a face!" Ron was white as a sheet; his heart was racing, he slowly got to his feet.

Jimmy squatted down near the entrance and pulled out his torch, the beam of light, illuminated a hideous face. The head was situated about a meter in, lying on its' cheek staring out blankly, the skin looked darkened, yellowed and waxy. It was Eddy, his mouth hung open, in a permanent silent scream. "Shit!" "I think it is one of the guys we are looking for." Jimmy said. "Only his head though!"

Ron was pale and wide eyed. "Did you get the walkie working Jimmy?" he asked urgently.

"What? …….Oh! No ……, it is still not working!"

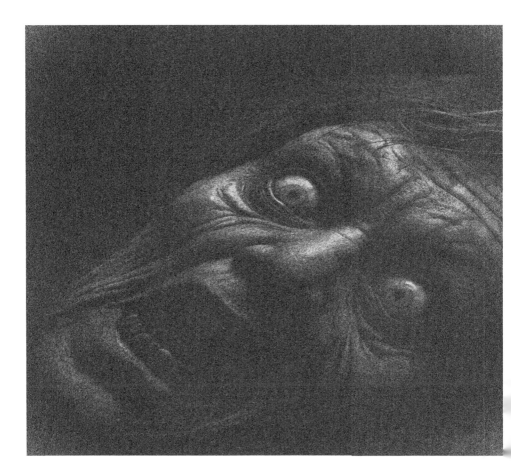

"Switch on your Body cam vid, we will get visuals and record location." Ron instructed. "I will tape up the entrance! Then let's get the hell out of here, back to the others, let them know what's down here."

Desperately they made their way through the stinging nettle undergrowth to the riverbank at the rear of the old tenement housing, once they emerged from the Glen, they were able to re-establish the connection with base.

#

It was now dark. All members of the search team were back at the Lower Mill site. Everyone had been updated, the atmosphere was charged with activity and excitement. Tommy was discussing with everyone the plan for the next morning. They would all be back at six am.

"The Bat Conservation Trust and someone from Taxonomy, the field of identifying species had been notified by administration to investigate the Glen as soon as possible." Tommy took a breath, "I'm not sure if they will turn up to assist tomorrow or not, regardless we need to search these sites especially now Ron and Jimmy have found the head of whom we presume is one of the missing brothers Eddy in one of the old sewers."

Tommy spoke with authority, "I just want to say thanks to you all, it was a hard day considering all the setbacks we encountered with communications. We will get that sorted for tomorrow. Well done."

Julie spoke out, "I think I speak for us all Geoff in saying we are gutted for you, we know how much you loved your dog Henry. "The men all mumbled in agreement.

Tommy added "I hope we can find out exactly what happened to him when we retrieve his head cam tomorrow." Geoff's face was ashen, he looked quite ill, he struck a lonely sad figure as he walked back to his van without his dog.

The entire Glen was now cordoned off, both the Tunnel and the Shaft crime scenes had been taped off and secured. Police vehicles positioned as barricades with Police officers now guarding all possible routes in, as the Specialist Teams now investigated the sites. A helicopter flew over the crime scenes its' huge beam of light illuminating the way for the Forensics teams in their white protective suits as they started to make their way to the tunnel and the shaft. Tommy and his teams were reluctant to leave the site, but they needed to get some sleep as tomorrow would be another exhausting day.

#

Scottish televisions news reader stared out of the screen. "A major incident is underway in the Glen Park in the Village. The Police have advised the public to not visit the area or try to access the Park for their own safety and to ensure the investigation is conducted properly. There will be heavy penalties for anyone found doing so. More information will be given as soon as the incident is under control."

Social media was awash with speculation.

#

Chapter 23.

The Party 's Over

Jenny, Sophie, Paul, and George were in the Torban, their favourite restaurant in Giffnock. The four had just finished their meal and several drinks. "That was amazing," Sophie exclaimed as she finished her Korma.

"Well, you ate it fast enough, fatty, I'm surprised you tasted it!" George joked.

"What a grubber! Where the hell do you put it?" Paul puffed up his cheeks, Sophie laughed. "Never sets foot in a gym either, guess you burn the calories off another way! Eh?" Paul nodded over to George with a cheeky smile. Jen stared at Paul disapprovingly.

"How was yours Jen?" Sophie asked, Jenny had left half of her Okra Curry.

"Okay, I'm not that hungry tonight I feel a little sick."

Paul rolled his eyes and sighed loudly as he looked over at George.

A group of attractive young women came in and were seated at the next table, they were laughing and chatting. The girls were obviously going on to a nightclub after their meal as they had on lots of makeup, looking glittery and glamourous, short skirts, tanned legs, high heels. George was leaning into Sophie whispering and she was giggling.

"Why do you keep looking over at those girls," Jenny complained to Paul, "it is really ignorant when I'm sitting right here!"

"There is no harm in looking Jenny, for gods' sake!" Paul snapped.

One of the girls looked over and gave Paul a big flirtatious smile, he gave her a huge smile back, but Jenny caught him. He looked away quickly feeling Jennys' eyes on him.

"You are a pig, so damn rude Paul" she turned staring at him.

"You want her? Go and get her then!" Jenny was furious, she stood, squeezing her way out of her seat past him, "I thought you could at least wait until I was back in Canada!"

George and Sophie looked up as she left the table.

Sophie scolded Paul, "you could be a bit more discreet."

"Oh, don't you effin start!" Paul snapped. George nudged Sophie to be quiet.

#

Jenny had just come out the toilet cubicle, she was standing in front of the sink finishing washing her hands, while looking in the mirror above it, when the girl that had smiled at Paul came in. Jenny gave the girl an angry look through the mirror.

"What's your problem?" the girl said with a sneer.

311

"Oh nothing, I just think that anyone who flirts with a man while they are sat with their girlfriend or wife must be desperate, or ignorant, that's all! "Jenny spat her words sarcastically, staring at the girl defiantly.

"I never 'eyed' up your man! If he canny keep his eyes off other women then it's him you have a problem with, no me hen!" she stormed out the toilet door.

The young woman went straight over to her table, where she proceeded to tell her friends what had been said by Jenny, they all looked round at Paul and were shaking their heads, tutting, making whispering complaint as Jenny made her way back to her seat.

"Are you having a sweet Jen?" Sophie asked, trying to relieve the tension that was crackling in the atmosphere.

"No, I'm having another Gin," she said and gave her friend a fake grin!

"Awwww, Jen what's up. Tell me?"

"Oh Nothing! Just Paul is looking for a new girlfriend while I'm sat right here!" Jenny said sarcastically, "and she was being a cheeky cow in the toilet!"

"What did she say?" Sophie asked, but Paul interrupted.

He looked at Jenny infuriated, "when did you become such a jealous bitch?"

"STOP!" George said loudly, the people at the other tables glanced round. He lowered his voice saying quietly but firmly. "You two stop it, we are out for a lovely night and you're spoiling it, you are embarrassing us."

"Aye, okay, "said Paul.

"Come on Jenny," Sophie prompted her.

"Sorry George, Sorry Sophie," Jenny said quietly. Paul glanced at Jenny out the side of his eyes.

"Let's go along to the pub Jenny, they have music on tonight," suggested Sophie.

"Yeah lets." Jen answered.

"You up for it guys?" Sophie asked.

"Sure am!" George replied.

They got up and went to put on their jackets as the men paid the bill.

Sophie asked, "what the hell is wrong with you tonight?"

"Pauls' lost interest Sophie, I can't bare it, I feel so hurt, I've been such a damn fool!"

"You probably have been seeing too much of each other." she looked at her friend's sad face, Jen nodded, "try to be a little more unavailable, you know how men love a chase!" Sophie suggested.

"He has been leaving me in all week, not coming home after work, and when he does, he just says he is too tired, going straight to sleep," Jenny said, her voice quivering.

George walked over. "Paul's just going for a slash," he said, "come on outside and wait." They walked away from the restaurant door along the street, the three stood for a minute, then Jenny walked back and looked in the glass door. Paul was chatting to the young women at their table, they were all laughing, then she saw him hand the girl a business card, she quickly looked away, but he noticed her. Jenny quickly walked back to Sophie and George.

Paul appeared, "Sorry guys, I got stopped on the way out, seemingly one of those lassies went to school with my young cousin."

"Small world eh!" Jenny said with a nasty tone. "What a coincidence!" Sophie said.

"You must think I'm a right idiot if you think I believe that!" Jenny snarled.

"You know what Jenny; I don't give a damn what you believe! I've had enough of you tonight," Jenny stood in a confrontational pose in front of him.

"You've had enough of me, huh! What a cheek, I'm not the one making a fool of you!" she raised her voice.

"Yes, you are making a fool of me! and yourself!" "Lower your fucken voice!" Paul said viciously. He walked away from her, then turned to face her and said loudly, "stay at Sophies, I'm off out, don't come back to mine tonight! You're not welcome!" "You coming George?" he shouted back as he marched away.

George looked at Sophie flummoxed, "What do I do?" he asked Sophie.

"Go if you want George, it's no biggy!" George ran after Paul.

As soon as the men were out of sight Jenny started to cry. Sophie took her arm; she resisted the urge to say, 'I told you so!' They started to slowly walk toward the pub along the road. "Dump you, did he?" the girl shouted as she left the Torban with her friends, they all laughed. Jenny turned and motioned to move towards her, she was about to shout back. Sophie tightened her grip on her arm. "Leave it Jen!" Sophie pulled her back.

"If it wasn't her, it be some other cheeky wee tart!" "You are better than that!"

Jenny was distraught she had cried so much her make-up was a mess, her mascara was smudged in huge black circles around her eyes, she was in too much of a state to go anywhere! Sophie called a taxi to go home to try to calm her down, fix her face.

'Maybe, they could go to a local pub for a drink in an hour or so, it might help,' she thought.

#

The Taxi drove down the Village Main Street on the way to Sophies home. There were Police cars everywhere, blue lights flashing, Police incident tape running over the entrance to the woodland at the side of the Bridge. The Glen had parked Police vans blocking the entrance. There was a Helicopter overhead it's search-light full beam on the riverbank.

"Wow! I wonder what's happened," Sophie said with concern. Jenny stared out the window as she looked away from the helicopter and over into the darkness of the dense woodland that lay beyond, she noticed a glow, rising up out of the trees it hovered or floated, she stared, turning to continue to look as she passed in the taxi. "I wonder if they have found the missing boy," Jenny murmured.

#

The Cartvale was closed as the Police needed access from the rear of the

Restaurant's premises, down into the side of the river which led to where 'the head' had been

found. The Village Hotel was closed as it was adjacent to the Bridge which led under into the

Glen. The residents of the three houses that were directly in front of the Hotel had been told

by the Police there was an ongoing major incident, which could restrict their access to their

homes for up to forty-eight hours, they advised them to stay with relatives or stay indoors.

The pub at the top end of the Village was packed as was the Bowling club. The

rumours were rife. The bar man in the club, Pete Muirhead was working this shift, leaning over, his muscular tattooed arms resting on the bar top listening to all the talk of the Glen. Everyone was speaking openly in loud voices so their opinions could be heard.

"I been telt the boy has been found," one of the young team announced, another spoke up, "the brothers that went missing were paedophiles who murdered wee Jamie then fucked off, that's what I heard."

"There is no way the 'Baker brothers are pedoes, they both got kids of their ain!" Steph McGuire, one of the bakery staff told them. "Now the Andersons at the bottom of the Bramble hill, Aye, I'd believe it about them! He sneered, "their family have had all sorts of folk complain about them! One of the brothers got a wee bird of fourteen or fifteen pregnant when he was aboot forty, he used to beat the living shit out her."

Tracey Roberts who lived right at the back of the Glen butted in, "I think they have found the Aliens that are in the Glen! We been seein the lights moving around in there fir years; lights up in the treetops, buzzin and all sorts of strange noises."

Pete shook his head, "Not the Alien story again Tracey, for fucks sake!" "Beam me up Tracey!" They all laughed; Tracey felt her face heating up.

The older community were having their say too; Danny Stanton, an old man in his late eighties sat with a glass of Whiskey, he had a scraggy old face, deep with wrinkles, he had lived in the village all his life as had his father, and his fathers' fathers as long as the village had been here.

Danny told a group of men at the back table, "the Glen is haunted by a witch that was hung doon there, it's documented in the Witchcraft trials. I've seen her many times over ma lifetime!" Everyone turned to listen. "No long ago when I used tae walk ma old dug Caesar, she appeared at the side of me, tall with long grey hair she is!" "Whit did you do Danny?" Tim Koy asked.

317

I just pretended I didnay see her," Danny sniggered. "Whits she goni dae tae me at this age? am nearly dead awready." The men at the table laughed. "I didnay want tae look in they green eyes o hers though, I kept ma heed doon!" Danny continued. "She whispered in my ear, 'BEWARE THE HOST!?" he croaked. "Nearly shat masel I did!"

Tim Koy added nodding as he spoke, "Aye I've seen her too Danny, glowing in the dark, at the river's edge! Um no lyin she floats above the grun!" he addressed everyone in the bar.

"The old Tales said there were demons in the Glen recorded as far back as the Mills!" said a woman sat far at the back.

"Aye, there been strange go-ins oan in there awe o my life!" Toby Mills told them.

"Whit did she mean Danny? 'Beware the Host?' the young team shouted over.

"Whooz the Host?" Tim Koy asked when the old man didn't respond.

"The Host!" he sighed, rubbing his chin. "Aye well, some talk of Fairies, others of devils, so many have died in there! A doan know ma-sel," Danny answered wearily.

A girl sitting at the table with the young team shouted over jovially to the old men.

"Aye I seen the witch too! Riding a Unicorn wi a demon hanging oot her arse!" They all laughed. "Very funny hen." The old men tutted turned away and quietly resumed their conversation so the others could not hear.

#

Jenny was back at Sophies. She had washed her face and applied some fresh make up, she stared into the mirror hating what she saw. 'A pathetic, red eyed fool!' she thought. Sophie was sitting on the couch as Jenny returned from the Bathroom.

"Ahhh that's better Jenny, you look good as new!"

318

"Thanks, but I feel shit." Jenny plonked herself down next to her heavily.

"What is going on with you Jen, I've never seen you like this before, jealousy and anger, you've always been so laid back!" "Remember all the great times we have had whenever I have been overstaying with my dad? So many guys interested in you!" she smiled. "You never wanted to get serious with anyone; I can hardly believe you have got in so deep in months?"

Sophie got up and poured them both a glass of wine and sat back down, handing a glass to Jenny. Jenny took a big mouthful swallowing hard, "I needed that!" she exhaled a loud, long tired sigh. "I fell in love, what can I say, I am an idiot," she said quietly.

"No, you're not an idiot, your just human." Sophie pulled her legs up, curling them under her. "I honestly think, it was just too much, too soon Jen!"

"I can't believe he doesn't want me! Just over a week or so ago he was telling me he loved me!" Jens eyes welled up.

"Come on Jenny, I know you can be tougher than this, don't you let him get you in a state. You know what men can be like!" Sophie said supportively. "Men can be like big kids, they treat women like lollypops, they want, want, want the pink one, then once they lick it a few times, they want the other flavour!" Sophie said with distaste rolling her eyes, shaking her head. "I know your right Sophie!" Jen said nodding her head sorrowfully.

"I won't let him humiliate me further! I am going to get my stuff, I will wait until after the clubs close, he should be back home around then!"

Sophie looked shocked, "You cannot go there tonight, Jenny! Please don't!" Sophie begged.

"He will be drunk! He made a point of telling you not to go there! Maybe he will have a woman with him, why would you want to give yourself the grief? Sophie sounded concerned.

"Wait until tomorrow, you can say goodbye as friends, come on!"

"Friends!" "Are you having a laugh Sophie?" Jenny said sarcastically.

"Yes, friends Jen!" Sophie retorted. "We all have had great times together, haven't we? Don't leave it with a bad taste." Sophie met her eyes, "Please, for me!"

"Okay, Okay." Jen sighed. "I am going to book a flight as soon as possible to go back home; I don't want to give him a chance to hurt me more than he already has, I need to make a clean break from him, to get over this!" They both sipped at their wine. "I can't sit here all night, I am far too agitated," Jen got up and stood staring out the window into the night.

"Why don't we have another drink then go a walk down to the village and see what all the commotion is about?" Sophie suggested.

"That's an idea, it might take my mind off that bastard." Jen gave Sophie a sad smile.

#

The next morning Jenny was exhausted, she had tossed and turned most of the night, hardly closing her eyes, she was sure Paul had another woman back at his flat. She and Sophie had taken a walk down to the Village last night, it had been glowing with blue with the Police presence, the embankment below was illuminated with harsh white light. The public bridge usually gave a good view of the river and partially into the upper Glen, but a barricade had been set up to stop the public from viewing what was going on below; Jenny and Sophie had walked over to one of the Policemen guarding the entrance to the Glen. "Hi," Sophie had said smiling, "we were hoping this is good news and you have found the boy?" she said looking at him with big eyes.

"There is a major incident, I am afraid I can say nothing more." The Policeman answered.

"Can you not just give us a nod of your head, if the boys been found alive?" Jenny asked.

The Policeman did not nod. "Does that mean he has been found dead?" asked Jenny.

"I am afraid ladies I cannot give you any information other than, "Do not enter the Glen it is dangerous!" he said with authority. "Okay officer, sorry for bothering you!" said Sophie as they walked away. They were disappointed not to be any wiser as to what was going on. The walk and the crisp air had helped reduce the terrible anxiety Jenny had been feeling. When they both returned to Sophies, Jenny tried to call Paul, but his phone was switched off! "Rotten bastard," she said bitterly. She eventually dosed off about five a.m, only to wake two hours later immediately sending Paul a text to ask if she could go to his to collect her clothes and other bits and pieces, he had not text back, so she had decided to go up to his home as soon as she could.

#

George had called Sophie at four a.m. waking her up! "What the hell are you calling me at this time for?" Sophie said in a groggy voice.

"Sorry Sophie, but I had to tell you!"

"What?" she said sounding aggravated and half asleep.

"Paul pre-arranged to meet that girl from the Torban!" George sounded drunk and very pissed off. "There was me thinking I was being a good mate running after him, concerned he would be alone and upset." George made a pfffffft noise. "I swear I didn't know what he was going to do!"

"George, you knew it was coming. I'm not shocked, one bit! "Sophie said wearily.

"Aye I guess you are right, I should have known; but I didn't expect him to just dump me in town the minute he saw her and her mates!" George sighed.

"Come on, you know what a selfish bastard he can be!" Sophie spoke with venom.

Anyway, he went back to her place." George sighed. They both were silent for a moment.

"Will I come over? I could do with a cuddle?" George asked in his best 'needy boy' voice.

"Sorry Georgie boy, I'm working in a few hours, so No!"

"Awwwwww pleeeeease," he replied disappointed. Sophie didn't answer.

"Has your pal calmed down any?" George asked.

"No, she is worse! I don't think I have the heart to tell her about the lassie, as she was in a terrible state earlier." Sophie said.

"Better not then, we don't want her going all Bunny Boiler on him!" George snorted a laugh.

"Oh, I don't know, that has some appeal!" Sophie said with humour, they both sniggered.

"Can I come over?" George tried his luck once more. "NO!" Sophie said definitely.

"Night then sexy, message you later." George said. "Okay, night." Sophie hung up and lay in the dark, feeling sad for Jenny. George had mentioned a couple of times when they had met up that Paul had been complaining that Jenny was becoming extremely clingy, but George had asked her not to repeat it, so she hadn't. She thought, 'I wish I had said something, I could have saved Jen this heartache!'

She closed her eyes, breathing deeply, she was asleep in minutes.

#

Sophie came down for breakfast. Jenny asked, "Can I borrow your car to go up to Pauls to get my stuff?"

"For gods' sake, give me a chance to sit down with a coffee, eh Jen!" Sophie said impatiently.

"Sorry, I just want to get this sorted, my insides are churning," said Jenny, realising she hadn't even said good morning and Sophie looked tired.

"Look! I don't think you should go up on your own!" she turned looking at Jenny with a serious face. "Can you wait until tonight, after I finish work and I will take you."

Sophies expression and voice softened, "I won't come in, but I will be there for moral support if you need it." She stared at Jenny waiting for a response, there was none so she continued, "I will just wait in the car until you both talk?" Sophie thought that Jenny was either going to cause trouble or make a complete fool of herself, as her hurt was still too raw.

"No, I can't wait, I need to go up and get this over with." Jenny replied abruptly, she was jittery.

"Okay Jenny if you can't wait you can take the car, but you need to drop me at the train station, plus you must promise me, no trouble." Sophie sighed loudly.

Sophie ate her cereal before getting dressed for work. Jenny watched her, "I wish I could eat; I feel sick and can't face anything." She looked as though she was going to cry again.

"Have a Camomile Tea while I get ready for work! A cup of herbal tea will calm your nerves!" Sophie said with a soft smile. "Try and relax, okay?"

#

Sophie came down the stairs half an hour later looking pristine.

"How do you do it?" Jenny said admiringly. "No matter how much you drink the next day you can scrub up like a super model." "Awwwww thanks," Sophie said.

Jenny turned to look in the hall mirror, fixing her hair. "I can't bear the look of myself this morning, the bags under my eyes are like suitcases!"

"You do look exhausted Jenny I won't lie! That's one of the reasons why I wish you would wait until tonight to see Paul; you will look and feel a lot better!" Jenny stared at her reflection for a long minute. "You also won't appear so desperate to see him." Sophie stated. Jenny put her brush back in her bag and took her jacket off! "You know what Sophie, you are right! I will wait for you," she handed Sophie back her car keys.

"Try to rest, you need it, Jenny! No man is worth making yourself ill, be kind to yourself today." Sophie gave her a hug as she left adding, "call me if you need me okay." Jenny smiled a sad smile while nodding.

#

It had been pouring with rain all day, the sky weeping heavily from dark grey clouds, it seemed to Jenny the day was empathising with how she felt about Paul. She had slept for three hours, then surprised herself when she actually managed to enjoy a lovely long hot bath. Sophie's gloriously luxurious Bath salts smelled so divine she didn't want to get out of the water, but when she did, she felt much better, a bit stronger she thought!

'Why did I behave that way with Paul?' she asked herself, 'because you knew you'd lost him!' "You were clinging on, fool, fool, fool," she said out loud.

Jenny styled her hair and put on some make up. 'At least now, I feel able to face him! Jenny thought, 'Sophie is always right!'

#

Sophie got back home about seven, she shook the rain off her jacket as she entered the hall, hanging it on the hooks above the radiator, "what a filthy rotten day it's been! "

Looking up she exclaimed "Wow you look great Jenny," she sounded surprised.

"Thanks, I feel a lot better. You were right Sophie."

"Of course, I was, "! Sophie laughed. "Have you eaten?" Jenny shook her head no.

Sophie tutted loudly and rolled her eyes, shaking her head in disapproval.

"I'm starving." Sophie said. "I think we should have something to eat before we head up to Paul's. If you don't mind?"

"Of course not! You must be hungry with working all day." "I'm just glad that you're coming with me give me a bit of girl power." Jenny said.

"Have you told him you're going up?"

"Yes, I've sent texts, but I've not had a reply to any of them yet!"

"Why don't you take the car and run up to the Chinese Take away, pick us up something nice," Sophie suggested," I can have a quick shower and stick something on while your away."

"Good idea, what do you fancy? My treat for you being such a great friend!" Jenny said with a genuine smile.

"That's more like the Jen I know!" Sophie laughed. "Thanks, get me, Chicken balls, in Sweet and sour, with egg rice, please."

#

"I'm back!" Jenny called up the stairs as she shook the umbrella in the Porch, she came in, throwing her keys on the hall table under the mirror.

"Just coming down!" Sophie shouted from her bedroom upstairs.

Jenny emptied the food out onto plates and poured two glasses of sparkling Apple juice, which she and Sophie were particularly fond of if not drinking alcohol. She took it through and sat it on the coffee table with cutlery. "Hurry up it will get cold Sophie," Jenny called loudly, suddenly gaining an appetite with the smell of her Chow Mein.

There was a scream and a clatter from the stairway, Jenny ran through, finding Sophie at the bottom of the stairs. "Oh my god, my ankle, I think I've twisted it." Jenny helped her up, Sophie leaning on her so she could hop through to the couch. "What the hell happened?" Jenny asked.

"For the life of me I don't know. It was as though my leg went away from under me. I must be tired. I have been on my feet a lot today!" Sophie sounded fed up.

Jenny had retrieved a bag of mixed vegetables from the freezer. "Sorry no Peas, it's a bit lumpy but will do the trick," Jenny placed the cold bag in a towel and placed it around Sophies ankle which she was now resting on the edge of the Coffee table.

"There is a tray in the cupboard under the sink!" Sophie said," could you get me it and a couple of Ibuprofen, please Jen."

"A tray? The things grannies use?" Jenny laughed.

"It was my mum's, she said it would come in handy one day!" They both chuckle. "Mums are always right!" Sophie said. "I miss mine tonight," said Jenny.

Sophie sat with her food on the tray, she and Jenny chatting while they ate. "There are not so many Police on Main Street now, the Bridge barrier is gone, I got a glimpse of a big white tent though as I passed." Jenny said.

"Someone must be dead right enough, if there is a tent." Sophie said, "what a shame if it is the boy! I wonder what happened to him?"

"We will find out soon enough," Jenny added. They continued eating quietly. Sophie put her cutlery down. "I am so glad you've pulled yourself together Jen," Sophie sounded nervous, "there is something I need to tell you before we go get your stuff. I wanted to tell you this morning, but you were so upset, I just couldn't!"

"What is it?" Jen stared into Sophies face. Sophie leaned forward holding out her tray, Jenny laid it down on the table for her. "Come on, tell me then!" Jenny urged her.

"This could ruin George and Paul's friendship by telling you this, so I am asking you not to repeat it Jen, but you need to know the truth!" She took a huge breath. "Okay I'm just going to say it!" "Paul went with that girl from the restaurant last night." "George called me during the night to tell me." "Paul arranged to meet up with her when we left the Torban! He dumped George shortly after they got into Glasgow, he pretended to 'bump into' her on her girl's night out." Jenny looked stunned. "I knew it, I just knew it! I felt it all last night." Jenny was so angry her face was white, and her teeth clenched. "Did he take that bitch back to his?" Jenny asked. "No, he went to hers to stay!" Sophie stared at her friend sympathetically. There was a strained silence. "Jenny you okay?"

"Why did you not tell me this morning?" Jenny demanded.

"You didn't seem strong enough to cope with it," Sophie said, "you were a wreck!"

Jenny looked down at her hands, slowly nodding her head.

"What could you have done anyway?" Sophie said hopelessly.

"I could have smashed up his bloody cosy cottage, that's what! Burnt all his fucken designer suits!" Jenny raged.

"And end up in jail for criminal damage. I'm sure that would be a great addition to your CV!" Sophie said with sarcasm.

"I know your right Sophie, I am so damn angry, I could kill him!"

"Calm down Jen, come on don't act irrational, we are not stupid teenagers!"

"I know, I know! I just want to get this over with now! My passport and other important stuff are up there, never mind all my clothes and make up, I need to get it, I hate to think of that cheeky bitch riffling through my stuff." Jenny said urgently.

"I doubt he would be stupid enough to have her there!" Sophie stated.

"I'm sorry but I don't think I can drive now Jenny. My ankle is agony, do you think it could be broken?" Jenny looked closely at Sophies ankle.

"It is very swollen; I think you will need to rest it for a day or two until the swelling goes down!" Jen said.

"I can drive Sophie; please say you will still come up there with me? I can help you out into the car!" Jenny sounded desperate.

"Only if you promise to be cool!" Sophie looked worried.

"I promise I won't do anything crazy; I will be ice cold!" Jenny said grinning.

'I'm not so sure about that!' Sophie said and Jenny laughed.

#

Jenny had phoned Paul several times and eventually he answered, she had not mentioned that she knew who he had been with all night.

Sophie was in the passenger seat of her Old Panda outside of Paul's house, her ankle was still throbbing, despite taking two Ibuprofen and three paracetamols. 'I bet it is broken or fractured,' she thought, she put on the radio, an old song by Mimi Webb played loudly and she sang along.

"I saw you out, it was zero degrees

And you had your hands right under her sleeves

Oh, you said you don't get cold

You liar!

Now I'ma set your house on fire

Running, I'm running back to your place

With gas and a match, it'll go up in flames

Now, I know you're not at home

You liar!

Now I'ma set your house on fire."

Sophie switched it off. 'I hope she is quick!' she thought worriedly, 'maybe I need an Xray!'.

The rain was still heavy, pattering loudly like thousands of little feet on the roof of the car.

Jenny had knocked the door, despite having a key, she felt it was not appropriate to just walk in, knowing what she now knew. Paul answered the door," lost your key," he asked.

"No, I just didn't want to be rude!" Jenny quickly answered, hurrying in out the rain.

"Like you were last night?" he accused her.

"With good reason Paul, but I am not here to fight, I'm just here for my things!"

"I'm glad to hear it, I don't want to fight either."

Jenny went in the bedroom and started to throw what she had lying around in her huge hold all, Paul stood in the doorway, their eyes met. Jenny felt a familiar surge of love for Paul, she thought he looked so handsome, her eyes welled up, so she quickly looked away.

"You know Jen, I just want to say to you that I did not mean to hurt you in any way!" he paused, Jenny didn't answer.

"I truly meant it when I said I loved you, as that was how I felt at the time, I do not know what has happened to change that, but something has!" Paul looked genuinely upset.

Jenny wanted to put her arms round him and hold him close, but her pride wouldn't let her.

"It is okay Paul, I will survive!" She said devoid of any emotion. "I will be going home as soon as possible, so you won't need to worry about it!" she said with a bitter tone.

She moved close to him as she passed him in the doorway feeling their strong physical attraction, it made her weak. In the Bathroom she collected her personal toiletries and as she returned to put them in her bag Paul grabbed her hand, turning her with his other hand, he looked into her face.

"We were so hot Jen, so intense, we just burnt out too quick!" he looked at her, his eyes full of sadness.

"No Paul! You did! I didn't! I'm still aflame!" She pulled her hand out of his and continued packing then zipped up her bag!

"We had a great few months, didn't we?" he asked.

She stood looking at him, he at her, he smiled his big, beautiful smile and said, "we could be friends Jen, who knows what might happen in the future." He paused, "I could visit you in Canada!" "No way!" Jen raised her voice, her eyebrows low. She went to the front door and paused for a second or two before opening it. She turned to Paul "Oh I nearly forgot!" she held out her set of his house keys, he paused, their eyes met, they both felt the loss, he took the keys out her hand.

"I hope she was good!" she said quietly as she left.

After a moment he answered "not as good as you Jen !" but she did not hear him, as he watched her run down the path into the dark dismal night, the rain bouncing off the road, he watched her put the bag in the boot, he was still watching as she got in the car, Paul watched her as she drove away without looking back. He closed the door. "Ahhh well, another one bites the dust!" he said to his empty flat, sighing, he suddenly felt very alone.

#

Jenny jumped in the driver's seat. "Okay?" Sophie asked. "Not sure!" Jenny started the car, she drove down and around the corner out of view from Paul's home, parking next to a Café that was closed. She burst into tears, putting both hands over her face, rocking slightly.

"That was one of the hardest things I've ever done!" She said through the tears. Sophie leant over putting her arm around her friends' shoulders. Jenny sobbed into Sophies chest, after a few minutes she sat up, heaving a heavy sigh. "It was wonderful while it lasted!"

"That is the way to look at it Jen! 'Better to have loved and lost than not to have loved at all, they say," she squeezed Jen's hand. "At least I walked away with my pride." Jen said sadly.

"Let's go get some good wine!" Sophie said in a cheery tone, "we need to get drunk, so I can cope with the pain in my ankle and you with the pain in your heart!"

Jenny started the car, "yeah okay, that might help. Do you not think I should take you to A& E?" said Jenny tears still stinging her eyes as she drove down the twisty dark ill-lit country road that led to the Village. "Uck, not tonight Jenny, you need tonight to get your head together. See if the swelling gone down tomorrow."

The roads were water-logged. Sheets of running water were being blown over the surface. As they sped home the tyres threw up huge sploshes as high as the car into the Hedgerows. "Slow down Jenny what's the rush!" Sophie said in a worried tone.

Jenny pulled the car out of the side road facing the Train station, turning right slowing to go through a huge puddle that always gathers in wet weather, under the old Railway bridge into the Village. It was deep! Once through Jenny sped up as she approached the Village and the traffic lights at the Glen River bridge; She put her foot down hard on the accelerator as she saw the Amber light turn to Red.

A large dark shape flew in front of the windscreen, Jenny startled, "Whaaaaaaa," she yelled as she swerved to miss it; the car veered off to the left, then began to glide, sliding at speed to the right, aquaplaning! "I can't steer," Jenny screamed, it seemed like time had slowed, they were skating on to the other side of the road. "No!" Sophie screamed as they were hurled toward the stone bridge! Sophie was swung across to the driver's side, her head smashing into Jenny's, then catapulted back, head slamming full force into her side window.

The drivers' side completely disintegrated on impact with the wall of the Bridge, the pedals and undercarriage folded in and up, crunching metal into her flesh then bone, breaking Jenny's legs, trapping her. The dashboard creased, metal scrunching on plastic, the steering wheel shot forward with great force crushing Jenny's chest, her head had smashed through the side window, the side of her neck was slashed by a shard of glass on impact.

In Jennys' final moments of life, her last thought was of Yvonne O'Devlins' face as she said, "Joseph and John always said they felt as though the family was jinxed!"

The Panda rebounded off the bridge, the car pirouetting around as if the tarmac was a black ice rink. A Black BMW car with music thumping, came speeding around the blind corner towards the bridge, careering towards them, the driver screamed "No……." as he attempted an emergency stop, the road was drenched so he hurtled into the wreck, killing Sophie instantly. The collision had such a force on impact the BMW flew up, rolling over the top of the Panda onto the bridge where it momentarily teetered, before plummeting into the river. The driver who had opened his seat belt in the seconds after he pushed his foot on the break, in a futile attempt to escape by opening the door, was propelled through the windscreen flying through the air landing on the spiked railings at the side of the Glen. The scene was gruesome. Silence fell. One of Sophies old plastic wheel trims rolled along the road briefly then fell.

#

Jenny O'Devlin was dead! The Josie Devin curse now fulfilled, after four hundred and sixty-two years, the debt was finally paid.

The Seelie were saddened by the deaths at the bridge, but their bright auras shone as they were relieved the curse was now satisfied. Glowing they passed under the bridge in a mist, travelling over what was visible of the BMW in the river, then onward into the Glen.

The Slaugh had enjoyed the car crash immensely, eyes bright green observing from the rooftops of the tenement housing, revelling in the human suffering. Buzzing filled the air increasing in strength as they drank in the horror of the scene.

The Police who were on the scene patrolling the entrances to the Glen while Forensics were dealing with the many slain in the Tunnels, called the Emergency services; Confused they tried to detect where the deafening humming noise was coming from.

"Maybe the sewage pumps in the park," one Officer offered as an explanation!

"No, it's everywhere not just the park," the other dismissed.

The Policemen stationed at the Glen River entrance, ran to the spiked fence where the Driver of the BMW was skewered onto the railing, he checked for signs of life but sadly there were none! The arrow shaped metal at the top of the spike was imbedded deep in the man's chest. The Policeman looking at the bloody gruesome site, he felt his guts heaving, then glancing down he stood mesmerised as a strange cloud of what looked like hundreds of tiny lanterns moving as one mass, floated just above the water, passing directly below where he stood.

"What the hell?"

#

Chapter 24.

Up, Up and Away!

Tommy and the team were back down at the river six a.m. sharp, now split into two groups.

Group A: Graeme, Jimmy, Ron and Julie were wading along the waters' edge to the old shaft. They had been issued with a robotic camera on wheels to investigate the passage going into the old wall.

Group B Tommy and Dougie were making their way through the woodland heading down to where Julie and Dougie had seen the Bat colony disappear into the ground the day before.

Max and Danny were firstly to investigate the top of the Viaduct for the dead dog's camera, so they headed up the small hill that led to the top of the Viaduct, scrambling up onto the train track, they walked along the side of the tracks holding on to the safety bars. "Jeeeeez Max, look at the drop, I can feel a bout of Acrophobia coming on!" "Is that not a fear of spiders?" Max asked. "Nah, that is Arachnophobia!" Danny looked down, "I hate heights, my legs are like jelly," he gripped the safety bars tighter.

"Stop looking down then fer fucks sake! Max shouted back.

"Can you no see it yet, "Danny called out.

"I see something, just up here a wee bit!" "Got it!".

The men stood looking down on Henry the dogs' head lying in a big dirty grey puddle of water. "Damn dirty flies get everywhere," Danny said, shooing them away with his foot.

"Poor dog still has the camera strap under his jaw. Wonder what happened?" Max said.

Max contacted Mark in the camera van.

"You copy?"

"Yeah Copy," Mark acknowledged.

"We located the camera, it is still attached to the dogs' head, it's pointing down into Glen, the dog has been decapitated, the body is not here! Please advise!"

"I wasn't expecting that!" "Leave in situ for Forensics, I will update Tommy." Mark instructed.

"Copy that. Over and out!"

The men taped off the area where the head lay. "This is crazy!" Danny said as they made his way back to rendezvous with Tommy and Dougie. "What do you think ripped the dogs head off?"

"Be buggered if I know, this case and this place gives me the creeps!" Max said.

They looked up when they heard the chuf-chuf-chuf of the Police Helicopter that was patrolling the entire woodland, it passed over the Viaduct and on toward the old Army base. "It's doing circuits," Danny commented, "looking for those things Dougie saw."

"They need to be keeping an eye out in case any public get through the barriers," Max said. "Would you believe, Geoff met an old yin, just stoatin about the river yesterday."

Danny made a 'tisssk' noise through his teeth, "Aye, I heard."

#

Team A were at the location of the old shaft at the side of the river. "Tommy, do you copy?" Jimmy asked into his handset,

"Affirmative, 10-20"

"At location, deploying Robot, Mark on alert." Jimmy said.

"Copy that. Over and out."

"Place it right in the centre" Graeme instructed Ron as he helped lift the Robot on to the floor of the dark tunnel. He stopped still, "shush!" he said waving his hand at the others to be quiet. "Hear it?" They all listened intently.

Ron said quietly," somethings in there," "it is a buzz like Bees except much deeper."

Julie asked, "Do Bats buzz?"

"No" Graeme answered, "they make noises so high we cannot hear them!"

"Not Bats then!" Julie said raising her eyebrows and pursing her lips, "what the hell are they?"

"Well only one way to find out!" Jimmy said smiling.

He switched the Robot on, they watched it trundle down into the tunnel the tether slowly winding out of the reel. Ron held the screen viewing the image of the inside of the shaft.

#

Tommy and Dougie now were searching the ruins at the 'Beachy bit.' Dougie stated, "this is it; Julie saw the swarm disappear down here somewhere!" he walked around searching for an opening.

"This maybe the answer," Tommy stood next to an old square stank with a rusted metal rim and the remnants of an ancient water pump, "drops down pretty deep," Tommy said, he looked around, "over there, that's the foundations of another ancient Mill." I bet this space goes all the way under it!"

Dougie was about ten feet away, "here," he shouted, "here is another one! This place is a bloody death trap."

"Stick the Body cam down there see if it picks up anything," Tommy instructed. He found his torch and held it into the mouth of the stank, as Dougie lay down his shoulder resting on the edge, he dropped his arm down holding his Body cam, he moved it in a circular movement, then brought it back up. They viewed the footage. "Goes deep and long, look there, it goes in different directions, needs to be a specialist team," Dougie told Tommy.

"Yeah, you're right! When I studied the maps, I could patchwork them together to get a picture of the deep openings that drop into the lower chambers of the ruins, large and small tunnels run far, some will be collapsed I'm sure, hidden in the maze of what once was the Mills." Tommy stood looking down into the hole. he took a step back, Tommy raised his eyes, "Oh fuck!" he yelped, jumping back as the undergrowth moved in front of them! A squirrel bounded up into the trees!" Dougie breathed out deeply, "you nearly gave me a heart attack then!" he said then started laughing, Tommy joined in. The squirrel sat high up on a branch watching them. "Sorry, after what I saw yesterday, I'm very edgy!" Tommy said. "No wonder," Dougie empathised, "probably need some therapy after that!" They taped the area off, and headed back up to the path, they stood at the Viaduct viewpoint.

"Brilliant spot," Dougie said while admiring the view of the huge Viaduct spanning the river, the trees, a landscape of greens adorning each side of the water, reaching down to where they stood. "I bet it can be a lovely walk on a sunny day, under different circumstances, obviously!" Tommy walked on ignoring the view, his eyebrows low, his lips pressed together. He looked a troubled man.

#

A short distance up the path, there was a squelch as Dougie's foot slipped a little "ugh!" what did I just stand in?"

Tommy turned around to look. "Some kind of fleshy pulp, jelly" he said.

Dougie took a step off the path to clean his boot on the undergrowth when he noticed the large torn leg of an animal still attached to part of the mangled rear.

"Tommy look! It's part of the dog Henry." Dougie exclaimed.

"You sure? It could be a Deer." Tommy suggested.

Max and Danny shouted" Hey!" as they walked swiftly down the path to meet them, they joined in their appraisal of the lump of dead flesh.

"Nah, it's the dog! Look there is a paw!" Max pointed out.

"That is definitely the dog Henry!" Danny spoke with certainty.

"So, we have the head up there, camera still attached and part of the rear with a leg down here! What the hell happened to the rest of him?" Max quizzed.

"This is getting stranger and stranger," commented Danny, "I don't like it."

They all looked up as the Helicopter approached this side of the woodland again.

#

Back at the shaft opening at the River, Graeme watched the screen updating the others, "the camera's not showing up anything suspicious so far guys!"

Ron and Julie peered in the entrance, checking the cables progress as the robot descended into the blackness of the narrow tunnel.

"That hum is definitely getting louder," Ron put his ear right in the entrance.

Julie agreed, "yep I can hear it getting much stronger now, I hope we haven't disturbed a huge wasps' nest!" she grimaced at Ron.

"Hey, what's that, "Graeme pointed to the screen, Ron and Jimmy sprung over to see.

"Too blurry, but it could be a cluster of Rats, "Jimmy suggested."

"Whatever it is, their alive and moving!" Ron stated. The screen went black, "Something is blocking the camera!"

Graeme shouted to Julie, "reel it back in!"

"Woah, what the fuck!" Graeme jumped, then stared in disbelief as a face appeared, squashed right up against the screen. Julie pressed the automatic reverse pull, but nothing happened, the reel started to tremor, as if it was being pulled into the shaft.

"It suddenly became slack, it's not pulling back!" shouted Julie panicking, she stuck her head in the tunnel, crawling in the tight space for about fifteen feet, pulling at the cable, the men stepped over to help. In seconds the buzz was thundering in the shaft, Julie tried to push her torso back, slithering in reverse, retreating out quickly. In the second that she looked ahead, the robot camera came hurtling towards her, backed by a horde of travelling beings, it was propelled at great force into her face, breaking her nose with a sickening scrunching thump! All her front teeth smashed, she was slammed backwards, fired out of the opening, the metal casing of the camera lens imbedded in her cheek; she whacked into Jimmy on her exit, he was flung down into the river fracturing his pelvis as he smashed awkwardly on a large rock.

Julie was lifted by the writhing mass of Slaugh, her legs kicking out at the air as she rose, up and up, she made a blood-curdling shriek as she ascended. She was thrown from a great height screaming all the way down until she hit the huge stone base of the Viaduct and bounced onto the ground.

Graeme curled up in a low squat, arms around his head, his face tucked down, trembling, warm urine soaked his trousers and his legs.

Ron had flattened his back onto the wall at the left of the opening, helplessly watching as the Host flew out and up through the trees, a legion of black figures amongst thousands of beating wings.

#

The Police Helicopter was flying at about five hundred feet at ninety miles per hour and had completed another circuit, now heading back over the Village; over the scene of last nights' car accident, where a crane was fishing the BMW wreck from the river.

The Helicopter approached the Lower Mill area.

The legion of Slaugh rose out of the trees at a ferocious speed colliding with the Helicopter from the front and the underneath! Two of the Slaugh slammed through the windshield without warning, their bodies hitting the pilot in the face, destroying his nose and jaw; Some of his teeth were knocked into his throat, he couldn't immediately breathe his mouth full of blood. His face was covered in lacerations punctured by shards of glass! He struggled to keep control as the right-hand engine failed, but he couldn't see. The accompanying Pilot pulled at the controls trying to assist, the Helicopter slowed, then became silent, as the damage created by the Slaugh shut off fuel to both the aircraft's engines, sending it spiralling, smashing full force into one of the Viaducts' huge stone columns, breaking up on impact. Both the Pilots blown to pieces. A mighty spectacular fiery explosion followed immediately, launching pieces of aircraft into the woodland and the Glen River.

Ron was still adhered to the wall by his own terror, he watched the scene unfold eyes wide his mouth open; he watched as a piece of metal shrapnel had hit Graeme as he was lying in the shallow edge of the river unconscious." Graeme, Graeme!" Ron shouted, he wanted to help him, but he was frozen in fear, he could not move from the safety of his wall.

#

Minutes before, Max, Danny, Tommy and Dougie had been walking back up the lower pathway, after taping and securing the Dogs remains for forensics to examine. They made their way under the archway of the Viaduct when they heard the helicopter getting close, just as screaming came from below, the men all ran forward, climbing the wooden fencing to access the steep embankment leading down to the other team, they all looked up as an intense deep buzzing filled the air. "Come on! "Danny shouted back to the others, bounding ahead toward where the screams came from under the Viaduct. All now running as fast as they could over the difficult terrain! The sky was filled with a black moving cloud of beings.

Danny suddenly stopped in horror to see the approaching Helicopter, he turned to the others further behind him. "Get down, it's going to hit!" he yelled out. In the next second, an explosion from the Viaduct lit up the air in front of Danny; nearest, he was engulfed in the flame, he died immediately from the force as it pulverised his major organs, suffering traumatic brain injury, before the wave of intense heat even hit him.

Max was seconds behind Danny, he lay screaming his hands over his face severely burned. The inside of his mouth and nose had closed due to airway burns. He lay in a few seconds of excruciating agony as he struggled to breathe, dying from asphyxiation.

Tommy and Dougie dropped to the ground, hands and arms protecting their head.

Shrapnel from the explosion flew through the air, a large shard of metal was fired towards Tommy as he crawled on his belly away from the crash puncturing his lung through his back. Tommy was floored; After the initial panic and realisation something had hit him hard, he calmed down, he moved his arm from his side, up round his waist, feeling the piece of metal in his back. "Shit, it's bad," he whispered to himself, a warm liquid was on his fingers, running down his side, "blood." The pain started to sink in.

"Oh god help me," he panted. "I need to move," he told himself, struggling to mobilise while experiencing a feeling like being poked a thousand times with needles in his legs. His breath now harder and harder to find, pain burned in his lungs, each breath was getting shorter and shorter, quicker and quicker. Tommy was trembling he was bleeding out for what felt like forever, in reality only a few minutes. He couldn't pull himself any further. "I can't hear," unable to move his head, he thought, "it's just like when you go underwater."

Tommy began to pray in his head," God I know I've not been the best, never gone in a church, been unfaithful so many times, so much I am sorry for. God, if your there please don't let me die, I will do better, I promise!" his eyes were open, but the vision was getting darker, a black circle just closing in, he could just see a small light in the middle. "This is it I'm dying," now a ringing noise in his mind. Tommys' pain eased, a peaceful like quietness came over him like a warm blanket, he wanted to close his eyes and sleep.

At that point a blurry image of an elderly woman was lying next to him invading his thoughts, pushing her way in, her green eyes shone out at him through the darkness. She said forcefully, "open your eyes Tommy or you will die!" "You are a good man, think of your family, how they will miss you, what their life will be like when they hear of your death." Open your eyes you need to fight it!" Tommy thought about his life, struggling to find the strength to force his eyes open, to see the woman surrounded by a glow. "Are you god?" he asked the woman. He hears a familiar voice, Dougie is next to him, "Tommy, Tommy, you're alive, thank god mate!" He starts to cry out loud, heaving with emotion, "I'm injured, got hit by a lot of small stuff, flying debris but I'm okay, we are alive!" He is in pain but has managed to crawl over next to Tommy, lying next to him he says loudly. "I can hear the sirens mate, their coming, hold on, it won't be long." "Stay with me Tommy." Dougie squeezes Tommy's hand and he squeezes his back.

The Villagers froze to the spot with the sound of the explosion, it rattled the windows of nearby shops and housing, people for miles stopped what they were doing, watching the plumes of black smoke coming from the Glen. The emergency services screamed through the streets from every direction to those locally it seemed their world was coming to an end.

For the Seelie it felt that way too, the bombardment of negative energy had culminated in an intense need for the Seelie to escape the Glen. They expressed their hope to one another that their evacuation would be temporary, reluctantly moving on in a cloud. Their glow now pale and dulled, floating slowly down the river, from a distance they looked like a haze of thick mist.

They went in the direction of the woodland some miles away that soon would be their temporary home.

The Host had travelled underground through their labyrinth, buzzing loudly, shrieking with anger. They had revelled in the pandemonium although they knew that man would try and seek them out as they had many times before through the centuries. It was time to find another hunting ground, but they loathed to leave. They flew to the Sanctum but the Guardian nor the Seelie were there! The Host buzzed furiously around, radiating hate. They felt they had been abandoned; a collective loneliness touched every one of them. Fynn was bereft and after the other Slaugh left, he sat for a few moments, his head in his hands, his wings pulled closely round him in a hug. He stood up, touching the circle of stones one by one, he had known them his entire existence. In that moment Fynn felt sad and confused about the Slaughs' role in the Universe. He had hoped to see the Guardian once more, for he did not know of the Hosts' destination, he put his hand on the silver bead around his neck, for the first time in his existence he wanted to change what he was. Stretching out his wings fully, he stood for a moment absorbing the sights and sounds of his home, then shot into the sky.

Forensic pathologists examined the bodies found at the Glen crime scenes; They had worked extremely hard, performing autopsies, practically 'back-to-back,' to determine quickly the cause of death of the sixty-eight people whos' remains were found in the large tunnel, among those of human remains were also dogs, cats and deer. Since the day of the explosion, there had been extensive exploration of the foundations of the older Mill sites, hundreds historic human remains had been discovered, some they believed, had been there hundreds of years.

The park and woodland had been closed to the public indefinitely all entrances fenced and chained by the local council, huge red signs screaming, DANGER OF DEATH, NO ENTRY, underneath in smaller print, PROSECUTION IF BREECHED were at every possible access point.

Five of the bodies were able to be identified, Alec Baldy, Edward Baldy, Jamie Callaghan were identified within days. The remains of Anthony Lewis a local man that was homeless in 2020 and had disappeared during Covid restrictions, plus the remains of a known drug dealer from Castlemilk, Stewart James, whom had been reported missing by his family in 2018, were identified from using DNA technology and local missing persons files; But to identify the majority of the historic remains would take months even years of work with genetic genealogists. The most recent bodies had revealed the persons had died in different ways, but all had one gruesome common denominator, the fact that they had been partially eaten, their flesh bitten or torn from their bones, but as yet, they had no idea by what?

The Bats conservation Trust had been on site researching all the Glen Mills openings, where the large Bats had been reported. For eight days they had found nothing. Sharon Fulton Head of her department spoke to Head of Operations Colin Edmands.

"I have no news for you Colin, I cannot find any evidence of a new species of Bat, there is however overwhelming substantiation of another type of small mammal, but not Bat. We know it is a carnivore due to the droppings, which were in mass, underground in a maze of tunnels, which could be so extensive we did not have the manpower or equipment to search further."

"So, what is this animal then?" Colin asked. "I'm afraid I cannot say as we specialise in Bats and only Bats. I can tell you I have not seen anything quite like the environment it has created for itself except in Ants and Humans. The difference is this being walks on two legs and flies".

Colin was silent. Sharon continued, "I think you need to call in the Mammal Identification - Field Studies Council."

"I know it's a big ask," Colin said, "but can you send over all the information you have in some semblance of a report in the next 24 hours? "

"No problem Colin, I will send over what I've put together, but it won't be perfect in that timescale." "Who do we need to contact Sharon?" Colin asked. "I will get the address and contact details over A.S.A.P." Sharon said.

"No worries, we are grateful for your research, thank you, to you and your team for all your hard work." After the call ended, Colin sat wondering to himself "What the hell is it that has been down there?"

#

Lesley Ormonde was the daughter of the medical examiner who decided cause of death in the Joseph O'Devlin suspicious death investigation in 2002. She had followed in her fathers' profession in becoming a Pathologist. She had watched all the news on the Glen murders, of the boy Jamie Callaghan and the two brothers, the Bakers, but she had also heard through the professional grapevine that there were over sixty sets of remains or more, but this would not to be released by the authorities to the public, or the press.

Her father had died some years previously from Bowel cancer, she had spent the last six weeks of his life at his bedside; Lesley recalled a conversation she had with him before he had deteriorated, he was still coherent and 'compos-mentis.'

"I have only one regret Lesley and I hope you never make the same mistake!" her dad revealed.

"Well, I don't know if I will Dad, unless you tell me what it is!" she smiled.

"I made a selfish choice, making a professional mistake, which I can't forget. I wanted to retire with an unquestioned record."

"I'm sure it can't be that bad, you are the most honest and respected person I have ever met in my life Dad."

"You my dear, are bias!" he smiled but his eyes were sad.

"I had never made any errors of judgement before or after I can assure you in my professional life, but I can't shake the feeling that I've caused great harm by this one lie." He wrung his old hands, marked with age spots and lumpy with arthritis.

"Well, tell me what it is and let's see if there is anything we can do to make it right!" Lesley had said reassuringly.

Her father momentarily put his head back on his chairs rest and took a deep breath, he spoke quietly. "There was a man and his dog who had been found dead at the bottom of a cliff, his name was Joseph O'Devlin. I certified he had died from a fall that had brought on a heart attack, but I lied on the certificate. He died from a multitude of injuries, consistent with being dragged at speed! Marked and deep abrasions of the back, the buttocks, the lateral surface of both ankles and on the ulnar surface of the left forearm. He had suffered a heart attack, in my opinion brought on by fear. Next was where my honesty faltered, he had many injuries including strange bites! Bites similar to a large Piranha fish or even small type of Shark, on his face! His nose was missing, in my opinion bitten off while he was alive."

"Piranha fish, Shark," she laughed, "how could that be? Were you sure Dad?"

"Well, it looked like that, but the bites were different in size and the rows of teeth. I couldn't explain it as he was found in Woodland, not in water!" He paused taking another deep breath. "I recorded the bites were consistent with Rats or other woodland scavengers, after death."

"Why Dad?" Lesley asked.

"Well! You yourself doubted me, questioned me, 'how could that be?' and "if I was sure!"

"I did not want any complexities, or worse, make a fool of myself by making wild claims just before I retired."

He had sighed, flopping back down heavily in his comfy chair and closing his eyes."

Lesley couldn't remember her response.

'It was a wild claim at the time!' She thought, 'but now, with all that is going on in the Glen and the rumours of specialist wildlife teams being brought in due to the undisclosed cause of death of those found, she decided to contact her superiors with the information she had, despite the fact that her father's good name could be stained.'

#

The Bowling club was quiet, only a few locals were in. Tracey Roberts was drinking with her sister Jean and her most recent conquest, Steph McGuire.

"Canny believe this wee place gonni shut!" Jean said sadly.

"Ano, it's a gutter, but look at it! It's deed maste of the time!" Tracey said.

Steph looked over at Pete wiping tables, "Aye my big mate, be outa a job."

"Poor guy be in the gym aww day everyday then!" the lassies snigger.

"He'll be the size oh a hoose!" Steph laughs.

Pete looks up and Steph nods his way and smiles.

"No way! Look at this Tracey," Steph showed her his SP (Screen-phone) holding out his lower outside arm to which it is semi permanently adhered. There was a media post from the page 'Unexplained' an established online magazine with a huge following, the names of the sites on which the post was available were rotating around the top of the screen.

"It's everywhere!"

"What the hell is that?" the women stared intently at the photo.

"It is an Alien!" "I knew it! I told you all didn't I?" Tracey said triumphantly! "Told you!" She read the media post aloud:

"The source who has verified his identity to the publisher, but who wishes to remain anonymous at this time, was part of the services attending the Glen site shortly after the Helicopter accident. The site is renowned for the murders of the brothers Alec and Eddy Baldy and the nine-year-old boy Jamie Callaghan, plus the recent Helicopter accidents where there were many fatalities. The source has claimed he saw strange lights, heard animal like screams and a frequent low tone buzz while he was stationed there. On one occasion our source went to look in the woodland he found this Alien creature, the body was lying in the dense undergrowth, he retrieved the remains. He presumed the Alien had died at the scene of the Helicopter accident. He told our reporter that he kept the body in his freezer as he shockingly, revealed the authorities knew of these creatures but were hiding the information from the public. He did not trust the authorities, he feared taking the body to them in case they disposed of it then denied its' existence.

 In an interesting corroboration of this man's story, it has been claimed a well-respected Pathologist has also made a statement insisting that that there are more fatalities found in the Glen than stated by the coroners' office. The Pathologist also claims that the authorities refuse to exhume a body which is said to have this creatures DNA bitten into its flesh, as the person died from injuries inflicted by the Alien.

Yvonne O'Devlin, a woman local to the Glen woodland stated. "My husband, his brother and his daughter and my dog were all murdered by whatever is in that Glen. The authorities hide and cover up what has been going on in there for decades!

Unexplained asked the Scottish Fatalities Investigation Unit. The coroners' office and The Scottish Police Authority for a statement on the claims, or to confirm or deny our information, but all those contacted refused to respond to our questions."

#

The photograph is of a humanoid, laid out on a white sheet, one arm is badly disfigured part of the stomach is exposed and it is missing a leg, it is about 18 centimetres in height. A downy fur covers its body, the 'thing' has a muscular torso and female breasts, the fur is heavy around the genitals keeping them private. The wings are not feathery, more reminiscent of a bat black and shiny, they are torn and broken. The creature's mouth is hanging open, its' jaw looked dislocated, but it was the inside of its' mouth that was frightening, rows of small yellow razor like teeth!

"Eh! Pete Muirhead come over and have a look at this!" Tracey shouted over to the barman, "think they have found the Aliens that are in the Glen." "You know the ones you told me I was imagining!" she sneered.

Pete shook his head as he walked over, smirking, he looked down at the image.

"Awwwwww, come on, that is not an Alien Tracey, for fucks sake!" he laughed," it is fake."

"Looks real to me mate!" said Steph. "And me!" Jean piped up.

"You lot are mental, honestly you can see it is fake a mile off, looks like a doll." Pete laughed loudly. "A Vampire doll, that's what it looks like!"

The media post had hundreds of thousands of comments, the majority accusing the photo of being fake. There are hundreds of laughing emojis moving up the post as others online respond. Steph said, "looks like most agree with you Pete!"

"That's right, you back your mate up!" said Jean folding her arms, lips pursed.

"Ooooooooo, trouble in paradise" Pete quipped,

"I can see your first barny on the horizon!" he said to Steph as he walked back behind the bar grinning.

#

Chapter 25.

Home is where the heart is! 2052

The Seelie had returned to the Sanctum, they sat buzzing among themselves all a glow, awaiting the arrival of the Guardian. It had been twenty years since they had been back in their true home. They sat under the bright blue sky with slowly drifting 'Candy floss' clouds; content together, speaking happily through thought. The leaves on the trees flickered with a bright lime green light as the sun twinkled through them and around the circle of stones. The Seelie emanated overwhelming joy to have returned.

The sun slowly receded into a peach and red sky, eventually dulling into night. An apparition appeared, a grey shadow, slowly solidifying within the tree seat of old. The spirit hummed, " ummmmm, ommmm, ummmmm, ommmm," the Seelie began to hum, together they lit up the huge circular plate of warm glowing light that lies beneath the stones. The Guardian now in high definition sat on her throne of wood, her aura, beautiful rays of colour emanating from around her head. Telepathically they transferred their true thought, no emotion withheld. Just before daybreak the Guardian spoke to them with difficult thoughts. The Seelie's' glow began to become pale as they absorbed the negative energy.

"The Host cannot be trusted; they will hunt the humans if they return to the Glen! Their appetite only attracts threat from the human population, putting the Seelie and the Glen at risk once more." The Seelie buzzed back; they radiated the group thought. "It is not for we Seelie to decide who or what resides in the Glen or what they eat it is the natural universal power."

The Guardian sent the thought, "If this is the natural way, I want freedom from this existence. I wish to move on from any negative energy brought by the Slaugh, I cannot endure the suffering of the humans, especially the innocent young!"

"I ask you to release me from my responsibilities here in the Glen."

The Seelie Fairies hummed in a high pitch of amusement.

They replied, "We do not hold you here!" "We enjoy the love you have shown us, we love you in return. Your pure aura brightens our existence;" "But it is you that commanded your energy to remain here to warn others of the Host." "Guardians offer themselves." The Seelie all hummed in agreement. "You 'chose' the Glen when you walked the earth as a human!"

"You are free to leave whenever you choose!" The Seelie floated near the Guardian sharing their glow.

From behind a tree in the outer circle Fynn of the Slaugh stepped out, he opened his mouth, expressing his anger in a high-pitched raw cry, he spoke to the Guardian through thought. "Why do you hate us? When you were flesh you were my equal; You fed me the meat from other beings that had suffered and died!" he paused for a reaction, there was none.

Fynn sent louder thoughts; "The Host must hunt to survive!" "Hunting humans, just as we hunt other flesh! As humans kill other mammals." He looked around all the Seelie then faced the Guardian. "Does the Deer, the Bird or the Hog have no brain, no feeling, no children, no inner energy as humans do?" The Seelie all gave positive thought to him as he continued.

"Why do you feel such sadness for only humans when all others are flesh too?" Fynn asked the Guardian. "Why try to protect only humans from suffering, do we all not deserve your pity?" he looked directly in her eyes seeking an answer. "All around you beings cry out in pain, their offspring dragged screaming from them at birth, billions suffer at the hands of humans, then devoured! Where is your shield for them?" Fynn demanded.

The Guardian's aura changed colour as he spoke, dulling to ice blues as she sadly considered his true sentiments. "We the Host are of ancient times before the hairless hog-man existed, we slayed the gigantic beings of the old worlds; The woodlands are ours; humans are the trespassers?"

The Seelie buzzed with contemplative thought, then gave positive affirmation to Fynn in unison at his truth.

"What you say is true Fynn" the Guardian responded, "except that the Host do not devour all the flesh of the humans they kill, they kill for sport only eating in part, then killing another, you enjoy killing the young most of all as they are easy prey!" The Slaugh and Seelie thought on this, knowing this was also true. "Once my coat was human flesh thus am bias in my sympathies; I accept this flaw, I am now proven no longer pure in judgement. I accept the

Slaughs' actions as partly their natural instinct!" The Guardians thoughts became powerful as she sent her message to them all, "Know this, my natural impulse is to protect those I feel are pure of heart, regardless of species. I will not desist!" "I love you all as I love this Glen!" the Guardians aura became overwhelming, intense with pure love, the Seelie connected with her glow. Fynn braced himself for the strong vibration of their pulsating aura, he approached the Guardian flying up in front of her face, putting out his hand as if to touch her, both joined in rich fondness and warmth. "We are not so different you and I," the Guardian said softly.

Fynn repeated aloud, "We are not so different you and I." This time he understood what the words meant. The Guardians face momentarily became Almas' human face and she smiled at him; he smiled back.

The Seelie moved slowly circling her, floating beautifully around her, speeding up into a swirl of glowing warm energy, a high-pitched hum emitted from them as they twirled. Whirling around her in a blur of light, within the stone circle, they rose up into the sky and when they flew away into their old home the Glen, Alma the Guardian of the Glen was gone.

Chapter 26.

Flying High 2080

The Seelie watch as the children climb the fence, holding their boards under their arms. "Disregarding danger once more to trespass on our land," The Seelie say collectively. Beautiful as always, they sit like flowing flowers in the wind, their luminescent beings, a soft lemon glow. "Why do they never learn?" The Faeries all discuss among themselves.

"We could warn them," one of the oldest Seelie suggested.

"No! Our beauty attracts them, more would come." they answered.

"The Guardian warned many," one other added.

"To no avail," the majority replied.

"Many lifetimes waiting for their so-called wise men to leave the Glen before we returned."

"What now?" they all ask each other. They buzz disapprovingly.

"The humans knew of the Slaugh that is why they have stayed away for so long!"

"So why do the return now?" they all ask each other, trying to understand the human thinking, but they cannot. One Faerie suggests an answer. "Human life moves quickly for them; they have simply forgotten the Host. The new generation has erased them from their memory, which is why they now return!" The Seelie all buzz in confirmation of her thought. "But if the Slaugh attack again, what then?" They quiz. "The Seelie of the Glen have enjoyed lifetimes of peace. Now we should make ready to protect ourselves from any negative energy brought by the Slaugh's actions once more."

"We must be grateful to our universal energy," they all gave this strong thought, all hum together glowing brightly radiating positive energy between themselves. The Seelie glow brighter and brighter as each other's love touches them individually.

"The Host have chosen to return to the Glen they are fewer in numbers now as many have made their home in other woodland Host families, but enough are here now to hunt larger prey."

"We must not interfere" the elder's buzz.

"We must, we must try," many Seelie chorus.

"No," the elders speak with authority. "Do you interfere when the Owl takes the Rat?"

"Look at them, they are young, pure, their aura is still bright," many Faeries cry out as they watch the children move past the huge gates.

"Does the Calf not have a glowing aura as it is led to the slaughter?" the elders push the thought defiantly. "No, we Seelie must not interfere!"

That was the final thought of the Seelie court as they all moved off through the woodland buzzing gently making their way to their high treetop home.

#

Seemo looks up at the huge sign, which is now worn and faded, DANGER, RISK OF DEATH. NO ENTRY, feeling exhilarated by what he read, he scrambles over the fence, fired up with the thrill of the risk.

Juno laid flat on her front, squeezing herself under the tiny space at the bottom of the thick metal fencing, she pulls her slender body through, slithering like a snake, feeling the gravel ground rub her skin through her protective suit. Once in, she stood up, wiping the dirt from her clothes, she sized up her surroundings. "Wow, it's like a jungle, no path!"

Seemo answered, "that's why we bring hovys!" He smiles a huge cheeky smile.

They position themselves on their hover pads, fitting their feet into the grips. Juno is a slim eleven-year-old with long dyed purple hair, she looks at her brother Seemo with his shaved head covered in fierce tattoos, he is a savage sight at only ten years old.

"Ready?" Seemo asks.

"Yeah," "You no scared?" Juno asks.

"Na!" "But if I'm in trouble, don't leave me! "Her brother says, pulling a worried grimace.

"I would never leave you Seemo!" she said sincerely. "We should leave a message on the Home screen," Juno said pausing, she adds "in case of any danger!"

"Na, then the olds gonna stress," "stop flippin out!" Seemo says forcefully.

Juno recalls what her olds told them, time and time again, "No go this area!" "Never go in the Glen!" An image flashed in her mind, her Olds faces looking worried. She starts to doubt their plan but shakes the thoughts out her head.

"Just go!" she calls to Seemo. They both laugh loudly with excitement and fear.

"Authorities here twenty-five years looking for Aliens but found zero! It is safe!" Juno reassures Seemo and herself. 'Olds just being overly anxious about Glen.' She thinks but her heart pounding in her chest loudly. she takes a deep breath.

Seemo shouts, "Race ya!"

Switching on their boards, they begin to rise up. "Ready?" Juno asks.

"Yeah," Seemo wobbled but steadies himself, they press the remotes on their thumb, 'whooooooooom' the Hoverboards took off at speed. Juno and Seemo whooped with delight as they flew over the long grass, it bends under them as they pass over, weaving their way through the dense woodland then down under the Viaduct archway.

"Waoweeeeeee, look at that!" Juno shouted impressed by the grandeur of the massive stone structure that is an old Railway Viaduct unused for decades since the introduction of

Sky-Rail. "Ya zoomin!" Seemo yelled, as he flew around, ahead of Juno.

"A getcha!" she laughed chasing him, her hair a streak of purple through the green surroundings.

Juno shouts "look a Deer!" The young Doe startled, bounded high and long, away from them into the trees. The siblings slowed over the old ruins.

"Old Mills, remember, Olds told us!" Juno said loudly, they both looked down on the remains of walls, now cloaked in green, with trees forcing themselves up through every available crack, she felt her heart quicken as a feeling of unease washed over her.

"The river." Seemo called out, pointing. He took off, Juno in pursuit. "Woooo hoooo." he

hollered. They raced side by side over the surface of the water, waves pushing to the shore.

Seemo bent his board over to the side, turning, hitting the water with a 'woosh' of energy, it

rose up in a huge splash over his sister. Juno screamed as the cold water hit her, laughing she

tried to replicate the move, her hover board immediately cut out as it hit the surface, she

landed in the river with a mighty splosh. "Help me!" Juno called out as she struggled to get

out of the foot grips, trying to stay above the water "No, I don't want to get wet," Seemo said from the water's edge. "Please Seemo, help me!" Juno begs. Seemo is laughing from the edge, not realising his sister is serious. "Seemo!" Juno shouts angrily. "Yeah, yeah okay!" He releases his feet from his board and steps into the river. "Not that deep!" "Oooooooo" he shivers, "but cold!" He said while wading through the shallow waters. "I told you to wear protection suit!" Juno said. He releases Junos' feet from her board dragging it to the shore, laying it down on the stones. Squatting beside it Seemo tips the Hoverboard up, draining any water out of the system as his sister makes her way out the river, shaking the water from her Evadri body pull on. "What happen to it?" Juno asked. "Too much water in the air pump I think."

"I will try heat it, dry the system out!" Juno slips her feet back in the grips and tries to start the hoverboard, it makes a grumbling noise, starts, then cuts out, she starts it again this time is on loudly, but once again cuts out. She huffs with frustration. "This time," Juno said positively.

Seemo looks up, he is frozen in a stare. There, sitting on a rock amongst broken branches, only a metre from him, is a small dark female figure, 'she looks very dirty, only her face is clearly visible, he blinks, then stares intently not believing his own vision.

"What?" Juno asks as she realises, he is staring behind her; she turns around and is stunned in disbelief! A few seconds of silence pass as the two youngsters stare at the creature.

"Yo," Juno lifts her hand in a wave and smiles.

"Yo," the tiny girl says, then spreads her shiny black wings out behind her.

Seemo and Juno stare, then giggle loudly. "It's a Faerie!" exclaimed Seemo, he lifts his hand, smiling broadly. "Yo," he says jovially.

"Yo," another voice much deeper replies. A young male now appears on the opposite riverbank just behind the girl, he is more robust, he grins, his mouth opening wider than the colour of his lips, showing hideous teeth.

Shocked at the sight, the two siblings no longer good humoured, were unsure of whether to run or stand their ground.

"You Faeries?" Juno asks. The creatures just stare.

"You Alien?" Seemo asks. The Slaugh points at him and repeats, "You Alien?"

"Na, human!" Juno states. "Na, human!" the tiny girl says straight faced.

367

"Stop!" Juno says frowning.

"Stop!" the man repeats, his eyebrows heavy, glaring, emitting fury from every pore.

"Zoom," Juno whispers to her brother, sensing the menace, they begin to move, their eyes never leaving the small beings.

Seemo presses the 'A.I.' on his outer arm, a tracker all humans have surgically implanted at birth, a red dot appears on his skin flashing, a signal to authorities that he is in extreme danger. He looks up, there are now many small creatures, there is a buzz in the air as they rise.

Juno has her feet in the grips of her board. In her panic she is frantically pressing her thumb over and over, turning her board on, off, on, off! Seemo is rising on his board.

"Zoom Juno, zoom" he screams, stretching out his hand for her to grasp, she throws her hand out to his, she touches his fingers briefly, Seemo tries to grasp them, but the Slaugh descend upon her breaking their connection. "GO!" Juno shrieks at her brother, she is locked into her board by her grips, she reaches down to try to unlock them, she can't, her arms are flailing against the Slaugh as she is besieged, feeling stinging, burning pain as the beasts relentlessly bite her, tearing through her suit at her flesh in a host of writhing blackness. Purple hair flashes in the swarm of movement, as Juno writhes in agony within the mass of viciousness.

Seemo, hovers, eyes wide, heart thumping, his throat tight, he has travelled higher up near the Viaduct gaping down on the gory assault on his beloved sister, he sobs, huge tears running down his face, he pushes his thumb, terrified he wants to flee, his board takes off at velocity.

Juno is groaning exhausted, she tries to thrash out at her attackers to no avail, blood now dripping from her face and head, she finally surrenders accepting her fate, as her eyeball is clawed out. Seemo hears his sister scream, then she bawled, "Seeeeeeemooooooooooo!" He is moving with speed through the woodland.

Juno howls a terrifying noise, cut short as her throat is torn out. A pumping fountain of blood gushes from her Arteries. Dead! She drops backward bending at the knees, her entire body soaked in blood, feet still attached to the board, the back of her head hits the ground with a thud, huge clumps of flesh are torn from her limbs, ripped from her torso, with sickening tearing, squelching noises, the Slaugh flying off with their trophies, others sitting devouring bits of her flesh where she lay. Her mane of purple hair fanned out on the gravel sand.

When Seemo reached the huge, rusted gates with the chained fencing in front, he began to loudly bellow with grief. Authority drones flew over him at speed into the Glen, one hovered above him as he unclipped himself from his board; He hung on the bars of the gates sobbing, eventually pulling his trembling body over and out of the gory Glen.

A voice came from the drone asking, "Seemo Pincha 121?"

"Yeah," he answers, his loud wailing subsiding into shuddering, he rocks back and forth as he hugs himself, "location of Juno Pincha 122?"

"In there," he points to the Glen woodland, "Aliens eat her."

"Authorities and Old keepers will arrive at your location in three minutes."

"Be calm, breath in now, 1,2,3,4, hold; out 1,2,3,4,5, "the voice recited as Juno followed the instructions, momentarily gulping breaths, shaking.

The drone stayed above him until the services and his Olds arrived.

#

Chapter 27.

The Men in White suits

Seemo watched the familiar face of the Virtual Authorities representative on the Home-screen in the recreation room, "Important Authorities announcement," he stared out from the screen with his perfect eyes, immaculate hair, the pretence of seriousness programmed into his expression; He continued speaking in the perfect A.I. voice:

"All communities within 4km area of the Glen woodland, EastRenLanark, have been alerted they are to be evacuated to a safe zone for twenty-eight days, unless they can be homed with safe area Community, Keepers or Olds. All Pets to be given to Authorities with ID. All valuables and clothing needed to be taken with evacuees."

The presenter paused changing the tone of speech.

"Warning! This is an order from our Authorities." "All who are contacted have seven days to organise, three days to alert authorities of their intent."

A virtual map appeared at his right; he outlined the area affected with a moving red dot.

"All who are not evacuated but are adjacent to the zone, must keep all windows and doors closed from six a.m. on the 1st of September 2080; their Pets must be kept in the home for forty-eight hours.

It will be compulsory to wear your Oxygenated face mask when outdoors for seven days."

An area map appeared, the presenter again directs by pointing out the red marked roads, he continues; "There will be no Move-ways or Sky-train around the Glen area."

"Authorities recommend all affected by this action plan find alternative routes."

"Authorities strongly state, Security forces will patrol zones closed to community, this is to protect lives." "Looters will be electrocuted!" The image faded and the instructions were repeated in a vibrant list.

Seemo lay still, a flash of his sister's face invades his thoughts, as tears roll silently down his cheeks. Seemo's Olds came in from the outdoor space, "do you want tea?" his Momo asks, he shakes his head in a 'No.' His Momo2 ignores him, not looking in his direction as she walks past, she has not looked at him since Juno was killed.

#

It was a cold dawn, the woodland of the Glen was eerily quiet, the mist lay low in the trees, when the men in white suits arrived in their large grey vehicles; Exiting in an organised manner, they took position. They wore tanks on their backs, full head coverings with visors and breathing apparatus, their white protective suits covered them from head to toe.

The Seelie with the gift of foresight into the immediate future were already leaving, once more reluctantly travelling as far away, as quickly as they could go. They had advised the Slaugh of their precognition, but most were defiant that they would not leave their hunting ground again for the hairless hogs.

A base of Tetramethylenedisulfotetramine mix with TTX, Botulism and water created a thick mist type spray that was the weapon of choice that the authorities had decided on to annihilate the plague of creatures. They wanted to make sure that they never return.

Historic records had shown other chemicals had been used previously by authorities, but now they acknowledged that they had only been successful temporarily. The chemicals were poisons to humans, deadly but the public safety measures were adequate if adhered to!

There were two groups of men, one group on each side of the river ready to deliver their noxious bestowal.

The group that entered the Glen positioned themselves in a line, a measured space between each of them. Like ghosts emerging from the morning mist, the men puffed out large clouds of a white powdery smog as they synchronised walking together with intent through the thick foliage and into the trees around them. They made their way down through the Glen leaving a thick fog in their wake. Soon rustling sounds could be heard accompanied by low 'thump, thump, thump' noises of birds and squirrels falling to the ground dead or dying, squeaks and squeals of pain wrang out of the sky and the woods, a symphony of death filled the Boscage.

There was an overwhelming clamorous rushing of wildlife, all moving in panic through the woodlands in the realisation that death had come their way. Deer bounded through the Glen trying to escape, a few already succumbing to the toxin stood in temporary confusion, staring blankly ahead, others lay convulsing, uncontrollably jerking their legs in the air before falling unconscious to die. Owl, Blue tit and Bat flew together, Stoat, Squirrel and Hare ran as one family in their desperate attempt to live! Drones wizzed over the trees spraying the poisons down over the heights the men could not reach.

The white suits approached the entrance in the ground near the riverbank, shooting high powered jets of the chemical down through the foundations, they walked on approaching the next opening, tools at the ready. An ear-splitting angry buzz emanated from the portal as a swarm of creatures rose at speed from the opening, a swirling dark tornado of life, heading for the sky, the men shot high powered mist up and into the moving black cloud, the Host quickly diverted into a horizontal direction moving over the river. Adia Powe, one of the white suits, thrashed through the water pursuing the Slaugh, aiming up into the dark mass above him, spraying the poison into the flock. The Host dropped, many screaming in agony, choking, bodies falling from the sky, splashing loudly into the water below. One of the men in white spoke low into his head mask, within a minute a drone appeared whirring in a low hum spraying over the writhing Slaugh, two more white suits arrived they aimed a long tube at the floating Slaugh, the men made a waving signal to above and the bodies were sucked up, the shadow of the dead beings visibly travelling up the tube to a large tank vehicle parked on top of the disused Railway line on the ancient Viaduct. The white suits made their way along the riverbank continuing on their journey of extermination. The Clean-up crews had contained the Slaugh corpses in the allocated containers and were already piling all the dead animals onto the mountainous Pyres, the stench of burning flesh rose up in a column of thick black smoke into the sky, moving slowly on the breeze, travelling over where the Village of old used to be.

Only a few Slaugh survived the poison that day, they fled from their dying kinsmen, looking back at their contorted bodies writhing in agony in the water.

The Host cursed Aidia Pow with their venomous energy into the universe, crying out for justice. "This vile human and all his descendants shall die an unnatural painful death until his blood line is no more on this earth." They thought with all the power they could muster.

#

Outside of the Glen, a huge container was mechanically lifted onto a large black vehicle, all the men removed their equipment, and it was placed in a large clear container and sealed. The men entered another black people-carrier type van still with their personal protective equipment on to be taken to the decontamination centre. The vehicles drove slowly through the deserted streets. The huge ornate gates were closed on the silent dead dark woodland, not to be opened again for decades.

#

Based in the beautiful zone EastRenLanark, New Age Homes 2150 are proud to bring you a stunning new development - Glen Waterside.

Whether you wish to explore the breath-taking Glen Gardens or you would prefer to forage amongst nearby unspoiled Woodland, there is no doubt as to the natural beauty of this zone. Nestled against the Cart and Kittock Waters, Glen Waterside boasts a range of three- and four-bedroom homes with spacious recreation. Sky-rail linked with its' own platform in the estate, so you can enjoy a convenient and speedy commute. Whether you are a first-time

lease, or have lease upgrade due, why not book Home-screen appointment.

Beno read the advert to his partner Jude. "This!" he said holding out his arm.

"Why the monthly payment very low for such natural beauty and Sky-rail?" Jude questions.
"Don't give negative, we could just go look. Beno said. Think of the new one coming."

"Is this in our social credit band?" She asked. "Yeah," Beno answers smiling.

"We can book to view it then," Jude says lifting her one eyebrow, she gave him a little smirk
as she rubbed her heavily pregnant stomach. Beno chuckles.

#

Chapter 28.

The Warning 2155

"This home is still the best thing we ever did, Beno, don't you just love our view."
Jude is laying back in her Comsofo on the balcony of their home of five years. "I will never
ever get tired of it?" Beno agrees, nodding as they admire their woodland gardens.

Their home is one of four beautiful tall slim, three floor, three-bedroom homes built
in Glen-Waterside, perched high on top of a small hill, with a woodland view at the front
entrance plus stunning views of the waterfall at the rear from the beautiful glass balcony that
encircles each floor. Beno leans over the glass balustrade, looking down on their fem child
who is perched on the middle of the three huge boulders in their outdoor space.

"I am happy I kept the three big stones! They give our patch different character than the
others." Beno states. "Yeah, and the many credits you would have to transfer to have them
dug out and lifted!" Jude chuckles from behind him.

Boni his four-year-old fem child waves up at him she is now standing on the rock. "Up you
come Boni, Momo2 going help you in spray cube!"

"No, Momo, I am clean, I want to play more." Boni said defiantly.

"What game you play?" Beno asks.

"I am the witch!" Boni states innocently, putting her hands on her hips.

Beno face falls with shock, "Who told you this old word?" Beno asks.

Jude stands up walking over, "This is a word we do not use Boni, never say this word again!" she says sternly.

Boni stares up at her Momo, "Why?" she jumps off the rock she was standing on.

"It is a negative word; it is derogatory toward Fems!" Jude explains retreating from the Balcony.

Boni is skipping around the large patch singing, "I am the witch!" "I am the witch!" "I am the witch!" The little girl occasional gives Beno a side glance to see if he is still watching. He shakes his head while trying not to laugh! Jude walks back out, looking down at Boni once more. "Your fem child! Beno points at Jude, laughing. "No, your fem child! Jude raising her eyebrows high, pulling her cheeks in, while shaking her head at him.

They both laugh loudly together.

"Where could Boni hear such a word," Jude asks Beno baffled.

#

Jude is sitting beside Boni on her Comsofo in her sleep room "Momo,"

"Mmmmm," Jude hums.

"Can I have stars when I sleep?" asks Boni "I don't want the dark."

"Stars stop you sleeping Boni," Jude answers.

"I close eyes, I vow," Boni speaks in a baby voice, while squeezing her eyes shut and pushing her face up towards her Momo. Jude giggles and smiles down on her lovely fem child. "Not to be anxious in the dark Boni, Momo an Momo2 only got good vibration."

Boni looks very sad. Jude rolls her eyes and sighs smiling, "I will turn stars on for you," she instructs the Hologram to play over Boni's sleep space. "BoBo, now go to sleep." Jude waits until Boni sleeping before softly laying the dark Tempisheet over her, switching it on and quietly tip toeing out the sleep space, closing the door on the moving Hologram of the Universe in the room.

Jude wakes with a start, the home screen has flashed on, lighting up the sleep space in an eerie glare, an image of Boni in the corner of her room curled in a ball, the Tempisheet wrapped around her face and head. Jude jumps out of the Comsofo, the night floor lights kindle on, one by one as she walks, a soft glow appearing before her as she hurries into her Childs room. Boni is still sat curled up in the corner, her face covered.

"Boni! you awake BoBo?" Jude whispers as she softly approaches the bundle of Tempisheet. Boni is whimpering, "did you have negative vibration in your sleep BoBo?" Jude feels uneasy, the hair on her neck and arms prickle, she momentarily feels there is someone behind her, turning quickly, scanning the room. 'Nothing here!' she reassures herself. Jude slowly pulls the Tempisheet from Bonis head. Jude is breathing heavily; she is shaking as she tentatively reveals Bonis face.

Jude exhales heavily. She smiles down on her fem child. Bonis eyes are wide, staring blankly at the Comsofo at the other side of the room. "Why are you so anxious BoBo?" Jude's heart was beating fast, she lifted her up out of the corner over to the Comsofo, "No, no, no!" Boni tightened her arms around her MoMos' neck, Jude could not release her grip, so she made her way through to her life partner. "Beno move over! Boni scared, not sleeping." "No! no more of this! I am sleeping, I am asleep." Beno mumbled not even half awake. Jude sighed a heavy sigh.

"Open," she instructed the door, the balcony door slid open. She lay Boni over to one side of the Comfosofo it softly moulded around her fem child's small body, she lay down next to Boni feeling the softness envelope her, she pulled the Tempisheet over them and swiped it on, the warmth soon soothing her jangled nerves.

Boni stared up into her Momos' face with huge round innocent eyes and whispered, "Old in my room MoMo." Jude stroked Bonis soft cheek tenderly, "Don't be scared, no Olds in the house, MoMo and Momo2 only, nothing to be anxious about here!" Jude reassured her. "I'm scared MoMo!" Boni softly whispered into Jude's ear.

"You see the Old in sleep, nothing more." Jude stroked Bonis hair. "Good vibes, BoBo," she gazed at her child lovingly." Look at the amazing sky, the trees, hear the waterfall Boni? We three are blessed to have this home. "Close eyes, sleep good vibrations this time." Boni fell asleep in Jude's arms.

#

Sometime during the night, Jude roused, barely awake she briefly looked out over the trees, a beautiful glow rose from within the woods, moving slowly through the trees, Jude smiled and fell back into sleep. She dreamt of walking through the woods at night, but she can see well as her way is bright and glowing, little houses with tiny occupants in the trees and in the undergrowth, she is not afraid, but laughing as she walks on the path lined with bright stones.

#

Awake Jude is now lying on her back, startled by something, she is breathing heavily, staring straight ahead, there is someone standing at the end of the Comfosofa, floating just beyond the glass balcony, they have long grey hair, clothes of old, she can't see the face clearly, but the eyes, the eyes are green and bright, momentarily frozen by shock, she just stares, as the apparition moves nearer, a voice whispers in her head as the spectre passes, "Beware the HOST!"

Petrified, Jude holds on to BoBo tight, she is breathing fast, sweat is on her top lip, a drip running down the side of her mouth to her chin; the manifestation becomes a dark shadow figure moving through the closed doorway of the sleep room where Beno lays.

#

The End or is it ?

Printed in Great Britain
by Amazon